SABINE DURRANT

Finders, Keepers

HODDER

First published in Great Britain in 2020 by Hodder & Stoughton
An Hachette UK company

This paperback edition published in 2021

1

Copyright © TPC & G Ltd 2020

A CIP catalogue record for this title is available from the British Library

Paperback ISBN 978 1 473 68166 8

Typeset in Plantin Light by Hewer Text UK Ltd, Edinburgh
Printed and bound in Great Britain by Clays Ltd, Elcograf S.p.A.

Hodder & Stoughton policy is to use papers that are natural, renewable
and recyclable products and made from wood grown in sustainable
forests. The logging and manufacturing processes are expected to
conform to the environmental regulations of the country of origin.

Hodder & Stoughton Ltd
Carmelite House
50 Victoria Embankment
London EC4Y 0DZ

www.hodder.co.uk

For Joe

The central philosophical debate over mental illness is not about its existence, but rather over how to define it.

Christian Perring, *Stanford Encyclopaedia of Philosophy*

You get to be independent when you live alone. You get to be real individual.

'Little' Edie Bouvier Beale, *Grey Gardens*

Chapter One

Scotch-Brite Classic Sponge Scourers,
10 x Twin Pack, 20 in total

Mariticide, *noun*. From the Latin '*maritus*' meaning husband plus '-cide' from '*caedere*', to cut, to kill.

I was up early so I got to it before she could see. Red paint, this time, which seemed harder to remove than the white. Is that true? Never mind. Either way, it was a good thing I kept those scourers because it took four of them to get it off. It's a grotty fence, as Tom was always saying, the posts bleached and rotting, cracks stretching between the slats, and parts of the letters – the curl of the G, the bottom of the L – were painted on the overgrown ivy. When I'd finished, I picked off each adulterated leaf.

'YOUR GUILTEY'

I don't like it. It's unnerving. It smacks of mob rule, of a world in which a person who is accused of something, proven or otherwise, is expected to go around with a marker on their back. As if police, court, a trial, jail term (however it pans out), is not punishment enough.

I won't tell her, of course. She's had enough to deal with. Bad enough to have spent those nights in the cell at Wandsworth police station; then the misery of the full week at Bronzefield.

The terrible food and the screaming, the soap that stripped a layer of skin. I tried to visit, got all the way to Ashford on the train, with the Clarins cleansing milk she likes, but it turns out you need photo ID: a passport or driving licence, and I have neither. (How do people manage? If she ends up going back, I'll have to work something out.) Anyway, she's only just settling in here. The last thing she needs now is to feel got at.

Of course, it's just the daubings of some illiterate or – to be sympathetic – dyslexic. But as I crouched, my back to the street, bucket at my side, I felt unnerved, as if each car that passed was watching. I felt suffused with shame, too, the natural humiliation, perhaps, of anyone forced to clear up someone else's unpleasantness. And I felt strangely lonely. It was an accident, I've told everyone who asked. Innocent. Any jury will see that. Surely. I don't know why people are so odd.

Once I'd stowed the scourers and the bucket in the kitchen, I came out to find her loitering in the hall, asking petulantly for her breakfast. Normally I take it up to her on a tray, as I always did for Mother, but this morning I hadn't had time because of being busy with the fence. I shepherded her into the front room while I got it ready. She likes a particular type of granola, but we're running low (I can only get it by walking down to the big Sainsbury's) so I supplemented it with some of my Quick Oats. She didn't seem to notice. She ate without expression, gazing out of the window at the cars and the buses, the children on their way to school. She seemed to be in one of her fugue states. Shock, the doctor said. But I'm never quite sure.

Maudie was agitating to go out, and when I suggested Ailsa join us I didn't expect her to agree. She hasn't left the house willingly since she got here. There's always been some excuse: too tired, or her eyes hurt, or she might see someone she knew. Today the defaced fence must have given an extra force to my words, or perhaps I simply timed it right.

'It doesn't do anyone any good to be shut up all day,' I said and she spun round. 'OK': the emphasis on the K, as if she were doing *me* a favour.

I found her a jacket, one of mine, and a scarf, ditto. She has none of the right clothes with her, all too summery. The jacket, a maroon-coloured puffer, not 100 per cent clean, was bulky and she didn't like it. Her nose wrinkled and I had to push her arms into it, as if I were dressing a recalcitrant child. The black scarf passed muster. It's only polyester but it feels like cashmere and, as I searched for the keys in the hall, I caught her studying her reflection in a mirror, lifting her chin to rearrange it at the side of her neck. Some habits die hard.

I stage-managed the walk, of course, making sure to turn right out of the house so as not to pass her front door, down to the end of Trinity Road and then straight across there at the lights on to the common. I was keen to avoid the busy row of shops and cafes on Bellevue. The reporters have cleared off but she's right; you wouldn't want to make too much of a performance of it. She walked very slowly, and I hooked my arm through hers and pulled her along. I tried to curb my irritation. Baby steps, I'd said, but I hadn't meant it literally.

It was a crisp, blustery autumn morning, the sky frantic with clouds, the sun rushing in and out. I unclipped Maudie from her lead and she ran ahead across the grass: a patchwork of roving shadows. Ailsa's pace picked up on the main path and when I drew attention to the loveliness of the big tall chestnuts – they're beginning to catch fire – she made a murmuring sound, which I took to be agreement.

We should perhaps have turned round then, to quit while we were ahead. I blame myself that we didn't. I like to think I am in touch with her moods, but I was insufficiently alert.

I was trying to be jolly, chatting inanely about the cygnets on the pond, how big they'd grown, when I became aware of two women, both blonde, with small dogs on leads, walking towards us. It was like a magnetic field, the tension, the anticipation, in their silence. Ailsa did too, or maybe she knew them. She knows a lot of people. Her breath changed: a sharp inhalation followed immediately by a strangulated whimper. She leant sharply into me – I wondered if she might fall – so I hoisted her off the path, and across the grass to the bench under the tree, the one that faces the incline down to the water. She hurled herself onto it, taking up most of the room, her head thrown backwards so she was staring up at the sky, her neck resting on the metal. After a few moments, she said, with some petulance, that she was exhausted; she hadn't slept for days. And then she began to talk about Melissa: she'd emailed her again but she hadn't replied; she wasn't sure her messages were being passed on. It wasn't fair. She told a long anecdote about a birthday picnic for the twins and how jolly it had been and something about a beautiful tree house they had built in Kent.

I stopped listening, I'm afraid. I don't like hearing about Kent and I've heard a lot about the children recently. Also, I was pretty tired myself. I'm having to work at night, for obvious reasons. A couple of parakeets flew, squawking, between two trees. Maud was over towards the copse, taking those oddly prissy choreographed steps that mean she's stalking a squirrel. The light was buttery, with a cool sharpness to the air, the criss-cross patches of sky a lovely washed blue. Under our feet was a proper scrunch of autumn debris. I rolled the soles of my shoes over it, finding the noise satisfying. I thought about Ailsa's voice, how posh it is and how her sentences can turn up at the end; sometimes even in the middle. I wondered for the first time how it would play with jurors. Conclusion: not well.

When she first leant forwards, I assumed she was looking at my legs. I was wearing those zip-off trousers that are so comfortable for walking, and a section of my lower calves were on display. Her eyes were focused on the tiny scales – the completely perfect white circles that are evidence of age; idiopathic guttate hypomelanosis, to give them their correct name. I thought she might be about to comment – 'You must see my dermatologist' – so her words came as a shock.

'At first, I didn't . . . you know, it was as if he just had something stuck in his throat, or it was too hot, like he'd eaten a whole chilli or something. You know? But the water I gave him it was all coming out of the sides of his mouth . . . I mean, his tongue was—' She began scraping her top teeth along the surface of her own tongue, back and forth. I couldn't think what she was doing, until I realised with a sickening lurch that she was giving a demonstration.

'How awful,' I said. I had a panicked feeling that I should have been trying to record her, though I didn't know how subtly to get to my phone.

She plucked at the maroon jacket, scratching the fabric with her nails, and then scratching at her wrists. Her skin looks sore at the moment. 'And his pupils, Verity. It was so weird. They were just *black*, like an animal's, and he was clutching at his neck and his mouth was hanging open still, and all this saliva everywhere, like a dog frothing. You know? I've never seen it, but how you imagine a dog with rabies, like that. It was inhuman. He was writhing, contorting like his body wasn't his; his forehead was covered in sweat. He was still looking at me. The look in his eyes . . . And he had been so sick – it was all over his shirt and the kitchen floor, and I couldn't find any kitchen paper, so I was using loo roll.'

'Was he still at the table, at that point, Ailsa?' It was something the police had kept asking.

'I think he had left the table. He'd slid off his chair onto the floor.'

'So he was on the floor. And you were – standing? Or had you got down?'

Crows flapped in the branches behind us. Her voice rose. 'I'd got down. I'd got the water.'

'Oh yes.'

A flighty wind was playing in the tree next to her, leaves spiralling past her shoulders.

'If I'd rung an ambulance immediately would I have saved him? Was it already too late?'

I opened my mouth to answer, trying to control my expression. If only I had been near that night. If only I'd known he was home. 'I don't know.'

Maudie had disappeared from view, and even as I was concentrating on Ailsa, I made room for a small amount of mild panic. I fought the urge to stand up and call.

Ailsa's head was making small darting movements, her eyes flickering with shadows. 'They said the hemlock was what stopped him from breathing?'

It was a couple of seconds before I realised it was a question. I said: 'I believe it paralyses the nervous and respiratory systems, and that is what leads to death.'

Her hands had fallen limply by her side. 'I often said I wished him dead.' She had begun to cry. 'That things would be so much better if he were. But they're not. It's not fair. Everything always goes wrong for me. I wish I could turn back time.'

I felt impatient with her then and I stood up. 'We'd better get going,' I said crisply, and I pulled her to her feet – all those years fussing about her weight; I'm not sure these days she's even eight stone – and, once I'd pinpointed the dog, I sort of frogmarched her home.

6

She's asleep now. We've made her a nest in the front room, in one corner of the sofa, and she is conked out there. She was sweet when we got in. She held my hand to her cheek when I brought her her rooibos tea, said thank you for standing by her. I've been watching her – the tiny muscular flickers under her eyelids, the way her mouth opens, blown apart by her breath, then gently falls back into place. It's a dear little face, really, heart-shaped, with the widow's peak (ironic now) in her tawny hair, those distinctively upward-turning green eyes. The small dent of an old scar runs for an inch or so under her hairline. I don't know how it got there. There is so much about her I don't know.

She has a meeting with the QC this week. Until now I haven't been too worried; I've been complacent. I thought it would work itself out. I told myself nothing on the surface was wrong with their marriage – they were the perfect couple. The case would be dropped, I assumed, or dismissed; after expressions of unending gratitude for all that I've done, she and the children would move back next door. Now, I don't know. My head is full of thoughts. Who is she? How have we come to this?

Her tone this afternoon – I keep thinking about it. There was shock there, of course, and self-pity: her own particular 'why does this have to happen to me?' vein (the consequence, I think, of being slightly spoilt). And fear, and horror – watching Tom dissolve into something animal and unrecognisable before her eyes: 'like a dog frothing'. All of this is understandable. Each of us deals with trauma in different ways. And after what she's done for me, I'll forgive her anything. I really will.

My fingers are still raw from scrubbing at the graffiti. I keep wondering who could posibly have done such a thing? What are they trying to tell me? It's awful, but as she sleeps, and the night presses against the window, I feel scared for the first time. Have I made a mistake? It's just one thing was missing from her outburst this afternoon, the one thing you'd expect to find in a tragedy of this kind.

Grief.

Chapter Two

Caran d'Ache Swisscolor watercolour
pencils in metal box (pack of 40)

Anthropomorphism, *noun*. **The attribution of
human personality or characteristics to something
non-human, as an animal, object, etc.**

I am not the subject of this story, but I don't want to be elusive,
for curiosity about me to be a distraction. Possibly no one but
me will ever read this – writing things down has always been
a good way, for me, of making sense of the world. But in the
event my words reach a wider public, I thought, while Ailsa is
having a bath, I'd better record what I can about myself to get
it out of the way. All narratives are unreliable; we all have our
own axe to grind. It's important to be transparent, that's all.

My name is Verity Ann Baxter. I have lived at number 424
Trinity Road, SW17 all my life, give or take. One mother. One
sister. My father left when I was four. My mother died five
years ago.

I'm fifty-two.

I'm not a virgin. Sorry, if that's TMI, as Melissa would say.
But I don't want anyone claiming I'm a bitter spinster of the
parish or, as Maeve and Sue from my pub quiz team keep
insisting, that my interest in Ailsa is sapphic. It annoys me,

how our current culture bangs on all the time about inclusivity, but there's still an implicit prejudice against those of us who are child- and partner-free, as if our views aren't valid, as if we haven't earned the right to comment, without jealousy or longing, on the behaviour of others who aren't. I'm not at all prudish. I quite enjoy watching sex on television. Some of the happiest moments of my life were spent watching *Love Island* with Ailsa and her kids. Fact is, been there, done that. I've had enough sex in my life to know I'm not missing out.

Ailsa and I both had unconventional childhoods – it's one of the things that drew us together. Not unconventional as in glamorous, hippy parents hanging out in Marrakech, but unconventional in nurturing a sense in us as children of not quite fitting in at school, of being a little odd. Ailsa's mother was clearly an alcoholic – though her daughter is too loyal to say as much. Mine was an invalid, who suffered from fibromyalgia, a chronic condition characterised by widespread pain and a heightened response to pressure. It was unpredictable where it might flare, but her neck was a constant issue. She would need the support of multiple cushions, in a tier-like pattern around her shoulders, to sit at all comfortably. My sister Faith and I learnt from an early age to avoid any sudden movements, and to kiss her, when bidden, with a neat non-jarring purse of the lips.

Her illness may have got worse after my father walked out. I'm not sure. I have few memories of life before he went. Or of him. A certain aftershave pulls me up short, and fabric in a particular black and white dog-tooth check speaks to me in a peculiarly painful way. He worked for the gas board and I'm told he was from a lower social class to my mother, but family life, it turned out, wasn't his bag. Or that's the conclusion events have led me to extrapolate. One Saturday morning, when my sister and I were still pre-school, he went out to get a paper. The woman who ran the greengrocer – now a branch of Pizza Express – said she saw him getting on the 319. He was never seen again. That, at least, is the story my mother always clung to. I think she found the dramatic nature of it reassuring. I have a few memories that don't fit: the sound of them arguing long before he left, empty hangers clanging in the cupboard, and then, after his 'disappearance', a trip with him to the fairground, when I was tall enough to go on the waltzer. If such visits did exist, they eventually stopped. Maybe he moved away, or got bored. Sometimes I wonder if he is out there still, but he was older than Mother, and she was in her eighties when she died, so it is unlikely.

My mother never worked, because of her condition, and I have no memory of her drawing any benefits. Instead, after he left, we scrimped and saved, made do, waste not, want not, etc. We grew veg, and collected coupons; we took in ironing, we constantly recycled, 'upcycled' to use modern parlance, our own clothes. We didn't have a mortgage – my father had inherited the house, located on a main road, from an aunt. In those days, Tooting was nothing to write home about. Things have changed dramatically around me – 'Trinity Fields', I believe the estate agents are calling this patch now – though it's still extraordinary to me that anyone would spend as much as the Tilsons on a house here, let alone bother to dig out the basement.

It has taken me a while to adjust to the notion of 'neighbours'. We had no visitors from outside, when I was growing up, though our world was populated nonetheless. My mother's parents were killed in the Blitz, and she moved in with her grandmother, a strict Victorian, in Eastbourne. As a child she escaped her surroundings (sadness, fear, relentless boredom) by colouring them in with her imagination, and it was a habit she never lost. All her significant relationships were with creatures, both real and imaginary. She had a vast collection of woodland-related ornaments – rabbits a particular favourite – and she talked about hedgehogs and birds and foxes as if she knew them individually. 'Mr Hedgehog's been sent out on his ear to find some worms.' 'Oh look, cheeky Rufus Robin's come to see what's what.' If anything went missing in the house it was blamed on the Borrowers, the family of miniature humans who lived behind the skirting boards. She talked about them so often that when, visiting a school friend, I happened upon Mary Norton's novel, I embarrassed myself, and was subsequently the object of much scorn in the playground, by insisting the book was written about our house. You could pull a room to pieces in search of the lost item – a sock or a protractor, say – but if you found it, it wasn't down to your efforts but those of an invisible lodger called St Christopher. For anything more serious we called on our guardian angels – we had one each. It was mine, incidentally, not my mother, who sat by my hospital bedside after the removal of my tonsils.

Does it sound charming? It wasn't actually. It was more of a tyranny. Every item in the house had an animus. She would never leave an egg alone in the box 'in case it was lonely', and we used loose tea to prevent the upsetting tearing of conjoined teabags. The cushions on our sofa sat in preordained family groups; soft toys and old clothes were never thrown out. In my treasured box of Caran d'Ache, each pencil was worn down to the same level, even the white; she made me use each implement equally so as not to hurt any feelings.

Someone – a young doctor who visited her at home once and noticed her distress at taking a single tablet – told me it was a psychological disorder. Acute empathy of that kind, he said, wasn't easy; it was linked to over-sensitivity to slights. We agreed it was a reaction to her illness, the isolation of it. But

I've thought hard about this recently. Ailsa says it explains a lot about me. It's probably generic, a family trait.

At first it seemed as if I would escape. 'The clever one' in relation to my sister – 'the pretty one' – I left school for university, King's College London, the lucky generation that got it all free. I lived in halls, and then in student digs near Elephant and Castle, and had finished my degree and begun a doctorate when two things happened: my mother's ill health flared, and my sister decided she had had enough of being the main carer. As a result of both, I moved back home.

I was in trouble anyway. Like all family myths, my reputation as 'the clever one' had turned out to be an exaggeration. 'The slightly cleverer one' would have been more accurate. My thesis, hubristically entitled 'Culture and Cognition in Language Evolution', was proving beyond me. Deadlines were already being missed, emergency meetings made and ducked. I slunk home, resentfully watched Faith pack her bags for a new life in Brighton, while secretly nursing relief. If my mother was insufficiently grateful for my sacrifice, it suited me to resent that, too. I continued to resent it for twenty years, to blame her for the jobs I took, initially at the library, which didn't go well (the chief librarian hated me, and there were too many children) and then in the Leisure and Culture department at the council – where I was just as miserable. I harboured this resentment, like a trusted old rotting skiff, throughout the last decade, when I have been happily employed as freelance assistant editor to the editor of the Oxford English Dictionary. I have Fred Pullen, an old university friend, to thank for recommending me for this post, and it suits me down to the ground. It's a big old project we have embarked upon, the updating of the dictionary. It started in 1999 and goodness knows when it will be finished. Never, probably, which as far as I'm concerned would be convenient.

Basically I re-write the existing entries; other teams are in charge of the neologisms. I help revise the old definitions and, with the help of newly available sources online, update the quotation paragraphs (the 'QPs', as we call them) where necessary. It's ponderous work, sometimes thrilling, often dull. I find it satisfying.

She's out of the bath now. I can hear the thunder of water overhead, the clanking of the old iron pipes. That was a short dip even for her. It's the metallic rusty streak on the enamel she hates. She says it looks like blood. Nothing about my house pleases her. She can't help comparing it to the light, empty, knocked-through open spaces of next door: the reclaimed wooden floors, the steel framed industrial-style doors, the curated combination of old and new. My rooms are a hodgepodge in comparison. She used to care about sorting it out. She's given up on that now. My house is no longer a project, and nor am I. She has more serious things to worry about.

Tonight, I must keep her off her phone. She has a compulsion to look at Instagram, but it's her own feed she constantly scrolls through, revisiting happier days – her cakes, her house, her children, Tom. It's very sad. Other people's pictures are supposed to make you feel inadequate, not your own. I might try to get her to read one of the books I got for her out of the library: the thrillers she likes. There was a whole row of them on the 'just published' shelf. They seemed all to be about women who discover their husbands are psychopaths, but what can you do? Just reading this stuff doesn't turn you into a killer.

At the pub quiz last night, Maeve asked if I wasn't scared having Ailsa here. 'You don't know what she might do. What if she loses her temper? What if she turns on you?'

I smiled. 'We're friends.'

'How do you know? You're too . . .'

She didn't finish what she was going to say but I knew what she was thinking. I looked around the table, at the motley crew who come together at the Dog and Fox once a week, and saw it in all their eyes: that I was too trusting, too lonely, that I would take in anyone to keep the darkness from pressing in.

The bathroom door just rattled; I can hear the creak of floorboards. She has crossed the landing and is standing at the top of the stairs. If I listen carefully I'll know if she goes into Mother's bedroom. She started in there a few days ago, systematically working her way through the tallboy. I don't know what she was looking for. She got angry when I asked. No, she hasn't gone in there. Her steps are coming down; I can tell from the tentative rhythm of her tread. She says my stairs are dangerous.

I must make sure she eats.

I'll put this away now. I don't want her to know what I've been doing. And anyway, I've written enough about myself. I can see, reading back, that I quite 'got into it'. That's the problem with human nature. We all think our own stories are fascinating, that we are the heroes of our own little worlds. We all like the sound of our own voice.

Chapter Three

Numatic Vacuum Cleaner Henry NRV 620 W, red

Sialoquent, *adjective*. **Tending to spray saliva when speaking.**

I find it strange to look back at the person I was before they moved in. I feel almost sorry for myself, for my innocence. It was as if for my whole previous life I'd been holding my breath.

The first time I saw her she was standing in the middle of the pavement, arguing with a traffic warden. 'Oh my God, come on,' she was saying, both hands clasped together against one cheek, in a sort of winsomely pleading form of prayer. 'Come on, I was only, like, two minutes. You can't do this to me. My husband will kill me. Please. I'll move it now. Don't give me that ticket.' Her arms crossed her chest. 'Come on, tear it up. Please. For *me*.'

Next to her, half on the road, half on the pavement, was a lopsided navy Fiat 500. She'd clearly parked up to unload her shopping (their off-street already taken by their main car, a huge silver beast I believe one calls a 'Chelsea tractor'). Rookie mistake. We live on a red route and to slow the traffic down here is pretty much a crime against humanity.

'Oh, thank you,' she said, 'thank you very much.' He had slapped the ticket under her windscreen wiper and got back on his moped. 'Have a fucking nice day,' she called after him, raising her palm in a salute.

I pushed through my gate and onto the path. 'Bastards,' she said, noticing me for the first time. 'They're all bastards.' I only half smiled, and let the lock click shut behind me. I had no intention of agreeing. I'm not big on generalisations. I was already wary maybe; something about her coiled energy reminded me of Faith. Plus Nathan's worked round here for years. He's a bit of a sweetie.

She took a step towards me then and introduced herself. 'We moved in next door,' she said. 'Yesterday.' She pointed over her shoulder at number 422, as if I needed geographic guidance, and I said, 'Oh really?', summoning the requisite note of surprised interest. It's not unique to her, this tendency of people who have 'done up' a house to ignore their impact in absentia. Of course I knew they'd moved in the day before. The whole neighbourhood knew they'd moved in the day before. Most of us had anticipated little else for the last thirteen months *but* their moving in the day before; thirteen months of drills and bulldozers, the clatter of scaffolding, the whining of saws, the bangs and shouts and music and oaths of the increasingly frantic builders. I knew their taste – from the original iron claw-foot bath that arrived, the plastic shower unit that departed. I knew, for example, that their sofa and their washing machine came from John Lewis, and the coffee table and a weird headboard thing from Oka. I even, to be honest, knew her name, that she was Ailsa Tilson, in HR, married to Tom Tilson, a record company executive; that they had three children, including twins (possible IVF?), and that they were moving to London after a failed stint in Kent. Please don't think I had sought out this information. It's just what comes your way if you live next door to a building site for a year and you're not so inhuman you can't make the occasional cup of tea.

About me, of course, she knew nothing.

'I'm Verity,' I said.

Ignoring the 319 bus, still idling behind her car, she stretched her arm over the gate to shake my hand, and then left her elbow there, propped, like she was leaning on a desk. On first inspection, she had rather pointy features, with large nostrils in a sharply upturned nose, and skin tightly drawn across the cheekbones. I noticed her mouth had a prominent philtrum and a mole sat just below her lower lip. She was wearing a bulky khaki jacket with a fur-trimmed hood, a common garment among 'yummy mummies' round here, which is how I can date this encounter to mid-February, during the return of what people persisted on calling another Beast from the East. We'd had a couple of mild weeks, but a cold front had swept in more biting winds and freezing rain. It's hard to imagine it, after the summer we've just had, but I do remember I'd taken off my gloves to fiddle with my key, and my fingers were numb with cold. I was curious to meet her, but I was keener to get into my house.

She didn't ask me any questions, whether I lived alone or in a harem. Equally, she showed no interest in my property, which she might have done, as it is the mirror image of hers, or at least it was, before their 'improvements'. She didn't even glance up at it. At the time I interpreted this as self-absorption, but I know now it was simply that she accepts 'difference' without judgement. Instead she told me they'd decided belatedly to sand the living-room floor, and the constant noise was driving her 'literally insane'.

'Tell me about it,' is what I didn't say.

And then she hoisted her arm off my gate and said something about having to move the car before that cunt came back.

'Mind my French,' she said.

When her solicitor asked us the other day when we had first met it became apparent Ailsa had completely forgotten this encounter. She planted the beginning of our friendship a few days later – at the meeting about the trees when I was more obviously of use to her. So when I look back on this, I try to imagine it's as if I am watching her without her knowing, an objective witness, a jury member say, who doesn't know her history. I suppose it is obvious to say that if you can judge a person by the way they talk to waiters, a person can be measured even more accurately by their behaviour towards a traffic warden. I don't drive but I've noticed how parking tickets tend to provoke disproportionate anger, a strong feeling of abused entitlement, in their recipients. I think of Ailsa as empathetic, as one of the least judgemental people I've ever met; and yet her reaction to Nathan was complicated. I think it wasn't just the fine that got to her, but his resistance to her charms. Later I would learn how, as an only child, she felt responsible for maintaining the equilibrium at home; it was her own cheerfulness, her 'upness' that kept her parents together. On this occasion, her seductive powers failed. And yet how hard she tried to repress her panic – the almost perfect fusion of sweetness and sarcasm in her 'have a fucking nice day'. And then her decision to sweep across and talk to me; her pointless lingering despite the cold, the havoc in the road, the furiously beeping bus. Was it kindness? I like to think it was. Or was it perhaps my cool that pulled her in? She had sensed my disapproval and wanted to win me over. Why? A frantic desire to be liked, or a woman in desperate need of allies?

As for her use of 'cunt' (from the Middle English: of German origin, related to Norwegian and Swedish dialect *kunta* and Middle Low German, Middle Dutch and Danish dialect *kunte*)? Not a word one should usually deploy without being sure of one's audience. You could think of it as a hand-grenade or the kind of smoke-releasing canisters police hurl into a building before entering. Do your worst and see who's left. But equally it could have been a distress flare, fired from a lifeboat; a scream, if you like, for help.

I was to have no contact with my new neighbours for a week or so. Over that period, they had a wood-burning stove installed, submitted a planning application for a 'driveway turntable', which would allow them 'to enter and leave their property in a forward gear', and signed up to Mindful Chef, a weekly healthy food delivery service. They also spent a Saturday night away, during which their fourteen-year-old, Melissa – or 'Lissa', as she was shriekingly referred to – entertained a few friends, a couple of whom left empty beer cans and a discarded box of fried chicken in my front garden. Over that time, someone inside their property also disposed of two damaged picture frames from Ikea and a large red Henry vacuum with a broken nozzle.

It was Tuesday late afternoon when I came up against them again. I was working at my desk in the front room. The traffic is heavy at that time of day, and I was listening to Classic FM through my noise-cancelling headphones. I had just received a new batch of words – anger and angst and anguish; I remember this clearly – and was, with that nice thrill of fresh absorption, having an initial spin through the database. I didn't hear him at the gate, but I *felt* him at the front door. He used the knocker, despite the fact I have a working bell. Bang, bang: it was an alert that brooked no disagreement. The windows rattled in their frames; the very papers on my desk vibrated.

A fairy-tale couple, the *Sun* called them, and he was a handsome man, Tom Tilson, with foppish dark-brown hair, a broad jaw and blue eyes. I read recently that symmetrical features are an important factor in a person's attractiveness, and he scored highly there. He was dressed, as I was to later discover he usually was, in the kind of casual but fearfully expensive garb made corporately acceptable by tech billionaires: dark-blue jeans, white T-shirt, hefty trainers, though I always thought – poor lamb – he'd be more comfortable in a suit. He was rather thickset for my taste, with a softness around his neck and the open-pored complexion of a person who has lived to the full, those wide-set blue eyes of his chillingly pale. His looks were not going to age well, though it feels mean to say that now.

By the time I opened the door he had taken several steps back and was halfway down the path, legs apart, looking at the upstairs windows. My house had piqued his interest, if not his wife's. I pulled the door to behind me, in case he had any intention of peering in.

'Yuh,' he called, as if we were in the middle of a conversation. 'Need to talk about a few things.'

'And those things would be?'

'Let's start with the trees.'

His T-shirt had come loose at the side, and he made a big play of leaning sideways to tuck it in, at the same time making a noisy inhalation – a gesture that managed to simultaneously convey two things: a general superiority and a more specific air of exasperation.

I asked him what trees, and he said the trees along my back fence – 'The apple trees – are they? – and the holly; and ivy, it's a weed you know. I don't want it all spreading into mine. All far too overgrown, far too overgrown.'

When I gazed at him, he raised his hand in a fist to his head and tapped it up and down a few times, his elbow pointed out at an angle, making a large V. 'We should start to make some inroads.' He was annoyed, and the sibilant-heavy nature of his sentence caused a detectable spray of spittle.

Menopause – well, peri-menopause actually – can make me a little snappy, defensive maybe, and I'm afraid that 'we' didn't play well. I gave him short shrift and went back in and shut the door.

I feel bad about this. I don't mind being disliked, but this skirmish between us was to set the early tone of our relationship. Perhaps I should have made an effort to like him more, been more sympathetic to the trap of upbringing and education that made him what he was. The thing is it *suited* me to dismiss him as arrogant. It was a knee-jerk reaction. I felt under attack and I wanted an excuse to dismiss him. If I had been honest with myself I'd have recognised that the fiddling with the T-shirt and the egg-cracking on the head performance were self-conscious. He was pretending to be relaxed. He wanted his own way, sure, but he wasn't as confident of getting it as he affected.

So yes, I do feel sorry for him. Who wouldn't? And it's hard not to remember the *physicality* of the man, the flash of flesh above the waistband of his jeans, the hairs on the back of his meaty hands, the muscles straining beneath the white cotton of his T-shirt – a body that moved, that worked, that could make the decision to breathe deeply or throw its hands or weight around if it wanted. And I'm finding it hard as I write this not to think about that same body, cold and inert, guts spilt, prodded, poked, and sewn back together on the pathologist's slab.

Chapter Four

Ladies blouse from Next, pink, size 12

Trichotillomania, *noun*. **A compulsive desire to pull out one's own hair.**

I caught her in the garden this morning. She'd got out through the kitchen, though I thought I'd locked the back door. She'd found a couple of old beer crates in the side return and had stacked them on top of each other to look over the fence. She was wearing a dressing gown and some old slippers, her hair unbrushed. The dressing gown, made of pale-pink fleece, had scraped past a bramble, and a few dried leaves clung to the bottom.

Her ankles were bare for once and the electronic tag was visible. It's really quite clunky when you see it close up, grey and black, a bit like you'd imagine an early prototype of the Apple Watch to look. I could see the friction had caused an angry rash around the edge of the strap: another flare up of her eczema.

She spun her head when she heard my footsteps. Her lips have a naturally violet-red hue to them but this morning they looked almost blue. She said: 'I'd like to go next door and mow the lawn.'

'You know you can't do that. It's rented out. Someone else

is living there at the moment.' A French banker on a short-term contract; criminal how little he has got away with paying. At least he's hardly there. A family would be noisier. I think the sound of children through the walls would kill her. She needs the money. Plus it was part of her bail conditions that she lived elsewhere, a condition suggested not by the CPS, but by her own lawyer. 'It'll look better,' Standling had said, 'if you're too upset to go back into the house, if the associations are too painful.'

I didn't think it was a good time to remind her of that.

'I want to do some watering. It's been so dry and the amelanchier looks miserable. It has such a fine root system, very close to the surface. It's been disturbed so much. It doesn't need a lot of water, but it needs some. I don't want it to die.'

'Shh,' I said sharply. 'Keep your voice down.' I don't like it when she reveals too much horticultural knowledge. 'It'll rain soon. It always does.'

She turned back and, peering over again, cried, 'What have they done, Verity? Why have they destroyed my garden?'

I took a step towards her. I had a memory then of my sister on a climbing frame, and a second memory, a sensory one that felt like a thud in my biceps: the weight of her small body. 'They were looking for evidence, do you remember?' I said. 'They had to dig it up to take away some of the plants.'

She stared at me. Her eyelids quivered. 'I know,' she said. 'I saw.'

She hadn't, in fact. But she doesn't like to admit weakness. It's part of the new power play between us. The medication, the exhaustion of it all, has fuzzed her memory and she resents me for it. I don't mind. I take it as a compliment. It's the people closest to us who get the brunt of our irascibility. Fact is she had been at the police station, railing and shouting, the day the men came in the space-age suits. I was the one who watched from my upstairs window as they erected their poly-tunnel structure and obliterated the garden on which she had lavished so much love and money, leaving heaps of churned earth, jagged holes, gashes of lawn. It had been unsettling, creepy even, the methodology of their progress: starting at the back with the 'wildflower' bed, advancing to those 'mature' shrubs she'd spent so much money on, only at the end of the day reaching the terrace and the pots of herbs.

'You didn't,' I said. 'You weren't here.'

She twisted away from me, craning her neck, but her sight-line was restricted by the newfangled trellis she'd put up after she moved in. It's fashioned from horizonal strips of wood and she had to bend her head at an angle to line up her eyes with a gap in the slats. Maudie was nosing around at the base of the crates and a hazel branch, which had been pinned back by Ailsa's elbow, sprung forwards and swiped her across the cheek. She wobbled, the crates buckled and, jumping off, she threw out her hand, snagging the flesh of her palm on a thorn.

I like to think it was the shock and the pain that made her mean. 'I can't believe the state of your garden,' she said. 'It's so dark. The holly,' she said. 'And the apple trees and the hazel. How much nicer your own garden would be if you cleared it and cut them right back.' She looked around, her arms stir-ring the air in empty circles. 'Tom was right. It's out of control.'

The invitation had come sprawled on the back of a postcard: *Are you free Friday, early evening, for a drink? Say 6 p.m.? Pop in if you'd like. Ailsa and Tom (no 422) xx*

I'd studied it carefully. Her handwriting, not his, I was sure, due to the feminine roundness of the letters and the kisses at the end. The postcard was from one of those boxes of cards depicting notable Penguin covers. Fred had given me a carton a few Christmases back. I knew from experience you sent the best ones to people you liked, or wanted to impress. This was one of the dullest – no picture; a generic orange and white cover. Either they were getting to the bottom of the box, or I was a low-status recipient. (Incidentally it was the cover for Sinclair Lewis's *Mantrap*: let's not read anything into it.)

The wording made it sound as if it were a solo affair, but I wasn't sure, and I made some effort with my appearance. In fact, I bought a new blouse. It was a bit small for me, and rather *pink*, but it was the best Trinity Hospice could provide at short notice.

I left it as fashionably late as I could bear to and at 6.10 p.m. took the short trip from my house to theirs. The silver tractor was parked across the off-street with its boot wide open. Inside were crammed trays of bedding plants, stacked two layers high. I'm not big on flowers, so I couldn't tell you what they were; different shades of green, squat and small; some trailing, some bushy. I peered in. There was a rich smell of earth and plastic; I sensed the quivers of tiny movements, of caterpillars and aphids. In the front was an olive tree, bound in tape, reclining stiff and straight like a dead body.

A woman I didn't know opened the door before I had a chance to knock. She was wearing a denim mini-skirt, thick patterned wool tights, and ankle-high wellingtons, her hair pinned back in an unruly bun. She took a step back when she saw me and for a moment I thought she was going to shut the door in my face. But when I told her who I was, she gave me a long doubtful look and said, 'Yeah, OK then, feel free,' and went past me back to the boot. After a moment's hesitation, I walked in unaccompanied.

I'd been in the house once or twice when the builders were still at work, but it was the first time I had seen it in its finished state. My first impression was of a moment in a film, or a dream, when the character has left their body and finds themselves in a corridor walking towards a bright light. The walls were white and bare, except for a huge silver-framed mirror above a hall shelf; the chequered Victorian floor tiles had been replaced with large slabs of pale stone, which seemed to run infinitely, and through the door on the left I glimpsed, dangling from the ceiling, an enormous chandelier apparently fashioned from swan feathers.

The Herberts' kitchen, where I had sometimes been invited to supper, had been a fussy affair, full of knife blocks, and fridge magnets, spider plants and grandchildren's drawings, cookery books, pots hanging precariously from an elaborate contraption above the stove. In the lower panel of their garden door was a cat flap, the plastic still black from the muddy paws of their long-dead Siamese. The room smelt – always – of garlic and curry; maybe also fish.

The Tilsons had stripped everything out, knocking through the scullery and the lean-to, and the room now seemed cavernous. A row of shiny white units and a stainless-steel industrial-style range cooker took up the right-hand side, while the sink, garlanded with shiny taps, was positioned in a central island. On the left was a spotlessly clean white enamel wood-burning stove, not in use, and a long pale wooden table. Black steel-framed doors – what I later learnt to call 'Crittall' – now ran along the entire back wall, framing a rectangle of garden. The whole place smelt of linseed and lavender. If houses give clues to the personalities of their occupants, and the Herberts' interior told of retired academics with a big family and rich inner lives, this was like a show home, impossible to read. The Tilsons seemed to have stepped straight out of the pages of a magazine, to have sprung from nowhere.

I'd left the front door open behind me and the noise of the road – a constant background drag and whoosh, like the roaring of the sea – must have masked the sound of my steps because after I had descended the small staircase and was standing at the entrance to the kitchen, neither of them registered my arrival.

It's possible, now I recall the scene, that they had in fact forgotten I was coming.

Tom was standing by the table, reading the *Week*. Ailsa was in front of me, looking out into the garden. She was smaller than I remembered, in Lycra leggings, trainers and a zip-up top, a further garment tied around her waist (a common appendage, I later discovered, to cover her bum). In movies you know when characters are going to kiss because the space between them shrinks; here it yawned and stretched.

I cleared my throat and like deer hearing a dog, they both turned their heads. Tom flung his magazine down onto the table with a small splat. 'Hello,' he said. 'Welcome.' Ailsa raised a palm in greeting. I realised then she was on the phone.

'OK, so you'll get an Uber,' Ailsa said, trying to catch Tom's eye. 'You and Milly, right? An Uber, is that OK? I suppose so. No later than ten. I mean it. OK.'

She hung up, and noticing her hands were dirty, turned on the tap with her elbow; rinsing them, she addressed me over her shoulder: 'Teenagers! Do you have kids?'

'No, but I know it's the age when they start pushing boundaries.' I should confess here to a bit of a newspaper and magazine habit; Mother didn't let them in the house, but I've made up for that since her death. It's amazing what life tips you can pick up – particularly from the Sunday supplements. 'The important thing is to choose your battles.'

'I know. Right?' she said, with an emphatic swoop and a half-laugh, a sort of delighted chirrup, as if I had just given the most insightful advice she'd ever heard. It is a trick, I know now, that tendency to agree so fulsomely with the person she's with. But it was new to me, then, and immediately alluring.

Tom put his hand out to accept my gift – a box of mint-flavoured Matchmakers. He was wearing the same bulky white trainers, but a different pair of jeans, wider in the leg with orange stitching along the seams.

'We didn't get off to a very good start the other day,' he said. 'I didn't have a chance to introduce myself properly. I'm Tom.'

'And I'm Ailsa,' Ailsa said, switching off the tap and anointing her hands with thick cream from a tube.

'Yes. Verity. Verity Ann Baxter.'

'Nice to meet you, Verity Ann Baxter,' Tom said, giving me a wide, warm smile. He put the chocolates down and reached out his hand to shake mine. He was studying me now, with close attention. I felt a matching fuchsia to my shirt creep into my cheeks. 'What can I get you? Tea, coffee . . .?' He clasped his hands together, making a small clap. 'Gin?'

I hesitated for a moment and then said: 'A gin and tonic would be lovely.'

He found a glass in one of the high cupboards and held it to the light, checking it passed muster before pouring in two caps of London gin, and a slosh of tonic. The ice he removed from a drawer in the fridge with a small metal shovel. His movements were tight and precise. 'Now, lemon . . .' he said, finding a tiny sharp knife.

A shadow flashed across the window – the woman in the wellies coming from the side return with a tray of plants. 'Oh God, I should be helping,' Ailsa said. 'Come and see what I'm doing. It's so exciting.'

I followed her across the kitchen and out through the open door. The Herberts hadn't been big gardeners, but there had been grass, bushes and a shed. All that had gone. A wide terrace had been made out of the same large pale beige stones as the kitchen floor. Beds had been freshly dug and something at the end that was either a sunken trampoline or a pond. The sky was heavy and leaden, a typical March sky. A blackbird or two pecked in the churned soil, but otherwise it was gloomy.

'Isn't it great?' Ailsa said. 'I was quite Japanese zen in Kent, but at the back there I'm planting cow parsley, poppies, cornflowers; lovely meadow flowers like that.'

The woman in the wellies had put down the tray and, hands on her waist, was stretching out her back. 'Cornflowers aren't actually meadow flowers,' she said. 'They'd only last a year in a permanent meadow. They need the soil to be turned; it's why they used to grow in ploughed fields – before herbicides wiped them out.'

'Yes of course.' Ailsa was smiling. 'Centaurea cyanus are annuals, of course.'

'The members of the papaver are the same.'

'I should probably talk about wildflowers, not meadow flowers.'

'Don't worry. It's a common mistake.'

Ailsa was still smiling. 'Not so much a mistake. A slip of the tongue.'

It was the first time I saw Delilah and Ailsa together, and I noticed the tension in this dialogue. But it didn't seem odd. People as they get older often seem to get more competitive with each other: all those tensely polite debates about driving routes, and holiday destinations, they're often irrationally personal and invested.

'This is Delilah,' Ailsa said. 'She's a professional garden designer. I garden for love, she gardens for money. Anyway, lucky me, she took me to her nursery today; it's trade, so much cheaper.'

'We've got our work cut out for us.' Delilah lifted her chin, pointing to the back. 'It was very neglected. Also, a high water table.'

'Underwater streams,' I said. 'Tributaries to the Wandle. And when people dig out their basements, well, they get diverted.' I smiled. My intention was not to antagonise. 'It's the price of change.'

'You can't create without first destroying.'

'Like much in life,' I said.

Delilah gave me a long look. 'I think I've seen you on the common,' she said. 'Are you the woman who feeds the birds?'

'Sometimes I do, yes.'

She nodded, then turned back to Ailsa. 'Listen, babe, I've got to go.' She kissed her on the cheek. 'Don't forget the rest of the plants. Shrubs are being delivered tomorrow.' She walked away from us through the doors into the kitchen. Ailsa and I followed. 'Tom?' Delilah said. 'The olive's still in the front seat. If you're feeling strong?'

He was leaning against the island, looking at his phone. At this, he lifted his chin, raising his hand and waving goodbye without looking up.

Delilah flipped him the finger, which he must have seen out of the corner of his eye, because he flipped it back.

'Delilah and Tom are old friends,' Ailsa said. 'They were at school together.'

'We used to snog,' Delilah said, hoping, I think, to shock.

'Wonders never cease,' I said before I could stop myself. Ailsa, who'd been following Delilah up to the hall, turned with surprise as if she'd underestimated me. I winked at her and she grinned back. It's hard to put my finger on why it was funny, but it was the moment, I think, that we saw something in each other; a shared sense of the absurd, perhaps, an instinct to undercut the posturing of others.

'Guilty as charged,' Tom said as he handed me my glass – a large tumbler, with a diamond pattern pressed into it. 'My misspent youth.'

'I'm sure the statute of limitations on that is up,' I said.

Pulling out a chair for me to sit at the table, he made a comic rolling of his eyes. 'I hope so.'

Ailsa came back into the room and joined us. I nursed my gin. Neither of them, I realised, had poured a drink for themselves.

I began over the next few minutes to wonder if I had misjudged Tom. I rather liked the way he treated me – a mild sort of semi-detached wryness. I even rather enjoyed the questions he began to level in my direction. I didn't often get to talk about myself. How long had I lived here? All my life? No! What extraordinary perseverance. I'd looked after my mother? I was a veritable saint. No siblings? A sister – 'Oh, the one that got away?' I smiled in agreement. 'You could say that, yes.' I became numbed to more dangerous enquiries. Had I noticed that a window at the back of my house – on the second floor, to the right – was badly cracked? We shared a drain: any problems in the past? Would I mind if they sent a man to have a little prod? I did rear back a few inches then, concealing my alarm in a joke – 'A little prod?' I said. 'It's a long time since a man's given me a little prod.' Ailsa deftly swooped in. 'I just love Trinity Fields,' she said. 'Nicer than Balham where we've been renting. I can understand why you live here. I can't imagine myself ever moving away.'

Why, I asked, had they left Kent?

Ailsa looked down. She started fiddling with the pepper pot on the table in front of her, grinding a tiny bit into her hand and then dipping her finger into it and dabbing it on her tongue.

'Don't mention Kent,' Tom said.

'OK.'

'We needed a fresh start,' Tom added. 'Kent's not everybody's cup of tea. To be honest, I hate the place.'

A silence bloomed.

Ailsa looked deeply uncomfortable. She was fiddling with her scalp, fiddling with her hair at the roots, with tense, almost aggressive stabs.

'Ailsa, you're in HR?' I said, to change the subject.

She looked up then. 'I'm not working at the moment,' she said. 'Finding it hard to get back into it after the kids.'

I turned back to Tom. 'And you're in the record business?'

'No. No. Not really. I'm a lawyer. I specialise in entertainment law. I've started my own boutique firm. The music biz is certainly part of it. Musicians. Tech companies.' He nodded his chin at a bouquet of flowers on the counter, still in their cellophane. 'The occasional movie star.'

I was about to ask which florally grateful occasional movie star – anyone I'd heard of? – when the front door slammed and two children burst into the doorway.

They were ten, I knew. Max and Bea. They had that almost-but-not-quite symmetry of some twins, the sense that one – in this case the girl – was slightly more finished than the other. The boy was paler, and smaller. He had a bruise on his forehead, and one of his eyes turned down very slightly. The girl, freckly and robust, bounced in, ignoring me, a stranger at the table, and started opening cupboards. 'What is there to eat?' she said. 'I'm starving.' The boy stood shyly in the doorway, a pair of football boots in his hands dropping flecks of mud onto the floor.

Ailsa got up and took the boots off the boy, quickly sweeping the bits of mud into one corner with her foot. She cupped the back of his head with her hand, smoothing his hair while drawing him into the room. She introduced me, made him and his sister say hello and then busied herself, pouring juice and reaching up to a top cupboard for a tin of cake. 'Lemon drizzle,' she said, handing them a slice each. 'That'll keep you going.'

'I love a lemon drizzle,' I said. I was still watching the boy. 'As long as it's *moist*.'

'Moist!' Ailsa said, bringing it over to the table. 'How funny. Do you just hate that word too? It's the worst, isn't it? Moist.'

It is very her, now I think of it, that tendency to kill a joke by spelling it out.

'How can you hate a word?' Bea said. 'That's so random.'

'I don't like words,' her brother said. 'Most of them anyway.'

'That's an odd thing to say.' Tom furrowed his brow. 'What will our new neighbour think of us?'

'Max's an idiot,' the girl said, springing across to sit on her father's knee.

The room appeared to regroup around me, the girl's arms snaked around her father's neck; the boy standing quietly behind his mother's chair. His eyes seemed to sink, the skin beneath them to darken. Family dynamics are always of interest to me. I know only too well how alliances build, how parents, despite their avowals to the contrary, have favourites. I could do anything for my mother: wash her, read to her, bring morsels of her chosen meals, and it was always Faith she talked about. 'Oh, but of course Faith,' she'd say to visitors, 'has done so well for herself.' I know, too, how it isn't always comfortable being the favourite, how it creates its own pressures and resentments. 'She never sees me,' Faith used to say. 'It all has to be wonderful. There's never any room for darkness.' But then that was Mother all over.

I opened my mouth to speak, to say anything, really, to rearrange the atoms. I began explaining how, in fact, it was actually quite a coincidence because words were my *metier*.

'Your metier?' Tom said, in that same arch tone. I suspect he hadn't associated me with employment. He probably thought I spent my time making jam, doing crafts.

'Indeed.'

And I told them about my work as a lexicographer for the OED, that I was involved with the history of language, how words and meanings have changed over time, and that my job was to help record that.

I could see, like many people, they didn't really grasp it. They seemed to decide that I worked for the Concise English Dictionary, that my role was not to document the changing meaning of words but simply to *spell* them.

'We could do with some help with spelling around here,' Ailsa said, reaching one arm back to touch Max's leg.

'Max has a learning difficulty. Or a learning difference as I think we're now supposed to call it.' Tom laughed, not exactly unkindly.

Ailsa sighed. 'It means homework is torture. It's all spellings.'

'This week they're impossible,' Max said. 'I mean how am I supposed to learn, like, "accommodation".'

'Two cots, two mattresses,' I said.

He swung his head to eye me with suspicion. '"Necessary".'

'One cap, two socks.'

'Or what about, like . . .' He wracked his brain. '"Rhythm"?'

'If you could say a sentence without saying "like", it would be a start,' Tom said.

I thought for a moment. 'Rhythm helps your two hips move.'

Bea slipped off her father's lap and grabbed a rucksack off the floor. She pulled a piece of loose paper out and started reading out the list: '"Harass". "Embarrass". "Forty". "Excellent". How can Max not know "excellent"? Maybe because he never sees it written at the end of his work.'

'Bea,' Ailsa said warningly. 'Don't be mean.'

I started improvising, coming up with mnemonics for each of the words listed, sprinkling in as many swear words as I

37

could manage. Ailsa was looking doubtful but when Max started to repeat the spellings back to me, she laughed and said: 'Move in, please, and do his homework with him every day? I'll pay you! Don't you think, Tom?'

He smiled thinly. 'If I couldn't spell a word when I was his age, my father used to tan me until I got it right. That's one method.'

'I think Verity's is rather better, don't you? Well I do anyway.' She reached out and squeezed my hand. 'Thank you.'

I took another sip of my gin and tonic. It really was quite stonkingly strong. I sat back in my chair, crossing my legs at the ankle. I began to feel strangely comfortable, to imagine myself sorting out this little family.

'So, Verity,' Tom said. He'd been looking at me. 'You have a dog.'

'Yes I do,' I said. 'She's a terrier-cross, a rescue – wire-haired – big squirreler.'

'Is it squirrels then that he's barking at in the garden?' Tom said.

Ailsa was watching him, with a placid smile. Her fingers had begun again to fiddle with her hair, isolating a strand; she gave it a little tug. It was something I would later see her do often.

I put my glass down on the table. I'd left a ludicrous pink lipstick mark on the rim; I wiped at it with my thumb. 'Yes. Or foxes. She—' I paused for emphasis. 'Also likes a fox.'

Smoothing my skirt, I noticed a stain just above the knee where I had spilt some tomato sauce opening a tin of baked beans.

'One suggestion,' Tom said reasonably. 'One way in which the foxes might bugger off and the dog shut up is if you cut your garden back a bit. As I said the other day, it's only neighbourly of you to clear some of that undergrowth; all those weeds, goodness knows what's in there. We're trying to make a nice garden here and we don't want all that unknown stuff propagating in ours. The ivy's creeping everywhere. And those trees of yours – the holly, the apple, etc – they're blocking out a lot of our light.'

I rubbed my wrists where the elastic in the gathered sleeves on my new top had left a crinkled line of indentations. As the silence tightened, I was aware of something growing taut inside me too. How foolish I'd been to think they might be interested in my company.

I sat up straighter. I tried to think about the mnenomics and to be grateful for the gin. I smiled into their expectant faces and said, 'I'll have a little prune, then.'

Tom's jaw relaxed. 'That's great news.' He clapped his hands together. 'Super.' He nodded at Ailsa and, pushing his chair back, walked over to his phone which he had left charging on the side. 'If you'll excuse me a second,' he said. He began scrolling through his messages, then tapped out one of his own, his brow furrowed. 'What time's supper?' he said to Ailsa without looking up.

She sighed deeply. It sounded like a release of tension. She started sweeping crumbs into a little pile. 'When would you like it?'

He didn't answer.

When I got to my feet and said I ought to be going no one suggested that I didn't.

They both accompanied me to the front door – grateful, perhaps, to see me go, grateful certainly for the major garden decimation upon which I was shortly to embark (NOT!). On the table in the hall was a bag of old clothes – 'Heart Foundation' the bag said on the front. My eye must have rested on this a fraction too long, because Ailsa looked at me and her lips parted, as if she had thought of saying something, but hadn't quite found the right words.

I couldn't bear it, so I leapt in and told her the church was having a jumble and I could take it for her if that was easier, and she nodded, relieved even, and handed it over.

There is a lot to say about this first meeting. Certainly at the time I registered a sense of unease, of something being not quite right; definitely in Ailsa's behaviour, an impression she was subdued. But when I reached the gate, they were framed in the doorway; his arm was around her shoulder and she was leaning into him. What was it he said? 'A fresh start'. They looked like the perfect couple, on the threshold of their new home.

At the time it wasn't the dynamic between them, but my relationship with them on which I fixated.

They had already, you see, begun to draw me in.

Chapter Five

1 bicycle pump valve adapter connector, red

Petrichor, *noun*. A pleasant, distinctive smell frequently accompanying the first rain after a long period of warm dry weather in certain regions.

I saw Rose this morning at the post office; she was in the queue ahead of me, arms full of ASOS packages to return. Just another mother doing their teenager's dirty work. I thought of hiding, but in the end I butched it out. Of all the people who've betrayed Ailsa, she's the worst. I'll never forgive her for driving the children down to Tom's parents – who knows what poison they're dripping into the children's ears? What happened to them all? Where did they go? The women at her book club. The gang from Pilates. *Delilah*? Death is of course its own form of embarrassment. I think of all those neighbours who crossed the road to avoid me when Mother died. How much worse when the chief mourner is said to have hastened the death. What is due then? Commiserations or big congrats? I'm being facetious. But the instinct of Ailsa's friends to turn their backs, to say 'She wasn't who I thought she was' unsettles me. It's too tidy. No one seems to appreci- ate that maybe it's greyer and murkier; that she is still the same person, that maybe she's deserving of their sympathy, or empathy. I suspect none of them were ever proper friends; these relationships, like so much with Ailsa, were a chimera.

It was on the top of my tongue when I saw Rose to say something. Instead, I just walked past her, my face rigid.

Ten days or so after the gin and tonic, I was walking across the small triangle of common between the train station and the road. I'd had lunch with Fred Pullen, my old university friend, and I was in a frisky mood. We had met at Côte in Covent Garden. His treat. Wine had been drunk.

The boy was walking along the path in front of me, in a school sweatshirt, carrying a backpack. He had a stick in his left hand and he was swiping at everything he passed: trees, a bin, a bench, a lamp-post. Clack, swish, clack. The backpack was only half zipped, and on each second or third swipe, a small item fell out: a pencil, a screwed-up piece of paper, a satsuma.

I picked the objects up, one after another, and then quickened my pace, to draw alongside him. 'Hail fellow, well met,' I said.

Max reared away from my outstretched hand, dropping the stick in his alarm. He spun his head wildly as if in search of rescue.

'Verity Baxter from next door,' I said. 'She of the big elephants?'

He didn't seem to recall with quite the fervour I'd expected, but he did scoop up his lost property and then made rather heavy weather of unshouldering his bag and stuffing them back in. I suggested he zip it fully this time, which he did.

We continued walking. I asked him how he'd done in his spelling test and he told me he'd got 7/10 and Bea had got 10, but she always did better than him. I asked where she was, and he told me drama club and that he hated drama club because of the teacher – 'You think she's nice and then she suddenly shouts at you for no reason.' He let out a heavy sigh. Sometimes he cycled to school, he said, but his bike had a puncture and he'd lost the bit from the pump you slot into the tyre. 'I always lose things, my dad says. He says when he was growing up he had to do chores to earn nice things, that I wouldn't lose them if I understood their value.' I listened, solicited a few more details and when we reached my house, told him to wait on my front path. He seemed nervous, insisting on hovering beyond the gate. A minute or two later – really quite a stroke of luck that I laid my hands on it so quickly – I emerged with what I could tell from his gleeful expression was the required value.

He said thank you several times and promised to bring it back. 'Now I've just got my homework to get through,' he added, in a weary sing-song.

'Story writing', it turned out. He'd been told to finish his 'weather bank'. He'd started it in class and lots had already handed theirs in but – another heavy sigh, at the end of which he met my eyes for the first time: 'What exactly is a weather bank?'

I don't know what came over me, really. Partly it was the way his hair rose unbidden at the back: caused, I now know, by a double crown. Partly it was the reference to his father. I'm no expert but it doesn't seem ideal parenting to accuse one's child of 'always' doing anything. Mainly, though, it was the hopefulness of his expression – as if, after my success with the pump, this was another problem I could solve. I succumbed; to charm, or flattery, or out of sympathy or maybe it was the lunchtime glass of wine and, before I knew it, I'd volunteered my services.

Max had a key but he couldn't make it work, and eventually a girl came to the door, wearing school games kit and fluffy bedroom socks, eating a piece of toast. I knew this was Melissa: I'd seen her around even if she hadn't seen me. Her long dark hair was pulled back across a pimply forehead, her bulbous, snub nose appeared too large for her face. Her features always have a naturally sullen cast in repose, and she has braces. But she smiled widely when she saw me, practised politeness to a stranger on the doorstep, and when she did so the young Brigitte Bardot came to mind – making sense of the seagull row of boys who'd sat on my front wall the weekend her parents were away.

Ailsa was out, she told me – Wednesday was her 'food bank day' – and I wasn't sure whether to feel relieved or disappointed.

Max and I sat at the kitchen table and he got out a crumpled exercise book. He'd written a few words about a summer's day – 'The sun was like a yellow ball. The clouds were like cotton wool.' (I've corrected his spelling.) I suggested we start again, opting for bad weather and, with my guidance, he cobbled together a paragraph about a storm: rain 'like needles', 'scudding' clouds', 'furious thunder', wind 'pushing and shoving me like a bully', and afterwards the 'fresh grassy' smell of the earth. He had a list of 'language features' he had to include – similes, metaphors, personification and something alarming called 'wow words', all of which I found a little reductive.

I began to really rather throw myself into it. 'We'll give them wow words!' I said.

I didn't hear anything from next door for a few days after this. It was just one of many good deeds, I told myself, flung into the abyss. But on the Friday of that week, Ailsa popped a card through my door, thanking me sooo much for mending Max's bike and also for sorting his weather bank. 'His teacher thought his writing was brilliant!!!' She included her mobile phone number and asked if I would get in touch if I were at all interested in tutoring him on a more formal footing. Just for a few weeks or so until SATs. They could offer £15 an hour. He so rarely agrees to any help. If I had time, etc, etc. 'And I am hopelessly impatient' ('hopelessly' underlined three times).

Over the weekend, I let the card languish. I'd seen adverts for tutors on the community noticeboard in the big Sainsbury's in Balham. I knew £15 was way below market value. Also, in my experience any regular commitment can start to feel claustrophobic. I remembered that from the time I signed up to AquaFit at the leisure centre. But the idea didn't go away. It had been gratifying, even over one afternoon, to watch Max grow gradually more enthusiastic towards the written word. I felt sorry for him. I liked the thought of arming him in a small way, against the other members of his family. Helping my sister Faith with her homework, when we were teenagers, was always enjoyable. Her gratitude itself was rewarding. Also, even with my commitment to the OED, time did sometimes hang heavy on my hands.

I picked the card up to study it. This book cover was *Memory* by Ian M. L. Hunter, and included a picture of a finger tied with a piece of string. I imagined Ailsa taking all the cards out of the box and choosing the one she felt was most applicable. It was Max's memory, after all, she was concerned about. It was this that swung it, really, the notion that she had put care and thought into it. I rang her to accept.

'Really?' she said. 'That's fantastic news. You've literally saved my life.'

'Well not literally, I hope.'

'No, not literally.' She laughed, but then when she'd stopped, said, 'But no, seriously, you literally have.'

The following Wednesday, I turned up at 4 p.m. on her

doorstep, dressed in a manner I thought appropriate. My office clothes were not in the best condition; I couldn't lay my hands on the skirt and blouse that would have been perfect. But I spent most of Tuesday trawling the charity shops on Northcote Road and I'd found a couple of suits that were only a little big; not in the best nick, but serviceable. I would alternate.

I think I was hoping we would have a little chat first, but she was business-like when she opened the door. She was in gym kit, and in the short time it took to set us up at the table her phone buzzed several times. She took the call out in the garden eventually, smiling into the phone as she walked up and down across the terrace, occasionally leaning down to pick up a leaf. After a bit, she sat down on a step and hugged her knees. She played with her hair; not picking at it the way she had in Tom's company, but puffing it up, giving it body. I wondered who it was on the other end of the call who made her so relaxed, and I felt a little left out and jealous. Which was absurd.

Max wasn't an easy pupil, and after a while I became absorbed in trying to work him out. Faith was just lazy. 'Oh, you just do it, V,' she used to say, one eye on *Blue Peter*. Max's brain was clearly wired differently; sitting still was an effort for him. He had a comprehension, 'The Drummer Boy', to do, and I defaced the paper with different-coloured highlighters, to pinpoint the alliteration, the metaphors, etc. He worked better if I made him run up and down to the basement between questions. I discovered what interested him – not rugby, the sport his father wanted him to be good at, but football (Chelsea in particular), and dogs and an Xbox game called *World of Warcraft*, and also magic, and various Netflix shows, including *Stranger Things*, which I had read about in the *Radio Times*. I'm not bad on football – the tabloids keep me updated on the Premier League, and the glitzier players often have spreads in

Hello!. One of the questions was 'How do you think the drummer boy feels?' and I suggested he imagine the lad was a mascot for a big game, and he almost immediately picked out the relevant language, 'smiling triumphantly as tall men grin and nod', etc. The hour went quickly – for me at least – and when Max got down from the table, he seemed visibly relieved to have polished off a task that usually, I imagine, weighed on his shoulders for a full week.

'You're a star,' Ailsa told me, coming back in from the garden.

There was no mention of money. Perhaps this was a trial session. For the moment, it didn't matter. I'm not embarrassed to admit, I left with a spring in my step.

The following two Wednesdays, Melissa opened the door, calling for Max who gingerly made a cup of tea – they didn't own a kettle but used a special narrow tap from which spluttered boiling water: quite perilous. Bea, I learnt, had drama club and was dropped back at the end of the session. There was a little bit of awkwardness with the woman, 'Tricia', who brought her home on the first week. I'd left Max at the kitchen table to open the door, but she called for him to come up and see her and then gave him quite an interrogation: 'Do you actually know this woman?' Apparently satisfied, she apologised for doubting me, flicking her blonde hair behind her ears with shiny white-tipped fingernails, but after I closed the door I could hear her on the phone – obviously to Ailsa – explaining how she had 'felt uneasy' and 'needed to check it was "kosher"', that 'she' – i.e. me – was 'genuinely allowed to be there'.

Still no sign of any money, which was a little concerning, though I told myself perhaps I was to be paid monthly, as in a proper salary. I should have raised it early on, but I was enjoying myself too much, really quite throwing myself into it.

I looked online for guidance, read up on kinaesthetic learning and memory tricks on dyslexic websites and school hubs. I got him to talk about *World of Warcraft*, 'a land called Azeroth peopled by mighty heroes', and taught him some card tricks I remembered from my own childhood. We discussed the knockout stages of the Champions League and I found a football which we kicked back and forth while we went over his spellings. On the third week, I texted Ailsa to ask if I could bring Maudie, and when Max had written a whole sentence on 'Why *World of Warcraft* leads to limitless adventures' he gave her a single stroke, double if there were no spelling mistakes, and when he had completed a paragraph, with the requisite number of adverbs or prepositions, he and she had a game of ball. Something about the irregular reward system, and the sensory feedback, as with dog training, seemed to help his concentration.

I tended not to think too much about my environment while I was teaching. We kept our heads down. The kitchen was always spotlessly tidy and a little cold; I do remember that. Once or twice, I wondered whether to light the wood-burning stove, but on closer inspection, it seemed to be as yet unused, the pretty basket of logs and kindling next to it solely for show.

It was on my fourth session that things changed. Bea had just got home – my cue to leave – and I was packing up my papers and pens, when my phone rang. It was Ailsa. She was coming in and out of signal, but I quickly gathered she wasn't at her food bank but in town; she was at a job interview and they'd asked her to stay on. Melissa was at a play rehearsal, she said, and wouldn't be back until 9 p.m. though Tom had promised to be home by 6 or 7 p.m. at the latest. Could I hold the fort for an hour, tops? Did I mind terribly?

Amazing. I was an absolute angel.

When I hung up, I was alone in the kitchen. I could hear gunfire and shouts from the basement; shrill voices and laughter from the TV in the front room. I glanced back at Max's comprehension, unable to resist adding a full stop and altering a lower-case letter into a capital. It was early April and still light out, but the room was east-facing. I had taken my shoes off, and the limestone floor felt cool beneath my feet. I gazed out of the back doors into the garden. No one had said anything more to me about my overhanging bushes, but they'd had a go at them from this side – any greenery they could reach had been trimmed down to the height of the new trellis. The olive stood erect in a pale terracotta urn on the new lime-stone terrace, and several new shrubs had been planted, as well as lots of squat dobs of green. The back was still lit by the low sun; despite the towering wall of my trees, and next to the trampoline, someone had created a bed out of railway sleep-ers. Her wildflower meadow? Still empty, it was bathed in a shaft of golden evening light; I could see insects whirling.

I chanced the boiling-water tap for another cup of tea and then, clasping it in my hands more as a prop than refresh-ment, stared about me. On the counter, next to the stove, was a small lasagne covered in clingfilm. The week before it had been a chicken pie. Before that, a stir-fry, the vegetables neatly chopped in preparation. Was that odd, or normal, to be so methodical? I worked with a woman at the library who had OCD and she told me that, after cleaning her teeth in the morning, she would prepare her toothbrush for the evening – even in the knowledge it would dry out. I asked if she thought that otherwise she would forget? She said it wasn't about that, it was about fear and control.

The fridge was half empty: not much more than milk, orange juice, a bottle of wine, a pack of butter. No mint sauce or chutneys past their sell-by dates, no piece of old cheese disintegrating into clingfilm. I am not the best judge of these things but the pull-out cupboard that housed the PG Tips also seemed unnaturally neat, the boxes of tea lined up in height order. The other cupboards were the same: cereal packets, and jams perfectly displayed, plates stacked. Even the cutlery drawer was clinically tidy, none of the elastic bands and glue sticks, and muddle of tape measure and takeaway chopsticks that you find in most cutlery drawers. It's a long time since you've been able to open mine. The effect was disconcerting. I thought of that film *Sleeping with the Enemy*, when Julia Roberts knows her ex-husband has been in the house because all the labels on her tin cans have been turned to face the same way. Not that order necessarily indicated the presence of a psychopath.

I'd been down into the basement where Max had now escaped to, the week before. I knew it had an enormous screen on one wall and a large, pale-grey linen, L-shaped sofa; not much else. The double sitting room, where Bea was ensconced in front of the TV, was equally minimalist; white shutters, a light-blue velvet sofa, some sheepskin rugs, that dangly swan-feather chandelier. The back half of the room, which I could see up some steps from where I was sitting, contained a black upright Yamaha piano, nothing else. There were no pictures. It was only the downstairs loo that was decorated, exclusively with things from Tom's past; group photographs of his school rugby team and Cambridge college year, and a framed *New Yorker* cartoon of two cats waiting outside a mouse hole. Caption: 'If we were lawyers this would be billable time.'

Upstairs was uncharted territory; even the builders hadn't let me up there. My mind turned to it. I was about to say I didn't mean to snoop, but I might as well be truthful: I did.

On the half-landing were two doors; the first opened onto a bedroom, a mirror image of Faith's, but this one was square and bland and neutral. Next to this was a small bathroom decorated in shades of green and white; an unused cake of soap sat in a porcelain dish, both the dish and the soap shaped like shells. Half a flight up, the space had been reconfigured. The loft conversion had shrunk the landing, and whereas we had three doors, here were only two. The first opened onto the equivalent of my bedroom: a study containing a desk, computer, shelves of files, and neatly stacked piles of paper. The other door was closed. I hesitated for a moment before pushing it open.

It was a beautiful room – the same shape and size as my mother's – with three large sash windows (invisibly double-glazed, I knew from talking to the builders). A door led to an en-suite bathroom. Fitted cupboards ran along one wall, and to the right, facing me, was a light oak four-poster bed; one of those modern ones with posts but no curtains. A full-length mirror rested on a matching wood stand, and there were two bedside tables, but otherwise: nothing. An empty wastepaper bin. No baskets of make-up, or dirty socks. No cascading piles of books; no magazines; no overflowing boxes of jewellery or tide-marked glasses of water.

I crossed to the bed, and carefully pulled open the drawer of the closest bedside table. It contained a pair of Sony head-phones, an iPad and four passports. The cupboard beneath was empty.

I walked round the bed, to the side closest to the window, and this time I had to tug hard to open the drawer. It burst open to reveal earplugs and eye-masks, a charger in a silk bag, a vial of 'black onion oil', several boxes of prescription pills, tubs of vitamins – evening primrose and black cabosh. Books were crammed into the cupboard beneath. They were all self-help tomes – *Eat, Drink, Run: How I Got Fit Without Going Too Mad* and *You Are a Badass: How to Stop Doubting Your Greatness and Live an Awesome Life*. Underneath was a slim volume, *Bit Sad Today*, but that seemed to be a collection of essays.

A door creaked open downstairs and I heard Bea shout at Max to check the wi-fi. I'd been crouching but I stood up and shut the cupboard and slid the drawer in and made to leave the room. I was aware of suddenly coming back to my senses, of saying, 'What am I doing?' to myself. I can only think I had got swept up in my search for some sign of warmth, some indication that the Tilsons had stamped their taste, their *personality* on the place. Perhaps, as the house had sat empty for so long, I also had a sense of entitlement. Totally misplaced, of course.

Bea was still talking, but in a different voice and with long pauses and sudden giggles; she was on her phone. 'I know, right? It was *fierce.*' I tiptoed to the door and was about to leave, when I noticed through the holes in the wicker waste-paper bin a scrap of grey; it wasn't empty after all. I reached in – there were some scrunched-up tissues with what looked like blood on them. And a curled-up piece of thin, smokey grey, fabric which I unravelled: a cotton scarf, not square, but long and thin and badly damaged. Several jagged tears, or even cuts, ran along the edge of the fabric, and at one end was a dark reddish stain. But it might wash, I told myself, rubbing the cotton together to test, and when I had a moment, I could take a needle and thread to it. I put it in my pocket. Yes, I suppose looking back, I did already want a little bit of her. But waste not, want not: that was always our mantra growing up. And it's a habit I confess I have found hard to let go.

'Oh my God,' Ailsa cried, seeing me at the kitchen table. 'You're still here! I don't believe it. You poor thing.' She took off her wedged boots. 'No Tom?' She frowned. 'He told me he'd be home.' Her expression changed; she looked thoughtful. 'OK, so he won't even know I've been out. OK. Fine.' Then she smiled, recovered. 'I'm so sorry. What must you think of us?'

'It's quite all right,' I said. 'These things happen.'

She was wearing black tights and a loose charcoal-grey silky dress with a cardigan around her waist; it was slipping, and she pulled it up to re-tie it. 'The children must be starving. You must be starving.'

'I'm afraid I cooked,' I said. 'Bea and Max were asking for food, so I put in the lasagne. Was that OK?'

'Did they eat it?'

'Yes.'

'All of it? They're such fussy eaters. Bea keeps trying to be veggie.' She looked around the room, then she opened the fridge, and the dishwasher, and looked in the sink, as if she didn't believe me. In fact, the twins *had* turned their noses up. I'd thrown most of theirs away. I was the one who had taken the lion's share. 'I'm sorry,' I said. 'We didn't leave any for you.'

'I didn't need it anyway.' She patted her stomach. 'I'm on a diet. Thanks for washing up. I'm embarrassed, that's all. You shouldn't have had to. I'll just check on the twins.' She left the room then and I could hear her, clambering between the basement and the front room, harrying them both upstairs. 'What will Verity think of you, being on screens so long?' I was putting on my jacket, thinking how both she and Tom seemed to care what I thought of the children, and also if they minded so much about screens, perhaps they should buy a few *games*, when she walked back in and stood in the doorway. 'It's only eight o'clock. It's not even that late.' She looked disappointed suddenly, deflated; all dressed up, slightly pissed, no food to eat, the evening stretching ahead of her. 'Oh well.' She opened the fridge door and brought out a bottle of white wine, then reached up for a couple of glasses. 'You'll have a quick drink, won't you, before you go?'

I hesitated. I needed to get back to Maudie but the evening stretched long ahead of me. Smiling with what I hoped was devil-may-care abandon, I slipped back onto my chair. 'Yes. Why not?'

She brought the bottle and the glasses over and sat down next to me. 'What a treat,' she said, pouring it out. 'You're always rushing off [not true], so it's nice to have a chance for a chat.'

For a moment, I thought she would bring up the trees, but her head was clearly elsewhere, and for a few minutes she talked non-stop, about the guy she'd just been up to meet, how it wasn't exactly an interview, more of an informal chat; how brilliant he was, and unexpected, totally self-made, well, he and his wife, and how massively their company was expanding, and how he'd told her they always needed people, but she wasn't sure she'd sufficiently impressed, she'd been out of the job market so long; the children, and a few health problems, and elderly parents, both now sadly dead, and how she hadn't had it easy and how difficult it was being an only child. She'd done her best to impress, though, 'That's the thing about me, I always throw myself into things.'

I listened, and made the odd noise. I was interested by the way she spoke. She seemed oblivious to her audience, but occasionally her eyes darted to meet mine, and I think it was an illusion. Now I know her better, I believe it to be a habit she developed as a child, a means of blocking out the silence between warring parents. She got used to people being not so much a sounding board as an echo chamber for her own narrative. Listening, you get the impression half the time she is trying to convince herself.

'Anyway, it was good to be out. Just to get the Tube into town, to be in bars, surrounded by people, music. You forget what that's like. I thought, moving back to London, I'd be busier than I am. I've tried to sign up for things, but Tom's so often out, and I do seem to be spending a lot of time on my own, and I'm not very good at it.'

'I've always thought it important to like one's own company. You have to train yourself, but it's worth it.'

She looked at me carefully. 'Yes, I suppose so.'

'Anyway, hopefully you'll get the job!'

'Do you think? I mean I have got transferable skills. I've brought up three children, and managed a home.'

'Wisdom and life experience,' I said. 'They've got to be better than youth in the job market. If this chap is any good, he'll see that.'

'I hope so. Thank you.' She took a sip from her glass and then ran her thumb over the rim where her lips had been. 'You're on your own, you said, next door? Your mother died how long ago?'

'Five years.'

'Do you have any other family?'

'Just a sister. Faith.'

'And is she nearby? Do you see much of her?'

'Brighton. Not as much as I'd like.'

She considered me for a moment more and then she extended her hand and gave the lapel of my jacket a quick, brisk sweeping. 'Hairs,' she said, withdrawing it. 'Possibly dog.'

'Oh dear. And I was trying so hard to look smart.'

She smiled suddenly. 'For us? For Max? Oh, Verity, please don't worry about things like that. I want you to feel relaxed here. I'm hoping now things have settled down a bit we're going to be friends, in and out of each other's houses.'

I felt suddenly coy. 'I'd like that,' I said.

We talked a little more – about nothing, really; I told her about my arthritis and she suggested a few things: a hot-water bottle, arnica cream. At the door, she took both my hands. 'It's been lovely to chat,' she said. I could feel the roughness of her palms. 'Max says you're cool. And he's right.'

I was disarmed. I'm used to keeping myself very rigid. I'm not used to compliments. People should be careful not to splash niceness around. I'm reminded of Konrad Lorenz's imprinting experiment with goslings – how on hatching, they followed the first moving creature they saw. In their case him. Nothing was to break that bond until death.

I think it must have been talking about Mother that did it, but a tear was unexpectedly pricking at the corner of my eye. I flicked it away.

'Likewise,' I said.

Chapter Six

Tortoiseshell hairslide

Burgeoning, *gerund & present participle*. **To bud or sprout; to begin to grow.**

This morning, I came out of my front door to see Delilah standing on the opposite pavement, staring up at the house. A murder scene is a draw. When Ailsa was first arrested, people regularly gathered outside or drove slowly past in their cars. I thought I'd got used to it, but when I saw Delilah, the prickliness of it got under my skin. I decided I'd had enough.

'You should stay away,' I called, zipping up my jacket.

She waited for a gap in the traffic to cross over.

'Still with you, is she?'

'It's part of her bail condition.'

'She owes me a lot of money, you know. All those plants I bought for her on my trade account. She never paid me.'

'Well she's not in a particularly good position to do so now.'

'I want to see her, to find out if you can see it in her face, what she's done.'

'You don't know she's done anything.'

'He wasn't perfect. None of us are. He made some mistakes. But the night he died, he told me . . . oh, it doesn't matter.' She had begun to cry.

'You spoke to him the night he died?'

'I was dropping Max off.' She wiped her eyes impatiently. 'The police already know. Don't look so shocked.'

It's possible when she said what she said next, she was simply searching her own history with Ailsa for justification, using the tragedy as an opportunity to vent all the resentments she harboured about her friend. 'The thing about Ailsa,' she said, 'is she couldn't admit when things were going wrong. Everything had to be milkshakes and candyfloss.'

I said: 'She has always been lovely to me.'

Delilah had started to cross back over the road. But over her shoulder, she hissed: 'You hardly know her.'

I didn't expect to see Ailsa so soon after the evening I 'babysat'. I'm not so devoid of self-knowledge that, while her protestations of friendship may have impacted heavily on me, I expected them necessarily to have registered with her. But the next morning, having navigated my front path, she was at my door, holding out a bunch of tulips. It was a long time since anyone had bought me flowers – even at the height of our relationship, Adrian Curtis hadn't stretched to floral tributes – and I was so touched I nearly lost control of my face.

A skip lorry clanked and rattled past, followed by a bus. 'I feel guilty,' she said, thrusting them at me. 'You were in the house for hours yesterday, and you've made such a difference with Max.' She came a step closer. 'I haven't even paid you yet, have I? God. I'm hopeless. Sorry. Next week, I'll get to the bank. In the meantime I'd love to do something to say thank you: I could help you out here, for example'. She gestured vaguely at a few things I'd collected in the porch. 'And also what about lunch? Can I coax you out of your lair?'

'What, now?'

'No time like the present.'

Was it pity? If so, she concealed it. Flustered, a smile still playing havoc with my cheeks and chin, I agreed and left her on the doorstep while I quickly got myself together, emptying the sink and filling it with water to make room for the flowers, and sorting through piles until I found my purse, and changing out of the silver-grey Uniqlo crew-neck, which I realised had come in her bag of jumble, and into the festive pink blouse.

She had suggested a cafe in Balham and we drove down in her Fiat, parking at the back of Sainsbury's. She locked the car with her fob – it made a satisfying clink – and as we crossed the car park, I felt a leap of curiosity and excitement, the thrill of new possibilities. One minute I was a lexicographer at her desk, teasing out 'angry' as it relates to the colour red. The next, I was *a lady who lunched*. When a thin woman with blonde hair, emptying shopping into her boot, greeted Ailsa by name, and a Mini tooted, a hand waving out of the window, I remarked on her popularity. She laughed. 'Acquaintances, not friends. Anyway, five minutes later and we'd have bumped into chums of yours.' I'm sure she was already aware I wasn't big on 'chums'. She was just being nice. But it didn't matter. She was just one of those women who got noticed, I told myself, and I bathed in the warmth of her inclusion.

The cafe, which was newly opened, was decorated with naked bricks and industrial wall lights. Artificial plants hung upside down from baskets on the ceiling. It was busy, including several children who should surely have been at school. There was a small kerfuffle when we first arrived, finding space for my trolley. I don't know why I took it; silly of me. Finally settled, we sat at the far side, against the wall by the window. Ailsa ordered 'huevos rancheros' and, slightly bewildered by the available choices, I copied. When it came, a great mess of eggs and beans and chorizo, she tucked in voraciously. (I was soon to learn she either ate a lot or not at all; there was no middle ground with her.)

At first, we talked about Max. Tom, she said, was keen to hear about his progress. (Had he urged her to have this lunch for that reason? I hoped not.) I gave her my observations in detail: that he was very bright and creative and keen, but was slowed by a literal approach to language. When his teacher had recently told the class to 'take themselves to a beach', he'd been paralysed by confusion. She nodded and kept her eyes on me, her face very still. I said: 'He's fine when it's explained to him that what he's being asked to do is imagine. He concentrates much better when he understands what he's supposed to be doing. It's frustration that's distracting for him. I'm going to keep drumming in the kind of questions he'll get asked and teach him techniques to shortcut them.'

'He says you talk to him about football and *World of Warcraft*,' she said. 'It's so nice of you to take so much trouble.'

'I'm happy to help,' I said.

'Tom can't bear to see him doing so badly at school. His upbringing was very rigorous, really, very academically focused. His father was a judge and expectations were high: boarding schools and Cambridge and *the law*. Doing well was how Tom got his father's attention. They were shit parents really. You know, his parents wouldn't turn up for matches if he wasn't in the first team? It was a huge thing for him when he did make it in, and on the first match he was subbed off, and they left. Can you imagine? So Tom, I don't know, he associates success with love. He takes it personally that Max doesn't seem to want to try. And then he shouts at him, and Max is beginning to talk back, and, well, it all goes horribly wrong.'

I winced. 'Well hopefully, we can break the pattern.'

She pushed her plate away from her. 'Tom is talking about sending him to school.'

I was confused. Max was already *at* school. If I'd realised she meant boarding school, I'd have answered with more indignation. 'He's a gorgeous boy, sweet and engaging, and extremely bright. You shouldn't worry. He will be absolutely fine.'

She looked vulnerable; the skin beneath her eyes seemed to tighten; her eyes to magnify as if covered by film. I covered my mouth with my hand. What would I do if she cried? But she didn't. 'Oh, you are lovely,' she said. 'You say all the right things!'

'I mean it. I wouldn't say any of it otherwise. I'm not one of those people who compliments others just for the sake of it.'

Across the room, I noticed a small girl of about eight was staring at me. I brought my hand to my hair and readjusted the tortoiseshell comb – bought for a few pence at a 'tabletop sale' at the local church – that was secured there.

Ailsa smiled. 'I can see that.'

When the plates had been cleared and we were sipping small grey cups of coffee – 'flat whites', which I had always wanted to try – she told me about her own upbringing, in a village outside Guildford. Her mother was an estate agent and her father an accountant. They were comfortable materially but her parents fought a lot and finally divorced when she was twenty. They'd have separated earlier, but at twelve Ailsa was diagnosed with a rare chronic disorder – an inability to process copper, Wilson's disease – and the trauma of it brought them together. 'I was very tired and anxious but I was lucky because it was detected early. I'll always have to take medication, which is a shame, but.' She shrugged.

As I expressed sympathy, a slightly self-pitying expression came into her face. She always talks about being lucky, but I know deep down she thinks she's unlucky: this rare disorder struck *her*, and while it kept her parents together during her teens, it didn't work forever. Bottom line, her illness wasn't *quite* bad enough. In the cafe, I just admired her. But on occasions since, I have wondered if she subconsciously exaggerates things that have gone wrong for her – that it's her way of seeking attention.

'It was all rather grim,' she said. 'Arguments and slamming doors, my mother drank like a fish, and then two years after they finally split, she got breast cancer, which I'm convinced was caused by the stress of it all, and that was that. It knocked me for six. You know, she was relatively young and, being an only child, it was hard.'

'And your father?'

'My father moved to the Far East but he died, um, it must be eight years ago now. So, yes, I'm an orphan.' She let out a sigh, noisy enough to express self-mockery as well as regret.

I sighed too – the intention was equally comic – and she looked at me across the table. 'You too?' she said.

I felt uncomfortable. 'Oh. Me? I'm not sure. I think my father's dead, but I don't knew for sure.'

'Why don't you know for sure?'

I hadn't expected the conversation to turn – it had seemed fixed very much in one direction, and I'd been perfectly happy with that. So really, it was as a sort of distancing technique that I told the anecdote of my father and the 319 bus. I thought she would laugh and we could drop it, but she didn't. She looked quite serious. She said: 'And do you think that's what really happened?'

I laughed. 'I don't know. He took a suitcase if he did because his half of the wardrobe was empty.'

Her face didn't change. 'How awful.'

I looked down at the floor. I had a sudden image of my mother standing inside the cupboard, wailing and crying uncontrollably, the bare hangers clacking in her hands as she shook them, the shock of this woman, usually so composed, breaking down.

When I looked up, I started talking. 'My sister and I, we went to a jumble sale that Saturday; I think it might even have been the next day, and we spent all the money we'd saved on armfuls of men's clothes – some old boy must have died – and we filled that wardrobe, and when we showed her, she laughed and kissed our faces, and we had cake for tea, and it was all forgotten.'

'That's sweet and sad. What did she do with the clothes? Take them to the next jumble sale?'

I raised my palms in the air. 'We kept them all. Still there.'

'Verity. All these years, you've kept some random dead man's clothes?'

'Afraid so.'

'Verity. That's a bit weird.'

'The clothes cheered her up. They stopped her being sad.'

'You should have a clear-out.'

'Yes. Yes.' I felt flustered. 'I know.'

The waitress brought the bill and then went away again to find the machine. While she was gone Ailsa said gently that she assumed my mother had never married again, and I told her that was true, she hadn't.

'And your sister?'

'Faith? Married men, yes, but generally not her own.'

'And you?'

'No. Never fancied it.'

'Or maybe never met someone you fancied.'

The sun had moved and I was sitting in a triangle of light. I was facing the room and I fanned my warmed cheeks with my napkin. I tried to laugh, but didn't know what to say. Ailsa must have picked up on my discomfort because she filled the

63

silence. 'I've made terrible choices that way,' she said, leaning forwards as if in confidence. 'Probably including Tom.'

The waitress returned and Ailsa put first her card, and then her number into the portable machine. 'I was vulnerable when I met him,' she continued when the transaction was finished. 'I'd been having a bit of a tough time what with one thing and another.' She leant back in her chair. Delilah had introduced them, she told me, a great gang of them had gone out for drinks after work. She and Delilah were both working for an advertising company; Tom was in corporate law. It wasn't a natural fit. He was, is, an intellectual snob, and Ailsa, who hadn't been to university – 'as he's always reminding me' – had thought he was awful. But drinks had been drunk, shots even, and the two of them had ended up spending the night together, which wasn't anything she usually did, 'you know: have sex on the first date'.

As I say, I'm not without experience, but perhaps not as much as was needed in this context. 'When you know you know,' I said, as if I did, which I didn't.

She raised her eyebrows. 'Well if I'd been in any doubt before, I wasn't afterwards,' she said.

I laughed.

Looking directly at me, laughing too, she said, 'Right?'

'But you've made it work?' I said. The question was too personal – she'd only given me all those intimate details because she was worried she'd offended me. Too late: the words were out there.

'We have our ups and downs. He gets very stressed. There's a lot of pressure running his own business. He's put in a lot of his own equity. And, while it seems glamorous – drinks with famous people – in reality he's constantly chasing clients, sweet-talking, entertaining. He's just lost a big media client [she named a company which I associated with mobile phones] and he's feeling the hit. You know, *personally*.' She pushed her cup and saucer away. 'The house ended up costing much more than we expected. We've had to take out a bridging loan. It's all very stressful.'

'I can see why a job would help.'

It was perhaps an ambiguous comment, and she frowned. 'What do you mean?'

'Yesterday? When do you think you'll hear?'

She still looked confused. 'Yesterday?'

'Your interview, when they asked you to stay for drinks?'

She looked at me blankly for a moment. The tops of her cheeks, just under her eyes, were tinged with red. She did that combing thing with her hair, her fingertips playing with her scalp. 'Oh yes.' She breathed in, bringing her hand down to tap her stomach, as if suppressing a burp, and gave a little shake of her head. 'I've no idea. I mean, it was sort of introductory really. It might not come to anything. And then if it did, I'd have to work on Tom. We need more money but he's also quite old-fashioned in some ways; he likes the thought of me being at home. This job hunt – I might not tell him.'

A small alarm bell rang – maybe I already sensed something was off – but I didn't comment. I think it was then we both started collecting our things and stood.

Our parking was nearly up and we walked back to the car. We were both quiet. I think it had surprised us both how much we had revealed to each other, how a quick lunch had led to so many unexpected confidences. Out in the real world we felt suddenly sheepish. I had begun to fret a bit about work – I'm expected to submit between thirty and thirty-five sub-entries a week (separate 'senses' of a particular word) and I was behind. But as we drove back, she mentioned some forms that needed witnessing and I ended up going into her house with her, signing my name and address; it was something to do with their mortgage, I assumed. It didn't occur to me it might be about life insurance, not that it would have made any difference had I known. I do remember she told me she was addicted to 'to-do' lists; she had a special notebook and she showed me the latest page. We laughed at the juxtaposition of 'pick up dry-cleaning' and 'make a will'. And I'm sure we discussed wills for a bit, too, then; how we really should all make one. So, yes, I think that was when the idea to write a will myself was planted in my mind.

An article in the *Observer* at the weekend suggested you need eighty hours of contact to grow a friendship. It didn't go into details. I don't know, for example, whether you need to be continually talking for the hour to count or whether companionable silence also works. Jail time, for example – those long stretches of enforced togetherness – would that be applicable?

It's hard to know exactly how and when Ailsa and I clocked them up but I am confident that we did.

When I look back on this period, I think about greenery, the changing view out of my bedroom window, the houses that backed on to me obscured a little bit more every day. I think about white blossom, sudden bursts of perfume, and the birds – the air manic with different song, how I hadn't noticed they were gone over winter, until now they were back. I think about her garden, too. I could see it if I craned my neck, through the crossed branches of my trees: the tips pushing up through the earth, blossom bursting against a blue sky, that pretty little bush she had planted on my side, the buds unfurling, deep pink and white flesh breaking out of their furry cases.

There were cold days, too; suddenly bitter days that looked the same through the window as the warm ones – the sky blue;

the leaves acid green. It was only when you left the house bare-armed, the chill wind penetrating your cotton layers, that you discovered they were only pretending to be nice. Aggressive mimicry; you find it everywhere in nature. Spiders that look like the ants on which they feed, death's-head hawk-moths that emit the smell of bees so they can sneak into the hive unnoticed and steal their honey, weeds that spring up next to almost identical cultured plants, strangling them and draining the goodness from the earth . . . The world is full of predators or parasites gaining advantage by their resemblance to a softer third party.

I continued to tutor every Wednesday, still unpaid, and sometimes I'd even do an extra session if Max had homework he found difficult. I should have mentioned money, but it was awkward. She talked so much about being broke and, while I clearly had less to live on than she did, I got by. At some point I told myself, she would press a thick envelope into my hand and in the meantime I was so much more than just a tutor – part of the family almost. We'd always have a coffee, or a Rooibos tea, and a chat after a session and she began to knock on my door, too. The first time was to ask again about the trees at the back: 'Any movement on that?' But the next time, she'd made a big batch of chocolate brownies, and really they didn't need them all: Tom didn't like too many sweet things in the house. Or she'd drop round an Amazon package they'd taken in for me – I got a lot of Amazon packages, didn't I? Another book? Wow! – and while she was about it, had I walked the dog? She'd love an excuse to stretch her legs – and maybe grab a coffee. And I'd abandon my computer and put Maudie on the lead, and off we'd trot, regardless of whether I had already taken her out that day or not.

I know, looking back, that it seems an unlikely friendship. It's hard not to wonder about her motives. Pity definitely came into it. I'd be deluded to think otherwise. She felt sorry for me and thought of herself as taking me under her wing. But she was used to being around misfits: she'd spent a lot of time in hospitals and, as I've said, her mother clearly had difficulties. But I also genuinely believe she enjoyed my company. I'm a good listener and she intrigued me: already at that first lunch our conversation had roved into interesting areas. It had an exponential effect, too. The more we hung out, the more relaxed she felt, and the more she was drawn back. It's true of friendship in general: we all find security in the familiar.

I also think she was lonely.

I want to say we walked on hundreds of occasions, but it was probably five or six. It just seemed more: the novelty for me was dizzying. And walking can be oddly intense; the lack of eye contact often leads to easy disclosure. We talked a lot about Max. I'd fill her in on how I thought he was doing and she'd tell me what his teachers had said at school (upward improvement, definitely). She moaned about Melissa, how moody she was, and about Bea's new obsession with make-up and Instagram. Often, she was caught between Tom and the kids: he could be hard on them, particularly Max. 'It's projection. He sees himself in him, and he takes what he does personally.' She deeply regretted not having tried harder at school herself. Her parents had given her anything she'd wanted, but she was never pushed. Tom's parents looked down on her lack of education – she was never good enough for him – but in truth she herself also wished she'd gone to university. 'Not fair, really.'

It wasn't all one-sided. She was intrigued by my own life as a student: the days, I suppose, in which I almost got away. It fascinated her that I had lived more than fifty years in one house; it boggled her imagination. She wanted to know how the area had changed, but also what we had *done* all day, holed up, the three of us. I told her about the long afternoons Faith and I used to spend together, when we were still close, watching films, or listening to albums on the old gramophone – soundtracks mainly, *Oliver!* and *The Sound of Music* and something called *Jumbo Hits*, how we would dress up in our mother's clothes and dance, how we made a little camp under her bed and it became our refuge. I told her our mother was scared of the outside world, of germs and strangers, and how we learnt to keep anything bad to ourselves. I touched only lightly on Faith's decision to move out, but I told her about the dullness of the two long decades as sole carer, how I would look ahead at the hours, the days, the months, that stretched beyond and it would seem inconceivable that they would be filled, with just this, just that, nothing interesting at all. And how I would also look back at the hours, days, months that had passed and think the same; the impossibility that all that time had gone by, and I was still there and nothing had changed.

I also unburdened myself about my mother's physical decline: the thinness of her face and arms, the swollen flesh of her legs and abdomen, how she had resisted hospital, and how hard it had been making decisions on my own. Should I call an ambulance? Could I get in touch once again with the out-of-hours GP?

I remember exactly what she said because she jumped in: 'Brutal, Verity,' she said. 'Fucking brutal.' They were words that made no etymological sense and yet absolute sense; they landed on my wounds like a salve.

'And where was Faith when this was going on?'

'By then she hated coming to the house. Mother developed an ulcer on her leg that needed regular dressing and her head-aches had made her sensitive to light so we kept the curtains drawn. I don't blame Faith. Honestly, I really don't. I can under-stand why she had had enough, why she wanted a new life.'

'And her new life is, where?'

'Brighton.'

'Still?'

I nodded.

'Do you go down and visit her? Does she come up?'

Out of nowhere I felt a pressing in my chest, in my whole body. 'Not lately.'

We were walking on the path along the railway line and I waited for a train to pass, to strobe behind the railings. I waited until I could no longer hear it. 'We rather fell out after the funeral,' I said, 'the crem. I thought she would come back to live with me, now Mother was gone, but she had other plans. We had words. And that was that.' I didn't elaborate and Ailsa didn't ask. 'You poor love,' she said eventually, which was, as Chris Tarrant used to say, *the right answer*. Faith had always loved *Who Wants To Be A Millionaire*.

So, no, I didn't tell her everything – far from it.

Some of the time we just had a laugh. We chatted about silly, trivial things: rare in my life. 'Botox?' she'd say as we parted from one of her friends, and I'd give a thumbs up or thumbs down, regardless of the fact that I've never been quite sure what the effects of 'Botox' actually are. She'd ask me what I'd had for supper, and seemed gripped by the answer. 'Baked beans on toast. With cheese? Delicious.'

On one occasion, we bumped into the mother who had found me so suspicious the day she'd dropped Bea home. She was introduced to me as Trish. 'Of course, you know Verity,' Ailsa said. 'She's the one you almost called the police on that time.' We had a giggle after she'd scurried off. 'Fillers no?' Ailsa said, and I nodded energetically. Another occasion, we met a tall woman wearing, as was later explained to me, 'invisible' braces on her front teeth, who told us in three different ways how proud she was of her daughter, 'dear Soph', who had scaled some academic pinnacle despite setbacks

– bullying by people jealous of her? – along the way. As we walked off, Ailsa said, 'She always makes me feel bad about myself. Am I a terrible person?' I told her I thought she wasn't. 'Do you think *I'm* jealous of Soph's achievements?'

'No, I think she wants us to feel that, and maybe we should feel sorry for her for wanting it so badly. To be honest,' I added, to Ailsa's delight, 'she can fuck right off.'

Was there something I missed? Clues? I don't recall her talking directly about her marriage – the omission is itself telling – though she talked almost obsessively about her friends, often anguished by small slights. Someone had a coffee morning and didn't invite her. Delilah had put her down in front of Tom. 'She referred to having designed our garden, and I said, "It's a collaboration," and she said, "Yes babe, of course," but it was just the way she said it, the way she looked at him? You know? It's so typical. She always has to have one over on me. It's always him and her against the world.'

We can't all afford to sweat the small stuff, but I found it touching that she did. I enjoyed the novelty of involvement in that kind of trivially emotional nitty-gritty. It didn't occur to me this might have concealed something darker and more troubling.

There were moments when her responses were slightly off – 'Oh, sweetheart!' she might say, drawing the words out with an unnatural emphasis as if her mind was elsewhere. She'd told me more about Wilson's, how one of the effects was anxiety, and, though it was managed with medication, her mental health was something she referred to darkly now and then. I knew, of course (though she didn't know I knew), about the self-help literature by her bed (*Bit Sad Today*), the evening primrose, the black onion oil and the prescription pills. The primrose and the black onion were reported to be good for anxiety and depression (I'd Googled); the pills were Cuprimine (for the Wilson's) and citalopram, an SSRI.

One conversation in particular sticks in my mind. We were having coffee in one of the cafes facing the common when she told me she had conceived Melissa very easily, '*too* easily', but that later when it was time to 'extend the family' (an odd phrase, I thought at the time), it had become difficult. She had longed 'achingly' for another child and, in the end, had taken the fertility drug Clomid, and 'to my delight' discovered she was pregnant with twins. It wasn't that I thought her revelation wasn't genuine. I was sure it was. I just had the sense it was oft repeated, that her telling of it had become pat. Even the final sentence seemed loaded with cliché. 'The morning after they were born, I remember holding both of them in my arms, these tiny weightless bundles, and feeling complete. You know?'

I put my cup down on the table. The milk had separated and I'd noticed a yellow globule of oil on the surface. The sight reached inside me, revolved in my stomach.

'Oh God, sorry,' Ailsa said. 'It's boring for you, isn't it?'

I rolled my eyes. 'Don't be silly.'

'I mean I make it sound so glorious, but it didn't last.' She sounded genuine again. 'What I haven't mentioned was how traumatic the births were.'

'Traumatic? You mean premature?'

'Actually, only a little bit early – twins usually are, but nothing too dramatic. Why do you ask?'

'No reason.' I pulled myself together.

'You know, I'd great plans for a water birth and whale music – the whole shebang. But it was so long and difficult and painful, and the epidural came so late, and they had to use forceps – I think we were all traumatised by the time Bea – she came first – finally struggled into the world.' She began to recite the rest like a list: 'She was OK, but Max didn't feed, and I got engorged and then I was crying all the time and he started losing weight, and Tom was working such long hours and I found it so hard having twins with a toddler already ...' She broke off and wrinkled her nose, embarrassed.

I felt myself stiffen, the old dragging in my limbs, but I tried to smile normally.

'Basically I got a form of postnatal depression. If you ask Tom, he'd say I had a mental breakdown, the complete psychotic full-on craziness, but that's not true. It's chemical with me. The pills help – though I've stopped taking them. They make me feel blurry.'

Perhaps I should have focused on the delicacy of her mental state, not his *response* to it. Perhaps it was foolish not to have probed deeper.

This morning, as I watched Delilah walk away, into my head came a memory of an incident earlier this year. I had been in Ailsa's kitchen helping Max with his homework while she was trying to find someone to collect Melissa from a hockey match. No one had picked up her texts or answered her calls; she was getting increasingly anxious and tense. Finally she rang a parent she hardly knew. 'Could you ... OK. Never mind at all. Thanks so much, babe, another time.' Her voice was sweetness and light; you'd have had no idea how angry she was if you hadn't then seen her hurl the phone on the table and scream: 'Fucking unhelpful bitch.'

Chapter Seven

Four 10g sachets of Heinz Tartare Sauce

Neologism, *noun*. A word or phrase which is new to the language, one which is newly coined.

I saw little of Tom during this period, though I was aware of him. Our walls are quite thin. He was loud in the morning, the first up for a shower, his voice echoing over the gush of the water in their en-suite, his laugh – a guffaw, almost like a shout – particularly penetrative. Once or twice, I *felt* his presence. I'd be in the kitchen and I'd see thrashing in the undergrowth outside the window. Not squirrels, as I first thought (Mother's Squirrel Nutkin having a play), but Tom Tilson on the other side of the fence, tugging violently at the ivy, trying to see what he could yank down.

Sue told me at the pub quiz she'd seen him having a row with Gav, a local care in the community, who is often out asking 'for a couple of quid for a cup of tea'. Tom, she said, was laying into him, telling him he was going to call the police if he didn't clear off. We didn't like that, me and Sue. He was a bully, we told each other, the kind of person who was threatened by anyone who was different. But I saw him myself once from Mother's window, in a scene in which I was forced to feel sympathy. He was in the street with an elderly couple who must have been his parents. Both were smartly dressed, the woman blonde and pearled, the man tall, with the sharp bend between his shoulders that suggests scoliosis. 'This is us,' I heard Tom say, and his tone was both declamatory and hopeful. He was seeking approbation and, despite myself, I found this grown man's need for approval touching. I winced when I heard his mother's reply, sharp and querulous: 'Busy road.'

It wasn't until the end of May that I spent any time with him. He had been away – Cannes, for the festival. Just a few days before, Ailsa had asked if I would be an angel and tidy up my front garden while he was gone, 'to keep him off my back'. I'm afraid to say I put it off, and it wasn't until the Sunday that I found myself out there, having a little go. Ineffectual, I'm afraid. I'm not very good at getting down to things.

I heard them, but didn't see them due to the height of the hedge. Tom was first through the front door, clearly back from his trip. 'Oh, for goodness' sake,' he called back into the house. 'Do it later. It's not the end of the world.' Ailsa's voice next: 'Yes, yes, yes.' Other snippets: 'For God's sake, what's going on now?' And then: 'At last.'

They were in the process of having their drive-in turntable thing installed and their off-street area was closed off behind a corrugated-iron hoarding. Otherwise, they'd have got in the car and driven away without seeing me. But as it was, they walked out onto the pavement, the five of them, on their way to where they were having to park the Chelsea tractor on a neighbouring street.

'Oh, Verity,' Tom said, seeing me bending over. 'This is a turn-up for the books.'

'Nice to see you, Tom.'

He was tanned, tiny white crinkle lines at the sides of his eyes, which looked very blue. He tapped the top of the gate. 'Good,' he said, about nothing in particular, nodding.

Behind him, his family stood waiting. Ailsa was wearing too many clothes: black tights, a calf-length denim skirt, and her usual long-sleeved layers. 'We're going for a pub lunch,' she said. 'It's such a lovely day. We could all do with blowing away some cobwebs.'

'How lovely.'

'The Black Sheep on Wimbledon Common,' Ailsa said.

'I've always fancied Wimbledon Common; it's on my list, but I've never ventured.'

'You've never been to Wimbledon Common?' Tom reared back in mock alarm. 'It's so close.'

'It's not that close,' Melissa said. Her face wore traces of make-up that had been roughly removed – ashy streaks under her lower lashes, bloodshot eyes – and while I recognised the bottom of a clingy black T-shirt dress as one she had worn to go out in on a recent Saturday, the top of it was covered up by a big grey sweatshirt, the word 'Baggage' jaggedly scrawled across it in graffiti-style letters. She looked sulky, as if there might have been a row.

'Verity doesn't drive,' Ailsa said. 'And when her mother was alive she didn't like her going into public places. You're only just making up for lost time, now, aren't you?'

'Buses work,' I said. 'I'd need to get two, but I've often thought of doing so.'

Max had reached over the fence to pat Maudie. 'She could come with us,' he said.

'Well, I wouldn't like to . . .'

'No, you should.' Ailsa was frowning at Tom. 'Shouldn't she? She's done so much for Max. Yes. You must come!'

Tom seemed to find the suggestion almost amusing. He surveyed my front garden. 'Of course,' he said, eventually. 'You can finish up here later.'

Ailsa persuaded Melissa into the boot and insisted I took the front, while she sat braced in the middle behind. She seemed to be trying hard to make sure we all got on. 'How jolly this is.'

She made me tell Tom about my life as a student in north London, how one of my great friends was an Oxford professor. Tom had been to Cambridge, she said (though I knew that from the photo in their downstairs loo). 'Long time ago now,' he said, 'though funnily enough I just bumped into an old college friend, he's a film producer, in Cannes.' He told a story involving the Croisette and the red carpet, the *Vanity Fair* party. 'You ever been to the south of France?' he asked, and I told him I hadn't; after a moment's consideration I added that in fact I didn't actually have a passport, I'd never been abroad.

'Never?' Bea poked her head over my seat. 'Like never? Not even Italy? Or skiing?'

'Oh, for goodness' sake.' Ailsa pulled Bea back down. 'You sound like a privileged brat.'

'I'm not.'

Max's voice: 'You are.'

I was aware of a tussle behind me, knees digging through from behind, seatbelts stretching.

Tom changed gear. He was wearing a short-sleeved white T-shirt, and as he pushed the stick forward, his bicep bulged, freckles thrown into relief by the pale skin on his underarm. 'And how's your work, Verity? You busy? Any interesting wordage?'

I had that morning just started on 'Rodeo' and outlined my latest research – how in the previous OED, the earliest understood sense was of rodeo as in competition, but I had found a quotation that pre-dated it, indicating the first meaning was 'cattle enclosure'. 'So I shall restructure the entry, which is always thrilling.'

Behind us Max and Bea were still fighting, Ailsa increasingly strained, and if I were to be generous I would say Tom was attempting to put a stop to it, when he called back: 'Max? Are you listening? Quick spelling test. Let's see what difference all Verity's tutoring has made.'

He started shouting out random words. 'Competition?'; 'Quotation'; 'Enclosure.'

I couldn't tell you if Max was getting them right or not. I found the tension too much; he and I hardly did spellings by then, busy as we were with more creative endeavours. I began finishing the words for him. The car fell silent.

It was hard to park. Tom swore at a dawdling silver van and, once past it, slammed his foot on the accelerator. I've been in the car with Fred, one of the gentlest men on earth, when he flipped the bird at an octogenarian, so I do know the road can bring out the Mr Toad in the best of us. Even so. I began to wish I hadn't come.

It wasn't a great idea, if you ask me, this pub. The position was lovely, among a sweet row of cottages on the edge of the common, but it didn't have a garden, which I'd assumed was the point of the excursion. It was sombre inside. I blinked to adjust my eyes, aware, when I finally focused, that the few other customers who were in there were staring. (I was still in my gardening clothes.) Tom found an extra chair – utterly delightful to the people who surrendered it – and we squeezed around the 'special table' they'd booked. It was next to the large open fireplace, obviously not roaring that day, and there is always something depressing about an empty grate. The dining room was quiet, and smelt of old chips and mildewed hops. It sounds like I'm griping, and I don't mean to. Far be it from me to be ungrateful for a free meal. I just mean to convey the sense there was of an occasion missed, of having tried to surf some rather glorious wave to discover it has petered out long before reaching the shore.

Once we were settled, as if aware things were falling flat and trying to inject energy, Tom was a man of laughs and jokes and large gestures. He ordered wine, and Cokes for the kids, so charming to the waitress – 'You can dig up a bucket of extra ice? Oh, you are a complete star' – that she went quite pink. A toddler, running past, tripped just near us and he leapt to his feet – 'Whoa!' – to check he was all right and then chatted to the grateful mother for a few minutes about the stresses of the terrible twos. Seated again, and full of himself as a great dad, he pulled Bea onto his knee and told her to recite the poem she'd learnt for class assembly; she did so, coyly, with her hands around his neck. It was about daffodils and rabbits and being kind. He moved on to Max, suggesting he tell me about a touch rugby match he had played the previous day. Max, one leg folded painfully beneath him, did as requested, but stutteringly, looking to his father for prompts.

'And. Then. You. Scored. A. Try,' Tom finished for him. 'The point of that story, Verity, is that they won. You see, it *was* worth doing. He's always saying he doesn't want to play rugby but it's nice when you win, isn't it? Isn't it?'

'I prefer playing football,' Max said, with a sudden show of spirit. 'She knows.'

'Don't be silly. Yesterday's match was great. Fierce. Really lit. Melissa – is that the right use of contemporary parlance?'

Melissa, looking up from her phone, stared blankly.

'Come on,' Tom said. 'This is our chance to bring Verity into the modern world. What have you got for her, Melissa? Bea? Sketchy, savage, extra, epic . . . Verity's the woman who needs to know.'

I shrugged to dramatise my ignorance, but I'm not *unaware*

of the latest slang. Lexicology is, after all, my thing. Melissa didn't answer, anyway. She was back on her phone.

'Verity, would you please remove that electronic device from my daughter? What must you think of us?'

'I'm not getting involved,' I said, putting up my hands in surrender.

Ailsa wasn't either. She was busy *not* getting involved; that's what leaps out in my memory – busy making Bea sit down in her own chair, and busy removing unnecessary wine glasses, busy asking about the specials, and requesting a water jug, and then when the food arrived – fish and chips in various guises – busy taking peas off one child's plate and adding broccoli to another's, doling out French fries and rationing ketchup and rescuing sleeves from dollops of mayonnaise. Looking back at the dynamics of their marriage, the louder Tom was, the more coiled energy he displayed, the quieter she became. The problem is, I think her passivity irritated him, goaded him into becoming worse.

She had ordered a salad for herself, a chicken Caesar, which she picked at, leaving all the interesting bits, like the croutons, on the side. I'd opted for bubble and squeak with 'hen's egg' (aren't eggs generally from hens?); it came neatly moulded, with the egg poached on top. When I popped it with the tine of my fork, the yolk seeped into the potato, staining it yellow.

'It's nice to be able to thank you for all your hard work with . . .', Tom extended a finger in Max's direction. 'I've been hearing positive reports.'

'He's making great progress.'

Max continued to study his battered cod.

'Not sure we're making such great progress with the house, are we? Or the garden? I hate to bring it up again but you have to admit your property needs some TLC. We're spending so much money and time on ours, and, well, some people, I'm afraid, might say your side is a bit of an eyesore.'

'Tom,' Ailsa said. 'If we're not careful she's going to wish we'd never moved in.'

'I'd never wish that,' I said. 'I love having you next door. The chats and the walks, the trips to the cafe.'

'Trips to the cafe?' Tom wiggled his shoulders, as if to say, *Fancy*. 'Is that a regular thing?'

I took a mouthful of the yellowy potato mix. It tasted bitter, of the vinegar they'd put in the water when cooking the egg.

Ailsa cleared her throat. 'Not really. Once or twice a week.'

'"Not really"?' Tom turned his head to look directly at her. 'I wouldn't call once or twice a week "not really". So what's that? Ten quid, fifteen quid a week?' I wasn't sure if his gripe was semantic or financial, but he seemed to want to humiliate her in front of me. Now I realise I was invisible; my presence irrelevant.

'Lucky for some. And you pay, I assume? You can give Verity coffee at home. It's insane to spend money out. It's all very well saying once, twice a week, but it adds up. And if you're buying two every time – these days, Christ, that's almost ten quid.'

I put down my knife and fork. The egg had congealed around the corners of the plate. 'If Ailsa had a job,' I said, 'I'm sure you wouldn't begrudge her any coffees out she wanted.'

'Yeah. How's that going?' he said, swirling his wine glass. He took a gulp. 'All these "interviews" and "casual drinks", they're not coming to much. I mean Thursday – what time did they keep you till? It was past ten, wasn't it? Did you get the job?' He was one of those men, I realised, made meaner by drink.

Ailsa shook her head.

'No,' Tom confirmed.

The pub had filled up; there were a couple of noisy tables now, including one – outsourced from a group of adults – made up exclusively of rowdy children. Tom was sitting back in his chair, with his arms crossed. Ailsa was brushing imaginary crumbs into a little pile. I watched her. Did Tom want her to work, or not? She'd told me he was against it, and yet he seemed resentful that she wasn't trying harder. She was going to keep the job hunt secret, she'd said, and yet it was me she hadn't told about whatever job it was she'd gone for on Thursday. There seemed to be a lot of contradictions.

A young man with narrow hips and heavy sideburns came up and began to clear our plates. He and I had a little tussle over the spare sachets of tartare sauce (I'd made a little pile to take home and defended it vigorously) after which Ailsa began to help, scooping up dirty napkins and gathering scattered cutlery; there was a brief clash as she tried to pass this to him, and in the handover a knife fell into her lap. The waiter flicked the napkin off his shoulder and was about to dab at her thighs, but he stopped himself. 'Oops,' he said. 'Sorry. Got a bit carried away there.'

'Close thing,' she laughed, rubbing at the stain with her fingers.

'You don't need a cloth?'

'I'm fine.'

'Well if you're sure.'

'I'm sure.'

It was a simple, awkward moment. The only thing I can think of that's worth adding is that she continued smiling for a minute or two after he had walked off, and that, rather self-consciously, she rearranged the folds of her top, and gathered her hair to one side of her neck.

'Chrissake,' Tom said under his breath. 'I don't know what you think you're going to achieve. He clearly bats for the other team.'

'Well . . .'

'Unless you think your attractions will turn him.'

She got to her feet then, pushing her chair back and crossing the room towards a door in the corner marked 'Ladies'.

Tom laughed. 'What's Mum like?' he said.

Bea giggled agreeably. Melissa didn't look up from her phone, but the stillness of her posture suggested she was aware of what was going on, that possibly she found it not *lit* or *extra* or *epic* but *sketchy* and *savage*. Max was chewing the neck of his T-shirt.

Tom tousled his hair, then pulled the T-shirt away. 'Don't eat that,' he said, brow furrowed.

I was feeling quietly horrified and maybe Tom noticed. He became suddenly expansive again. 'If you're still hungry, we should have pudding. Pudding!' he said loudly, catching the waiter's eye. 'Chocolate cake and ice cream? What do you say? Verity?'

I told him I had had, as my mother would say, an elegant sufficiency.

'Jolly good.'

The waiter came over then and Tom ordered brownies with salted caramel ice cream for the children and – to me – 'Coffee?'

Quickly, I shook my head. *Fuck no*.

Ailsa didn't come back until the puddings were half eaten. She had rearranged her face and said a few things that sounded pre-prepared about the nice soap dispenser in the lavatory – innocuous and dull, their only purpose to let us know she was all right. Tom asked her if she wanted a pud – 'It's not too late' – and she said she didn't, or rather she said, 'I mustn't.' But Bea had pushed her plate away, finding it too rich, and Ailsa picked at it continually for the next few minutes. 'Lovely,' she murmured. 'Mustn't, though.'

Tom paid the bill – huge tip, I noticed.

I was thanking him and telling him how delicious it had all

been – when I followed his gaze. Ailsa was still at it, picking away, doing that thing some women do, of eating lots of tiny pieces under the pretence that tiny pieces 'don't count'.

'I thought you said you didn't need pudding,' he said.

'I don't.'

'Well don't eat it then,' he said.

A deep flush spread across Ailsa's cheeks. It looked as if she had been slapped. She opened her hand, and the crumbs fell back onto the plate.

The children were subdued in the car, which I've learnt is a sign: like birds falling quiet before a thunderstorm. I looked out of my window. Tom threw a few idle comments in my direction. How would I be spending the rest of this fine day after my fine repast? 'Sorting out the front, obvs, and then maybe finding your way to attacking the back?'

I felt trapped, furious that he was making me feel in his debt, when I was the one who was owed money. I would have raised it, if I hadn't worried it would get Ailsa into trouble. 'Not all of us are as obsessed with tidiness as you are,' I said eventually. 'Some of us find all that a bit bland. I've never been into a house as neat as yours. Was Kent the same?'

He didn't answer and an atmosphere entered the car, as if something was holding its breath.

Tom took a call the moment he was out on the street and he strode ahead of the rest of us, speaking apparently into thin air – though actually into a small speaker clamped to the top of his T-shirt. 'Pay or play,' he proclaimed. He raised his hand above his shoulder, and without turning around, pressed the fob he was holding to clonk-lock the car. 'As long as the money's deposited in escrow.'

Ailsa was doing up her shoelaces, so I couldn't see her face.

'Thanks for coming,' she said. 'I really appreciated it – though I'm not sure any of us were at our best today.'

'Ailsa.'

She straightened, shrugging apologetically. 'I irritate him at the moment,' she said. 'There's a lot going on, and he's not good at dealing with pressure.'

She didn't meet my eye. I realised she was actually embarrassed; that, for all sorts of complicated reasons, she cared what I thought of him. So, despite myself, I took a few seconds to consider my answer. I didn't mention alcohol.

'It's very common, particularly among men,' I said. 'There was this thing on the radio last week about anger, how anger works to energise some people when they're stressed; their cortisol levels drop when they've lashed out and then they find it easier to focus on the task in hand. In those cases, anger actually serves an important purpose.'

She gave a brief nod. 'It's nice of you to give him the benefit of the doubt. It's what I love about you – you're brutally honest, but also generous.'

'Though he was being an arse,' I couldn't resist adding.

She lifted her finger and tapped the air, smiling despite herself. I had cheered her. 'True that.'

We walked together in silence along the pavement to join the main road.

'Sometimes I'm not sure I should stay married,' she said.

There was a gap in the traffic, and she gripped my elbow to steer me across. Tom and the kids had already gone in, and we stood for a moment, between our two houses. She was still holding my arm, but she was looking over her shoulder down the street towards the common. 'Listen,' she said, eventually. 'I fancy a walk. If anyone asks, could you say I was with you?'

'I'd *love* a walk,' I said.

'I just fancy being on my own?' Her sentences were going up at the end. 'Do you mind?'

I spoke too quickly. 'Of course not.'

She dropped my arm and turned her head away again.

'See you later,' I said. And then because she was still standing there, gazing into the distance, I decided to hug her. I'm not a big hugger, but I'd noticed that she always threw her arms around people if she bumped into them when we were together, and I wanted to make a gesture, to show my allegiance. I took a step towards her, extended my arms and held her awkwardly, feeling how delicate her shoulders were, beneath her layers. It was only for a second, and I only pressed lightly, but when I moved away I was sure I caught on her face a wince of pain.

Chapter Eight

Pale grey scarf

Recalcitrant, *adjective.* **Esp. of a person or animal. Obstinately disobedient; uncooperative, refractory; objecting to constraint or restriction.**

Ailsa's meeting – or 'consultation' – with the QC took place today. She took a mirror from the bathroom and rested it on the window ledge in the front room to put on her make-up. It was quite a performance: the contortions, her eyelids lifted and stretched as she applied a shadow and a liner. Maybe her hand was shaking too much – the strain of concealing emotion – but when she'd finished, the proportions seemed wrong; the powder settled in her pores; the blusher looked painted on.

She didn't want to go alone. Lawyers intimidate her and fair enough, she's spent enough time being bullied by Tom's father. She'd wanted to get an Uber, but I persuaded her the Tube would be quicker and we took the Northern line up to Embankment, and then changed onto the Circle line, alighting at Temple.

We got a little lost, finding the right chambers, and wandered, buffeted by a brisk wind, under towering plane trees, up stone steps, past fountains and through courtyards, along rows of black railings. Our footsteps echoed and jackdaws cawed, heating vents hummed; there was the occasional smell of cabbage and boiled pasta. It was inappropriate but I did feel a slight thrill – it was my first time at the inns of court and it reminded me of visiting Fred in Oxford: the same mix of architecture, the same sense of hushed scholarship, the same preponderance of balding men in cords.

John Standling, her solicitor, was waiting for us on a bench when we finally found Terrace Court. I've met him a couple of times now, at the police station, and at the plea and trial preparation hearing, and he seems a decent enough man. He's in his mid-forties with cropped ginger hair, a very straight mouth – literally no curve to his lips at all – and a pinkish round tip to his nose, rather like that of the actor who played Pod in the film version of *The Borrowers*. He has the traces of a Mancunian accent (flat vowels), which I approve of, and an owlish air, accentuated by rectangular steel-topped glasses.

He leapt to his feet when he saw us, pumping our hands up and down, and muttering, 'OK, OK, grand,' under his breath. He was the duty solicitor the night Ailsa was charged, and most of our encounters are underpinned by the sense that for him, her case (murder!) is quite a coup. Shortly after she was first arrested, I caught sight of him outside the police station, talking on his mobile while pacing up and down. Glitzier lawyers had already begun to circle like piranhas. To Ailsa he'd been all politeness and legal restraint, but as I passed, I heard him hiss to whomever it was he was talking to, 'I'm fighting the fuckers off,' and I was quietly impressed. Ailsa's decision to stick with him is mainly financial – his offices are behind a grimly anonymous shopfront in Clapham Junction, and he's priced accordingly – but I like knowing he has something to prove.

This morning, he led us through a modern glass door into a tall red-brick building, and up a flight of stairs carpeted in royal blue, to the first floor. We waited in a grey antechamber, a bit like a dentist's waiting room only with worse magazines

(*New Law Journal*), until a tall, lean man with a hooked nose and thinning hair walked into the doorway and stood there, as if striking a pose. Robert Grainger QC, I assumed: the man described by Standling as 'my first choice for murder'.

Ailsa had met him once, and he greeted her with an air of restrained professional courtesy, like a head teacher meeting a parent who's come in with a complaint. He shook Standling's hand, then he turned to me and said baldly: 'And you are?'

'This is Verity Baxter, the neighbour with whom Mrs Tilson is residing.'

Grainger looked at me carefully. 'You're not a witness?'

'No. I gave a statement to the police, but it wasn't very helpful.'

I found my hand reaching for the back of my head, patting down the hair there. I washed it this morning before setting off, but the water was cold and my head was sticky with soap. I adjusted my glasses, squeezing the little bundle of Sellotape that secured the arms at each side. I put my hand out, but as he didn't proffer his, I made to put it in my pocket, though it was too full.

His eyes narrowed. 'So, just to be sure: you're not the neighbour who has given evidence for the prosecution?'

Standling took a small step forwards, knocking his shin on the low magazine table. 'That's the other side. Mr Andrew Dawson. Verity is a friend of the family, but she was out on the evening in question.'

'Pub quiz,' I said. 'Every Wednesday.'

He nodded. 'OK. I need to check, you do understand. It wouldn't do for myself, or Mrs Tilson, to be having any contact with a material witness.'

'I'm an immaterial witness,' I said. It was a stab at a joke, and it covered my unhappiness that I *wasn't* a witness. 'I didn't know Tom was in the country. He was supposed to be away.'

'Right, OK.' He cut me off. 'Well if you're all right waiting here, Mrs Tilson will be out in a while.'

The three of them left the antechamber and through the open doorway, I saw them enter a room opposite. The door closed decisively, but I could still hear Grainger's voice now and then, a general burr and the occasional ejaculation. 'That's very important' and 'I'd like to be clear', and something that sounded like 'good God'. In court, it's obviously an advantage to have a voice that travels. But he seemed to do an awful lot of talking for someone who was in this instance being paid to listen.

I sat alone on a black leather chair, nursing the bottle of water I'd brought with me. On the ledge outside the window, an enormous white seagull perched apparently motionless. The room smelt of stale chicory. I recognised the particular reek from the coffee machine at the council; the drop that fell from the black plastic funnelled neck onto the hotplate if you took the jug away too soon, the hiss and ensuing stench of it. In the doorway, a woman in a black gown was talking to a young man with a neat beard about a Netflix true-crime drama. He caught my eye and said: 'Can I get you anything? No? OK,' adding, 'Your sister won't be long.'

My sister. I thought for a moment about times when I had waited for Faith: in the street outside her first job interview aged sixteen at the local hairdresser (I combed out her hair before she went in); on a chair at the bank while she opened her starter account; in the foyer at the centre during her driving theory test. I hadn't realised at the time, but I was her enabler. Each wait was a step towards her escape.

'Ailsa's not my sister,' I said, but he'd gone.

About forty minutes later, the door opened, and the three of them stood in the hall. Ailsa's mascara had run. She was holding out one palm as if proffering it to shake, and scratching it, back and forth, up and down. Her eczema flares up under stress. Grainger patted her on the shoulder and then walked through the door into the 'private' section of the building. When I reached them, Standling was muttering: 'OK, OK. Grand.'

'How was that?' I said.

Ailsa was already heading for the stairs. 'I'm fucked,' she said.

Hand on heart, I have tried not to think too hard about the question of Ailsa's 'guilt' or 'innocence'. I don't like to think of it in those terms. The most plausible explanation is a mistake; I really believe that. It's what she screamed the day they finally took her away, and the fear and panic and grief in her eyes: well, it was enough to persuade me, if not the arresting officer. She is not a bad person. There is room for doubt.

Until recently, as I think I've said, I've had faith in the legal system. Ailsa would not go down for this. The status quo would be restored. But as we walked to the Tube, the three of us, I had the feeling things were beginning to unravel, not quite in the direction I had hoped. If I was going to help her, to take control, I needed to do it now.

I waited until the pavement narrowed and Ailsa was a few steps behind to ask Standling if he had time for a quick coffee.

He took a look at his watch, a flimsy electronic Casio, narrow for the thickness of his wrist. 'Er . . .'

'It might be useful,' I murmured, 'for us to compare notes.'

He must have seen something in my expression because he froze for a second and then nodded curtly. 'Yup. Let's do that.'

The cafe, a greasy spoon, was tucked between the Embankment and the Tube station, one of those small forgotten corners of London. 'Come on,' I said to Ailsa, who was still lagging. 'Don't know about you, but I need my shot of caffeine.'

It isn't the sort of thing I usually say – it's more her, really – but she didn't demur. I almost wished she had. The passivity is a coping mechanism, I'm sure, but it comes across as sulkiness. Standling took up the rear. 'Oh, are you coming too?' she said, only just noticing. 'Do I have to pay you for that?'

Standling laughed awkwardly. 'I'm sure we can come to an arrangement,' he said.

'I am married to a lawyer,' she said. 'I know all about bill-able hours.'

She had crossed her arms; her frame was all defensive angles and sharp points. She was so brittle, I was worried she might fragment.

'It's not quite the same these days, as I'm sure your husband told you.' He had gone pink at the mention of Tom, or her use of the present tense. 'It's more often a flat fee. I mean, there are problems with accountancy always, but . . .'

'Yes, I know,' she said. 'Problems with accountancy. It was quite our thing.' She smiled, her lips stretched tight across her teeth.

We had taken a table near the counter – it was at right angles to the wall, with a fixed banquette on either side of it, a 'booth' I suppose you'd call it. She and I sat together on one side; Standling asked us what we wanted and went to the front to order.

The table was clean, but a little sticky. It smelt of damp J-cloth. A laminated menu offered a wide range of fare, includ-ing the handwritten addition of 'spicey chiken'. Ailsa rested her arm along the back of the banquette, and looked to the other side of the room, to where a man in a suit was eating a full English.

When Standling sloped in opposite us, I said, wishing I could jolt her to make her pay attention, 'So what happened in there? Where are we with everything?'

He tapped his finger against his upper lip. 'Mrs Tilson. Ailsa. Are you happy for us to discuss this now?'

Ailsa shrugged. 'You can say anything you like in front of Verity,' she said. 'She doesn't count.'

'Well, Silk explained the criminal justice system to Mrs Tilson. He ran through what the next few months will involve, the process going forward, how, as we know, there are now five months until trial; he reminded us of stage 1, the date for primary disclosure from the prosecution and stage 2, the date for service of the defence case statement, and then 3 and 4, when we both have the chance to ask for items that appear on the schedule of unused material. And then he reminded her never to lose sight of the theatre of it all. What she wears, how she carries herself; it's all important. Once the trial starts, he said, one of the twelve will always be looking and judging.'

She rolled her eyes. 'It's not as if I don't know that.'

'That's what he meant,' I said. 'No rolling of eyes.'

She held her head very still then, keeping her expression pointedly bland. Her body language was really very concerning.

I turned back to Standling. 'What about the case? We're going for an innocent plea, yes?'

He looked at Ailsa enquiringly. One of her shoulders rose very slightly and fell. Almost uncooperative, but not quite.

'Mrs Tilson is maintaining she has no knowledge of how the toxic alkaloids made their way into Mr Tilson's, um, supper.'

'So, an accident,' I said. 'An accident. Ailsa?' I smiled at her encouragingly. 'You must have gone into the garden and picked what you thought was coriander. Unfortunately, it wasn't.' Ailsa was still looking at me blankly. To Standling I said: 'I don't see what the problem is. I don't see why it's even going to trial. It was just a mistake.'

Standling pushed his glasses further up the bridge of his nose. He sighed, his nostrils pinching. 'Unfortunately, the prosecution thinks otherwise. They are claiming premeditation. They have a witness who says Mrs Tilson was a competent gardener, who knew the difference between a poisonous and a non-poisonous plant.'

'What witness?' I asked. 'One of the children?'

'No, no.' He shook his head. 'Everyone's always reluctant to call kids. They're notoriously unreliable, liable to agree with anything that is put to them. Um.' He opened his briefcase. 'Sorry . . . let me just . . .' He rifled through some papers and then put them away. 'Mrs Delilah Perch; she's the witness here.'

'Delilah. Tom's ex-girlfriend. She's not objective.'

'Do you think she has it in for me?' Ailsa asked. She sounded detached, as if the thought didn't upset her. Again: not a good stance.

'She was in the house that evening,' I told Standling. 'Has anyone considered *she* might have done something to the curry?'

'What motive would she have?'

'She and Tom went way back—' I broke off. One has to be careful.

After a few moments, Standling referred again to his notes. 'The prosecution is claiming Mrs Tilson would have sustained injuries herself if she had *accidentally* touched the plant. There would at the very least have been lesions on her skin. The conjecture is that she wore gloves.'

Ailsa turned her head and looked at him directly for the first time. 'I did wear gloves,' she said. Her voice was clear, and defiant.

I caught my breath. I wished again that I had managed to school her beforehand. She was playing this wrong. All wrong.

Standling swallowed hard, his Adam's apple moving. 'Yes, I know. The police found a box of unused disposable gloves under the sink.'

'It's because of her eczema,' I said. 'She would have been cutting onions and chilli. I mean . . .' I shook my head a few times to try and convey my exasperation with this line of enquiry.

Standling adjusted the arm of his glasses. 'The question is: what happened to those gloves? If they had been worn innocently – the Crown maintains – she would have simply chucked them away. But if gloves were worn, they've gone missing. SOCO went through the kitchen bin and the bagged-up refuse in the wheelie bin outside and found no used gloves, so if she did wear them to cook – as she has consistently maintained – they have been disposed of elsewhere, which, as you know from your conversations with the police, Ailsa, has left them unsatisfied.'

Again, I watched Ailsa while he was talking. She was fiddling with the cuff of her sleeve.

Standling stroked his chin. 'We should also think about the fact that there was a half-empty packet of coriander in the fridge – a receipt for which, along with the other ingredients, was found in the bottom of a Waitrose bag, dated that morning. Forensics found the same coriander, which was grown in Spain – amazing, the detail they can unearth – in the pot of curry. I suppose also . . . this is only circumstantial. But we should think about why you didn't eat any of the food yourself.'

'Here you go, my darlings.' Three coffees had arrived, as well as a plate bearing a sultana scone. The waitress who brought them, a young blonde woman with a black stud in the middle of her chin, put my cup down a little roughly and I was preoccupied for a second with mopping up a pool of spume.

'Thank you,' Ailsa said. She smiled sweetly. It was uncanny how quickly her tone could change. But this was better; much better. That sweetness, if only I could bottle it.

'She doesn't eat,' I said when the waitress had gone. 'I mean she does, but she's a bit odd about food. Aren't you, Ailsa? You're always on a diet, or trying to cut down, or you used to be. You make bargains with yourself – had cake, won't have supper.' I turned back to Standling. 'That makes sense, doesn't it? And also motive. Don't they need motive?'

He nodded. 'There was the shouting and the high-pitched scream the neighbour overheard that morning.'

'"I wish you were dead,"' Ailsa offered for him.

I took a gulp of my coffee. Standling tipped the sugar out of the glass dispenser into his spoon and I watched as he poured it into his cup. The sugar rested on top of the foam, suspended for a few seconds, before it sank.

'Financial difficulties,' he muttered. 'Mr Tilson had substantial life insurance – recently extended.'

I nodded. Those forms. I remembered signing them now.

Ailsa stood up suddenly and sidled out of the banquette. She asked if she could use the toilet, and the waitress lifted up a section of the counter, then she went through a door at the back of the cafe. Standling craned his neck to watch her go.

'So what?' I said quickly. 'Is it too weak a defence? An accident, I mean? Be honest, are you thinking about a plea? You don't seem convinced.'

'All we have to do, as I have said, is unpick their case. We don't need to come up with anything of our own.' He had sliced his scone in half and was trying to butter it, but the butter was hard and the scone was breaking up under his knife. 'The worry is not knowing what else the Crown has up its sleeve. We'll know soon.'

'So.' I took a deep breath. I'd thought hard about this. 'What about arguing self-defence?'

'Ms Baxter, there is no evidence Mrs Tilson was under attack – no defence wounds, no sign of provocation and this type of, um, death . . . well, it would be hard to argue that it transpired from a moment of madness.'

I laid my hands flat on the table. 'I've been reading about coercive control. There was that case recently, wasn't there – the wife who killed her husband, but who got out on appeal on the basis she had been ground down by long-term hidden abuse.'

He breathed out deeply, half-groan, half-sigh. 'I don't see how it would apply here.'

I told him then about the weird order in the house, Tom's obsession with an empty fridge and clear surfaces, how he didn't like to see Ailsa eat. I told him about the way he undermined her and the children in public. He was a bully. Something had happened in Kent, where they'd lived before. I didn't know what it was but it was like he was holding her hostage.

'She hasn't mentioned any of this.'

'Isn't that the thing with coercive control? The abuser saps your confidence so deeply and so relentlessly that you lose perspective. You stop trusting in your own judgement. You start to think you are as worthless as they say you are.'

'Nothing came up in the psychiatric review,' he said. 'Obviously a history of mental health issues, but it's important for our purposes that we play those down. We could look for witnesses, but . . . it would be hard to prove. Physical abuse is easier. It still plays better with a jury – that she feared for her life, that after years of abuse, she snapped.'

'What if it wasn't just mental? What if he hurt her physically, too?' I said.

He crossed his arms around his body then, and bowed his head. 'Can you expand?' He looked quickly through to the back of the cafe. I turned my head too. The toilet door was still closed.

'She always wore long sleeves, and trousers or tights, even when it was hot. I'm thinking maybe she had bruises on her legs and arms and was hiding them.'

'Nothing you ever saw, on her face for example?'

'He would have been too clever for that. I found some bloody tissues in their wastepaper basket and also a scarf with what looks like blood stains on it. I kept it and I found it again last night. I thought I'd lost it, but it was in a box under my bed along with . . . well, you don't need to know the details, but here it is.' I pulled the piece of grey fabric out of the pocket of my jacket and handed it across the table to him.

He took it, with some reluctance. 'I suppose I could get someone to analyse it. Though I'm not sure what that will tell us. Even if it is blood, it could just be from a nosebleed.' His mouth suddenly tightened into a smile. 'Hello. All good back there?'

Ailsa had appeared next to me on the banquette. 'What have you got?' she said. 'What's she given you?'

I put my hand on her arm and kept it there even though she tried to shake it off.

'It's a blood-stained scarf. I found it in your house and now I've given it to Mr Standling.'

'When did you take it from my house?'

I didn't know how to signal to her I had her best interests at heart. Instead, I smiled quickly at Standling. 'Ages ago.'

Something vulnerable flashed into her face and then vanished, covered over by scorn. 'Verity, what is this? I thought we were past this.' And then to Standling. 'You do know she's insane.'

I tried to laugh it off, and shortly after he stood up – he had a meeting to go to. When we got to the entrance of the station, I wondered if he would come on the escalator with us, but he took the stairs – leaping ahead with great lolloping strides. On the Tube, she seemed suddenly weak, so when we got out, I waited for a bus to take us up the hill. I didn't trust her to make it on foot.

Chapter Nine

1 fold-up metal garden chair
1 Russell Hobbs Powersteam iron, flex broken
5 melamine plates with a sunflower pattern
1 child's tin globe, rusty and with a divided
Germany, but in working order

Gallimaufry, *noun.* **A heterogeneous mixture, a confused jumble, a ridiculous medley.**

Ten days went by after the pub lunch without me seeing Ailsa. I wasn't concerned at first. I had other distractions, viz the revisions to my most recent words – 'angry', 'angst', etc. The comments from my editor were unusually sniffy: 'Old-fashioned phrasing'; '1838 needed'; 'Three errors! This will not do, Verity'. Since the Tilsons had moved in, my concentration had lapsed.

I didn't tutor Max the first week as he had a rugby match after school, so I had no direct contact with any of the family until Melissa let me in the following Wednesday. 'Hiya!' she said brightly. She was wearing school uniform, the grey skirt just reaching the top of her thighs, her black tights nearly all ladder. 'How are you?'

'I'm very well, thank you,' I replied, scanning her face. She had just plucked her eyebrows and the skin above her lids looked raw. She looked very like Ailsa; the same tawny eyes, the same sculptural pointiness to her face. 'Your mum in?'

'No.'

'Is she at her food bank?'

'Maybe.'

'Or another job interview?'

'I don't know actually.'

'Is she all right, Melissa?'

'Yeah. She's good,' she said in that fake-upbeat way I had begun to distrust.

She hovered, though, chewing the side of her thumb, as if she had something to ask. Finally, she said: 'Verity, I just wondered. I'm doing a project for my GCSE Art. The title is Dreams and Reality. I've drawn the outline of a head, and I was thinking of filling it with newspaper articles – about global warming and stuff. It's just Mum said I could ask . . .'

I waited, and when she didn't say any more, I said: 'Of course.'

'It's just, I need lots of newsprint, headlines and pictures from as many different sources as I can, to get different type-faces, and I don't know whether you need them or anything, but those plastic crates in your porch area, they've got loads of old magazines in them. So I wondered . . .'

Carefully, button by button, I undid my jacket, as if I intended to take it off, which I didn't.

'If you weren't using them, if you were thinking of throwing them out . . .'

On the table in their hall was a pile of that day's post, a couple of bills, and some flyers in an untidy heap. I touched one with the tips of my fingers. It was an advert for a 'top to toe' cleaning service. I slid it along the wood until it was aligned with the pizza leaflet, and a stapled brochure promoting special offers at Lidl.

'I'd love to be able to help, Melissa,' I said. 'I might need them so I'm not sure if I can give them to you today.'

'OK.'

I pulled my fingers back from the table. 'Let me have a little sort and I'll see what I can do.'

'Awesome,' she said doubtfully.

'OK.' I nodded and she went upstairs.

The kitchen was spotless as usual. There was no sign of any supper; I suppose, looking back, that was odd. Out on the terrace sat two large bags of compost, and a black plastic tray of what looked like herbs. She had been in the middle of planting them out – one of the bags was open and there were several trails of earth on the stone slabs.

Max was on the floor. He had upturned his school bag and was rifling through his books; some of the lined paper had come detached from their stapled spines. 'I've lost my maths homework,' he said.

'Do you need your maths homework this minute?'

'It's got to be done now. I'm supposed to have done it. I couldn't do it yesterday and I meant to ask the teacher today to help, but I forgot. Now I can't find it. Oh, here it is.'

He grabbed a loose sheet from the floor. It was crumpled, and he laid it on the table and tried to smooth it with the flat of his hand. 'Can you help me do it? It's equations.'

'Not my strong point, maths,' I said.

'Can you Google it, like Mum does? Or BBC Bitesize. She said she'd be home in time to help and she isn't.'

'We're here to do English,' I said. 'I've prepared for our lesson already.'

I produced a piece of paper from my own bag, on which I had typed: *Tension in the room was rising. She looked from face to face and saw the same closed expression. They didn't believe her. They didn't want to hear her side of the story.*

'I'd like to see you continue this piece of writing.' I put it down on top of the maths sheet. 'Using your best sensory descriptions, the longest words you can think of.'

He tried to push it off. 'I've got to finish my maths.' His eyes looked small and anxious. There was a cut in the middle of his lower lip.

I wish now I had been more flexible, but mild anxiety about Ailsa had left me tired and scratchy and I told him I was here to do English and he could do the maths after I'd gone. It wasn't a good session and it was with relief at 5.55 p.m. that I began to pack up my briefcase. Max was writing out his spelling corrections when the key turned in the front door. Max knew first, picking up like a dog those tiny gradations in timbre that exist when different people perform the same actions. What was the distinction? A slightly heavier touch – his hands always seemed rather clumsy – or a more, or perhaps *less*, forceful push? He didn't have to get his weight behind it like she would.

'He's early.' Max slid quietly off his chair and began to stuff his scuffed-up work back into his bag. I found myself tidying the table. I'd already put my papers in my bag, but I straightened the matching wooden pepper and salt pots – one of them, I noticed, still had the price tag on the bottom.

'Ah.' Tom stood in the doorway to the kitchen. He'd had a haircut, and his newly shorn neck looked pale. He put his bag down. 'La Verité. Looking very spring-like, if I may say.'

I suppose he was referring to the colour of my jacket, which was primrose yellow. I'd seen it hanging on the railings by the playground and, after three days, considered it unclaimed.

'Thank you,' I said, giving a little sweep of the table and standing up.

'Where you off to?' he said, as Max tried to slip past him. 'No hug for your old man?'

Max briefly buried his face in the buttons of his father's white shirt.

'I'll check over that maths in a minute, when I've had a word with Verity. I assume you've finally managed to finish it.'

Max ducked under his arm, muttering something that sounded suspiciously like 'Bloody fucking no'. His footsteps on the stairs sounded light and fast, panicked; the scrape of his hand on the bannister, a thud when he jumped the last two steps.

Tom must have heard what he said because his face tightened. He turned to me: 'No dog today?'

I knew I was being mocked, but it was hard to pin down exactly how. I said, 'It's my fault Max hasn't done his maths. I'm the one you should be cross with. It's just we were doing English and he's doing so well.' I took a step towards the doorway, but he was still blocking it. It was the first time I'd been alone with him since our initial meeting on my doorstep and I felt intimidated. I could sense the coiled energy, anger, and the unhappiness of the man.

'I hear what you say,' he said, which is what people say when they're not listening. 'It's just the maths is important too. I'm doing my best to help him. Maybe you should give me some lessons. It's very frustrating. He can be rude, as you just heard.'

'Maybe just be a bit gentler?'

I could tell he didn't like that because he breathed in sharply. 'Anyway. As I've got you, I, um, I notice you didn't find your way back to your front area the other day. I'm all for live and let live, but something's blocking the drains. You must have noticed? The smell's getting worse.' He was about to say more, but his phone made the sound of a quacking duck and he took it out of his back pocket, holding his hand up, signalling to me to stay.

After a second or two, I sat down on the nearest chair.

'Absolutely not,' he said, brushing past me, turning his back. 'He's not to speak to the press. No one at all. OK? Keep him indoors if necessary. I don't care what they're saying. They are not controlling the story. We are. Until the police . . . Yup . . . I know.' He was inspecting the surface of the counter, rubbing his finger over an invisible stain; then he walked to the back doors and slid them open. Frowning, he stared down at the spilt earth.

'I don't care what Fitz says. He should have asked her age.' He spun round and came towards me then, sitting down in the chair next to me at the table. His mouth did strange things, I noticed, when he was talking, the teeth sliding sideways, one canine more prominent than the other. 'Yeah, well, I'd recommend from now on he keeps his trousers zipped,' he said.

He put the phone back in his pocket, then rubbed his forehead with the ball of his hand and sighed. I was aware of an exhaustion, a desperation even, beneath the surface. 'One of my clients, a well-known actor who shall remain nameless, is in a bit of hot water. A one-night stand that went wrong.'

'Oh dear.'

Fitz. Fitz Conroy, presumably. The *Radio Times* had just done a big thing on him.

He stared at me then, his stare intense. 'What is it with people and fucking one-night stands?' He sat back in the chair and breathed out from his cheeks, puffing out the small space above his upper lip then releasing the air with a squeak. He was wearing a button-down shirt today, pale-grey cambric with a crest on the top pocket. It was a replacement for another cambric shirt – a bluer one with a frayed collar that had been in the bag of jumble. The blue would have brought out his eyes. The grey made him look harsh and sallow.

He inhaled deeply. 'So yes, I have concerns. I realised at lunch the other day that you and Ailsa have been spending a lot of time together, that you've become quite . . .' He searched for the right word and when he found it, he emitted it with what was almost a little cry of surprise: '. . . *close*.'

I nodded to confirm his choice of words, feeling the heat rise in my neck. When I am anxious I sometimes clamp my left thumb in my other hand and tug on it. I'd been too aggressive; a muscle gave a crank of pain.

'So I'm checking she's talked to you again – about clearing up a bit, getting to the bottom of the drains, etc. Yes?'

'I haven't seen her since the lunch, actually.' I weighed my words carefully. 'We went for a walk when we got back. But I haven't seen her since.'

His eyes had been flicking all over the room while he'd been talking – at the sink, where a tap dripped, at a torn scrap of ruled paper stuck under a chair leg – but for the first time, he fixed them on me. 'Where was this walk?'

'Just round the common.'

'And she didn't talk to you about anything in particular?'

'No, nothing memorable.'

I stood up, muttering about Maudie and her supper time. My jacket pocket snagged on the chair, but I managed to get out of the kitchen and up to the front door and out and round, and to the security of my own house. Once in, I stood against the wall in the hall and felt the fabric of my own building – my post, my papers, my possessions – press in on me, like a blanket, like a protective vest.

That night was pub quiz at the Dog and Fox, and I was grateful. I've come to rather depend on it. It's my ballast, my lode star. If I'm having a bad week, I only have to count the days until quiz night and life feels more manageable. I'm part of a random team – resident oddbods, put together by Phil the landlord early on: me, Maeve and Sue, who share a stall at the antiques centre, and Bob, who owns a lot of lockup garages. We don't have much in common but when we're round that table, with our minds, our memories, a few pens and some scraps of paper, things fall into place. They take me as I am without any baggage, and I like that.

In the five years I've been going, it's become more popular. A gang from one of the local estate agencies has started coming, the agents in their late twenties and rather rowdy. There are teachers from Hazledown Primary, and some older couples, filling their evenings now their children have flown the nest. It's a draw now, like a trip to the theatre or bowling. Something you might do as a one-off.

Which is why, that Wednesday, on the table next to us, I wasn't surprised to see a group of women in silky tops and big earrings who hadn't been before. They were drinking Pinot Blush and you could tell they were new because they were planning to order food, and if there's one thing I've learnt in my years of doing the pub quiz it's not to order food. One of the women, a curvy brunette in tight skinny jeans, was standing up, waving a menu in front of her face. 'OK – so let's share the fried Camembert; the garlicky mushrooms and one Greek platter, but let's ask them to skip the tzatziki and add extra halloumi.' I was conscious that two of the women were looking at me. I could feel the heat of their gaze, the pulse of their concentration. But I kept my own eyes averted, a smile on my face, to show I was impervious to the attention. After leaving Tom, I'd had a go at cutting my hair. My mother and I kept our hair long – she thought it was cruel to take scissors to a living thing. I looked it up on the internet and I've adopted the traditional pudding-bowl method. I've got quite good at it, though sharp scissors help and I can't always get my hands on a fresh pair. That night, my hands were shaky, and the shortness and irregularity of the fringe was, perhaps, more eccentric than I'd intended.

The curvy, tight-denimed brunette had crossed to the bar and was in dialogue with Phil – thrashing out her various requests – when I heard my name.

'Verity?'

At first I wondered if I might have misheard. I certainly didn't want to look if so. But then it came again.

'Verity?'

Bob and Maeve, who had been bent over the sheet for the picture round, raised their heads.

So I did look then, with mild panic, and scanning the group, recognised a couple of women on the next-door table: blonde hair, white-tipped nails – the mother who had objected with such officious self-congratulation to my appearance at the Tilsons' front door; and next to her, lips scarlet, a bob of springy curls artlessly bouncing free from a large hair clip: Delilah.

'I thought it was you.' Delilah smiled. Her eyes lingered on my companions. Bob carries some weight and Sue, who has an issue with her thyroid, is never without her fingerless gloves, frayed and rather soiled. I felt a shameful lurch of embarrassment. How I'd wished I'd been on the table of narrow-trousered estate agents, or even the teachers with their bulging bags and general air of exhaustion. (How badly that wish reflects on me.)

'What are you all doing here?' I said, stupidly.

'Class night out. It's great, isn't it? Not that I know anything. My general knowledge is terrible. I've warned these guys. I'm going to be hopeless.'

'Not the whole class,' Trish said. 'Just a bunch of like-minded souls.'

'How nice.'

The curvy brunette clomped back from the bar and sat down with a big collapsing movement, the air of someone who had just climbed Everest and been underwhelmed by the view. 'They're out of Camembert,' she said. 'And the Greek platter comes with nachos, not chips.' I was poised to turn back to my table when I realised Delilah was still looking at me intently.

'How are Mr and Mrs Tilson?'

'Tom seems fine. I haven't seen Ailsa for a while.'

'You've become friendly, I hear.'

'Yes, I think so. I hope so.'

'She's an odd one. Rather *elusive*.' She seemed pleased with her choice of words. She rested her hand against her forehead. Her fingernails were rimmed with dirt. 'Is she happy? I don't know. She doesn't seem it. And Tom . . . Poor Tom.'

'Are you talking about Ailsa?' Trish interrupted. 'She only came to book club twice, and yet she made such a fuss about joining.'

'Plus she didn't even read the book,' Delilah said. 'It was obvious her heart wasn't in it.'

The table had gone quiet. 'She's a bit flighty,' another woman said, her open mouth revealing a plastic covering to her teeth – of course: dear Soph's mother. 'When she first moved here, she begged to join our Pilates class. Sonia went out of her way to make space for her, even though the studio only really fits five, but she hardly ever comes.'

'So selfish,' Trish agreed. And they began to talk among themselves, not directly criticising Ailsa but talking in general about behaviour they deemed unacceptable in a friend.

The quiz started up almost immediately but for the whole of the first round, I was aware of the conversation on the next table starting and flaring and being suppressed, like random flare-ups after a forest fire.

In the half-time break, I stood on the pavement outside with Maeve and Sue while they smoked their roll-ups, picking tobacco now and then from the tips of their tongues. The conversation – they were bickering about their van, whether to get it serviced before their next trip to France – didn't need my input. I was thinking how Ailsa hadn't lived in the area long, her roots here were shallow, these friends of hers didn't know her well. I could see Delilah and Trish and dear Soph's mother and all the others through the window – passing round the wine, screwing up their noses at the mushroom pâté. I'd imagined Ailsa the centre of all this, the queen of her little world. I'd been wrong.

When I walked behind Delilah heading back to my table, she put her hand out to stop me. 'Don't tell Ailsa you saw us,' she said. 'Be a love.'

I was home that night at about 11 p.m., and the shouting started soon after. Or maybe it had been going on the whole time; the walls had absorbed it, but now they had got close to the back door. 'I'm not going to ask you again. Just tell the truth.' Tom's voice, bullying and boorish, repeating the same phrases over and over again. I thought about the children upstairs, pressing their faces into their pillows. How Ailsa had grown up with arguing parents, how patterns repeated. When I was a child, I used to line my stuffed toys along the bottom of the door, block out the noise that way. Should I go next door and knock? Take the children from their beds? My heart rate, already raised, raced at the thought; my hands trembled. What would I do? Where would I take them? I couldn't bring them *here*. I was a coward, and I did nothing.

I fell asleep, hours after it had gone quiet, and dreamt vein-like cracks appeared across the ceiling, that it began to creak and then bow, and that as I watched, small droplets began to swell on the base of it, turning gradually to thick yellow globules and I felt a drip and I knew that any minute, with a crash of plaster, and a flood of water, the ceiling would fall. The fear, the dreadful anticipation, woke me and I touched the wall above the bed and for a second the coldness of it felt like damp, and I felt quite sick at the thought of telling Mother, until I remembered she was dead. I remembered she was dead *before* I remembered it was a dream, and the relief of the first outweighed the relief of the second.

The next day, I watched Bea and Max leave for school. I knocked on her door, but no one answered. I texted 'Hello? Fancy a walk?' No reply. I tried to distract myself with work, but I stared at the screen, reading without reading, searching without digesting any of the answers. The area where I keep my computer needs a clear-out, but I collected a pile from one place and put it down in another. I stared out of the window.

I went for another walk, down to Lidl, where I bought some of the hazelnut chocolate she'd told me she liked, and up and down the long wide streets on the far side of the high road in the area estate agents call the Heaver Estate. When I was growing up, the wide red-brick terraces were divided into bedsits but now they're in the second or even third wave of re-gentrification, and I wasn't surprised, halfway up Louisville, to come across a small yellow skip, insecurely covered with tarpaulin. A basement was being dug out and the homeowners had used the building work as a spur for a clear-out.

Normally, a discovery like that has a positive effect on my mood; the satisfaction sits in my chest, settles there and expands, rolling around the nerve endings, cauterising any pain. Not that day. When I got home, I stood in the doorway to Mother's room and imagined myself collecting clothes, finding bags and boxes, without moving. I looked down at my top and noticed I'd picked up a mark from the rung of a garden chair I'd carried back: the scythe-shaped streak of rust looked like blood.

When the doorbell rang, I assumed it was my Amazon delivery. I was expecting Walter Isaacson's biography of Leonardo da Vinci, a tome too hefty for the letter box. The chain was on, and with the new stiffness in my forefinger and thumb it takes me a minute, reaching up, to unhitch the knobbly end from its slotted corral. Then I turned the latch and opened the door.

It was Ailsa.

She looked at me without smiling. 'Can I come in?'

Chapter Ten

Folding wooden dish drainer from Habitat, hinge broken

**Tsundoku, *noun*. The act or habit of piling up newly
acquired books. From the Japanese '*tsumu*', to
pile up, and '*doku*', to read.**

'It's not a good time.' I stepped out into the porch, closing the
door behind me. On the other side, the dog had started barking, jumping up, her nails scratching at the wood. The air was
warm out, warmer than in the house; the light seemed suddenly
different, bright and clear, like when you arrive at the beach.
Ailsa had been fixed in my mind as I'd last seen her: pale,
blotchy around the eyes. It was a shock to see she looked well.
She'd had her hair cut and it bounced just above her jawline.
She was wearing cowboy boots, and a cream dress with
broderie anglaise and other fussiness across the chest.

'Are you working?' she said.

'No. No I'm not. But I . . . it's not a good time,' I said
again.

'It's just I've been so busy. Just one thing after another this
week. I've been meaning to come round for a chat. I feel
terrible that I haven't come sooner so I thought I'd just invite
myself in for a cup of tea. We're having a party and I wanted
to talk it through with you.'

There was a drop in the traffic. On the other side of the road, the street cleaner rolled noisily past.

'Or do you have people?' she said. Her eyes landed on the stain on my top, and then rested on one corner of my mouth. I raised my thumb before I could stop myself and felt stickiness there, a tiny bit of toast in the crease.

'Do I have people?' I tried to make sense of her words. *Did I have people?* She knew my people were dead, or gone.

She was waiting, fiddling with the ribbons that dangled from the neck of her dress.

'I don't,' I said, understanding at last. 'I . . .' I shook my head. 'I don't have people here at the moment.'

'Verity,' she said. She was looking into my eyes, my small hard eyes, her foot resting on one of my crates of magazines. 'Verity. Please let me come in.'

It started in the depths of my chest, and it rose, until it was between the back of my throat and my nose and it felt unmanageable, gloriously monumental and yet dreadful.

'Just let me come in,' she said. 'Verity. It's time. It'll be OK.' She took the key out of my hand then and inserted it in the lock and turned it. I felt powerless suddenly, drained. All the force and energy seemed to come from her as she unlocked the door, pushed it back as far as it would go, which was only a crack really, and slipped through.

I didn't have a choice but to follow.

I bent down first of all to talk to Maudie, who was leaping up, tugging with her paws at my legs. I occupied myself with calming her, which was obviously a displacement activity for calming myself.

Sometimes, when the door is closed on the street, the house seems in contrast very quiet. It wasn't quiet now. It twitched and rustled. There was a roaring in the walls, a creaking in the beams, a groaning. Ailsa hadn't spoken.

'When I said it wasn't a good time,' I managed to say, 'it's just that I'm having a bit of a clear-out.'

'Oh, Verity.'

She still hadn't moved; her eyes were travelling to the floor and up to the ceiling, from place to place, alighting for a moment on one spot and then shifting and alighting on another. I found myself itemising the immediate points of reference: a pile of papers to the side of the mat, comprised of flyers and the free magazines and handwritten notes for missing cats, and a pile of jiffy envelopes and loose packaging and Amazon cardboard sleeves that were waiting to be recycled, and a pile of post I hadn't yet opened, and a pile of post that I had and which was now waiting to move to the front room to be dealt with or filed. And the piles of miscellaneous kitchen equipment that I hadn't yet found a place for, and a haphazard heap of boxes that other stuff had come in that were too useful to be thrown away. And plastic bags containing I didn't remember what, some of them piled up almost to the ceiling, and at the back there, at the bottom of the stairs, some new additions, including two large white picture frames from Ikea, and a Henry vacuum with a broken nozzle, and yesterday's haul: a fold-up garden chair, an iron, five melamine plates with a sunflower pattern and an old-fashioned child's tin globe.

Her neck tipped and I saw she was craning to look between the bannisters to the stairs. 'Books,' I said. 'I've run out of space in the shelves. Those treads are a useful place for books. It's not like they're used for anything else.'

She had brought her hand to her mouth.

'It's all got a bit out of hand,' I said. 'It's run away with me rather.'

'Oh, Verity,' she said.

The heat in my neck rose. I had an impulse to sink to the floor, to bury my face between the two closest plastic bags and to stay there until I heard her leave. But I could only stand, next to her, alongside everything. 'The thing is,' I said, 'I just need a chunk of time, and as you know I've been very busy recently. It's hard enough staying on top of my work for the OED.' I laughed, or it was supposed to be a laugh. Ailsa was very still.

'How has it got like this?' she said finally.

Again I tried to laugh. If we could make light of it, it wouldn't be so bad. 'It's just crept up,' I said.

'What is all this stuff? Where is it all from?'

I swallowed. 'Life.'

She bent down and poked into the top of one of the kitchen boxes. Her expression was appalled. 'I mean – these . . . why?'

'Takeaway cups,' I said. 'They're always useful.'

She pushed them to the side, picking up something else and dangling it from one finger as if she didn't want to get too close.

'That's a good colander.' I took it out of her hand and clasped it to my chest. 'It's a proper one. Lots of them are plastic these days, and the handle bows when you pour boiling water into them. This one' – I tapped it, holding it more tightly – 'it's enamel. Solid. Someone had thrown it away and I hate waste.'

'It's old,' she said. 'Dirty.'

'It just needs a bit of wire wool.'

'Why is it out here in the hall? If you wanted it, you could keep it in the kitchen.' She stirred the surface of that particular box. 'This stuff – Verity. This old tap . . . this hose thing . . . what is it?'

'It's for attaching to the bath so you can wash your hair.'

'These?'

'Radiator caps.'

'It's all just rubbish.'

'It's not just rubbish. Most of it has a place – and will be useful. I just need to have a clear-out elsewhere so I can create cupboard space.'

I threw the colander onto the top of the box with some force. I wanted her gone now. Two steps and a 180-degree turn and she could be out of the front door. If I put my hands on her shoulders, I could steer her in that direction, *push* her.

And she did take two steps, but not towards the front door. She side-stepped – which wasn't necessary, she was making a point – along the path between piles towards the sitting room, and then she swivelled and put her hand on the door, and I couldn't stop her, I realised, even if I got there in time. She pushed and it opened a small way and she put her head round the frame.

Sometimes I imagine I can see the room as it was before, the bones beneath the swelling flesh: the two floral velour-covered armchairs, and the matching sofa with its patterned scatter cushions; the fireplace with the tiles down both sides and the mirror above it; two side tables, one round, the fringed table lamps, and the desk and chair in the window. Watching her peer in, I could pretend to myself that that was the room she was observing, but I knew when she withdrew her head and I saw the distaste on her face that she hadn't seen that room. She had been too distracted by other things: the bags of clothes and the piles of books, the towering heaps of pens and correspondence mingled with half-drunk mugs of coffee; the uneasy darkness – the lamps were long buried – and the dust. I knew plates and cutlery sat in teetering piles and collapsed mounds on the table and floor, and that some of the shoes and clothes I had come across recently were stacked on the chairs.

'Verity,' she said again, and for the first time since she had been in my house I heard reproach. 'This is where you work?'

'Yup. On the desk there. At the computer.'

She put her head back in as if she wanted to confirm, and

when she brought it back, she said, 'How can you even reach it? All that crap.'

'Everything in here is important, Ailsa,' I said. 'I receive a great deal of correspondence. Back and forth. The slips. Obviously, there is some filing to do. But it's all vital to the process. I do need to keep the documentation.'

'All of it.'

'Yes.'

'But the books. The plastic bags. The clothes. There're so many of them.' She raised her voice. 'It's a fire risk. You're lucky you haven't . . .' She stared at me, and then something came over her features, and she softened. 'It's a *health* risk.' She rubbed her forehead. 'What else?' she said. 'What else?'

'Nothing,' I said. 'That room's the worst.'

But she didn't take my word for it, and took several stumbling steps, kicking a plastic bag out of her way, and followed a path to the back room. 'Don't,' I said. 'There's no point. That room isn't used.'

She was picking things up and moving them to make her journey easier. 'What's this?' she said, handling a long stainless-steel rod. It was from the Herberts' shower – the one she had ripped out and replaced. I shook my head slightly and made a face as if it was too complicated to explain, and she flung it carelessly down to the side. It landed on a collection of plastic crates, and slid sideways with a clatter. When she reached the door, she turned the handle and the door gave maybe a couple of inches. 'I wouldn't,' I said, seeing she was about to give it a shove with her shoulder.

'You can't even get in this room?' she said.

'It's never used.'

She took to the stairs then, before I could do anything. Reaching her hand over to the bannister, she placed her feet gingerly, one after another, on the few inches of bare carpet

– as far as the half-landing. I needed to stop her. Faith's room is there. I let out a shriek. She put her hand on the handle.

'Don't,' I said. I began to come up the stairs after her. I'd raised my voice. 'Can you come down now, please.'

As she descended, taking care not to trip, I could see her struggling to find the words to express whatever she was feeling: how about *repulsion* and *disgust* and *disappointment*? I knew things could never be the same between us again. I had lost any credibility, all equality as a person, as a friend. All gone. I could do nothing now to redeem myself except claw back a small amount of dignity.

'Ailsa, you're quite right,' I said, when she was standing next to me. 'I need to have a jolly good sort-out, and seeing things through your eyes has clarified that. I've got this latest batch of words to finish and then I'll start. It's just a matter of finding the time and getting down to it.'

She rubbed her hand across her forehead. It left a smear of dust like a bruise. 'Where do you cook?'

It crossed my mind to lie, to make some arch comment about not knowing one end of a saucepan from another. She knew how it was: I ate out or 'ordered in'. I could even hear myself say it, repeating something she'd told me about her twenties in Fulham. '*All that was in my fridge was a bottle of tequila and six vials of teeth-whitening serum.*' But her head had made short shifting movements, like a small bird, and she had seen the kitchen door, which was propped open with the fold-up aluminium chair under the handle, and she picked her way back towards me, on the path she had created, and then out again at ninety degrees towards it. She paused to pick up a wooden drying rack. 'This is ours, isn't it?' she said.

I looked at my feet. 'You were throwing it away.'

'But Verity, it's broken. The hinge doesn't work. It doesn't stay upright.'

'It just needs a screw,' I said quietly. 'Or a piece of string.'

She put it down, but carefully this time, as if I had begun to get through to her. I could talk about our throw-away culture, my abhorrence of consumerism and its attendant wastefulness, the importance of recycling, the protection of the environment, but even as I began to shape the requisite sentences in my head, I knew they didn't sound right.

She had reached the kitchen door and again I found myself unable to move towards her. If I didn't look into the room, I could block my mind to the reality. But I couldn't prevent an image searing itself on my brain: a splatter of tomato across the floor. I'd dropped a tin a few days previously (possibly longer than that). She was only in there a few seconds, but her expression was different when she came out. She didn't look at me. Perhaps she couldn't. She rested the tips of the fingers of one hand on the end of her nose. She came towards me, laid her other hand on my sleeve, and exerted a small amount of pressure. She pulled the front door towards her and manoeuvred herself out, into the fresh air, and the hand that remained gestured at me to follow.

'Let's go next door,' she said when we were standing next to each other on the path. 'Let's go and have a cup of coffee.'

I knew what she wanted. She wanted to get as far away from my house as she could. She wanted to put distance between her and it. She wanted to remove the smell of it from her skin. But it wasn't what I felt, despite the incapacitating block of humiliation that was lodged, rigid, in my belly. I felt the shame emanating from the bricks, and I wanted to stay close to my house, to protect it and shore it up, to reassure it.

'I've got things to do,' I said. 'I haven't got time for coffee now.'

She looked over her shoulder and then back at me. The left sleeve of her dress had a smear of dirt above the cuff. She inhaled deeply and said in a rush: 'I'll help you. I'm going to help you. Even if we just started with the kitchen, we could make a difference to your quality of life. I'm not sure it's safe for you to cook in there. I mean do you use those microwaves?'

'Not yet, but one day I intend to.'

She shook her head. 'Why?'

'I don't know. Microwave popcorn; I've always wanted to try that. And there's a Sainsbury's ready meal – Singapore noodles – and it's the only way to cook it. They only need mending, a part or two.' I felt suddenly fierce.

'But if you wanted a microwave you could buy one. I mean, I think you can get them for about thirty quid now. The ones you've got in there have been thrown away for a reason. They don't work. You could electrocute yourself trying to use them. Or set fire to the whole house. It would go up like a tinderbox. And the smell . . .'

When I didn't respond, she said, 'Can I ask you, Verity – are the rooms upstairs the same?'

I tried to smile. 'Same as what? Full of microwaves?'

'Full of so much stuff.'

'No,' I said. 'No. No. No.' Her expression said she didn't believe me. 'No,' I said again.

She stared at me, fiddling again with the strings on her dress, twirling them around her finger. 'It'll take us no time at all to clear it out. You only have to look at it with objective eyes, and you'll see when it comes down to it, it's all worthless. It's just rubbish.'

'It's not just rubbish,' I said. 'It's not worthless. I agree it's out of hand, but there are books here, documents, things, that I need. Some of these things are precious.'

The pity for my house and my possessions, the loyalty, had strengthened, turned to something rigid like iron. I didn't care if I never saw her again.

But she took a step towards me then and rested her hands on my shoulders. I don't know whether it was the smudge on her forehead or the look in her eyes: compassion, kindness. And it turns out that rigid thing wasn't iron at all because I bowed my head. I think my eyes were tightly closed; I felt a strong surge of motion sickness, as if the earth and the sky were changing places, and whatever compass we hold in the centre of our chests to tell us what is up and what is down was spinning out of control. She said, murmuring, like reassurance, not provocation, almost like a lullaby: 'You need to want to do it. You need to want to change. It has to come from you. But if you want me to help, I'm here.'

I felt myself sink into her, her hands like struts. If she took a step to one side, I knew I would fall.

She let me rest there for a minute or two. I could hear the street cleaner coming back. And then she tried to pull away, ducking her head to try and look into my eyes. 'Do you want me to help?' she said.

And, with the ground unsteady beneath my feet, and her hands still braced against me, all I could do was nod. And when I'd nodded once, it was easier to nod a second time and then a third, and then I found I couldn't stop.

Chapter Eleven

A tin of Del Monte Peach Slices in Light
Syrup, sell-by date APR 2008

**Perishable, *adjective*. Liable to persish; subject to
destruction, decay or death. Of a foodstuff or other
organic substance: naturally subject to rapid decay.**

The following day, I got up, dressed and walked Maudie early:
a series of actions determined more by muscle memory than
intent. It was warm, the beginning of June, and I sat by the
pond, dog at my feet, to delay my return. The water was busy,
fanned with ducklings and other fowl. A heron perched over
by the reeds on one leg. The male swan swung past on patrol.
As I stood up to go home – I could think of no alternative – I
noticed in the scuffed grass beneath the bench a small shoe,
soft green with a tiny button as a clasp; a baby must have
kicked it off. Useless on its own. I picked it up and, though the
day was to be quite momentous, when I think back on it, it's
the smooth spongy feel of this shoe in my pocket I think of
first.

   She had told me 10 a.m. and it was twenty past when I
reached my gate. I had dressed smartly, in one of my jacket
and skirt arrangements, my own form of armour, but she was
clad in a faded navy boiler suit thing not dissimilar, now I

think of it, to the protective clothes SOCO later wore to remove the evidence from her house and garden. She was on my front path when I walked up, unravelling some of the tarpaulins and peering underneath.

'Ah,' she said, laying down a piece of timber. 'I thought you'd done a runner!'

I let a beat pass, tried to smile. 'If only.'

She raised her head, looking at me doubtfully. Her hair was pulled back in a scrunchie and her face without make-up looked pinker than usual, her eyes rounder, less upturned. 'Listen – all this . . .' She pointed to the planks, and bicycle wheels underneath. 'Tom's right: it's a fire hazard.'

I clambered past her and put the key in the door. She'd left a red bucket on the step containing bleach, a canister of kitchen spray, black bin bags, newspaper, J-cloths. I stepped over it. I had it in mind suddenly to close the door after me, but I could hear her steps behind, the scrape of the bucket; I smelt a waft of bergamot and lime. I turned sharply. Perhaps it was the new haircut, the uniform aspect of her overalls, or the determined set of her jaw, perhaps it was the weight of the fortnight in which I hadn't seen her, but it was like being jostled by a stranger, an enemy. I began to try and push the door into her face, but she was stronger than me, and I was restricted by the lack of room in the hall. I minced back a few inches and she managed to get in.

'We're not going to do anything you're not comfortable with,' she said, shutting the street out.

I took a sharp breath through my nose, feeling myself shudder. The house felt stuffy, thick with warmth, almost solid. A weak light picked out the cobwebs that laced the cornices; in patches the wallpaper had bubbled and blistered. As if through her nostrils, I could smell a rancid sweetness.

'I know it's hard.'

I forced myself to nod.

'The kitchen, then? It's what we've agreed. Yes?'

The restrictions in my throat prevented me from speaking. She waited a few seconds until I managed to move my head, then gave a confirmatory nod and shuffled her way towards the back of the house between the boxes of kitchen equipment on one side and the vacuums and garden furniture on the other.

I followed her and stood in the doorway as she manoeuvred along the gully between the table and the counter, and put her weight into pushing open the back door. The cupboards were full and the table and other surfaces crammed with excess packages and tins. Small electrical appliances – some kettles and toasters, a food mixer, etc – took up a portion of the floor space, and my collection of pots, saucepans and utensils were heaped along the counter and on top of the stove. Food had been left out. The walls were grimy with dirt. The splatter of tomato sauce was, dismayingly, much more extensive than I'd remembered, flooding down the door of the oven, and over the floor and back up across the cupboards.

After taking a few deep breaths at the open door, she put on her rubber gloves, asking if it was OK to make a start on the fridge?

I must have made some sign of agreement, because she filled the bucket with soapy water and unravelled a black bag from the roll and then, kneeling on some newspaper, began to remove items from the shelves. 'I'm going to throw away anything past its sell-by date, Verity. Is that OK with you?' An answer seemed not to be needed because, her face half averted, she continued to put food into the bag: a lettuce and a cucumber that just needed the outer layers removed, a packet of butter, and an only half-used tin of Carnation milk; and then, with small clinks, a jar of black olives, and raspberry jam, and anchovy paste, some pickled walnuts, a bottle of mayonnaise, and products I had, in truth, forgotten about, including a green slab which I think, a few months previously, had been a half-price packet of Wiltshire cured ham.

I was trying to breathe. I knew I should be thankful, and yet I was unable to summon up any sense of gratitude. As the bin bag filled, I began to twitch my head, and fidget with my hands, my shoulders knocked against the doorframe and I took a step into the room, my hands gripping the wooden backs of the stacked garden chairs, and then a step backwards. I rolled my foot against the edge of the bottom microwave, pinning it there. I rubbed my hand across my ribcage, to try and still what felt like impossibly rapid movement. I swallowed several times. It had got warmer in the room, despite the open back door. A vegetal, sulphurous smell filled my nostrils.

She washed out the fridge with soapy water and then she sprayed it with Mr Muscle, scrubbing at it with a J-cloth. She put a few things back – a jar of Nescafé, an unopened carton of long-life orange juice. Then she stood up and, without asking, reached over to open the cupboard next to the fridge.

She peeled apart another bin bag, taking some time to rub one end to separate the sides, and began dropping in tins – baked beans, chicken soup, peach slices in syrup.

I pushed forwards and snatched out the tin of peaches. 'These are fine,' I said, sharply. 'There's nothing wrong with these.' They were Faith's favourite. She liked them with Ambrosia Rice Pudding. I'd got both in for her when I thought she was moving back. Ailsa was probably about to chuck that away too. I reached past her and began searching the cupboard.

'These are all rusty, Verity, past their sell-by date. They're spoiled.'

I'd found the Ambrosia rice and I held both tins to my chest. 'You're being over-zealous,' I said. 'No one cares about sell-by dates. They're just a way to make us buy more things than we need.'

Now I had stood up to her, I felt quite aggressive. 'I don't mind you throwing some things out,' I said. 'But this is just ridiculous.'

She folded her arms, her yellow rubber hands clamped in her armpits. 'I understand. It's part of it, don't you see? You're both attached to and overwhelmed by your hoard. You're fearful of the emptiness associated with clearance. This stuff – you see it as part of you. You've used your hoard to avoid confronting emotions that are difficult for you, to funnel anxiety, and it's hard, Verity. It's hard. All that anxiety is going to come flooding back. The grief for your mother, the row with your sister. But I'm here and we'll do it together.'

I didn't like the way she spoke: the practised use of 'your hoard', the overly dramatic repetition of 'it's hard'. I didn't like her bringing my sister into this. She had done some research and was enjoying the sound of her own voice, her intellectual engagement with the subject. She was pleased with her cod psychology, her sense of herself as my redeemer.

'I can tell you've been on Wikipedia,' I said. 'What did you search? Hoarding Disorder? I've watched the TV shows. This isn't what this is.'

'It's something *like* that.'

'It isn't. I'm not that kind of person. I'm not *ill*.'

'No, you're not. You're a wonderful, highly functioning individual. I'm sure the reasons for this go deep, way back into your past.'

'Like what?'

'You've told me about your mother's anthropomorphism of inanimate objects. I've been thinking too about that story you told me. The time you and Faith filled the wardrobe with old men's clothes – her reaction to that. She was touched and must have been cheered up for a bit but in your eyes the *stuff* made all her grief for your father disappear. I can see how very early on you associated possessions with keeping emotions at bay. But Verity' – she gestured to the room – 'it *is* a condition. It's not normal. Isn't it helpful to know that it's a psychological disorder, that you don't have to live like this, that we can do something to combat it?'

'A "psychological disorder"? Our culture's obsessed. It's all a matter of definition, Ailsa, and you can only define something by what society considers "normal", which is itself contingent on the whims and subjective values of the time.' I was, as I often do, taking refuge in language, but my voice sounded unnaturally brittle. 'I mean for goodness' sake, homosexuality was considered a "psychological disorder" until the1970s.'

'But if you're not happy, if it's impairing your quality of life . . .?' She trailed off, eyes cast down. She didn't know how to speak to me now; none of this fitted within the parameters of the friendship we had forged. She didn't have the sophistication; the *education*. I felt the mean vindictive satisfaction of that thought, an internal venomous glee at using her own insecurities against her.

'I *am* happy,' I said.

'OK.' She began to wind up the roll of bin bags; they didn't coil flat, but bunched and bulky. She gave up and put them down, still not meeting my eye. My triumph began to fade. 'The only thing I do need to say,' she said, 'is that the externals at least, the fabric of the building, the drains, the front garden – before our party, I've promised Tom . . .'

I drew myself up, pushed my shoulders back. 'None of this is any of Tom's business.'

She moved her hair away from her face with the heel of her hand. 'Well it sort of is, isn't it? We share a party wall, the drains.

He's unhappy with the smell. He thinks there's some sort of serious damp issue, or a blockage. He's talking about bringing in the council. So far I've managed to persuade him that we could deal with it quietly between ourselves. But if you and I can't come to some sort of compromise.' She blinked, as if clearing her eyes. 'I'm worried about how far he might take things.'

Her head on one side, she rubbed her fingers, small circular massage movements, into the crinkled lines across her forehead. Something black, a small piece of gunk from the lid of a jar, adhered to her cheek. She picked up the roll of bin bags, and her eyes flicked to the kitchen door. Mentally, she had already walked through it.

And it seemed, with an acute, sudden intensity, vital that she shouldn't. I dropped the rice and the peaches back into her bin bag. 'I'm sorry,' I said.

I reached down to fish the J-cloth from the bucket and, turning away from her, crouched to begin rubbing at the tomato on the oven door. It was dried on, engrained, but I kept at it, using my nail to dislodge the edges. It was disgusting how long I'd left it. Not days, or weeks, but months. Maybe years. I didn't turn round; I hardly breathed, but I heard a top cupboard open and the rustle of plastic, and finally a reassuring clunk.

She worked all day. I won't say I found it easy. She piled anything she considered 'rubbish' in bags along the front path, and I admit that, while they were there, I felt connected to them by invisible elastic, highly conscious of their presence, and drawn to them, rather as if it were Maudie she had taken outside and left, feeling that nobody would expect me to let them stay out there for long, that there was a deadline to their exile.

In the kitchen, where piles had multiplied and plastic bags bloomed, clear space began to appear. The table and chairs became accessible and the floor tiles were revealed beneath their screed of dirt to be a terracotta red. The cupboard doors were scrubbed down with less success – perhaps the detergent had been too strong because some of the old cream gloss paint got stripped away with the grease, and the streaks of dark pine underneath looked a bit like mould. But God she worked hard. I don't know why I find that so hard to admit. All those sentences I've just written in the passive. Anything to avoid placing her at the centre of it. My own muddled resentment and guilt, I suppose.

Late in the afternoon she went out into the garden, perhaps just for air, but after a few moments she poked at the pile, unpeeling the Herberts' shower tray and glass panels and carrying them, one by one, into the side return on the far left – on the boundary with Sanjay, my neighbour on the side. He's lived there for years, and never complains. She had already brought out some of the garden furniture from inside the house and in the small clear space she erected a metal table, using a brick to balance out its uneven legs, and sprang apart two of the wooden chairs.

I'd been watching her from a window in the bedroom, where I'd been banished after a dispute over a SodaStream, but she called me down then and by the time I emerged, had made us both a cup of coffee, using the last remaining kettle, the lone jar of Nescafé.

'How do you like that?' she said, putting the tray down on the table. 'Your own little outdoor area.'

Bees buzzed in the undergrowth. Tiny midges whirled in shafts of light. In the linked arms of trees, blue tits darted and squeaked. From afar, the garden might look abandoned, but close to, it seethed with life; woodlice lurked, ants scurried, worms uncurled. Even on a dry day, it was damp.

'Tom would like us to tackle out here,' she said.

I perched on the edge of the chair and took a sip from my mug. It was white inside; the tide lines had gone. But the coffee tasted chemical; there's always a quid pro quo. I wanted to mention it, I *longed* to complain, but I managed not to.

In my pocket I felt for the small shoe.

'You all right?' she said. 'Not too traumatised?'

'I'm sorry I was difficult,' I said. 'Really I would have found it very hard to get going on my own. I'm grateful. I'm sure you've got so many things you'd rather be doing.'

She looked at my face carefully and then, the tone of her voice tailored to mine, said: 'Not at all. I'm grateful for the distraction.'

We sat for a few moments in silence. I tried to remember what we usually talked about. I wanted to be her friend, Verity Baxter: supportive, wise, witty neighbour. But the role was no longer mine to play and I was acutely aware of the loss of it, of my standing as someone whose judgements and opinions still had value.

I longed to resume our usual idle chatter; who had had Botox and who hadn't. When I spoke, though, I sounded peevish. 'I don't feel I've seen you properly for ages.'

'I know. I'm sorry. I've been rushing around here and there. Quite a few job interviews. Been doing a lot of Pilates. Book club.'

'Oh really?'

Nothing in her expression suggested she was lying.

'Yes – busy bee.'

'I've been worried about you. You didn't seem yourself in the pub that day. And since then I've had the impression you and Tom aren't getting on as well as you should.'

She looked quizzical. 'What do you mean? How've you gained that impression?'

'Well . . .'

'You been spying on us, Verity?' She sounded light-hearted, but I wasn't sure.

'No. Of course not.' I felt horribly self-conscious. 'It's just . . . well, you know . . . sound travels.'

She nodded. 'Oh, I see. OK.' She slunk her shoulders lower in the chair, stretching her legs to rest them on the bar beneath the table. Lightly, as if it were insignificant, she said: 'It's a bit stressed at ours at the moment. Tom's having a difficult time at work. Tempers have flared more than usual.'

'I've heard the odd fight.'

She began to run the pads of her right fingers in circles over her left palm, not quite scratching. 'Yeah, like all couples.'

I plucked up my nerve. 'Is he ever violent towards you?' I said.

'No! Verity! What do you think? No!' She laughed quickly. 'He's a complicated man. When it's going well, it's fantastic. You know, he has so much energy. He can be very funny, you know, life and soul. But he's working long hours, desperate for new business. Money is – well – we're in way over our heads. God knows how we're going to dig ourselves out of this one. As a result, I've hardly seen him recently and when I do – when he's as tense as he is now – all sorts of other things come into play. He can be such an arsehole. But, Verity, I'm no angel.'

'You are to me.'

She half smiled, considered me. 'You have no idea. I don't know whether it's because I was so seriously ill as a child – faced my own mortality.' I noticed that little expression settle again on her face: self-pity and valour. 'I get overwhelmed by life, swept up in things, make mistakes.'

'I'm sure you don't.'

I wonder now if she decided to tell me what she did for one

reason only: to prove she was still my friend, to make me feel better about myself.

She angled her face so she could look into mine. 'I don't tell many people this because it's not important. It doesn't change anything except that it makes me feel . . .' She pressed her breast above her heart and screwed up her face; a gesture that conveyed an intensity of emotion if not the emotion itself. 'As I say, I don't want to make a big thing of it, but . . .'

'What?' I whispered.

A flush rose on her neck. 'It's nothing. It's just, my mum had just died, and I was leading a bit of a rackety life when I met Tom. The thing is, I was already pregnant.'

I began to murmur a response, something stupid like *Oh, I didn't know* but she spoke over me. 'Many men would have run a mile when they found out. He didn't have to stay. And I'm grateful to him for that.'

'Oh,' I said, trying to sound several things at once: concerned and yet unconcerned, aware of the consequence of his actions while equally conscious of the insignificance of hers. 'So who is Melissa's real father?'

Of course that was the worst thing to say. Her brow creased. 'Tom's her real father. It was a one-night stand. It's not important. Well – not to her it isn't. From the moment she was born, it was irrelevant. It's just . . . what am I trying to say?' She took a breath, started again. 'It's irrelevant to Melissa and Tom, but to *me* . . . every tiny detail in a relationship has an impact, any shift in the balance, and in this case something as simple as gratitude, it can make things uneven and that causes problems. I've been feeling very trapped. He hasn't wanted sex for months . . .'

Remembering this moment, I feel almost repelled by my inability to behave naturally. I tried to make my expression concerned and knowing, but my face felt tight and wrong.

She lowered her head further. I could see tiny brown flecks in her eyes. Her lip twisted. 'Listen, I'm going to tell you something else. I've got to tell someone. But if I do you've got to promise to keep it to yourself.'

'What?' (*What next?*) I moved my face closer to hers. A cobweb had caught in her hair and my fingers twitched to take it out. I think she was about to speak but there was a noise then – a scrape and rattle; the sound of a back door opening. Bea's voice in the garden: 'Wait. What?' Tom's, distant but echoing, in the kitchen. 'Where's your mother gone now?' Ailsa let out a sharp breath. 'They're back,' she said.

For a minute, though, she didn't move. She stared out at the vegetation, at the thigh-high brambles and bindweed, the giant heads of grasses and wildflowers, the vigorous acid green plant with its pointy, sticky leaves that crept into every gap. I followed her gaze; it was focused on the back corner, where the apple tree bows down to kiss the rising undergrowth; the brambles reaching up into the branches to pull it into its embrace. In the warm air, with tiny shifts and rustles, the whole garden seemed to expand, to move as one, like netting or a web.

Ailsa was still staring. 'Tom says you could hide anything out there,' she said. 'And no one would know.'

Chapter Twelve

My grandmother's inlaid writing slope, poss Regency?

Codependency, *noun*. Excessive emotional or psychological reliance on another person, typically a partner or close relative . . . reciprocal dependence on another's neediness.

The problem, looking back, is that, like a patient on the operating table, their organs balanced in the surgeon's gloved hands, I was weakened by her entry into my house. I lost perspective; *grip*. It triggered obsessional thoughts in me; I ruminated on things all night, pushed them endlessly round and round in my head. Ailsa was right, Tom was Melissa's father; the existence of a biological father (*who?*) made no difference to that. And yet – it did add a layer of complication. *Hadn't he recently said something bitter about one-night stands?* She'd talked about her postnatal depression and the problems they'd had conceiving. Had both facts fuelled in him a sense of unfairness? Her revelation about their non-existent sex life; linked or unlinked: was his bullying the frustration of a man who couldn't get it up? And what was the secret she'd been going to tell? I thought I'd got close to her and yet I didn't trust her. What were her motives in telling me this now?

When I sat at the kitchen table in the morning, I tried to feel calm. I remarked out loud on the space available for my feet. But the emptiness unnerved me; I was aware of the filth along the top of the window, of the smell: disinfectant and dog food and something baser that got into your nostrils and clung and bloated. People think loneliness is like boredom, but for me it's more like agitation. After a while, I began to think there wasn't much point to a table if it was somewhere one would sit alone.

At 11 a.m., I took Maudie for a walk, comforted to see out the front the reassuring heap of black bin bags that would stay, she had said, until I was 'ready'. I scooted round the common. Though smartly dressed, I was wearing my usual trainers, so for some of the distance, I took it at a half-run. Maudie, poor old girl, struggled to keep up. This is relevant because it shows a) how anxious I was, if Ailsa did come, not to keep her waiting, and b) what a short time I was absent from the house.

When I saw the open gate and the bare front path, the stepping stones, the grass between them, my first instinct was to throw myself to the ground and scream. Don't worry, I didn't. I know how that sounds. I put both hands on the fence and bent forwards, lowering my head over it, so the top bar was pressed into my abdomen. I let out a long low groan, a bellow, like a cow that's lost her calf. She had promised me, *promised*. It was the betrayal that got me, the knowledge they'd watched and waited, that I'd been played. A bus hummed. The church bells rang. I didn't hear Ailsa until she was right on top of me. 'So Tom took the stuff,' she said breathlessly. 'I couldn't stop him. I know we said we'd wait. I'm really sorry. Verity. Please. It'll be OK. Look at me.'

My eyes, I'm afraid to say, were full of tears – anger at being misunderstood and panic, as well as an overwhelming sense of loss.

'I'm sorry,' she said again, her voice urgent, her hand an insistent pressure on my shoulder. 'Listen. Please. Dear old V. Let's go in before he gets back.' She was so close to my face I could smell the tea on her breath. 'I'm on your side.'

Perhaps I should never have let her in, that could have been the end of it, but I did let her in, and we sat together at the little table. Now she had cleaned the windows, the light in the kitchen was harsh; she looked tired, shadows under her eyes. A tiny cut on her lower lip. I should have asked how she was – found a way to ask those questions that piled up in my head. Instead, I was weakened. I let her take control. It stopped being about me and Ailsa or Ailsa and Tom and became about Tom and me. This room: the war office. My house: the campaign. Armed conflict underpinned her language. She referred to him 'bringing in the heavy artillery'; how we should 'put up a defence'. It weakened me, won me over. It's only now, looking back, I realise I should have thought more about who was the vanquisher and who was being vanquished; who was abusing whom.

She stood up and placed her hands firmly down on the melamine. She was 'mine' again for the day. Tom was taking the kids for lunch at his parents in Berkshire. Where did I want her? Don't worry, she wouldn't go upstairs. She knew Faith's room was out of bounds. (I'd locked it now and hidden the key.) Father's study was beyond her, which left the hall, the stairs and the sitting room. The party wall was a matter of concern. Also: finding the source of the smell. But yes, for now, all good. 'Right. Let's get at it,' she said.

Her mood was very different that day. No more confidences. She worked with a sort of happy frenzy; almost manic. She sang, scraps of old pop songs, and told me I was brilliant. It was even warmer than the day before, the air mushy like rotting pears, and yet she wore a long-sleeved shirt, I remember that, and now and again I saw her wince and rub her shoulder. I went in search of Nurofen, and in a box of sewing kits, found half a packet of Valium, left over from Mother. She declined – 'I'm off my own pills,' she said, craning to look out of the front window, 'I'm not taking someone else's' – though she urged me to take a couple. She said it would help me to relax. The rest is a bit of a blur. I know I sat on the chair at my desk and that she talked to me about various things – for some reason the words egodystonic and egosyntonic float into my head – and occasionally she would bring me an object she had unearthed: my grandmother's writing slope, for example. 'It's rather lovely. Is it rosewood and ivory? Regency, maybe. If you don't mind, I'll get it valued.'

I dozed off and when I opened my eyes, her face was peering into mine. 'Something's come up,' she said. I struggled to sit, but she was already at the front door. It slammed, the gate jangled, and a few seconds later, I heard her door slam too. It was only early afternoon, I think; not much later.

The stillness of the house pressed in. My head was befuddled. I should have been working and yet I felt edgy, unstable. I wandered to the kitchen and drank deeply from the cold tap. I stood in the garden and, above the mildewy dank fetor of rotting veg or, yes, maybe drains, I wondered if I smelt toast. I went back into the house and into the hallway, hovering. She had stacked some cardboard boxes by the door and I found myself unpacking the top one, finding Brillo pads, some serviceable towels, a pair of Faith's slippers. I hid these under the sofa, and then I went upstairs and sat on Mother's bed.

It was comfortingly full in here. I felt the touch of my mother's knick-knacks, the photos and old birthday cards; the soft toys on the bed, the shelves of china animals. Whimsies. I picked up a squirrel. Its tail had broken and been stuck back on and I picked at yellow flakes of old glue. Tiny taps and squeaks came through the brickwork: Ailsa was just the other side. The floorboards creaked. I could hear music – what was it; Mozart's *Requiem*? – and the gush of water in the pipes. With my ear pressed to the wall, I felt the vibration of a distant hum; the tumble dryer on its endless hot rotation. I picked up her voice too: urgent and slightly panicked, 'Yes, I know,' a nervous laugh abruptly cut off. Her steps across her floor, the groan of a cupboard opening, small clatters. And then louder thumps as she took the stairs, the rattle of the front door. I got to the window just in time. Hair shiny, a shoulder bag slung across a summer dress, she turned left onto the pavement, and set off in the direction of Tooting Bec.

For the next week or two I was absorbed by the question of whether she would come or not. I thought and worried about her constantly – a distress only temporarily eased when she was in my sight. But her visits were erratic. I was like the dog, or Max, waiting for the validation of an irregular reward. Sometimes she left shortly after she arrived, saying she had to see someone, she'd come back – occasionally she did, often she didn't. Unable to work, I'd sit by the window, peering out. It didn't occur to me to wonder, or to ask, where she went. I knew she was busy. Three children, and a party to plan. Again, in that, I was passive, like a faithful dog. Not that I liked what she did in the house. I hated it really. But her visits, the kindness they imbued, gave a new shape to my days, and in that sense I longed for them as much as I longed for them to be over.

The heatwave had begun properly. Bluebottles droned at the windows; a wasp crept in through a crack, and buzzed angrily, knocking its head against the glass as if it could bore its way out. The rooms were hot and airless, the sun filtering in only drew attention to the grime that furred the walls. One day Ailsa washed them, but to my eye they looked worse afterwards, not better; uglier and more ashamed. I felt the same, constantly on edge with a sour combination of humiliation and rancour. I would follow her around, helping or obstructing; she kept telling me to go out, to leave her to it. She was brisk, distracted; I think she regretted the confidences of the first day. We never again returned to them. Once she said, 'I'm a terrible mother. No, I am,' when I demurred. 'You have no idea.' If I began to ask anything further, she'd skate the subject away. I begin to wonder now, what complications in her own life she was guarding; at the time I was numb to such sensitivity, my empathy blunted, my interpretation of her behaviour guided purely by self-disgust. It seeped in, poisoned the atmosphere. I assumed she was repulsed by me, that her underlying emotion was embarrassment, and I didn't try to get through to her as a result. I regret it hugely now.

On the rare occasion that we did talk with any intimacy, I was the focus. Two conversations in particular, both distressing, stick in my mind.

It was a Tuesday afternoon, and I had been talking about *Jackie* magazine; how Faith used to read it in secret. (It wasn't the sort of thing our mother approved of.) Her favourite part, I told Ailsa, was the before-and-after makeover spread where some hapless female in a baggy dress and ill-fitting glasses was given an A-line skirt and a new pair of specs, discarding the severe oblongs for something that brought out the 'heart shape' of her face. Sometimes, she'd test the theories out, using me as a model. It would make her laugh.

'I'd like to say you were conducting as dramatic a transformation here,' I said. 'But I know I'm making it hard for you.'

I was fishing. Earlier that morning, she'd discovered the towels and slippers, etc, under the sofa, and given me a lecture about my tendency to 'churn'. She hadn't spoken since.

We were in the front room, sorting through miscellaneous piles of papers, and stationery, and she opened and tried to close a lever-arch file, before laying it on the chuck pile. Then she sat back on her heels and wiped her wrist across her forehead, stretching up the lines, making a quick, hard flicking movement from the temple.

'Does she look like you?' she said.

I thought she meant Mother. She'd found some old photos of her, 1970s sepia prints of Mother holding one of our cats to her cheek. 'Who?'

'Faith. There're no pictures here of Faith.'

After a long moment, I said, 'We both had very long hair as girls.'

'Was she already keen on hairdressing? Did you plait each other's hair and things like that?'

I hesitated. I remembered the silkiness of Faith's locks through my fingers, the slip of it; the fiddle of securing the elastic, her face twisting, gurning when I pulled it too tight; her widow's peak, so similar in fact to Ailsa's; the funny wonkiness of her teeth. 'I used to do hers,' I said, shutting the image down. 'She didn't like touching my hair. She said it was too crinkly.'

'And your mother – I know she wasn't well, that she didn't leave the house. But did she join in? Did she play with you?'

'She did. She had long hennaed hair and she liked Faith to put it in pigtails.'

Ailsa wrinkled her nose. 'That sounds very jolly.'

In that moment, I was acutely aware of the reality of it, how the refusal to admit anything emotionally unpleasant had created its own burden, how the jolliness was its own form of darkness. It had suppressed anything raw or real, disappointment or frustration or sadness, like a chlorophyll-soaked cloth across the mouth. I thought that that was why Faith had left – choosing to cut hair, an act of violent rebellion, and I thought about the years in which I'd lived with it, and how next to the ulcers, and the headaches and the sensitivity to light that kept the curtains drawn, hardest to bear of all was the suffocation.

'It was,' I said.

'You really haven't seen Faith since the day of your mother's funeral?'

I'd been putting a lid back on a pen and for some reason I couldn't get this lid to fit.

I stabbed the point of the pen into the soft part of my thumb. 'Well, I saw her immediately after – as I said, she came back here and we argued but I haven't spoken to her since.'

'What was the row about? Was it this?' She widened her arms, raised her hands to the walls. Her expression said she wouldn't have blamed Faith if it was.

I didn't answer for a few seconds. I put the pen down and rubbed my hands up and down the front of my thighs, and then the back of them, squeezing the flesh above the knees. I allowed myself to picture Faith standing in the hall, the disgust on her face. The image was like a wound. 'Yes. No. She knew it was like this, though she hadn't been here much in the years leading up to Mother's death. She started poking about, talking about selling. Trying to go into rooms. I had to stop her, put my foot down. It all got too much for both of us. When she left, she said she was never coming back.'

She searched my face. 'Neither of you have tried to build bridges since?'

I was sitting on the floor, leaning against the wall, the ridge of the windowsill hard against my skull. I put the box of pens to one side and laid my hands flat on the carpet. It glittered with tiny particles of dust. 'Not really,' I said. I wrinkled my nose. I could feel a sharp prickle at the top of it. I closed my eyes to stop them hurting.

Ailsa stood up then, and came over to sit next to me. She was wearing black trousers and a pair of those French elasticated plimsolls that have two rows of holes, but no laces.

'It's not surprising you've hunkered down a bit,' she said softly. 'You lost your mother and then fell out with your sister. And let's not even start on your father walking out on you when you were tiny. It's understandable if you have abandonment issues.'

I read somewhere that our personalities are shaped, more than by genes or parental influence or life experience, by our relationship with our siblings. In my case, Faith, the pretty, bubbly one, did the talking, while I weighed my words carefully, or not at all. Wisdom counts for nothing in the face of effervescence. It was irrelevant how 'clever' I was; she was the one who got to give a shape to our existence, to define it and record it.

I realised it didn't matter if I answered Ailsa or not.

'Abandonment issues,' I repeated eventually, enunciating carefully.

She flexed her feet. She wasn't wearing socks and I could see she had recently shaved, but had missed a few stray hairs on the soft patch of skin above the bones of her ankles.

I'm trying to recall if it was that afternoon or the next when she came across the postcard from Adrian Curtis. Possibly it was the next, because I remember she was tetchy, and she had been kind to me the day we talked about Faith. By then, you see, it was no longer my humours we trod around, but hers. Perhaps it's human nature; perhaps the moment I accepted her help this was inevitable. I was mindful of how far she was putting herself out on my behalf, so was acutely aware of every shift in her mood. I began to worry that my presence irritated her, to notice how often she tried to get rid of me. She'd send me on errands – more bin bags, more Mr Muscle – and if I came back too quickly, she would be in a different part of the house. I'd locked Faith's door – when I passed it, I felt the presence of what was inside – but I might hear her footsteps in Mother's room. It would be at the front of my mind to ask what she was doing, but somehow when she came down again, brushing a cobweb from her hair, or releasing a 'pouf' of exhaustion, it felt rude to do so, not my place. 'For God's sake, chuck,' she would explode. 'Chuck, chuck, chuck.' Desperate to appease her, I became cloying, reiterating endless expressions of gratitude: 'I don't know how I'll ever repay you.' The first time I said this, as she was loading the boot of her car, she hugged me and said, 'It's what we do for our friends.' So I suppose that's why, the following day, I said it again, for positive re-enforcement. Only she didn't hug me the second time, and in fact on the third utterance, her tone was clipped and she said, 'I'm sure you'll find a way.'

Was it then I began to think about money? Or was it when she mentioned how much the house was worth, how, 'Now one could see the bare bones', it might be worth getting it valued. I think she used the word 'goldmine', or perhaps that was the visit she scrubbed down the mantelpiece and stood back to admire it. 'Lovely old marble,' she said. 'Verity! Who knew? What else have you got hidden here? The fireplace alone is probably worth a fortune.'

It was the first time I realised that, of course, I was not entirely without means, and that maybe there was a way I could show my gratitude.

I remember now: it was a Wednesday the day she found Adrian's note. I'd taken Maudie next door to spend an hour or two to help Max with his homework and that was nearly always a Wednesday.

When I'd left she'd been up a ladder cleaning the picture rail, but on my return, I found her sitting on the sofa. Her crossed feet were resting on my mother's needlework stool, and next to her was the plastic crate containing some of my correspondence. She was leaning back into the cushions, elbow resting on the arm, as if she owned the place.

It's odd, looking back, that I wasn't cross. The crate contained personal letters, birthday cards and the like; I would get to it in my own time. I had told her that. And yet, I didn't see it as an incursion. I had already begun to cede my independence to her.

She looked up when she saw me in the doorway and held up a postcard. Across the front of it was written 'Six Wonders of the Isle of Wight'. A smile played about her lips. 'Adrian! Who's Adrian?'

I unclipped Maudie's lead. 'Adrian Curtis. The man I met at the council. I told you about him.'

'Tell me again.'

I stood in the doorway. 'He worked in the planning office and we got chatting in the canteen – he asked me to pass the salt and then we both moaned about how hard it was to get anything out of the shaker. He asked me out for a drink and then I suppose in modern parlance we dated for a bit.'

'What went wrong?' I noticed again the points of her cheekbones, the upward turn of her eyes. She fanned the postcard, as if drying the ink. It was one of those multi-photo cards, depicting six famous Isle of Wight landmarks: the Needles, Tennyson Down, Newport High Street. 'He says he's missing you, looking forward to Wednesday, with three exclamation marks.'

I thought back to the night I'd spent in his room in the tower block above Southside shopping centre, the stale smell, the overly soft texture of his sheets, and for some reason, I remembered the tea he had brought me in the morning; the white scum that floated on the top of it as if he hadn't let the kettle properly boil. I thought about his pale narrow chest, his lashed eyes, fish-like, without his glasses and then I thought about a conversation I'd had in the early days with Ailsa, how worldly I had tried to sound, with my 'when you know you know'.

'It didn't really work out,' I said.

'"It didn't work out"?' There was something mocking in her repetition, as if how *couldn't* it have worked out? A man was interested in me. What more did I want?

'He wasn't for me.'

'Verity Ann Baxter, are you by any chance a little too fussy for your own good?'

She wasn't listening or engaging. I felt a surge of irritation then. I'd had enough of her teasing. Just because I lived *like this*, as she put it, didn't mean my responses weren't valid. My back teeth felt as if they were glued together. I tried to speak without dislodging them. 'It was a horrible time,' I said. 'I hated working at the council. I hated everything about it.'

'I'm sorry,' she said. 'I didn't mean to pry.' She took the necessary steps to reach me at the door and she put her arms out. 'What am I like?' she said.

The realisation came like an explosion in the chest, painful and yet glorious. I don't know why I hadn't noticed before.

My sister, I thought. My sister.

Chapter Thirteen

Karrimor Grey and Blue Waterproof Hiking Trainers, size 6

Surreptitious, *adjective*. Taken, used, done, etc by stealth, secretly, or 'on the sly'; secret and unauthorised; clandestine.

Two things.

Yesterday, during a perfectly nice supper, Ailsa suddenly put down her knife and fork and said she'd had enough of 'this ready meal three-for-two shit'. She'd go to the supermarket herself, she said, and pick out some nice vegetables. 'What's in season? God, I don't even know. Where are we?' It's the second week of October and I told her as much.

'Runner beans, still. Maybe. Leeks. Squash. I'll go tomorrow.'

I picked up her plate and put it in the sink. She's been different since her meeting with the QC. She's more alert, as if she's planning something. It's making me uneasy. 'I'm not sure that's a good idea,' I said, running the cold tap over it, watching the red-tinged Chinese noodles swirl down the drain.

She didn't answer, and when I turned round, I saw she had opened the 'notes' app on her phone and was writing a list.

I've started getting up early to work and this morning she came in, a couple of hours before I expected to see her. I've been sent a new batch of words, 'wick' and 'wicked' and 'wicker', and was looking through the file of original slips – the quotations from novels, newspapers, etc, sent in to the OED by readers for the first edition – when she came and sat next to me and started asking me questions.

At first I was touched, pleased she was showing an interest.

I showed her how the adjective 'wicked' in its first documented appearance, 'wickede', referred exclusively to the devil; how this expanded over the centuries to include the supernatural, and then evil, as in unnatural, and then more recently it came to be used as an intensifier.

'When do you think was its earliest use to mean cool, or excellent?' I asked.

She shook her head. 'I don't know. The 1980s?'

'Aha.' I showed her the slip on which, in the original reader's spidery writing, was written the quotation from F. Scott Fitzgerald's 'This Side of Paradise': 'Phoebe and I are going to share a wicked calf.'

'That's taken you by surprise, hasn't it?' I said. 'Published in 1920!'

Her eyes darted to the door, and that's when I noticed the white envelope in her hand.

She said, with what sounded like pointed composure, 'I'm going to walk down to the post office. I've written to the children asking them again to meet me. I thought if I wrote to them directly, without going through Tom's bitch of a mother, it might actually happen this time. If I go now, I'll catch the first post.'

I am glad she's focused and trying again with the children. But at moments like this, an image flashes into my mind: her departure from Wimbledon Magistrates' Court. I'd watched from the pavement as they dragged her down the steps, her head flicking from side to side, feet kicking out at her escorts. It was a struggle to get her into the van; one arm free for a moment, she pulled away and banged her head repeatedly against the doors.

So yes, I'm glad she has a project. But I wish I knew her motives. This – after yesterday's shopping list. It's best to stay on the safe side. Standling and Grainger's application for bail made a big play on the fact that, as a mother, a pillar of the community, she was not going to make a run for it.

She rattled the latch for a minute before she realised it was locked. We had words, but I think she came to understand my position. In the end, I went to the post office for her. I don't want to take any risks, that's all.

I didn't see much of Tom while Ailsa was helping me with the house. He was busy, either at the office, or at various social commitments – Henley, Hurlingham, Ascot, events for which he had to 'fork out'. (Even in this day and age, apparently, a certain sort of business is to be conducted, or courted, over the equivalent of a round of golf.)

I wonder how hard Ailsa had to work to keep him away from me.

When I think back to my state of mind at this point, I admit that, rightly or wrongly, I was obsessively vigilant. Listening at the wall, I learnt to distinguish their different treads: Melissa's fast, a headlong dash; Bea's quiet and light; Max's uneven, clumsy, accompanied more often than not by the scrape of an elbow along the paper. Tom's steps were the heaviest, his presence the noisiest. His mood deteriorated over this period, noticeably so. The success or not of his day was obvious in his moment of re-entry. A hefty push of the door and a shout hello: all would be well. The tinkle of the key on the shelf, the click of the door closing, his steps were silent then. I imagined him creeping along the hall, edging down the stairs into the basement, to catch someone out – Ailsa or a child, doing something they shouldn't: watching TV, or playing video games, or internet shopping. My ear pressed, I'd hear raised voices then, tears, a fight, usually with Max. I noticed Tom often repeated the same phrases. 'You're banned. I told you on Saturday. You should have listened. You're banned, as I told you on Saturday.' The same words in circles. On the third repeat you'd begin to feel bludgeoned.

One evening, Ailsa and I were standing on my doorstep, tussling, if I remember rightly, over an old cat basket. I looked up and there was a figure on the pavement, behind the hedge between our houses, a shadow emerging from between the timber resting against my fence. Sunglasses. Blue jeans. White shirt.

'The front door is wide open,' he said.

'You're home early.' She was trying to sound cheerful.

'I said, the front door is wide open.' He repeated himself in the same flat, reasonable tone. 'It's wide open.'

'Max has only just gone in.'

'So he's decided to leave our house open to anyone who wants to help themselves to anything they can get their hands on?' He pulled at the hedge, privet bunching out of his knuckles.

'Seconds ago,' she said. 'I'm almost there. It's been seconds.'

'I don't care how long it's been,' he said. 'It needs to be shut at all times. The door can't be left wide open for anyone to walk in. I'd have thought that was obvious to anyone who wasn't a fucking moron.'

Ailsa was looking at me, her eyes narrowed, anxious but smiling, as if it were all a bit of a joke, and I was either so scared of him or so in thrall to her, I smiled back. I colluded. I don't know which of us felt more ashamed.

The date of their summer party crept up without me really noticing. She mentioned it a few times – who was coming, who was doing 'the nibbles', how annoying Delilah was being about the flowers – but I didn't pay that much attention. Until the last minute, I wasn't even sure I was invited. In fact, I don't think my attendance was intended. It was accidental.

The day before the date in question, a Friday, a man came to my door. He was wearing a black suit, his hair slightly damp; under his arm he was carrying a small brown attaché case. 'Miss Baxter,' he said in a tone that was both profoundly serious and cheerful, almost skittish. 'If I may. I've just come from a meeting round the corner with your neighbours, the Swinsons – do you know them? No? And I said to myself Pete, it would be remiss not to check in with Miss Baxter, so here I am, just wondering whether you had time to think any more about my proposal?'

'How do you know my name?'

'We met once before, do you remember? Peter Caxton from Equity Release Freedom dot com?'

He must have seen something in my expression, a hesitation, because he snapped open his attaché case and, balancing it on one knee, started handing me pieces of documentation on which figures were printed in neat lines. I took them. He was talking still, listing the reasons why it was a good idea, how beneficial it would be at this point in my life, how I would maximise my advantage, my profit, how I would be realising my assets.

He must have come to the house in the weeks when I was first here alone; it was all quite a blur. You lose your brain a bit after a bereavement; things drop through the holes.

I could see from the leaflet in my hand that he was offering something called 'a home reversion scheme'. I'd get a lump sum; they'd get the house, though I could live in it 'for my lifetime'. He was still talking, spinning his spiel, and words and phrases reached my brain: 'ready cash', 'an opportunity to do something for oneself'. And I had started thinking. 'An extremely viable proposition': yes, maybe it was. In Ailsa's hands, the house no longer felt as safe as it had. Perhaps I could leave it behind me. I could travel. Not a cruise, as he was suggesting. But there were places in the UK I'd always wanted to visit. The Lake District. I could go on one of those organised hikes Fred was always advocating. Hell, maybe I could even apply for a passport and join Sue and Maeve on one of their antique-buying trips to France.

'Hello there?'

Ailsa pushed the gate open with a clang, and came towards us. Caxton clunked shut his briefcase. 'Right, I'll leave that with you,' he said and began to back away. 'Afternoon, ladies.'

As he passed Ailsa, he cocked his head – if he'd had a hat, he'd have tipped it – turned left and was concealed by the hedge.

Ailsa looked annoyed. 'Who was that?'

'Something to do with Equity Release Freedom?' I inspected the masthead on the documentation. 'ERF,' I said.

Ailsa frowned. 'Interesting that he scarpered when he saw me. People like that – they prey on the vulnerable.'

'It's a big house,' I said.

'Well, if you are thinking of trading down, please don't do anything involving ERF. You would talk to us before doing anything, wouldn't you? I mean, we might be interested. Particularly after I've . . .' She finished her sentence with a gesture, holding her palm upwards, as if she were holding a tray of drinks.

I looked at her, puzzled. She was always saying how broke they were; how could they possibly afford it? But she was smiling so I gave a little bow of acquiescence.

'OK.' She inspected the front garden. 'So much better out here now,' she said. 'Nothing to put off our guests!'

A step away, almost as an after-thought, she said: 'You are coming, aren't you?'

I let out a little laugh.

'Because of course you're invited. Saturday night? Tomorrow?'

I began to mutter about having a lot of work, that maybe I could pop round for the first hour or so, happy to help out, to pass round nibbles, that I wasn't sure I was presentable, but she cut across me. 'Listen – if you can spare a few minutes, this afternoon, pop round. Maria, my hairdresser and beautician, is coming.'

'Your hairdresser and beautician!'

It was the sort of phrase we found funny if overheard. She flushed as if she realised too late. 'I have to do what I can to distract from this.' She made a gesture with both hands, signalling up and down her torso. 'You know, when you carry weight like I do, it's more necessary than for others. It's important – Tom wants me to look my best. He's got potential clients coming, Ricky Addison, you know the guy who makes the cookery show, and . . . yeah, people, as well as friends. Anyway,' she looked into the hedge, smiling, not making too big a thing of it, 'she gives me a very good rate and it would be my treat. What do you say?'

I won't go into too much detail. I spent most of the hour wondering why I had been invited; was it kindness or necessity? Would my presence at the party otherwise be an embarrassment? At first I sat on Ailsa's bed while Maria, a brusque Spanish woman with elaborately tattooed forearms, finished putting colour in Ailsa's hair. Before this point, I'd had no idea how extensively it was dyed. 'Grey as a tabby cat,' Ailsa insisted, her face pale and puffy with her apparently artificially honeyed bob concealed beneath serried flaps of silver foil. 'You'd die if you saw me as I really am.'

Maria combed my hair until it lay flat across my forehead and scalp and she and Ailsa decided I should grow out the fringe, but a few layers would be a good idea. They'd taken off my glasses. 'I'm in your hands,' I insisted gamely. I wanted to be loving it, to take pleasure in the kind of 'girls together' pre-party experience you get in romantic comedies. I joked about the *Jackie* before and after, wondered if she was doing something for my 'heart-shaped face'. But I didn't enjoy it. The way Maria's fingers gripped the shafts of my hair, like those clips you get for plastic bags, recalled past occasions when I had watched Faith practise her scissor skills through the window of the hairdresser. I felt a squeeze of loss and then a grim chill settle in my heart.

Afterwards, deemed by both to be 'much more presentable', I let Maria 'tidy up' my eyebrows with strips of wax. Agony. Ailsa seemed to care a lot about what I planned on wearing. She ran through several of my options with Maria and eventually the two of them decided the pink blouse and the recently unearthed pair of jeans, but maybe not the denim jacket. And shoes – flip-flops, or sandals, they suggested, as long as I painted my toes. 'Don't wear those old trainers,' Ailsa said, and then laughed. 'As if!' I replied. She gave me a lipstick she didn't use any more and on the doorstep, joked: 'Nothing to frighten the horses.' For all her attempts to seem light-hearted, I got the impression she was deadly serious. Appearances, I told myself, matter when you are married to a man like Tom.

On Saturday, the activity started shortly after lunch. Two women turned up in a blue Berlingo van and offloaded poly-thene-wrapped trays and Tupperware. Ailsa went out in the car and shortly afterwards Delilah arrived on foot, her arms full of flowers. Tom opened the door and a little while later I heard them in the back garden together. She was asking him where he wanted pots. 'You better ask the guv'nor,' he answered. 'You wuss,' she said and it struck me how relaxed they sounded, how his voice was loose; how she spoke on the gurgle of a laugh.

I felt a growing agitation, a tightening of nerves, over the course of the day. When it was time to get ready, I thought again about Ailsa's bossiness over my outfit. Was she fearful I'd embarrass her? Or had she, in a kind way, anticipated my stress and tried to ease it? I put on the top, and the jeans, and applied purple varnish to my toe nails from Faith's box of make-up, but I lost confidence in the flip-flops. Nobody wants to see a middle-aged woman's feet, even when they are daubed with plum. At the last minute, I tried out Ailsa's lipstick, but I wiped it off and lay down on my bed, overcome by a memory of the last time I had put on so much make-up, feeling it creep into my thoughts.

I stayed there for a couple of hours – Maudie curled up next to me – listening to the music, the bass thumping through the brickwork, the chatter slipping through the cracks in the windows, until eventually I gave myself a talking-to. Ailsa would be hurt if I didn't attend. A party was an enormous undertaking at the best of times, let alone when your marriage was in trouble. I owed it to her to at least show my face.

Two people were leaving as I arrived, the door opening, a blast of light and noise behind, and his arm around her shoulders, tripping down the steps towards me, the swish of silk, the click of heels, laughter around the corner.

A woman in a black trouser suit held the door open and a man stepped forwards, holding a tray bearing glasses of prosecco. I took one, and the door closed behind me.

The house was dark and yet bright, lights flashed, candles flickered, shadows looming. Vibrations shuddered through the floor; there was a sharp, disorienting smell of spiced orange. The kitchen was a throng of bodies, backs of heads, flicking hair, limbs and heels, voices and laughter.

I turned into the sitting room, joining a crush of people – a few of whom I recognised, including several of the women from the pub quiz, and Sue and Andrew Dawson, Ailsa's neighbours on the other side. I smiled but they didn't respond; I'm invisible to them, or at least they pretend I am – which I suppose has its plus points (they've never complained about my clutter). It was loud, a wall of voices and music, the occasional shriek. I stayed by the door, touching the wood behind me with the tips of my fingers. It felt damp. I could stay here for a little while, and then creep back to the safety of my own house. It was too crowded for Ailsa to know if I had come or not. 'What a squeeze!' I imagined myself telling her the following day. 'Such fun. I had a *ball*!'

A tray passed and I took a canapé – mushroom? No, fish! – and stood there, smiling as if I were having a lovely conversation with myself. I nodded my head and clicked my fingers a bit to the music. Hits from the 1980s; I recognised some of the playlist from my own student days.

People were dancing at the other end of the room, and I edged along the wall to get a better view. Two women in jeans and tiny tops were camping it up, trying to involve Bea who, flouncy in a red party dress, was giggling in the corner; a man with a goatee was wiggling his hips. And in the middle were Ailsa and Tom.

She was in a bright, long-sleeved kaftan, purple and turquoise swirls, her feet bare, her cat-like eyes flicked with heavy eyeliner; Tom was wearing a flowery blue shirt, crisp at the cuffs and collar: both of them a burst of colour. He was swinging her round in a cack-handed attempt at a jive; she was tripping over his feet, and they were laughing, the two of them, moving together and apart, as if they didn't have a care in the world. They seemed grounded, smiling, happy, united.

I stood still for a moment or two. Tom had his arm around Ailsa's waist and he suddenly threw her backwards; causing one of the women to lurch out of the way. Pulling Ailsa towards him again, he held her close for a moment, hurled her away, held her to him.

It was a performance, I realise now, a public display. They knew they were being watched.

Delilah was standing alone across the room, leaning against the far wall holding a glass of prosecco. Her hair was pulled back in her usual bun, with its artless tendrils, and she was wearing dark-red lipstick and a white satiny dress. I was struck by the expression on her face. It wasn't wistful, or resentful, or anything I could quite put my finger on. It was just something in the relationship between her eyes and her mouth, the position of her chin, but I got the impression she was breathing carefully.

The song ended, and a slower ballad came on. A guitar and a sad voice singing about his English rose. Tom bowed out, raising his hands to Ailsa in apology, and left her, brushing past me down to the other end of the room, and then out into the hall. More guests had arrived. I could see his arms raised extravagantly in greeting, hear the dry bark of his laugh.

Ailsa hadn't noticed me. I hoped she wouldn't. I didn't need to speak to her. I would wait a few minutes until I could be sure Tom had left the hall and then I would slip away when no one was watching, and indeed I had begun to sidle in that direction when I saw Max coming up into the back sitting room from the kitchen, holding a tray. His hair was gelled – you could see the comb marks – and he was wearing a button-down blue and white check shirt. My heart turned.

'Would you like one of these?' he said, holding out the tray.

'Max! How lovely! What are they?'

'I think it's roast beef in Yorkshire pudding? I'm not sure.'

I took one, dipping it in the pot of horseradish sauce. 'I think you're right,' I said. 'Are you having a nice time?'

'Mum says the people who make that cooking show have just arrived, so I thought I'd go and . . .' He held out the tray and I nodded, and watched, as he ducked between arms and squeezed behind backs, tray held up at a precarious angle, towards the door out to the hall.

He got there just as Tom was bringing his guests in.

I know more about them now: Ricky Addison and Pippa Jones of the successful production company 'Stirfy TV'. At the time, I only got a brief impression; he was plump with a shaved head and an air of extreme confidence; and she was floaty and hippy-ish. Tom swept Pippa in under his arm, but he was looking over his shoulder at Ricky, laughing at something he said, playing mein host, or the sycophant, somewhere between the two, so he didn't see Max bearing down with his tray of horseradish and beef.

Max took a step towards them, just as Tom, his head still averted, took a step towards him. There was a crash and an oath and the dynamics of that corner of the room changed – people moved away, others crouched down, choux pastry rolling over the floor and Max repeating he was sorry, and Pippa's voice: 'It doesn't matter. Forget it. Forget it.' Ricky laughing and Tom swearing and flapping at Pippa's dress with a napkin.

'Apologise,' Tom said to Max and Max, mortification sounding like anger, said, 'I have.'

'Again,' Tom ordered.

'I did,' Max said, his face red.

It was easy in the chaos that followed, the scuffle for cloths and dustpans, to scurry past them all. I took the stairs and reached him just as he was about to lock himself in the bathroom.

'Max,' I said, getting my foot in the door. 'Let me in.'

His face appeared around the corner, his eyes pinched, his lower lip wobbling. 'Why?'

'I need to talk to you.'

'Why?'

'I just do.'

He opened the door and I closed it behind me. He sat down on the floor, curling up into a ball. He had a grease stain on his new shirt.

'I'm useless,' he said. 'I ruin everything.'

'You're one of the least useless people I know. You're a superstar. God.' I pulled down the toilet lid and sat on it. 'If you knew what terrible things I've done, you wouldn't believe it. This is nothing. You said sorry several times, I heard you. It's over now, everyone's forgotten it already. It was a mistake – not even your fault actually. People need to look where they're going when there are canapés around.'

One of the buttons was undone and in the gape his chest looked pale and white.

He looked up at me. 'I hate my dad. He's always so angry.'

I laughed. 'Oh, I wouldn't worry about him!'

'They're the really important guests – they're the point of the whole party – and I ruined it for him.'

'No!' I sounded as dismissive as I could. 'They can't be that important. What's as important as his own son? He knows that, if he has any sense at all. Next time you need something to write about, write about this! Humiliation, embarrassment, mortification – all good wow words. Remember how it feels inside and think of how to describe it. Honestly, nothing makes one feel more in control than finding the right words for a horrible experience – it begins to feel like you're writing about someone else and it stops hurting.'

He let out a noise, half-laugh, half-groan.

A desire rose in me then to hug him, to hold him, to make his sadness go away, but instead I stood up.

'What do you think? Shall we go down and join the party?'

He scrambled to his feet. 'I'd rather watch a movie but I'm not allowed.'

'I'm sure it's fine. I'll square it with your mum.'

We left together and I covered his back while he scurried down into the basement. I had a strange disembodied feeling walking into the kitchen, as if I would trip and fall face first into the crowd. The table had been moved to one side, and was covered in bottles and glasses. I could see Ailsa standing there talking, and I managed to cross the room and reach her without mishap.

'Verity!' Ailsa was a polished sleek version of herself. 'You came! I'm so glad!'

My fingers fiddled with my new layers. 'Of course.'

She pointed down and said in a tone of total outrage, 'Trainers!'

'No one can see my feet.'

'They can smell them! Joking!'

'You've got so many friends,' I said. 'So many people I've never seen before.'

'I know. Hell. It's awful!'

'Who are they all?'

'Parents from school, old friends of Tom's, *clients*.' She gestured out to the terrace where Tom was holding court, Delilah in the crowd around him. 'It's all worthwhile because Ricky turned up. The party can be deemed a success – though God.' She leant forward to whisper. 'Bloody Max spilt a tray of food all over him.'

'It was just an accident.'

'He's so clumsy, that boy.'

'He didn't mean it. He's mortified. He's watching TV now. I hope that's OK.'

But she was looking over my shoulder, searching the crowd. 'He's wonderful, Ricky. Of course I knew him first. It was my introduction that ... anyway.' Her eyes became suddenly wide. 'Lucinda! There you are! See you later, Verity. I'm so glad you came. You're my wing woman.' She mouthed: 'Debrief tomorrow, yes?'

Out in the garden, I saw Tom disentangle himself from a group and come back into the kitchen, his arm over Ricky Addison now, whispering in his ear. It was dark out, but fairy lights twinkled in the bushes, also some real fire things on sticks. Perhaps I could make my way out there. I took a few steps in that direction, squeezing between the table and the counter.

'Hello!'

The woman I had pushed into was small with white-blonde hair, and a prominent overbite. 'Susie,' she said. 'We met once with Ailsa in Sainsbury's car park.'

She introduced me to the people she was with, a tall thin couple called Liz and Will. 'They're friends of Ailsa and Tom from Kent.'

'Kent,' I said. 'I've never really understood what happened there.'

Liz kept smiling, keeping her head on one side: 'What do you mean?' she said.

'Ailsa said "it all went wrong". I've never quite understood what she meant.'

Liz darted a look at her husband, who pointedly looked away. 'Her house was so gorgeous,' she said. 'They did such a good job with it.'

'She's good at doing up houses.'

'She certainly is. I know she was sad to leave it.'

I kept looking at Liz, trying to keep my gaze level. 'So why did they?'

She took a sip of her drink, holding the glass to her mouth longer than was necessary. 'Why did they what?'

'Leave Kent.'

'Oh.' She shrugged, and let out a little laugh. 'Life's complicated. We miss her!' she said. 'We all love Ailsa. Tonbridge's not the same since she's gone! Do you want another drink?'

I shook my head and she and Will, after conferring, headed over to the bar area.

Tom was leaning at the bottom of the steps up to the hall; Ailsa was back on the dance floor. I craned my head. She was entertaining Ricky now, the two of them dancing together quite closely; her head was back, her eyes closed.

I set off with purpose in the opposite direction up the steps onto the terrace, through the smokers and shouters and onto the grass, and once I was there it was easy to keep going, ducking between the shrubs and under the decorative wrought-iron arch, to the 'wild meadow' at the bottom of the garden. It was fuller and richer than the last time I'd given it any attention. I sat on the raised railway sleepers they'd erected around it; I smelt creosote and soil; my ear was tickled by the floaty grass things that took up much of the space. Their house was as loud and fluid and bright as one of those party boats you see passing on the Thames – a stream of noise, voices and music, a streak of light against the dingy river. I could only see the top half of my house beyond the trees, but it looked black in comparison, gloomy and uninhabited, the brickwork stained, the window frames grey and splintered. The sash of Faith's window had clearly slipped, leaving a foot-long gap between glass and wall. Several slates were missing on the roof. Tom was right – it was probably letting in damp. I thought again about Peter Caxton's proposal. If I had a cash injection, I could mend the broken gutters. I could patch the property up, make it more habitable.

I curled my toes, shuffling my shoes against the chipped bark.

Had Ailsa been serious? Did my feet in fact smell?

The light on the lawn flickered, sent finger-shaped shadows. The music had got louder – a wailing blur. I didn't want to go back now. I thought about trying to clamber over the fence, but it was too high to scale, even if, when I reached the other side, I could get through the brambles. No, I should go back, see Ailsa again. Her wing woman. Kent. What *had* happened there? I thought about how hard she always tried to pretend everything was fine, and how vulnerable she was beneath her façade. And poor Max, too. Tomorrow I should offer to help clear up, maybe in the different surroundings of her house we would properly talk, I could see if I could get through to her, help her navigate a way out.

I stood up, brushing the compost off my jeans. I looked down at my trainers – at the stringy particles of bark that clung to the soles. And then, I stood very still. Beneath the throb of the party, the pulsing rise and fall of it, I caught something else; movement perhaps, a different quality of sound. The iron arch sighed, swayed; there was a murmur, a rustle, a loud inhalation and then a giggle.

'We're safe,' Tom said, his voice slow and suggestive. 'The shrubs are protecting us.'

A few seconds in which no one spoke. More rustling and a click, the sound of deep breathing.

I kept my feet as still as I could. By moving my head, I could get Tom in my line of vision. His head was forwards, almost touching a woman's, and his hands seemed to be cupped over hers.

He straightened up and she let out a sigh. 'Delicious,' she said. Delilah.

She had her back to me, but she held her cigarette out at shoulder height in the manner of a 1920s debutante.

'Don't tell Johnny,' she said. 'You promise? He'd kill me if he found out.'

'Our little secret,' Tom said.

Smoking. That's all it was. All smokers seem guilty and skulking. It's the nature of it.

'Need to do some work out here,' she said. 'Ailsa's wilderness is getting a bit overgrown.'

'It's all the bloody weeds creeping under the fence, self-seeding from next door. I'm sure I hear rats there too.'

For a few moments neither of them spoke, and then Delilah said: 'How's it going with Ricky Addison?'

He exhaled slowly, in stages; trying to blow rings. 'I'm making such a dick of myself. He's only here because Ailsa asked.'

'He didn't have to come.'

'They've had a lot of international offers. It would be a lot of business – it's worth the humiliation.' He took another drag. 'You're cold.' She told him she was fine, but he rubbed his palms quickly up and down her arms. 'You need more flesh on you,' he said.

She laughed, flicking her ash into the flower bed. 'Eyes.'

'If you must wear such a low-cut top.'

His hands still holding her arms, he shifted her into the side of the archway. She giggled. I held my breath. They were inches away from me. If either of them turned their heads, they would see me.

'Kiss for old times' sake?' he said.

She slipped from under him then, started swaying back down the lawn.

'Not fair,' she said over her shoulder.

He pushed himself upright. The archway rocked, the shrubs next to it rustled, and he followed her back towards the light.

Chapter Fourteen

Pret Jambon-Beurre

Superior, *adjective*. In ironic use. Characteristic of or designating someone who thinks he or she is better than someone else; having or displaying a high opinion of oneself; supercilious, condescending, patronising.

She took over the cooking last night, something with broccoli and pasta from the Fat Flavours, Thin Thighs website: I'm amazed she can bear to look at it, after its connection to Tom's last meal; I suppose it's a sign she's feeling more herself. No word yet from the children, but she is optimistic. She told me while we ate that she'd had a long conversation with Standling (when?) and that he told her he should have good news soon.

I went to bed straight after. It's not like me. A dull persistent pain bloomed in my temples. My vision was odd. She helped me upstairs. She brought me a cup of herbal tea and sat at the side of the bed. I must have passed straight out. When I woke a few hours later, she had gone. Had the dog barked? No, I could hear noises in Mother's room: the vibrations of Ailsa's steps; the creak of the cupboard door, a muffled bang as an object dropped. She was looking for something. I don't know what. I could ask, but I'm a bit scared of her when she's in this mood. In the end, I put in earplugs, which I haven't done since she arrived. The enforced deafness makes me feel vulnerable. Also, I prefer to be alert in case she needs me.

On the Monday after the party, I had lunch with Fred, my old friend from King's, to distract me. We met once a month though since Ailsa had started taking up so much of my time, I had been harder to pin down.

That morning I set off with purpose. Fred would be a useful sounding board. He had no connection with the Tilsons, lived some distance away and had more experience and wisdom than I did in the relationship department. For the sake of full disclosure, I think I should admit I was looking forward to having something interesting to discuss with him. A small dishonourable part of me felt important; glad, for once, to have a drama of my own to share.

He had come to London, as he regularly did, to do some research at the British Library. Usually he treats me to what he calls 'a slap-up' at Côte in Covent Garden. But it was so warm that on Monday he suggested we meet outside Pret at King's Cross station and buy a picnic.

It was a bit stressful choosing, with office workers and people rushing for trains, so we didn't have a chance to talk properly until we were sitting on a bench in Granary Square, that bright new space they've created out of urban wasteland. It's really quite the scene up there: fountains erupting out of pavements, steps fashioned from artificial grass, brickwork so scrubbed and clean the ancient warehouses look modern; even the stretch of canal, once grimy and syringe-scattered, runs sleek and shiny as if moulded out of metal.

It didn't take long to eat our food. I am partial at Pret to the Jambon Beurre, not a big mouthful, and Fred, who is a fussy eater, made quick work of his simple cheese and butter sandwich which is, I think, intended for children. He rolled up our rubbish and placed it in a nearby bin, and sitting back down, mopped his brow with a large white cotton handkerchief he had taken out of his top pocket for the purpose. We were facing a row of orange deckchairs in which office workers were sunning themselves in various states of déshabillé. Next to their acres of exposed, reddening flesh, our sartorial decisions must have looked incongruous. Fred was wearing a lightweight checked suit, a floral shirt and his trademark cravat, while I was in a corduroy dress from Ailsa's jumble, with the primrose jacket. Hot but smart.

Fred was in a cheerful mood. His book, on Renaissance swear words, was going well and he and his boyfriend Raoul, a classics don, were off to Italy that weekend to walk the Cinque Terre. He outlined in detail their decision to stay not in Levanto but Sestri Levante (more restaurants, bigger beach), and for a while I found it hard to get a word in edgeways.

'So we're both looking forward to it,' he said. 'Getting out the old walking boots. Working up an appetite. Liguria, you know it's where pesto comes from.'

'And I thought that was Marks & Spencer.'

'Ah, very funny.'

Two small children ran giggling into the small fountain spumes. Their mother unhitched a younger sibling from a buggy and he toddled in after them, stomping his bare feet up and down, as if he were marching on the spot.

I noticed Fred frown with mild distaste. 'So how's Maudie?' he said.

'Bit of arthritis,' I said. 'But otherwise good.'

This, I realised, was the usual pattern of our meetings. He would arrive bursting with anecdotes and plans and prospective jaunts, and only when his stories ran out would there be a pause and he'd ask first after Maudie, and then my job.

Pause.

'And what news from the OED?'

I told him about the latest notes from my editor – a close friend of his. I let him bitch for a bit, with equal quantities of rancour and fondness. 'He's always so pedantic,' he said. 'The tedium of that prissy attention to detail. I don't know how he does it, day in, day out.'

I let that lie for a second.

Fred didn't seem to notice he might have offended me too. 'It's about time you came down to the office for a visit, isn't it?' he said. 'You must let me know when you next do and we can meet up in Oxford. Raoul would love to see you again. Or just come and see us, when we're back from Italy. It'll be August before we know it.'

'Yes. I will. I've just been busy. Yes, quite busy, really.'

'Oh, that's good.' He sounded pleased. 'Anything in particular?'

'I've been seeing a lot of Ailsa – you know, the woman who moved in next door. I told you about her.'

'The people who made such a terrible racket and mess, whose son you were helping with his English?'

'Yes.' I felt the slight irritation of a story being anticipated, or of when a friend relates back something you have told them with none of the original nuance. 'Them.'

He raised his eyebrows. 'How did the boy's A level go?'

I decided not to correct him. 'Well. I think it went well.'

'Oh, Verity. I do hope they've been paying you.'

I looked away, hot under the arms, flustered. 'She pays me in kind. She's always buying me lunch, coffee. We're in and out of each other's houses.' I didn't say anything about the clear-up. He had never visited me at home – the very idea was the definition of agony, like being peeled from the inside out. 'It's lovely, actually, to have a new friend.'

Over the years Fred has been a big campaigner on my behalf. When Mother died, he said he understood how hard it had been, as her main carer, to carve out a life of my own, and that now she was gone I shouldn't – I think his phrase was 'shrivel up'. He took it upon himself to research clubs and activities suitable for the single person in my area. The AquaFit class at the leisure centre was not a success, but the pub quiz was a lifeline.

He didn't speak for a moment or two. Behind him a child clapped. A flock of pigeons, spooked, flapped into the air, and landed a few feet away. 'That's nice,' he said eventually. But he didn't sound as if he thought it was at all nice.

'Yes. She's really warm, full of life.'

'That's nice,' he said again.

'But also thoughtful and troubled. She has a few mental health issues and her marriage . . .'

'Oh you're no one without a few mental health issues these days.'

This wasn't proving nearly as enjoyable as I'd anticipated. I ploughed on. 'Something is horribly wrong in the house, in her marriage. The family. On the surface they seem normal, but . . .'

'But what?' He sounded irritated.

'Well, to begin with, she told me the other day that she was already pregnant when she met her husband. Her eldest isn't biologically his.'

Fred shrugged. 'I don't see that it makes much of a difference. It's the case in lots of blended families. Life is complicated, Verity. It's not all Janet and John.'

I felt immediately vexed, misunderstood. I knew that, and

173

now I was the focus of his moral scrutiny, not the Tilsons. 'But the father's such a bully. They're all terrified of him. Well, not the little girl, and actually maybe not Melissa. But the son – Max – he's horrible to him.'

Fred swept some invisible crumbs off his trouser leg. 'Families are tangled and intricate and contradictory. You know that as well as anyone. Remember how awful your mother was to your sister until you came back and then, as soon as she was gone, she became the favourite?'

He'd derailed me again. I closed my eyes for a few seconds to recover, hearing my mother in my head, her voice querulously asking after Faith, repeating examples of her beauty and charm, how good she was at cooking, how gentle she was with a Tubigrip elasticated bandage. But that was just the three of us. What did I know about family?

'The thing is I'm not even sure he's faithful,' I said. 'I saw him at their party in the garden with another woman.'

'Ah. Doing the beast with two backs? He's doing the dirty on her and you're trying to decide whether to tell her? One word of advice: no. Keep out of it at all costs. It's never a good idea to interfere in other people's affairs. If I were you, I'd keep myself to myself.'

'They weren't actually . . . It was just the atmosphere, the sense that something was about to happen. I have that all the time, that they're poised on the edge of disaster. I keep thinking I should be doing more to help her, to give her a way out.' And then responding to a deep pang of longing that had for some reason risen inside me, I added, 'In some ways, actually, she reminds me of Faith.'

He winced. 'And that's a good thing?'

Fred had never liked Faith. When she used to visit me at King's, she'd take over, within minutes making her presence felt, not just as the prettiest but the loudest and the drunkest in the common room. The college parties weren't good enough; we'd be off up to Camden on the bus to some club she had heard about, and Fred and I would sit in the corner talking about semantics while she and the others drank and gyrated and disappeared to the toilets to get up to goodness knows what.

Behind his head, the sun glinted on the warehouse windows. He put his hand on the sleeve of my jacket, his fingers long and white, the cuticles neatly pared around the moons. 'I'm sorry to say it, but maybe the last thing you need in your life is another Faith.'

Over the years, it had suited me to let him turn Faith into a cliché, to extrapolate an airhead from the airy eighteen-year-old (and even then she hadn't really been airy; she'd been troubled and fierce and undisciplined, but also funny and honest and sweet). I had been selective in what I'd chosen to tell him. It's too easy to give an incomplete version of ourselves, and others. It had given me a small vicious pleasure to laugh at her silly, frivolous, boring job as a hairdresser; I hadn't told him about her growing roster of private clients, that she had done magazine work and cut hair on stage in front of hundreds of people at conventions, that she had travelled widely for work and for pleasure, that when I had last seen her, she had had a lover and friends and a rich, full life. It came to me, sitting on that bench surrounded by office workers, that actually Fred wasn't always right, that sometimes my desire to please him had held me back, that all those years ago, I wouldn't have minded doing the gyrating and the goodness knows what myself.

I tried to smile. 'I've become very fond of her, and her children – the boy Max particularly. I want to help her.'

'I just think you've got enough on your plate.'

'Like what?' I noticed the thinness, then, of his upper lip. 'What have I got on my plate?'

He didn't answer, just churned his mouth in circles, his eyes pained and kind. 'People take advantage of you,' he said.

'No one is taking advantage of me,' I said.

He was jealous, I told myself, as I strap-hung on a sweltering Tube home. Our relationship was based on convenient lies. He said he didn't want me to be lonely, but it suited him to think of me as dependent, and sad and small. Well, things changed. People moved on. Maybe I'd had enough of Fred. Maybe it would be a good idea if we didn't see each other for a while.

Chapter Fifteen

Swallows and Amazons series: incomplete set (*Pigeon Post* missing). Jonathan Cape. In publisher's green cloth bindings, some with illustrated dust wrappers.

Suspended Animation, *noun*. The temporary cessation of most vital functions without death, as in a dormant seed or a hibernating animal.

Ailsa says it's because of me that her work on my house stopped. It's not true. The only time I barred her path was when she tried to take away the box of Arthur Ransomes. No, she may not like to admit it, but she got bored.

It was gradual, now I look back on it. Her visits had already tailed off, though it was that week when I realised it was over.

It's awful how the walls compress when you're waiting. She sent me a text on Tuesday asking if I would be in. I'd replied, 'Yes, all day!', which was too vague. Her response, 'Good. Will pop in', equally so. I didn't think it mattered at first. I was working on 'clever' – a juicy little word – a surprising late arrival in our vocabulary, cited in 1682 by Thomas Browne as peculiar to East Anglia; probably related to the Middle English 'clivers', meaning claws, talons, clutches (which casts the phrase 'clever devil' in an altogether different light). Normally, it would have absorbed me but as often happens when Ailsa is concerned, concentration evaded me.

I waited all day. I'm not a big believer in intuition but I do associate a sense of dread with this day in particular, a deep, dirty, stagnant anxiety, a teeming or gnawing under my ribcage. I'd told myself I wouldn't tell her about Tom – I'd decided Fred was right – but I needed to see her to reassure myself it was the right decision. While I waited, I felt useless. I scrunched and unscrunched my hands, cracking my knuckles, squeezing the flesh on my fingers. The house seemed to respond, to seep and rot, a sweet meaty odour caught at the back of my throat. The pile of plastic bags that had collected over the previous week came alive in the heat, tiny shifts and adjustments. When I moved a Toby jug containing pens, an earwig unfurled. Maudie was scratching to reach something under the sofa. Behind the wainscot I imagined I could hear scuttling.

I took the key from the tin where I'd hidden it and went upstairs to Faith's room. It was a long time since anyone had tried the key and the lock rasped, stuck. I jiggled, finally getting traction; it released and, pushing, I caught sight of a few inches of flock wallpaper, before the bottom of the door snagged on a fold of carpet. I nudged it harder, but it wouldn't move; I'd have to get down on my knees, and wriggle my hand under the door to free it. I thought for a second and then I closed the door, locked it, and returned the key to my pocket.

Mother's room was still crammed: her piles of paste jewellery on the dressing table, her plaid gown on the back of the door, a cream quilted garment referred to always as her 'bed jacket' on the pillow; knick-knacks, an army of childhood toys, bodies in heaps, defeated, on the shelves. I picked up a dusty lion, and a long strawberry-blonde hair was caught in the polyester fur – a fine thread, sixteen inches long, frail and yet here it was, even after all these years. The light glinted on its kinks. My heart began to swell with a fresh sense of loneliness and despair.

It was coming up to 5 p.m. when the doorbell rang. The hours of waiting dissolved, suddenly meant nothing. With indecent haste, I rushed to open it.

Tom was standing in the porch. His hair was dishevelled and he had a scratch across his cheek. He was already turning away.

'Tell Ailsa I'm home, could you?' he said. 'Only for half an hour, so I wouldn't mind a quick chat. I'm out again this evening. Client drinks.'

'Ailsa's not here.'

He slowly twisted until he was facing me. Carefully he rubbed the scratch on his cheek. 'I thought she was supposed to be spending the afternoon with you. I thought she was finally getting to the bottom of the smell.'

His complexion was grey with tiredness and there was something vulnerable in his expression. For a second I felt sorry for him, but I thought about his drunken grope with Delilah and pulled myself up.

'Nope,' I said.

He stood for a second or two, his eyes half closed. He started nodding. 'Fine. OK. Whatevs.' He took a step back and raised both his hands to his head, elbows out, as if to take up as much space as he could; to intimidate me, I suppose. 'But listen – I've had enough. This can't go on.' He made an expanding balloon-like gesture with his arms. 'The stench. It's coming through the walls.' He wrinkled his face in disgust. 'I've looked it up. I think it's dry rot. Fruiting bodies.'

I made to close the door.

He took a step forward. 'You've got worse, not better,' he said. 'You're ill. Ailsa's efforts, they've made no difference. I

179

mean – what's this?' He pointed. His voice got louder. 'Where's it come from? What is it?'

I didn't answer.

For the record it was a rotary clothes dryer I'd found down by the railway line on my way back from lunch with Fred.

'Let me in.' He took a step towards me, looming into the porch. 'I want to *see* what's going on.'

'No.'

'I'm going to report you to the council. I'll have you evicted if nothing else. You're a danger to the community.'

Trembling, I managed to get my weight behind the door.

'Last chance,' he said.

I upped my listening that evening. Scraps, mainly. Clunking on the piano (Bea?). A door closing too loudly (Melissa?). Tom and Ailsa's voices, quiet. Mainly, a deadly silence interrupted only by the scrape of their kitchen chairs on the limestone tiles, the chink of cutlery, an occasional clearing of a throat.

I was convinced the next morning I would pull back the curtains to see someone from the council staring back at me. Adrian's pale moon face.

Instead, I heard a tapping, regular and insistent, like the light hammering of a nail. I was using a glass, then, and when I held it to Mother's wall I realised it was intercourse. A male grunt and a female cry gathering in intensity. So relations had resumed, I thought. But how awful, how humiliating for her, after how I'd seen him behave. I slid the glass away then, threw it down, with shame and embarrassment.

A few hours later, Ailsa texted me: 'Sorry about yesterday. Held up.' Naturally, I replied generously: 'Couldn't matter less.' She followed with another: 'Have to cancel Max's session today – late notice. End-of-term madness! My bad!'

Stupid of me, I know, to have been upset. It took me a few minutes to compose both myself and my response. In the end, I wrote: 'No problemo!' and signed off with an 'x'.

That afternoon, for something to do, I took Maudie and caught the bus down to Clapham Junction for a new ink cartridge, then walked back. It was a warm day and the common was busy. Brueglel meets Richard Scarry: small children haring along on scooters, legs dangling from trees, a mishmash of balls and dogs and picnics. The light was hazy, more white in the sky than blue. The leaves overhead looked limp, poised to wrinkle; the grass a vast, dried, pale-olive prairie.

I was passing the ice-cream van, temporarily blasted by heat from its generator, when I heard my name. 'Verity; coo-ee.'

At first I thought I was hallucinating. It's always a surprise to see in the flesh someone who is occupying your mind. But in a group under the trees between the path and the pond, Ailsa was kneeling and waving.

Acutely self-conscious for several reasons, I made my way in her direction.

'Verity,' she said, smiling brightly. 'I thought it was you.'

She was with seven or eight other women, a few of whom I recognised – Delilah and Trish and Poor Soph's mother with the invisible braces, and various others from her party. They were staring up at me, silent but smiling, a forty-something corps de ballet. Delilah was leaning back on her elbows, her face turned to the sun. Otherwise, I remember a lot of legs in white jeans and unsuitable shoes. The blonde woman with the prominent overbite – Susie? – was wearing a puffy pale-pink blouse you might describe as 'milkmaid'.

'We've just had sports day,' Ailsa told me, her hand held over her eyes as a visor. 'It's why I cancelled. Sorry. Join us!' She was still smiling, but there was something forced in the way she was talking. A fake brightness.

'That's very kind,' I said, clipping on Maudie's lead. 'But I've got work to do. I'm in a bit of a hurry, in fact. I was in the middle of printing and I ran out of ink.' I lifted the Ryman bag to illustrate.

'Oh go on, do.' She was patting a space next to her, as if I were a small child. 'I haven't seen you since the party. Sit down, even for five minutes.'

I faltered. I'd been so anxious about her and yet here she was. Poor Soph's mum was smiling up at me, teeth bared, the sun giving a milky tinge to her invisible braces, and I thought about the bored, petty bitchiness in the pub. Delilah, I noticed, hadn't even registered my arrival. Ailsa didn't feel comfortable with these women. I felt renewed goodwill. Her wing woman; that's what she'd called me. Moral support – at the very least, that I could provide.

She scooted up and I stepped into the space, feet together, and then slunk down, sitting with my knees bent to my chin to take up as little room as possible. Maudie lay down on the grass next to me and when I was sure she was settled, I slipped the handle of the lead around my foot. In this strained position, I was aware of the waistband of my trousers cutting into my gut, gaping low at the back. I tugged my top to tuck it in and cover the area of bare skin. Ailsa patted my shoulder. 'Gosh, you must be a bit hot in that jacket,' she said. 'Do you want to take it off?'

'I'm fine.'

'You're wearing walking boots too.'

'They're comfortable.'

A brief kerfuffle as provisions were shunted my way – a small plastic cup of rosé, a pot of supermarket hummus, and some cold sliced pitta bread to dip into it. I took a few sips of wine and, having already eaten a tin of baked beans before leaving the house, nibbled on a piece of pitta. The big talk on the rug was school reports: they'd been given them at pick-up in envelopes; some people had opened theirs but others, including Ailsa, were waiting until they got home. She rolled her eyes. 'When I can do so with a stiff drink.' Lowering her voice: 'I mean, Bea's will be fine, but . . .' She looked at Max and mouthed. 'I feel sick.'

Delilah and Susie of the pink top began moaning about a school email urging them to keep up their children's maths and literacy over the summer. 'Ridiculous,' Delilah said. 'I mean, *how*?' rejoined Susie in the pink.

A dark, bird-like woman who had been introduced to me as 'Rose who works full time' said, 'You live next door?'

'Yes.' I cleared my throat, adding unnecessarily, 'I'm Ailsa's next-door neighbour.'

'Verity grew up in Tooting. She's lived here *for ever*.' Ailsa said. She drew the last word out, turning the 'ev' into quite a drone.

'How rare,' Rose said. 'I can't imagine what that must be like. My husband and I were based in north London before moving to Wandsworth and when I was growing up we lived all over for my dad's work. I never feel I belong anywhere. To be rooted, to be properly grounded. I don't know – it shows you're a much more loyal sort of person. It must give you some sort of inner decency, don't you think?'

Ailsa said: 'Verity is incredibly decent.' She gave my hand a quick squeeze. 'She's very long-suffering.'

I took another sip from my goblet, biting the plastic between my teeth for a second, enjoying the sensation. We were on a slight hill and the grass stretched before us, past the bench, down to the pond, a little slimy but bristling with reeds and insects and waterfowl. I felt a wash of pride in my longevity and, yes, my *loyalty*.

I asked Rose what children she had and she said two: a teenage girl a year younger than Melissa, and a boy, Ferg, in the same class as Max. 'You?' she added.

'Just me,' I said. 'I was my mother's carer until she passed away. Not that that's relevant – though she was quite child-like.'

Ailsa dipped a chip in a pot of violently red sauce. 'You have a younger sister, though, don't you? You sort of brought her up.'

The word seemed to stick to the front of my mouth. 'Yes.'

'Where is she now?' Rose asked.

I pressed the goblet to my lips hard, hearing my breath as it hit the plastic. 'Last I heard she was living in Brighton.'

'That's nice. I love Brighton. Does she have kids?'

I felt a solid lump at the back of my throat, a stirring of the old panic and alarm. 'No.'

'Verity hasn't seen her sister for a bit.' Ailsa said. 'They fell out.'

'I'm sorry,' Rose said. 'I shouldn't have asked.'

I tried to rest my plastic cup down on the rug, but it wouldn't stay upright. 'It doesn't matter.'

I did take off my jacket then, though I was careful to keep my arms close to my sides, aware of sweat. The conversation moved on, Rose and Ailsa talking about their own children, joining in the moan about the summer homework. Rose's work was 'full on'; she was a lawyer in a big City firm. Ailsa asked if she had any breaks to look forward to, any holiday plans, and Rose said they were going to Cornwall. 'Oh yes,' Ailsa said. 'You have a place. By the sea? *Lovely*.'

Max, a smattering of sunburnt freckles across his nose, was sitting with Maudie now, stroking her chin. Dear, sweet Max. Always so gentle.

'What about you?' Rose asked, drawing me back into the conversation.

'Holidays aren't really my thing,' I said.

'Oh I *love* holidays,' Rose said, making it sound like a question of taste, a choice.

As I write this, I realise I sound judgemental. I don't mean to be. I never disliked Rose – even later. She is just as much a product of her life and upbringing as I am. But I suspect it's one of the things that drew me to Ailsa, and also what made life hard for her. She didn't want to be a victim of her child-hood or circumstances; she wanted to be better, different, *more*. She fought against the restrictions; it's an instinct that has brought out the best in her, and the worst.

'Ailsa?' Rose was still on the subject of holidays.

'Oh yes.' Ailsa had been watching me, but she smiled brightly. 'Nothing too exciting this year, really. Tom's rented a cottage. Somerset.'

'Oh, when?' I said. A holiday? I hadn't imagined that. 'How long for?' I already felt the lurch of their departure.

'Saturday. We've booked it for two weeks. Tom wants to invite potential clients. Ricky Addison and Pippa Jones, who make the cooking show? They've got a place down there and he's trying to get them on board. It's tax deductible, I suppose.' She rubbed her arm. 'What about you, Verity? Do you ever go away? Fred? Does he invite you?'

'Not really.'

She was studying me. A beat passed. 'You look upset. Are you all right?'

Rose had started talking to Susie and I said quickly: 'Tom came round yesterday. Did he tell you?'

'What did he want?'

'He wanted to know where you were. When he found out you weren't with me, he was quite aggressive I'm afraid. He said he was going to ring the council, and it's put me in a bit of a tizz.'

I could feel her eyes on me. 'You mustn't worry about that. Have *you* ever tried ringing the council? If you ring the number for Environmental Services, as he did, and press six or whatever it is for "filthy or verminous property", there's a recorded message that begins: "If you have immediate concern about the safety of a child . . ." I don't know if it's a mistake or whether it's intentional; whether knowing about a child who's living in a filthy house takes you to the top of the complaints queue. Either way it put Tom off. He flung the phone down in disgust, so you're off the hook for a bit.'

I let out a deep sigh. It shuddered through me, almost overwhelming.

'Oh, poor Verity. I'm sorry about Tom. I'm sorry he was rude. I'm going to have a word. He promised me he would keep out of it. You've been worried and I haven't been any help at all. It's just been one thing after another. The party, finding this house for Tom – big enough, nice enough to pass muster. And I've been busy myself doing the garden for Ricky's London flat. But I should have popped round to check on you.'

I felt my shoulders sag. Her life was so *full*. She was *fine*. Parties, Somerset houses, Ricky's London Flat. How foolish to think she needed me, that I made any impact on her life at all.

I sat there after that for as long as I could bear to. Ailsa joined the general conversation, which seemed to be about end-of-year presents for teachers. She made a joke about a circulating scented candle and found a funny video on her phone which made everyone laugh. Watching her, I realised she wasn't an outsider after all. She fitted right in. It was her trick of friendship to make you think she was who you wanted her to be. When I decided I could leave without being rude, I collected my jacket, pulled the lead off my foot and stood up. I heard the crunch of plastic and a yelp from Rose. 'Sorry! Work beckons.' I managed to scatter some general goodbyes, disentangle a reluctant Maudie from her love fest with Max, and was soon heading back along the main path in the direction of Bellevue Road. Near the lights, I sensed footsteps behind me, but it was only a runner who gained, overtook and jogged past, leaving only the tinny vibrations of headphoned music in their wake.

When the bell went that evening, I was still braced for a visit from the council, so I opened the door reluctantly, with the chain on.

Tom and Ailsa were both standing there. He was holding out a bottle of wine, and she was clutching a small white booklet which she waved in the air.

'Max's report,' she said, as soon as I'd released the chain. 'It's so much better than last term. They're thrilled with his progress. A five for English, effort and achievement. But also maths – better, two threes. And the teacher's comments are just great: how his confidence has come on in leaps and bounds and . . .' She flicked to a page and started reading, '"He's not afraid to plumb his own experiences and emotions".'

Tom was nodding, also pleased, and I smiled broadly. 'I'm so glad,' I said. 'He deserves it.'

'So we are here to thank you' – she nudged Tom to hand me the wine – 'and Tom wants to apologise for being rude yesterday. Don't you, Tom?'

'Yes.' He cleared his throat. 'I'm sorry. You got me on a bad day.'

I eyed him. The bottle in his hand was wet with condensation, straight from their fridge.

'And we've got a suggestion.' Ailsa had slipped her hand through Tom's arm. 'I know you won't take money but we'd like to thank you so, we wondered whether you'd like to come down to Somerset for a couple of days? It's a big house and we haven't got guests the whole time, and you say you never take a holiday: what do you think? You and Max could do a bit of literacy. It would do you good to have a few days out of London.'

'It might give you a bit of perspective on your own house,' Tom said. 'It might inspire you. You might come back with a renewed sense of vigour.'

I looked down at my feet. Hard to describe the combination of emotions – mortification and embarrassment, and a sort of confused delight. Somewhere in there, history was being rewritten but it didn't matter: the force of other emotions swept away any unease. I couldn't possibly, I told them. It was 'too much of an imposition'. They waved my objections away. 'It'll suit us all,' Ailsa said. 'It's mutually beneficial.'

It was settled.

Chapter Sixteen

Canvas 'grip' overnight bag

Mini-break, *noun*. A short holiday, esp. one lasting two or three days and spanning a weekend.

Maudie and I got the train down: a very ordinary train, rather rackety and grubby and uncomfortable for a journey of that length. I had made some sandwiches, but the carriage was full and, in the end, I found myself too inhibited to open my Tupperware (people can be funny about the smell of egg). The headphones of the woman next to me emitted a tinny, high-pitched cacophony which prevented me from concentrating on my copy of the *Week*; as, I confess, did a persistent anxiety that Maudie might not be able to hold it in. In the event, she did, proving that not everyone or everything in life lets one down.

I was relieved to see Ailsa there to meet me when I came through the barrier of the small, isolated station. She was in the big silver car and she beeped and waved, then threw open the passenger door. Maudie leapt straight in and I followed, hauling myself in by gripping onto the back seat. Ailsa made a joke about the size of my luggage, and then put her foot down, swinging out of the car park and up to a roundabout, and then along a dual carriageway. I clutched

Maudie to me as she spun the wheel tightly to the right, and then roared past a school, and a pub and a garden centre. It was only when we were on a narrow lane with high green banks, the car a great hulk, that she spoke again. 'Journey OK? Not too stressful?'

'Yes. Everything was . . . easy, thank you.'

'You all right?' she said. 'You look even thinner. Have you lost more weight?'

'Oh, I don't think so.' I got under Maudie to unzip my waterproof jacket. 'I've been feeling a little tired, so it's lovely to get away.'

'I'm so glad we're able to give you a break,' she said. 'I should tell you, though, we're quite a full house. I got the dates muddled. It's much pokier than the website led us to believe, which is a bit rich seeing as it costs a fucking fortune.' She glanced at me and then back to the road. 'Technically, dogs aren't allowed. But I'm sure we can keep Maudie on the down-low.'

'Oh, I'm sorry.'

'No. No. It doesn't matter.'

'I can't believe I didn't check, Ailsa. I'm so sorry.'

'Don't worry! It's fine.'

'I can always go back.'

I found myself trying to zip the jacket up again. I had slotted the pin into the metal bit at the bottom, but on the first try the pull-tab wouldn't budge. I yanked it several times before getting it to work. Then zipped it up again to my chin. I was feeling close to tears.

'It's lovely that you've come, with or without the dog. Max will be thrilled.'

The hedgerows had begun to press in. Foliage scrunched and scraped against my window. Leaves, torn off, straggled from the wing mirror.

'Now.' She reached a junction, indicated, and turned. 'I

have to warn you we're quite a crowd. Delilah's here on her own. She and her husband Johnny are having difficulties. He's taken the kids away this weekend and she was at a loose end. Also Rose – you met her at the picnic – invited herself en route to her house in Cornwall, so she's here with her husband and two kids.'

'The house by the sea.'

She glanced at me. 'Good memory, yes. So she's got Fergus who's in Max's class, and we were wondering if it would be OK to include him in your literacy camp? Rose was so impressed by how Max's academics have improved.'

Literacy camp? *Academics*. I hadn't realised it would be quite so formalised. 'Yes. Of course.'

'Super. Anyway, who else?' She sighed theatrically. 'Yes. Ricky and Pippa – did you meet them at the party? They rang to see if they could come to lunch this week instead of next. She's adorable, and they have a tiny little baby who is just to die for. I know Ricky better – you remember, I've been helping him with the London garden. It would have been much more convenient if they'd come when asked but Tom wants their business and we didn't really have a choice.'

There was a break in the hedgerow, a gate, a flash of field. She was slowing down.

'We're here.'

The house, an elegant pale stone building, nestled in a dip of the landscape. The back wall edged directly onto the lane, but at the front it was open and wide, a proper Georgian façade, with those lovely Somerset floor-to-ceiling sash windows. Wrapped around it was a wide flagstone terrace, edged by fecund flower beds and a long lawn rolling down to a row of trees – I could hear a rushing; was it the wind, or was there a river behind? – with a sheep-pocked field on the other side, a single tree on the summit standing out against a mackerel sky, like Jesus on the cross.

It was deserted at first glance. On the terrace was a fire pit, full of burnt charcoal and sweet wrappers, and on a bench an empty coffee cup and a plate, smeared with what might have been the remains of some cake. Ailsa pointed over to the left, beyond a long lawn, poppies and roses and statues, to a tennis court, nestling in a hollow of land. Two figures were waving racquets in the air. 'I'm back!' Ailsa yelled, and the taller of the figures raised both arms to serve, and smashed the ball to the other end so hard his opponent, Delilah, dodged it with a little skip: 'Bastard!'

Ailsa shook her head. 'The kids are at the pool,' she said, 'which is through there.' She pointed to a gate in a row of thick trees, on the same side of the house as the tennis court, but further over and higher up the gradient.

There was birdsong, low wood pigeons and tweeting tits, and a pleasant buzzing of insects. The sky was magnificent, blue, streaked with clouds. I laid my bag down. 'How wonderful it all is,' I said.

'Would you like a swim?'

'I haven't brought a bathing suit.'

'Oh, we can always lend you one. But in the meantime, I'll show you where we've put you, shall I?'

I picked my bag back up and hauled it over my shoulder. 'Lay on, Macduff.'

She took me along the terrace; not through the open French doors of the house, but down a flight of wide steps made of railway sleepers and gravel that carved their way through long grass, and round to the far side of a small low-slung structure; a barn, I supposed.

'You're in the piggery,' she said. 'Don't laugh. It's a lovely little annexe. We thought you'd be more comfortable out here. A bit more independence.'

She opened a door and, lugging my bag, I followed her directly into a long narrow guest room: double bed and a chest of drawers at one end and, at the other, a table, on which lay a pad of paper, a row of pens. Around it, I noticed, were three chairs.

'We thought you could do your sessions out here – nicer for the kids to have a designated work area; keeps the rest of the house clear and . . .'

'. . . untainted by the horrors of literacy.'

'You got it. OK – so shall I leave you to freshen up for a bit? And then, I don't know – if not a swim, do you fancy a walk? I'm longing to stretch my legs.'

'Perfect,' I said.

After she left, I moved a pile of towels, and lay on the bed. Maudie jumped up too, almost certainly verboten, and curled up next to me on the pillow. It was a pleasant enough room – carpeted and clean – and it was good to have a bit of space to myself, if that's what she meant by 'independence'. I would have been overwhelmed to meet everyone all at once, to have been thrown into conversation. And yet here, on my own, I felt oddly empty. It was all so oatmeal. How bare the walls were. Not even a picture. The clock next to the bed was an alien modern cube. I slid my legs off the bed and pulled open the top drawer – nothing. I decided to unpack, to fill up some of the spaces, and had a glass of water from the tap in the shower room. I found my egg sandwich and ate it at the table, feeling hungrier when I'd finished than when I'd started. What could I do if I got really hungry? Nothing. I hadn't been shown the kitchen. We hadn't passed a shop. 'A couple of days', she had said. A couple was two. But people can be so vague with language; a couple/a few – they have become interchangeable. It had seemed a disappointingly short trip in the planning, but now I was actually here the time loomed

193

ahead dark and unknown. I mean, how long should I sit here? She'd left me to freshen up 'for a bit'. Ten minutes? Half an hour? More?

When I finally left the piggery, and walked back up the path, I found her waiting for me on the terrace. Cries and splashes carried in the air from the pool. She was alone, sitting upright on a bench with her hands clasped between her knees; she was staring across the valley at that single tree on the horizon, her features slumped, her eyes hooded. Her expression was dull, vacant. When she saw me, she jumped up and seemed to put on a smile, sort of shake it onto her face. She had changed her flip-flops for trainers and a small rucksack was strapped to her back. 'There you are! Have you been having a nap? Tom and Delilah have gone for a swim, but I said I was waiting for you. Let's have this walk, shall we?'

I gabbled apologies, and we set off, past the cars, up to the lane. She said it didn't matter at all; we were on holiday, it's not like she had anything else to do – well, apart from cleaning up and cooking, and she'd had enough of both. At the top of the drive we turned right onto a bosky lane, and almost immediately crossed a stile to the left, onto a footpath along a field. Maudie was tugging to get free, making a frustrated rasping noise from her throat, and I bent down to unhitch her from the lead.

Ailsa said: 'I'd keep her on, if I were you. There are a lot of sheep around and the farmers aren't mad about dogs on the loose. We don't want her getting shot.'

'Maudie shall not be shot,' I said, borrowing from Dr Johnson.

I'm not sure she got the reference. 'Let's hope not,' she said.

The path was narrow and overgrown and we struggled along it in single file, Ailsa in the lead, the dog next, me dragged behind, between a field and a scratchy hedgerow and then under a line of lime trees, through shadow and sunlight, until we reached a four-barred gate to our right. Beyond was an open pasture and here the path widened and we could walk abreast. To our left, overhung with trees, the occasional willow, a small river meandered. To the right, a meadow of long grass, rampant with daisies and buttercups and poppies, followed a gentle incline towards the dark clustered shadows of a small copse. There was the liquid sound of water, the general hum of insects, the occasional loud and purposeful low-flyer zooming by close to one's ears. High above us swifts screamed.

'How's the week been?' I asked.

'Fine.'

It was warm, if not as hot as it had been. A tepid breeze rustled in the willows. The sky had clouded over – the mackerel scales multiplying as they tend to, in thick waves across the sun.

'Is Tom a bit less stressed about work?'

'Well he's happy to be away if that's what you mean.'

'Is he really pleased with Max about his report?'

'Yes, what a relief.'

As the path turned away from the river, the gradient steepened. We walked in silence – just the sound of our breathing. When we reached the brow of the hill and were almost into the dappled shadows of the trees, I paused, and she stopped too. We both turned round to look back down the meadow, the swaying grass, the long-stemmed buttercups and daisies, to the house beyond, glimpses of roof, and trees and wider glinting water. She took a few deep breaths. 'Fucking relief to get away from them all.'

'Oh dear.' I pushed my glasses up my nose. 'You do seem a bit out of sorts.'

'I'm fine,' and then again, drawing the word out, 'I'm *f-i-ne*.' She let out a puff from her cheeks, a sort of harrumph. 'It's harder work than in London, that's all. And I wasn't expecting Delilah to turn up as well. Did anyone ask me? No, just fait accompli. Yes, everyone's having a lovely time, but does anyone think about all the fucking catering?' She rubbed the palm of her hand with her thumb; then scratched it in little controlled circles. 'Sorry, itchy. Chopping onions yesterday. So many mouths. As far as they're all aware, the meals just arrive – as if by magic. You know?'

Aware I was another mouth, I kept it shut.

A fly was buzzing around her face and she waved it away. 'I'm a grouch. Sorry. Not sleeping. It can happen if I'm off my meds, which I think you already know I am. Don't for Christ's sake tell Tom, by the way. He'll kill me.'

'Oh dear, it all sounds a bit stressful for you,' I said. There were things I could have said, *asked*, but Maudie was still making that strangulated panting sound; it was taking all of my strength to keep hold of the lead.

'Oh, let the dog off,' Ailsa said, as if she was the one whose patience was being tried.

I bent down to release her; but the strain in Maudie's neck tightened the collar and I found it hard, with my arthritis, to get my fingers close enough to unclip the clasp. It was a struggle, but finally, like a greyhound released from the traps, she propelled herself forwards, and was gone, head down, whipping through the long grass, back towards the river.

'Fuck,' Ailsa said. 'Where's she going? Is she going back to the first field? Did you notice if there *were* sheep in it?'

'I didn't see.'

'Would she chase them? We should have checked if they were there. They might have been clustered by the far fence.'

'I don't know.'

'I think there might not have been,' Ailsa said. She rubbed her chin. 'The farmer was around yesterday, but . . .'

I couldn't wait to hear any more. I began to stumble back down the path, the earth beneath my feet uneven and pitted.

Grass whipped at my calves; my glasses knocked against my nose. Why had I let her off? Why had Ailsa suggested it? It had been insane under the circumstances. *She might be shot.* I shouted, 'Maudie, Maudie!', my breath ragged, a hot pain in my chest. I could hear Ailsa, but her voice sounded a long way away. She wasn't running. She wasn't panicked. She didn't care if Maudie was shot or not. It would be a minor inconvenience to her, that was all.

When I reached the river, the pain had widened under my ribcage. 'Maudie,' I panted, my heart pressing against my sides. I raised my voice: 'Maudie!' Had she gone through to the other field. Any second would I hear the sound of a gun? What would I do? Was there a vet? Would we get there in time? I could hear the crackle of Ailsa's steps, the hush of her breath, and I began to run again, tripping over the uneven ground, almost falling, vision blurred with tears; my heart loud in my ears.

And yes . . . I knew I was ridiculous, *foolish.* The moment I caught sight, through the overhanging yellows and greens, of Maudie's straggly white coat, her head down as she gulped water from the stream. The moment I called again, and she lifted her head and hurtled back, tearing through the entrails of the willow, and reached me, panting, her sides heaving – yes, in that moment I knew I had made an idiot of myself. Furiously, my heart still pounding, I clipped the lead to her collar. I bent over myself, leaning my elbows on my thighs to try and recover my breathing.

'There she is.' Ailsa had caught up. 'Panic over.'

'Panic over,' I managed to repeat, fingertips pressed into the corners of my eyes.

She patted my shoulder. 'Poor Verity,' she said.

'I'm fine.'

'You look very pale.'

I shook my head.

'You're shaking.'

'Better in a minute.' I rubbed at tiny bubbles of blood on my ankles.

'We should probably wander back now anyway.'

I straightened. 'Yes.'

She began to walk ahead and I followed. 'A nice cup of tea, when we get home,' she said. 'About the one thing Delilah seems able to do unaided.'

I made a noise at the back of my throat.

A few minutes later, she lifted her chin and looked back at the field. 'This is what I call a proper wildflower meadow. I might have to dig a bit up to take back to my own.'

'No cornflowers,' I managed to say.

'You're right. No centaurea cyanus.'

I swallowed. 'They need annual ploughing so they're not technically *meadow* flowers at all.'

Ailsa laughed, looking back at me from under her lashes. 'What I love about you is you don't miss a *thing*. She's quite annoying, isn't she?'

'Maybe not my cup of tea.'

'Thing is I have to put up with her because she and Tom have always been so close.'

I let a beat pass. 'Too close?' I ventured.

She moved her head to look away. 'They've known each other a long time – they were neighbours as kids and mucked about in tree houses and stuff together, and then later, before university, they dated for a while. She's always been a bit in love with him, and he tends to play up to it. He's a terrible flirt.'

We had reached the four-barred gate. I stopped and leant into it. 'Oh, so it's nothing serious,' I said.

She looked back at me. 'I hope not.' She laughed. 'Otherwise, I'd have to kill him.'

I wish I could be sure of what happened next. It is so hard to be certain, particularly when certainty is as important as it is now. Although I recall details, it's possible I dreamt it.

What I *remember* as happening, is that I stretched out my hand to cup one of the tall lacy flowers that were sprouting in a hollow between the river and the gate, lifting their heads towards us. 'Lots of cow parsley in my garden,' I said. 'It's rampant. But it dies so quickly when picked, doesn't it?'

Maybe it wasn't cow parsley. Maybe it was buttercup or harebell or foxglove. Lots of wildflowers have doppelgangers. I'm sure I can come up with other examples if I try hard enough . . . I've just Googled: morning glory and its treacherous cousin bindweed. There you go.

Whatever it was, Ailsa pulled me from it. 'Don't touch. Even brushing against it can give you blisters on your skin.'

I inspected my hand. I felt a curling of unease, thinking of my own wild damp garden. 'How can you tell it's not cow parsley?'

'You just can. If you look closely enough. It's a slightly darker green, and the leaves are more feathery. Also' – she bent to study the stem – 'you see those purple blotches on the stalk? Cow parsley, which flowers earlier in the year, is pinkier and also slightly hairy. If you were to crack it open, you'd see the cow parsley stem is triangular, while hemlock is round and hollow. And it has a nasty smell.' She wrinkled her nose. 'It smells of mouse.'

Mouse. I wish it hadn't stuck with me, but it did. *Mouse.*

Chapter Seventeen

Wonders of the World Top Trumps

Nocturnal, *adjective*. Of a person: that engages in an activity or occupation by night; preferring to be active at night.

The house was bustling with activity when we got back. Wet footprints criss-crossed the terrace and over chairs were draped various towels and teenagers. Voices came from the kitchen and Rose, in a sundress and a large hat, came out holding a mug in one hand and a biscuit in the other. 'Oh, two more for tea,' she called when she saw us. Music was playing – what I have since learnt was the soundtrack to *Hamilton* the musical; though there was also something tinnier emanating from the direction of Bea, who was on her phone at the top of the steps.

Rose, finishing her biscuit, gave me a one-armed hug and Maudie her hand to sniff before stroking her: the sure sign of a dog person (possibly that's also why I give her the benefit of the doubt). Tom and a man who must have been her husband, Gary, came out of the house to greet us too; both pale and fleshy in shorts and slightly too small polo shirts, sunglasses strapped across their heads. Tom appeared to be letting his beard grow. He winked at me, clearly putting all threats and intimidation aside for now. 'Tea?' he said. 'Or something stronger?'

'I've just used the last of the milk.' Delilah had followed him out of the kitchen. Her hair was loose and crinkly and she was wearing a frothy 1950s-style swimsuit, a towel around her waist.

Ailsa smiled brightly. 'I'll pop back to the shop,' she said, in a resentful sing-song. 'Keys? Tom? I'd better go now; it's getting late. A meal for eleven won't cook itself.'

'Or maybe Verity would like a drink? We could crack open a bottle? DL [he named a famous British actor] has sent me a rather special bottle of champagne.'

Ailsa cleared her throat.

'I'll fetch the milk.' Gary hung his arm over Rose's shoulder as if to say, *Look, happily married couple, helpful husband, grateful wife.*

Ailsa smiled. 'Well, that would be so sweet of you. And let's save the champagne, shall we, for later? Verity's got to tutor those horrors so she needs to keep her wits about her.'

'We get it.' Tom rolled his eyes. 'Too early for champagne.'

'So kind of you, Verity,' Rose said. 'I've been hearing about how much better Max has been doing since you got your claws into him. Boys! Are you ready?'

I had sat down at the garden table but I stood up quickly. I hadn't realised the 'work' would be starting today – though I supposed, if we were to fit in more than one comprehension, we did need to crack on. Also: claws?

'Dinner's at eight,' Ailsa said.

Max and Ferg, who had been playing Top Trumps, were not particularly enthusiastic about the new direction of their day. I recognised Ferg from the picnic on the common. A good foot taller than Max, he was wearing slip-on sandals with sports socks, a combination so ugly and pointless it must have been dictated by fashion. I realised quickly he was one of those earnest fact-collecting boys, whose life's work was to compare his own knowledge of things with that of the person next to him. Before we'd even arrived at my room, he had caught Max out twice, once by declaring the Devil's Causeway to be in Northumberland not Wales and the second time by asking him what he would find if he went for a walk on Jupiter.

Max looked doubtful.

'It's called the red planet, isn't it?' I volunteered.

'It's not the red planet.' Ferg looked even more pleased with himself. 'No. That's Mars. Though Jupiter does have the Great Red Spot.'

'Red soil?' Max suggested.

'Nope.'

'Red rocks?'

'No.'

'I give up.'

'You *couldn't* go for a walk on Jupiter,' Ferg responded with glee. 'It has no solid surface.'

'Oh.'

'So you *couldn't* go for a walk on it because you couldn't *actually* walk.'

'Oh right.'

'So you *couldn't* go for a walk even if you wanted to. Do you see?'

Neither of us answered.

'So when I said if you go for a walk on Jupiter, you *couldn't*.'

'Yup,' I said. 'You're very clever.'

We'd reached the door to my room, and I stretched my arm past them to turn the handle and let them in.

'Ugh, what's that smell?' Ferg said.

I slipped past them and scooped the remainder of my egg sandwich from the desk, crumpling the greaseproof paper into a bundle in my hands, and putting it in the small pedal bin in the bathroom. 'Crumbs from my lunch,' I said. 'Tomato and egg.'

'Why would you have tomato and egg?' Ferg asked, venturing into the room.

'Egg because I like it. Tomato for one of my five vegetables a day,' I said, pulling out chairs to indicate they should sit.

'A tomato's a fruit!'

'Five a day can be fruit or vegetables,' Max said. 'So it doesn't matter.'

I could have kissed him.

'Right, we're going to do a comprehension,' I said. 'Luckily I brought two copies – one for myself – but you can have that one, Ferg, and I'll read it over your shoulder. We're going to use PEA. Point. Evidence. Analysis. Max, you remember? It's that method we found on that prep school website. Yup? What about you, Ferg? Is it a system you're aware of?'

He said he wasn't, shifting in his chair as I explained it to him, not happy to have been found wanting in the knowledge department. In his set, Sharks, apparently they follow 'the 1234 method'.

His eyes shifted to Maudie, who had leapt up onto the bed.

'Right, well we're using my method today,' I said.

'The dog shouldn't be on the furniture,' he said.

'I know.'

'She's a stray,' he said.

'No, she's not. She's mine. A stray's a dog that doesn't have an owner. She was a rescue when I got her. But she's not a stray. She's got a microchip and I think that is the definition of a non-stray.'

I shouldn't have contradicted him. I don't know what got into me.

He brushed his fringe away from his forehead. 'She is a stray. Tom was telling my mum and dad about her when you were walking.'

'She's not a stray,' I said, reaching into my suitcase for the copies of the comprehension.

'Tom said she was. Tom said Ailsa was always collecting wayward strays.'

The pages of the comprehension, which I'd printed out from the internet, were doubled and I carefully divided them into two sets. The air in the room felt acrid; my mind focused on the ball of clingfilm resting at the bottom of the bathroom bin.

'Waifs and strays,' I said, laying the print-out on the desk in front of him. 'I think you'll find that's the correct phrase. It's "waifs and strays" Ailsa collects, not "wayward strays".'

The term originates from the fourteenth century, from a legal privilege granted under the Crown to lords under Anglo-Norman law, a 'waif' being an item of unclaimed property found on a landowner's property while a 'stray' any domestic animal – a cow, say – that had wandered onto that land.

I knew Tom and I hadn't warmed to each other. But I didn't like the thought of him *talking* about me. Who wants to be thought of as a waif – a thin, shoeless ragamuffin? Or a stray – cow or dog or otherwise? Well, I was anything but. I had my own house, thank you very much. And, even if I *were* a waif *and* a stray, I'd like to know what long ranks I was joining. Who else had she 'collected'? And who was he to dismiss what I assume were nothing other than unlikely friendships? It said more about his contempt for Ailsa than it did about me.

I almost didn't go up to the house at 8 p.m. In the end, hunger won out. I had only had that one sandwich all day; even the promised cup of tea had never materialised. These days, I am very well aware that I irritate Ailsa. 'Stop fussing,' she said to me this morning, when I asked if I could bring her a piece of toast. But in my opinion it's better to bombard one's guest with offers of nourishment than to neglect them.

The low murmur of voices reached me as I climbed the steps; a burst of laughter, the chink of glass on stone. A bird, clucking, flew low across the lawn. It was still light, but the house was lit up and fairy lights were strung over the bushes. Bea, Melissa and the other teenage girl were in the kitchen – I could see them through the window at the table on their phones – but everyone else was outside on the terrace, around the fire pit. Gary and Rose were next to each other on the bench, opposite Delilah and Tom on wooden chairs. Max and Ferg were crouched between them, poking sticks at the smouldering logs. Ailsa was closest to me, on one of the deckchairs, lower than the others, and at a necessarily backwards recline.

I hesitated at the top of the steps. I hadn't realised a change of costume was in order. The women were in dresses, both men in brightly patterned shirts. Ailsa was wearing a neon pink cotton kaftan. It was tighter than her usual decorative sacks.

She startled when she saw me standing in the shadows. 'Not Maudie,' she said – too quickly. 'She's not smelly.'

'I like Maudie,' Rose said. 'We're talking about someone else's dog.'

'The farmer's,' Delilah said.

Tom smirked.

'How's life in the pigsty?' he said.

'The piggery,' Ailsa corrected.

'That's what I meant.' He stood up and dragged another chair across from the table. 'Tutoring go OK?'

'Very good,' I said, sitting down in the chair and nodding my thanks.

Gary looked up from his paper. 'I hope Ferg acquitted himself.'

'He certainly did.'

Tom let out a mannered groan. 'I expect he showed Max up.'

Max, sitting on his hands, hunched forwards. I resisted the temptation to stroke his head. He threw his stick in the fire, and watched it burn.

'Not at all,' I said. 'They were both equally focused.'

Tom poured a glass of champagne from a bottle on the ground, and handed it to me, balanced on the palm of his hand. 'There we go, my dear,' he said, putting on a posh voice and bowing obsequiously. 'Thank *you*,' I said, trying to match his tone, but getting the intonation wrong and sounding like a schoolmarm putting a naughty child in their place. Ailsa caught my eye and winked.

Tom sat back down on the chair next to Delilah. Her dress had a long slit and she was rubbing the side of her thigh as if massaging the muscle.

One of the logs sent off a spark.

Rose apologised to me for their presence, 'for gate-crashing'. They were heading down to Cornwall the following day, where Gary and the kids were to spend the summer. She herself could only take two weeks out of the office. 'Muggins here has to work,' she said, 'to keep the rest of my family in the manner to which they are accustomed.'

Ailsa asked a few questions about the Cornish house. Had they knocked through to make a bigger kitchen in the end? What had they decided about the barn? Planning permission was OK for that, was it? Even in an area of outstanding natural beauty?

'How lovely,' she kept saying, even when Rose had just mentioned the need for a new roof. 'How love-ly.'

Gary was sitting on the other end of the bench from his wife. The Saturday newspapers were in a pile next to him, the sports section on top. He looked up, aware maybe of having not been part of the conversation, and said, 'Verity, Rose tells me Ailsa's been helping you do some work in your house?'

I took a sip of champagne. 'Yes. Not a new roof. She's been helping me declutter.'

'Declutter?' Tom let out a derisive laugh. 'Sorry,' he said, catching Ailsa's eye. 'Sorry. Not funny I know.'

'Oh, but it's quite the thing now,' Delilah said. 'Decluttering. There's that programme on Netflix that everyone's watching.'

'Marie Kondo,' Rose said. 'You have to hold each object in your hand, and work out if it sparks joy.'

'Or rage,' Ailsa said.

Rose lay her arm along the back of the bench and smoothed down her husband's collar. '"Have nothing in your house that you do not know to be useful or believe to be beautiful." Isn't that what William Morris said?'

'Apparently so,' Ailsa said. 'Though we all have different ideas of both beauty and utility. And Verity's don't always coincide with mine.'

She smiled at me. She didn't mean to be sharp. She was playing to the gallery. I thought about Faith again, how when we were young she could be lovely to me when we were alone, but when people were around I was often the butt of her jokes. I sat on my hands, the wooden chair rough beneath my palms. I curled my fingers until I felt the flesh catch on a splinter. 'You never know when something might come in useful,' I said. 'A hammer isn't useful until you have a nail to bang in. Tweezers aren't useful until you have eyebrows to pluck. And you might not realise the utility of something – an iron rod, say, or a piece of rope – until for mending purposes you're looking for an item of that exact nature. And of course,' I was stuttering but I needed to carry on, 'beauty is relative even to the individual. One day one might profess oneself ready to die for ferns and palms, the next cornflowers and daisies.'

Ailsa stood up and said she had to get the food on. I offered to help, but she shook her head. 'I'm in control,' she said. 'I'll call you when it's ready.'

She went through the open doors into the kitchen and we heard the oven opening and the hiss of hot fat.

I felt Tom's eyes on me. He said: 'Verity's house is apparently an absolute treasure trove of useful and beautiful items, as well as items that are perhaps less useful and less beautiful. But what I want to know is what she keeps in the upstairs back bedroom. No one is allowed in it at any cost. It's kept locked.' He lay his finger beneath his nostrils and turned to look at each of the others in turn.

'We all need a room of our own,' Rose said. 'I don't like anyone coming into my study. Not even Gary. In fact, if I have a home office in Cornwall – which is the eventual plan with the barn, it's going to be kept locked at all times.'

I looked across at her gratefully. I said, 'It was my sister's room, *is* my sister's room. No big mystery. No dead body, or Gothic torture chamber or whatever it is you imagine is in there.' I let out what I imagined to be a tinkling laugh. 'Just my sister's room.'

'And your sister doesn't let anyone in?' Gary lifted his eyes again from the newsprint.

'Her sister doesn't live there,' Rose said. 'They're not on speaking terms.'

Gary groaned. 'Oh God, family fall-outs, awful.'

'What did you row about?' Delilah rested her elbows on her knees. 'Anything in particular?'

'Yes.' A low pain spread beneath my ribcage. My breath had started coming in constricted bursts. 'No.'

Ailsa came out of the kitchen then, carrying a big plate of food, her pink kaftan covered by a large blood-stained apron. '*À table*,' she said in French.

I stood up, with relief, and followed the others over to the garden table. Tom sat me on his right-hand side, like the guest of honour, and Ailsa carved the meat. It was delicious – thick slices of beef, with a watercress sauce, and several salads. The night darkened slowly and more wine was poured. I didn't talk much, but I felt included that evening. Nobody mentioned Faith again, or my house, or my garden. It was just light-hearted easy chat about children and animals, village fêtes and local castles, the seaside, bread-making, everything and nothing.

At one point the conversation turned to the next day's lunch guests.

'They're charming,' Tom said. 'Both of them.'

Rose raised an eyebrow. 'As well as rich. How convenient.'

'I hear he's a terrible shagger,' Delilah said.

'That's an ambiguous comment,' Gary said. 'If ever I heard one.'

'Either way,' I said, 'it doesn't bode well for Pippa.'

And when everyone laughed, I felt their warmth and fundamental kindness.

'She's sharper than she looks,' Tom said.

I dropped off quickly – in this case aided by the champagne and the red wine – but woke up, wide awake, an hour later. I lay there in that strange bed, mind curled around horrible thoughts and memories. I kicked off the sheets, my nightdress damp with sweat, and eventually got up and opened the door. It was dark outside, the shed opposite a low black shape. I stepped out, aware of my own breathing, of small rustles and creaks; the scrape of my own feet; and crossed the small yard. The house above me loomed against the inky sky. I sat down at the bottom of the flight of steps, my knees against my chin, enjoying the cool of the stone. The garden wasn't quiet, but full of little rattling, rasping sounds: scurrying nocturnal beetles, or leaves falling. It was a moonless night but my eyes began to adjust. The curtains were drawn at all the windows. I could see a small fractured glow from the fire pit, and over to the right, a distance from the house and in a patch of shadow, the glisten of a single fairy light.

It was moving slightly in the breeze and for a moment, I wondered why it would shine on its own like that. Perhaps it was solar-powered and it had a stronger internal mechanism or battery than any of the others. But, as I stared, it swung violently to the right, and was extinguished. And the bulk next to it shifted, too, and it came to me, with a sharp intake of breath, that it hadn't been a fairy light at all but the end of a cigarette.

It's foolish at my age but my first response was to be aware of the thinness of my nightie. My arms were clasped around my knees and I pulled the fabric tight across my calves, bunching it with my hands at my ankles. I clenched my buttocks. I felt suddenly chilled, both vulnerable and embarrassed, as if I had been caught somewhere I shouldn't be. I breathed quietly through my nostrils, staying very still.

'So yeah, me too. Yeah.'

It was like a whisper I caught then – a nothing, I couldn't be sure it was anything at all.

'Yes. If we can.'

There was no mistaking the shape of the body now, his arm-swinging gait. He had detached from the darkness of the bushes and was moving across the terrace, his voice a murmur. The white background of his patterned shirt gleamed like phosphorescence. He passed in front of the fire pit and there was the sound of a bottle being knocked over. He paused, bent to right it and then began to move away from the house again, taking a few steps to the front of the terrace in my direction. When he stopped next to the olive tree, I heard leaves rustle, saw a branch sway as he touched it. I could smell the woodsmoke on his clothes, the spice of his aftershave. He said, 'We'll have to try,' on a sigh through his teeth. I held my breath.

Behind him was a grating sound, a rattle – a door opening – soft steps, the clink of the bottle once again knocked over, a muttered oath. A hiss: 'Tom.'

'Gotta go,' he said.

The shape came closer, bare feet and legs, a night-shirt. 'Who are you talking to?' Delilah's voice.

'No one. Work.'

He raised his arm, holding his phone away from her and she tried to reach across to grab it. 'You look guilty.'

'I'm not.'

'Who were you talking to then?'

'None of your business.'

She took a step aside. 'I don't trust you, Tom Tilson. I never have.'

'Fuck you.'

'You having an affair?' she said.

'You leaving Johnny?' he said.

'You leaving Ailsa?'

'Fuck you,' he said again.

Now I've written them down, the words on the page look confrontational. But it wasn't at all. I don't know how to convey the ease of it.

He sunk onto the top step then, folding himself into a seating position. His knees were bent and he let out a small groan, twisted sideways to get comfortable. She stood above him for a few moments, and then he reached out both of his hands and placed them on her hips. She let out a gasp, or a laugh, somewhere between the two, and he drew her down until she was kneeling beside him. One of them said something – him, I think – but she lowered her head towards his, and I didn't hear any more talking then, confrontational or otherwise, but only the soft suck of lips on lips, the sweep of hands in hair, the quick urgent rasp of clothes, the slide of skin on skin.

Chapter Eighteen

A bottle of Paul Newman's Own Italian Dressing

Anaphylaxis, *noun*. An acute reaction to an antigen (eg a bee sting) to which the body has become hypersensitive.

I was chilled when I finally crept back to bed, stiff too from the prolonged stillness of my posture. Heavy petting, I suppose you would call it, of the type banned in municipal pools. Or frottage – a word no one has asked me yet to update, but which I see from my online OED was first documented in 1933 by H. Ellis as a form of aberrant sexual behaviour: 'the special perversion of f— consists in a desire to bring the clothed body, and usually though not exclusively the genital region, into close contact with the clothed body of a woman.' They finally broke off, in the end, by a sort of mutual consent – murmurs and groans, to my relief if not theirs, persuading each other to stand up and return to the house.

Lying on my bed, I was appalled by what I had seen and heard, but I would be lying if I didn't also admit to a sense of satisfaction – vindication, the relief of having been proved right. Ailsa needed to know; I'd have to tell her. But I thought about the SSRIs and the self-help books, all the cooking, the constant diets; the thing she'd said that very day: 'I'd have to kill him.' It was bitterly cruel. Perhaps ignorance was kinder. I pulled the sheet up and then minutes later kicked it off. No, I had a moral responsibility. And yet – to be the messenger . . . no one wanted that. Better to know, though, than live in ignorance.

Dawn was creeping into the room under the door, at the edges and bottom of the blind. I was eager to get on with it now. Should I wait until nine? Maybe earlier; eight might be acceptable. I stared at the electronic clock, willing the numbers to turn over. I would dress, go up to the house and ask her to come for a walk. I thought about which words to use, how to phrase it. *I wish I didn't have to tell you this.* I began to imagine ahead. She would want to leave. The train would be easiest. I pictured the two of us sitting in the carriage on the way back to London, Ailsa next to me where the woman with the tinny music had sat. She would probably cry, thank me for standing by her. I would take her hand. Max: perhaps we'd bring Max. She'd move into my house when we got back; both of them would.

Light was pooled on the pillow when I opened my eyes. A noise had woken me. I sat up. Maudie was on her back legs, scratching at the door. The numbers on the clock read 11:12.

I leapt to my feet, head swimming. My clothes were scattered on the floor, and I gathered them and got dressed. My lips were dry, the roof of my mouth scaly. I opened the door into a burst of sunshine and let Maudie out into the yard; she crouched to relieve herself. It was a blue day, achingly clear. A dove cooed on the roof of the shed opposite; jackdaws clucked. The events of the night felt muddled and vague. I tried to focus my mind. What should I do? Oh lord. I couldn't find her now, claim urgency. 'Something awful happened. And I wanted to tell you. But first I needed a lie-in.'

I gave Maudie her breakfast and shut her in the room. And then I slowly climbed the steps to the house. Whatever I did, I couldn't skulk all day in the piggery.

When I got up onto the terrace, it was deserted. No one was on the tennis court; no sounds came from the direction of the pool. And on the driveway, the gravel showed tyre marks, but both cars had gone.

I let myself into the kitchen. Several mugs and a pile of dirty cereal bowls were perched on the counter next to the Aga. I opened the dishwasher, thinking to put them in, but it was full of clean things. Instead, I sat on a stool, wondering what to do. I couldn't think where they'd disappeared to. Had they waited for me to wake up? I tried to remember if we'd planned a tutoring session. Dear God, let no one have come down to check on me, opened the door, seen the room in a state of disarray. They'd have gone – where? To church? No. Shopping? Maybe. A tiny worm of a thought: had one of them mentioned a market? A flea market? The thought grew into a certainty.

I stood up and opened the fridge. A stench. A stainless-steel container took up the bottom shelf; it was wet and gunky with raw chicken, knobs of garlic, red powder and thick slivers of lemon. People – those clients of Tom's – were coming to lunch.

I closed the fridge, found a clean bowl and poured myself some Special K. I ate it dry, standing at the sink. Propped against a pot of jam was a cookbook open on a page for 'Catalan chicken'. When Ailsa got back, she'd be stressed, in a rush to get the cooking on. I wouldn't be able to talk to her. It would have to wait.

I left the empty dish with the others on the counter and looked around. The kitchen opened into a small hall, and I walked into it; the stairs curled up to the left, the sitting room was straight ahead. I poked my head in: it was square and smartly decorated, with an empty fireplace and a stiff-looking blue linen sofa and matching chairs, thick floral curtains and a lot of crimson velvet cushions. It smelt odd, musty and sweet like old pillows. Someone had been watching television – a plaid blanket lay crumpled on the floor, and a carton of Cadbury Heroes was on its side on the coffee table, with its lid off.

I paused at the bottom of the stairs, wondering whether to risk it. I was curious to explore, but if they came back and found me in a bedroom, it would seem as if I were snooping. My hand was on the bannister, and I was peering, head tipped back, which is probably why the sound reached me. It was so very quiet and muffled that for a moment I thought it was just the squeak of a window, or the creak of a door. But then it came again, and it was the kind of noise that you have to strain your ears to catch, but when you do you realise it's only the tips of it you're catching, that there is a low hum below, almost inhuman, animal-like, and yet at the same time the essence of human. A high keen, a catch, a whimper.

I didn't hesitate. It was instinct. I took the stairs two at a time. I knew it was Ailsa; there was no doubt in my mind. I recognised the register of her voice and I understood, with a flood of certainty, what had happened. She'd found out. Something had alerted her. She'd seen them last night or he'd told her this morning. And now they were gone and she was up there, alone.

I reached the landing. Several closed doors faced me, but the sound came from the far right, from the bedroom over the sitting room. The door was ajar, and I stepped towards it; the sound louder now. I paused again, still doubtful. I didn't want to interfere or embarrass her, and yet the thought of her sad and desperate was unbearable. And so eventually I did push open the door, though I didn't immediately step into the room.

The bed was against the wall on the far side, between the two windows. Ailsa was lying in it alone, on her front, her face to one side on her pillow. Her body was humped in a strangely contorted position under the covers, her arms beneath her, and her eyes were closed. I remember noticing the phone on her pillow, how the screen was lit. The sound was coming faster now, little regular pants, and I was aware also of a low buzzing.

The blood rushed to my face. I brought my hand to my mouth. I think a yelp of embarrassment might have risen to my throat, but I managed to suppress it as I backed out of the room, and pulled the door to.

Over the course of that day, I kept remembering the exact moment in which discovery coincided with *fear* of discovery; the pall of horror, even as I saw her, that she might see me. It was a particular kind of mortification, and it was later to become muddled in my mind with my knowledge of Tom's affair. I had watched them both in secret and it led to a sort of self-disgust that was to contribute to making me feel unwell.

It was a matter of minutes before cars rolled into the drive, doors slammed, gravel crunched. I was sitting at the kitchen table, pretending to do the crossword, when in a blast of noise and bags, they barrelled in. The kids ran off for a swim, and Rose and Gary went upstairs to pack. Tom and Delilah began to distribute the shopping: another giant carton of milk, a pat of butter, a dirty-looking lettuce, some Neutrogena hand cream, and a rectangular box bearing the word 'Bodyguards'.

Tom, putting the lettuce on the counter, said, 'You missed a great trip, Verity. The Barcombe flea. All that tat, right up your street.'

'I shouldn't have slept in,' I said. 'I'm sorry.'

'No one's judging,' he said to me. 'The boys were delighted with their reprieve.'

Delilah, in cropped jeans and a lacy top, was moving lightly around the room, quite a spring in her step. ''Scuse us,' she said, squeezing in front of Tom to open the fridge. She was spooning coffee into a cafetiere when Ailsa walked into the room, her hair damp from the shower.

'Just in time,' Delilah said, too brightly. 'Coffee?'

'Yes please. I'd love one.'

Ailsa pushed past her and swung open the dishwasher; she began to empty it, clattering plates into the cupboard.

'I didn't know where anything went,' I said.

'Never mind,' she said. 'I'll do it.'

'I found you a chemist,' Tom said. He pointed at the 'Bodyguards' box on the table. 'Vinyl, not latex, but they should do the job.'

'Thank you.'

She took the lid off the hand cream, squeezed some out into her palm and rubbed it into both hands. Then she pulled back the lid of the box and peeled out a pair of thin cream gloves – identical to the ones doctors wear for a medical examination – and snapped them on. She twiddled her fingers in the air, like an evil scientist planning their next move.

I laughed, to make up for not emptying the dishwasher. But Delilah had put on a sympathetic expression. 'Poor you,' she said. 'Have you thought of . . .' She began to list various homeopathic remedies. I wasn't sure how Ailsa received them – she had her back to me, first referring to the recipe book, then taking the plastic container out of the fridge, placing each piece of chicken on a stainless-steel tray, and finally putting that in the Aga, closing it with a slam.

I continued to take refuge in Saturday's crossword as lunch preparations intensified, shifting, when I got in the way, to the table outside. I was aware that I could have been helping, but I didn't know how. I had a strong and vexatious memory of my first few days at the council, knowing I should be doing something and yet too self-conscious to ask what. I felt a familiar paralysis in my limbs, the same embarrassed rigidity in my cheeks. Adrian Curtis came into my head and I felt sick. Gary, laying out the cutlery, asked me perfectly pleasantly what train I planned to get – clearly under the impression I was leaving that day. Lifting the newspaper to make way for a knife and fork, I explained I thought I had another night and he said, 'Cool,' but after he had gone back into the house I felt a wave of shame at my ineptitude, a sense that things were slipping away from me, that I was doing everything wrong.

We were already eating when the guests arrived. The kitchen and terrace had smelt delicious, of roasting juices and onion and then very slightly less so, of burnt garlic. Opening the Aga, Ailsa deemed the chicken 'utterly ruined'. Rose and Gary were restless, eager to get on the road to Cornwall before it got too late, and the children, according to Ailsa, were 'starving', which seemed unlikely as they had been eating bread and Nutella all morning. Tom, who had been up to the lane several times to check – what, that two media millionaires weren't sitting in a hedgerow? – eventually agreed that we should start without them.

We left spaces that made the table look as if it were missing teeth. Tom sat at the top, with a gap to the right of him, and Gary one beyond; to the other he had Delilah, Rose, an empty seat, and then Ailsa. I stayed at the far end, with Max on one side of me, and Melissa on the other. I was happy to be distracted by the children. Max and I played a game I'd borrowed from Radio 4 in which I gave the definition of three words and he had to decide which one was made up. Even Melissa and Bea joined in, though Ferg said it was boring. At the other end, Tom chewed with an aggressive churning of his jaw, making a point of the meat's toughness, and Ailsa's eating was at her most unhappy; she gave herself a minuscule portion but picked at the dish of potato dauphinoise, digging her nails into the burnt bits around the edges until, despite her initial good intentions, she must have eaten her own body weight in potato dauphinoise. Delilah told a long story about a party she and Tom had gone to as teenagers, how they'd missed the last bus and had had to walk home: it was so boring that even Rose found it hard to respond with any enthusiasm.

It was a relief when we heard the sound of a car pulling into the drive and purring to a halt. Ricky leapt out first, and immediately strode towards us, head ducked, arms rotating: half-dance move, half-semaphore.

Tom jumped to his feet, knocking his chair over, and the two of them met by the front door of the house, slapping their arms around each other in an overly jovial greeting. 'We've started without you,' Tom said, and then in a mockney accent I'd never heard him use before, 'Soz, mate. You snooze, you lose.' Springing away, he made the sign of an 'L' with his thumb and forefinger. Ricky, who was wearing tracksuit bottoms and a tight black T-shirt, caught him in a headlock. 'Grrr,' he said. He was looking at Ailsa over Tom's shoulders, and he winked. She quickly turned her head.

Behind them, Pippa, having checked the contents of the papoose strapped to her chest, was walking towards us, long-legged and long-haired, in floaty white trousers and a white top.

'Hiya,' she said, waving her fingers. 'I'm so sorry we're late. It's all my fault. I was awake half the night so I was slow this morning and then I misread the postcode.'

Her eyes were extremely clear and blue as if you were look-ing at them through a magnifying glass. Her voice was soft and airy, with flat Essex vowels.

Everyone got to their feet and paid court for a few minutes, peering in at the baby and lamenting over their journey as if Ricky and Pippa had just trekked barefoot from the North Pole. Ailsa was at her most gushing. It was so kind of them to come. She and Ricky had had another meeting, it transpired, about the London garden. Was he happy with the plans? Had he shared them with Pippa? Was she loving Bath? How often did she get up to London? And was she still working? She was? And the baby just fitted in. How marvellous. How *jolly*. She was at her most cloyingly fake and it was unbearable to watch. Bless, she kept saying. Bless.

Ricky complimented her on her dress. She'd changed into a long green silk wrap thing with straps. 'Gorgeous,' he said. 'That's your colour. Hope you're keeping a close watch on this one, Tom.'

Ailsa looked pleased, and then embarrassed. She clasped her hands in front of her.

Eventually, the newcomers sat down. Melissa, Bea and Max were exhorted to clear the dirty plates and bring out the clean ones. I got up to help too. (Maudie was asleep in the shade, muzzle twitching and making tiny circular movements with her paws.) Ailsa said, 'Can you bring out the salad? It's on the side.'

'Of course.'

'And the dressing!' she called after me.

The bowl of lettuce had been sitting on the kitchen counter in full sun and was looking floppy. I found the dressing at the back of the fridge – I assumed she meant the Paul Newman's – and I slopped some into the bowl. But when I laid it down on the table in front of Ailsa, she sniffed and said: 'What did you use? Oh no, really? I meant the homemade dressing. It was on the side.' She pushed it to the centre of the table. 'Sorry, everyone.'

I sat back down at my end. It felt hotter than before; my bra was sticking to me, and my forehead felt damp.

A few minutes later Ailsa said that since the kids had eaten, perhaps we could squeeze in 'another session'. Ferg was resistant – 'not that again' – and today Rose, who had drunk several glasses of rosé, didn't seem in a mood to insist, but to my gratification Max seemed quite happy to accompany me and Maudie back down to the piggery.

He picked up a stick and slashed at the long grass as we walked down the steps. 'Anything rather than sit any longer at that boring table.'

'It was hot, too, wasn't it? Sorry Ferg isn't coming.'

'I'm not. It's nicer without him.'

It was stuffy in my bedroom, and a bit messy. I'd left a few clothes lying about and Maudie had found a J-cloth under the basin in the shower room and had torn it to pieces. I began to pick up the clothes and collect the bits of shredded blue while Max sat at the table.

'We could play that game where we make up long words,' he said.

'Or we could go for a walk?'

I put Maudie on the lead and we turned right out of the piggery, across to the far side of the yard, and took a small path behind the barn which led down to the stream – a tributary, I think, of the one along which Ailsa and I had walked the day before. It was a shallow, stony sort of stream, straggly and shaded by great towering walls of trees. The light was limpid and we walked on the garden side of it for a bit, the water to our right, until at a narrow section we reached some stepping stones which we crossed gingerly over to the other bank. We stood for a moment or two in a sunlit clearing. Noises from the house reached us: the drone of voices, a pick-pock from the tennis court; Bea squealing, a splash. Insects buzzed. A dragonfly skittered.

'I'm not going to play *World of Warcraft* any more,' he said. 'Dad says it's rotting my brain.'

'Oh dear. Do you think it is?'

'I don't know.'

In the distance, some way down the valley, there was the sound of a tractor.

'It's good to game less if it'll please your dad,' I said.

He had picked up a stick and he swished at some large cow parsley heads. 'Nothing I do ever pleases my dad,' he said. 'He's never going to like me.'

His tone was easy. If he had sounded more upset, I might have put more thought into my answer. But my head was still thick with what I'd heard the night before. I said, 'Your dad doesn't appreciate what he has.' Max looked at me – and I saw the appeal in his eyes but again I missed my chance. 'I appreciate you,' I said, 'and I'm not properly family so it counts double,' and then I changed the subject. 'That cow parsley looks suspiciously like hemlock.'

He walked off up the path then and I followed. It became more overgrown, brambles and long grass, huge thick flowerheads scratching Max's bare legs, and we doubled back on ourselves and turned left on the track up the field that tilted, across patches of thorny scrub and broom, towards the single tree. I tried to think of something that would count as work, and together as we climbed we made up a story about a spaniel who ran away from a home where he was mistreated, and went to live with some foxes in the country. We were supposed to come up with a sentence each, to take it in turns, but Max began to take over. The spaniel got caught up in a pack of beagles, forced to hunt one of the foxes he'd made friends with. I can't remember it all now – though I typed a copy for him when I got back to London – but it was rich in sensory and emotive detail: the conflict between the dog's excitement in the chase, his *instinct* to kill, and his emotional connection with his prey, was really quite inspired. It makes my spine tingle thinking about it.

'That's brilliant,' I said.

'How would it end?'

'I don't know – maybe you could circle back to the beginning in some way.'

'Like he takes the foxes back to the home where he was beaten and takes his revenge?'

I laughed. 'I love a revenge story.'

Max stopped in his tracks. 'Was that, like, literacy?'

'It was indeed.'

'Wow.'

'My work here is done,' I said.

Melissa and Bea were in the kitchen when we got back. The dishwasher was whooshing and the drying area by the sink was a rickety pile of upside-down dishes. Melissa told us Rose and Gary and their kids had left, and that 'Mum and the guy' were playing tennis. Delilah was having a lie-down. 'The others', she said, were up at the pool.

I'd found a bowl which I'd filled with water for Maudie and she was gulping it down messily. Bea, who had crouched down to stroke her, asked if she could take her for a walk around the garden.

I agreed. I shouldn't have. It left me idle, hot, aimless. If I'd still been holding Maudie's lead, I wouldn't have gone up there. I wish I hadn't. When a house has been busy with people, and then some of them have left, it's hard to adjust to the change in numbers. I was curious to see the pool. But I should have done the maths.

The terrace wrapped around the house, and at the far end of it, around the other corner of the building, was a square lawn with stone steps running across the middle. Beyond this was a row of tall, thick bush-like trees – the crown of each trimmed into a round shape – and in the middle of these was a wrought-iron gate decorated with hearts and leaves.

It was closed and as I pushed it open, the prong at the bottom of it dragged against the ground where the grass had become worn away; as a result I pushed too hard and, once free, it sprang backwards on itself, swinging into the foliage so that, after stepping through, I had to turn round to release it. The leaves brushing against my fingers were thin and dark, pointy. The shape of them was familiar, but I couldn't immediately recall what the tree was called. I had a feeling it was poisonous; certainly I associated it for some reason with death.

It was the pool I noticed before anything else. A long oblong, with the water on a level with the edge, it was disappointingly green and dark, murky even; not what I thought of as a proper pool. To my mind, if you're going to go to all the trouble and expense of having a swimming pool, you should make sure it's a proper blue: the blue of aertex shirts, and melamine picnic plates, of 1950s summer dresses, and the shutters on French houses. Not this dreary school uniform *grey*.

Most of the water and half the lounging area were in the shade now; which was why, presumably, the beds had been moved into a cluster on one side. A crowd had been here: there were trails of towels; a bikini top spreadeagled on the ground like the guts of an animal; a wine bottle on its side; empty glasses in the pots of lavender; a tub of melting ice cream.

But there were only two people here now, and they were both staring at me.

'Good afternoon, Verity,' Tom said. He was sitting on the edge of one of the sunbeds, with his back to me, his head awkwardly turned. He was wearing nothing but swimming trunks, and the position in which he was sitting had pulled them low at the back, so I could see the line between his buttocks.

'Hello there.' Pippa was lying on the next bed beyond him, only inches away, her shoulders bare, her legs long and white and naked. She had hardly moved. 'How are you, then?'

I could have turned round and gone back through the gate. It was my immediate instinct, to flee. And yet by doing so I would compound the intimacy of the scene I had interrupted. Because it *was* intimate. I had no doubt of that. They had stopped talking when they saw me, and I had a sense now that their voices had been low, and private. The water glinted in the corner of my eye; bottomless depths. Beyond were more of those trees with their intimations of death. A sleepy wasp crawled along the edge of the ice cream. But she had spoken to me; I had no choice but to keep moving forwards. Tom got to his feet and it was only as he did so that I had a full view of Pippa: the strap of a crimson swimsuit pulled down entirely on one side – she was feeding the baby.

Tom took two steps towards the pool and sort of slid into it from the vertical; hardly making a sound, only a slight splash, more of a watery quiver. His head emerged and he shook it and then crossed his arms on the edge of the pool facing Pippa, his chin resting on his hands.

I had no idea what to do with myself. I walked slowly, as if I were just taking some air and had wandered in this direction as part of a general garden tour; I let out a sigh meant to express appreciation of the view, of the day. I kept my eyes averted from Pippa, but I was aware that her face was tipped upwards and I was almost sure she was looking at me. 'Here you go,' she said. 'There are some down here.'

I saw then that she had gingerly manoeuvred her right leg off the side of the lounger, and with her foot, she was steering a plate in my direction. And then, still holding the baby in the crook of her elbow, she dropped her spare arm and started fishing under the lounger, her hair slipping sideways, her neck white and long, as she reached for a used bowl just out of her reach.

'Yes, of course,' I said, taking a quick step towards her. 'I'll take it into the kitchen.'

'Oh, could you? Thanks so much. You're brilliant.' She was pleased with herself for being so kind to the help. Her hand was still groping at empty space, but then she let out a cry. Her body crunched forwards and the baby detached. 'Ow, ow.'

'What, what?' Tom pulled himself out of the pool.

'Ow, idiot. Just when I . . .' She was half laughing but then her face contorted. 'Actually. Ow.'

She hauled her legs to one side and stood up, flapping her hand, bringing it to her mouth and away, moving from foot to foot, agitated. She was still holding the baby in the other arm, but loosely, and it had started emitting small angry cries, its neck bent back.

Tom was standing beside her now. 'Are you all right?'

She was looking closely at her hand, at the skin between the index finger and the thumb.

'Been stung. Shit, was it a wasp or a bee? I'm allergic.'

'I don't know.' His wet trunks clung to his buttocks. The elastic in the waistband had left a row of red marks on his skin.

'I need my EpiPen,' Pippa said, a new note of hysteria in her voice. 'It's in my bag. Where's my bag? RICKY!'

'Is it here?' Tom was looking under the lounger. 'No. Where is it?' Pippa's head started making odd jerky motions as she tried to control herself. Her eyes flicked from where I was just standing, hopeless, over to Tom still crouched on the ground, back to me. I took a step towards her. She was panicking properly now. I felt I should perhaps stroke her arm. The crying had got louder, and more insistent, and as I reached her she suddenly thrust the bundle at me. 'Here,' she said. 'Can you just hold him?'

And in my hands, out of nowhere, was the baby, skin and flesh and bone – not bundled, but loosely tied together with a dangling piece of muslin and a white babygro, its arms and legs tiny and wrinkled, like the arms and legs of a shrunken old person. The face was scrunched, eyes closed, toothless mouth open, chin vibrating, and nobody noticed as I stood there holding this noisy creature, a possession so precious to its owner, and yet me not knowing what to do, breathless, shaking, totally ill-equipped for the task. Tom, with a backwards glance, was on his feet now, hurrying Pippa through the gate. They were both shouting for Ricky, and I could hear Ricky shouting back, a battering of feet, movement, activity – beyond the gate at the house, a door slamming. Here by the pool it was still just me and the baby, who was crying now, thrusting backwards into an arch, impossible to hold, bony and delicate; no longer complete, not a wrapped package, but dissolving into a collection of shaking limbs and neck, the head falling to bang against my chest, a smell of sour milk – and chlorine, the treacherous water gleaming beside me. I tried to stay still, to hold its head still against my clavicle, but it twisted away, so I began to move my hips from side to side, my hand trying to keep the head still, the dusting of black down under my fingertips, and somehow my thumb brushed against the soft breach of tissue at the centre, the ghastly pulsing abyss of the fontanelle. And it wasn't just stress I felt then, the normal everyday panic a screaming baby inspires in everyone around it – on a bus, say, or in the queue at the post office – but something more precise and physical: a wave of sickness, not in my head, but in my body.

'Here. Let me take him.'

Hands scooped the baby off me, deftly collecting the muslin from the ground and re-wrapping it, and I don't know what happened next, but the noise from the baby eventually slowed to a hiccup.

But it was too late, too late for me. My mouth and nose were pressed into the synthetic fabric of the lounger, my knees against hard stone. And I kept my face buried there even when Ailsa was patting my back, pushing a glass of water in front of me, urging me to sit up. At some point, the physical distress I'd felt began to ease, but I didn't raise my head for a little longer because, as so often happens when one has made a scene, mortification had taken over and it seemed better to keep my face hidden.

We all agreed later that I'd had a 'funny turn'. It was the phrase Ailsa chose, and it was perfect: benignly comic and vague enough to cover a multitude of sins. It was better than 'Off-legs', which was what had come into my mind: a phrase health professionals use, as in the case of my mother, to describe a deterioration in the health of the elderly. Ailsa had wanted to call a doctor – she remembered my breathlessness on our walk – but I assured her I was OK. I would see my GP when I got home. Tom gave me an odd look, his eyes narrowed. He muttered in Delilah's ear and he made a little tipping motion with his hand to show he thought I'd been on the sauce.

Pippa was fully recovered by then; she'd fully recovered even before the EpiPen was unearthed at the bottom of the nappy bag. And in fact it was never deployed – adrenalin not being necessary in the case of a bee-allergic being stung by a wasp.

Ailsa didn't leave my side, even as Pippa and Ricky and the now sleeping baby were taking their prolonged, drawn-out leave. ('I wish when people said they were going, they would just go,' she murmured.) She sat by me at the garden table while I drank the sugary tea she'd forced upon me, watching me carefully. Once she even patted my leg. 'You must look after yourself,' she said.

'I will.'

'Ask if you ever need anything. Don't just . . .'

'Of course.'

'Anything, Verity. I mean it.'

A thought came into my head then. It was an old thought, like an enemy, that slipped into cracks in my mind, waiting for the middle of the night or a moment of lowness to pounce. And because she was being so nice to me, I let it out into the light.

'If anything happens to me,' I said. 'Would you look after Maudie?'

'Yes, of course.'

I felt all the horrible emotions of the last twenty-four hours, the sense that she had slipped away from me, dissolve.

She had put me in the formal sitting room, and a little later Melissa and Bea came in, snuggled under blankets, and switched on *Love Island*. I don't suppose it's a surprising admission to say it wasn't my thing. But I didn't care. I was so grateful to feel included, so giddy with relief, nothing else mattered. Tom's infidelity – everything that needed to be told: for now it could wait. On the sofa, with a plaid rug pulled over my knees, a toffee gumming my jaws, I even re-cast in my memory the moment I had walked in on Ailsa. It seemed touching. If she had seen me, she should know it didn't matter, that I wasn't shocked. Good God, no.

I wouldn't have imagined such a sterile room could feel so cosy but that's the effect of people, I suppose; that's what happens when you're part of a family.

Chapter Nineteen

5 wire coat hangers, tissue attached

Trepidation, *noun*. Tremulous agitation; confused hurry or alarm; confusion; flurry; perturbation.

Standling rang yesterday to say that, as a consequence of Ailsa's letters, Cecily Tilson had agreed to a supervised visit with the children. A date has been given at a contact centre in Vauxhall. I watched Ailsa carefully while she took the call; her face went ashen and then quickly red, the colour leaching back in across her cheeks. A blush is made of blood: one forgets that. After hanging up, she bowed her head for so long that, until I'd coaxed out of her what he'd said, I thought something awful had happened, that there had been another death. She was in her spot on the sofa in the front room and she pushed her head back into the cushions, raised her fingers to flick back the lace curtain. Light trickled in.

'Fuck, Verity,' she said, finally. 'I don't know if I can do it.'

I patted her shoulder. 'Of course you can. I'll be there. I'll look after you. I always do.'

They dragged, the ten days they were still away and I was back in London. I tried to keep busy. I went to the pub quiz but Maeve and Sue had decamped to France for the summer and it was a flaccid affair. Fred usually invites me down to Oxford during his long holiday but there had been no word from him since our picnic at Granary Square. It's an indication of my state of mind that I didn't care.

The house reproached me for my absence. Thieves had been into the front garden and stolen the rotary dryer, and a mini-fridge. Also some of my timber and a lawnmower. Inside, the smell was worse – it clawed at the back of your throat, particularly on the upstairs floor. The wallpaper was disintegrating, the wall behind it black and mottled, dirty with mites. Outside the bathroom, a strip had peeled entirely back, and hung over the dado like a filthy stocking. On the bedroom ceiling, dark-yellow drips had started appearing. I put saucepans down and tried to ignore it.

I didn't feel myself at all. Ailsa was right about the weight. I did seem to have lost a bit recently. A floral Jigsaw skirt from Cancer Research gaped at the waist. I had to fix it with a couple of safety pins. I had less energy than usual and at night my heart would seem to beat alarmingly fast.

It was listlessness that took me into Collard & Wright. The office is above a nail bar on Bellevue Road, and the name is printed in old-fashioned black typeface on the first-floor window. I must have walked past it every day for twenty years. One dull afternoon I found myself ringing the buzzer and walking up the stairs. The son of the founder, Richard Collard, was on a tea break and could see me then and there. It's very straightforward, making a will. I answered lots of questions and he jotted down the answers in black biro on a foolscap sheet and a few days later, I returned to sign an official typed-up form. In the event of my death, I wanted the cheapest coffin (cardboard) and a quick cremation: no fuss. I bequeathed the fruitwood chest of drawers in Mother's bedroom to Maeve and Sue, a dark oil painting of a portly gentleman holding a quill pen to Bob, and to Fred I left the books – he'd enjoy sifting through them. Everything else, my share of 'house and contents', in recognition of the close bond between us, I gave to Max – to be held, until he attained his majority (in this case twenty-one), by Ailsa.

She deserved it, I thought as I strode home, after everything she had done for me. It would give her financial independence. Freedom. She could leave Tom. How much easier, after the divorce, to live next door, so much less disruptive for the children; a loose form of the arrangement I've read about called 'nesting'. I enjoyed thinking all this. I began to imagine her delight at discovering this good fortune – tempered, of course, by sadness at my passing. My generosity would add a new intensity to her grief, and as the years went by, she would often dwell on our time together, with a tear or a smile. During this reverie, at the back of my mind, I suppose I must have been aware that pre-deceasing her was far from a given. But this awareness was very much at the back of my mind, in the further recesses, shoved against the far wall like the operating instructions for defunct kitchen equipment.

Outside the dress shop on Bellevue Road, a pretty establishment with a fondness for slogans like 'LOVE', was a pile of bin bags filled with folded-up cardboard. I was having a celebratory pick through (they often throw away perfectly serviceable wire hangers), when I heard my name.

I straightened.

'Hello, Verity. No dog today?'

It was Delilah. She was in shorts and walking boots, carrying a large polystyrene tray of white flowers. Her van was parked in the waiting bay; she had left a trail of dried globules of compost.

'No,' I said. 'She's at home. Somerset took it out of her a bit.'

'Don't think I've ever seen you without a dog attached.'

'Well . . .' I began to retort that was blatant nonsense, but I stopped. What was the point? She was lightly mocking me, that was all it was. Some little private joke she and Tom shared.

I glared at her instead. 'You appear to be dropping earth,' I said.

'I'm doing the window boxes for the wine bar next door – I did them a couple of months ago, but they need refreshing. It's where the smokers stub out their cigarettes. All that artistic endeavour and they just think they're giant organic ashtrays. Anyway. Yeah. I've got the contract for most of the restaurants around here.' She rolled her eyes as if to say, *Busy me*.

I thought then how keen Delilah always was to shoe-horn self-promotion into conversation. 'Glad to hear you're so successful,' I said. 'I'm surprised you have time in between canoodling with other people's husbands.' Only I didn't have the courage to say the last bit.

I stuffed the hangers I was holding into the pocket of my mackintosh and was about to move past her, but she put her head on one side and said, 'Lovely house, wasn't it?' She placed the tray carefully on the pavement.

'Yes, I felt very privileged to be included. It was kind of Ailsa to invite me.'

'She's good on the saintly gesture, is Ailsa. Mind you, I'm sure it suited her too. Nice to have an English tutor and a doting slave on tap.'

A woman on the other side of the glass was holding a dress to her body in front of the mirror, twisting her hips. 'I'm happy to help out however I can,' I said. 'She has a lot going on. Someone has to keep the show on the road.'

She laughed. 'Oh, Verity. You really have swallowed it whole, haven't you? She likes to maintain she's so busy and important but she's off all the time, having fun, doing her own thing, whatever that might be, while quietly, behind the scenes, without letting anyone know, Tom does everything. *He's* the one keeping the show on the road.'

I lowered my eyes to the plants at my feet; I could see an insect, a green beetle with a shield-like shell, crawling along a thin tendril.

'I know what's going on,' I muttered. 'Between you and Tom. I'm not blind.'

My face had got very hot and my heart was pounding. The top of the hanger was digging into the flesh on my hand and it felt as if it were drawing blood.

'I don't know what you mean.' She bent down to pick up the tray, her hands gripping the far side, fingers splayed. 'The problem with you is you think you know everything, but you don't notice what's happening right under your nose.'

I was expecting the Tilsons back on the Friday but by Saturday night there was still no sign. With the blinds pulled shut in all the windows, upstairs and downstairs, the house looked asleep. Dead, even.

I picked up my phone several times to text her. 'Looking forward to seeing you,' I wrote and then deleted. 'When are you back? Can I get milk?' also written and deleted. She hated neediness. Perhaps I'd got it wrong and they had the house until Sunday. Or they'd be back any minute now. I'd hear the engine roar onto the off-street, and stutter to a halt.

An ambulance shrieked past the house, and quickly after, a police car, its light pulsing red against the walls of my front room. I looked on the BBC news website for a fatal accident on the A303 and when nothing came up I felt only temporary relief.

Sleeping in your clothes saves a lot of time in the morning, and I was through the door with Maudie just after dawn, out on the common as the sun sent pink streaks across the sky. Walking is a natural sedative, and I ended up doing a big circuit, down to Clapham Junction and up and down the gentrified backstreets 'between the commons'. They're more concerned with loft conversions than dug-out basements in Nappy Valley, as the estate agents call it: another bedroom for the baby. Still, it made no difference to me. Whatever the type of improvement, householders still see the advent of builders as an opportunity to empty their cupboards.

I wasn't home for several hours. Sod's law, they'd drive up just as I was approaching my front gate. I saw the flash of Ailsa's face in the passenger window as the car slowed. I'd longed for this moment, agitated with anticipation for it, but now I wanted to hide. Using the legs of a stool, I pushed the gate open and scurried up the path, pulling Maudie behind me and dropping a few items as I fumbled for my key. I left everything in a heap in the hall and went up the stairs to watch them from Mother's window. Car doors were flung open and Melissa and Bea, boxes of food, suitcases and, last of all, large black plastic bags which – I now know – contained plants all emerged. Tom was shouting at Max: 'For God's sake, can't you take anything out without dropping it?'

She didn't come round to say hello – too busy, I was sure, unpacking, washing, re-nesting. It didn't matter. The relief that they were safe was enough.

The following morning, I was at my desk in my dressing gown trying to do some work, when I heard her voice, out the front: '. . . and then round you go,' she said. 'Like magic.'

A man's voice then. 'Between seven to ten per cent. No question.' I ran upstairs to look out of the window. The man was wearing a suit and holding a clipboard. Ailsa was showing him the parking turntable. He was staring up at the house, and then over at mine. I drew back so he didn't see me.

It took me a few minutes to throw on some clothes, but by the time I was on the path with the dog, they'd both gone.

Chapter Twenty

Gluten Free 4 Multiseed Sandwich Thins

Homeless, *adjective*. Having no home or permanent abode; spec (of a person) having no home, shelter, or place of refuge owing to destitution, living on the streets.

It was warm, walking down to Balham, particularly in the cardigan I was wearing, but the full heat of the day hit me when I turned the corner at the Tube station onto the high road. The sun glared over the railway bridge, the air thick with particles, rich with exhaust and urine. A pigeon pecked at a paper bag outside Costa, its feet mutated. Two men were collecting signatures for a petition against the Heathrow expansion. Kids and women with buggies loitered by McDonald's.

I began to regret coming. My limbs felt heavy, as if they were filled with sand. But still no knock on the door from Ailsa, and I'd needed to distract myself. Tutoring would surely resume that week and I decided to buy Max some new stationery. He likes a nice new pen.

Outside TK Maxx lay a bundle of dirty cloth: a woman, swollen legs splayed out across the pavement. About my age, she was wrapped in too many layers – a dirty sleeping bag coiled behind her head. She had a dog with her, a collie cross

I think, and I let the dog sniff my hand and tried, unsuccessfully, to engage the woman in conversation. We're all so near to the edge, I thought, as I moved away; just a couple of wrong turns, a few doses of bad luck, and everything can fall away.

The breathlessness got worse as I waited to cross the road. I stared at the ground, at a cigarette butt, at the blue streak of bike lane, the wheels of a huge delivery lorry, the rattle of its towering metal sides, its exhaust. When the beeps told me to cross, I put one foot in front of the other, struggling a bit.

Entering the store, the smell of bread and fruit and refrigerated meat clogged my airways. I tried to cough, but I couldn't. Someone had rammed a trolley into the back of the line by the door and the whole procession rattled violently, shifting forwards towards me. The self-service tills emitted a constant high-pitched squawk. A child in a buggy threw a plastic cup and it skidded across the floor and under the display of flowers. A kid about Max's age whizzed past me on a scooter. It was all movement and humming and words. *Can Britney report to the kiosk? Can Britney report to the kiosk?*

What is wrong with you, I told myself. Box files. Highlighters. Get to it.

A few more steps and I stopped again. A sharp pain in my chest now. Nausea. An extreme sense of tightness and panic. I put my hand out to balance against a shelf. 'Deliciously free from' read the sign above it. Free from what, I was thinking as the world went black and white. I had an image of the woman outside, her legs across the pavement. And that's the last thing I remember.

An expanse of speckled tile. A dust-ball. And a coat button. Or was it a Rolo? Perhaps a lone sprout. A sign closer to me read: 'Warburtons gf 4 multisd swch thins 172g'. Incomplete words. Had I had a stroke? A soft, itchy texture under my cheek with an intense smell: synthetic perfume, sweat, something cloyingly sweet like custard.

'She's coming round,' a voice said.

A woman brought her face close. 'You're all right, darling.'

Or perhaps it had been a question: 'Are you all right, darling?'

I tried to answer, but my throat had closed. I panicked, struggling to get up, and a paper bag was brought to my face and the same voice told me to breathe in as deeply as I could. An ambulance was on its way, she said. I wasn't to be alarmed. But she said it in a way that made me realise she was alarmed, that it wasn't that there was nothing to be alarmed about, but that alarm would make whatever it was worse.

A blur after that. Swirling. Noises. 'Prosecco on offer'. The boy with the scooter, staring. Can Britney report to the kiosk? The homeless woman's swollen legs. And then a bluster of activity, movement, new voices. Hands cupping my head, cold straps, a mask across my mouth. A taste, chemical and cool, a small release. My shirt buttons undone. One. Two. Three. Cool air between my cheek and the custard-smelling fabric, legs up, and onto a stretcher. And then movement above: a strip of white light, the ceiling tiles, and pipes – a whole world of shapes and gullies and bulk up there. PRICE LOCKDOWN. And out, and up a ramp and into what I now know was an ambulance.

I don't like to make a fuss, so I'm not going to go on too much about what happened next. I didn't die – but you know that because you're reading this.

I remember very little of the journey to hospital. No siren or screaming or pumping of chests. Mainly I concentrated on taking in what I now know is albuterol, an intensive blast of the drug you get in a common or garden inhaler, while they concentrated on saving my life. Turns out they did do that. The heat, and the stress, my increased anxiety, had led to compromised lungs, narrowed airways, tightened muscles, restricted airflow, etc, etc. Arriving at hospital I was swung in, past the drunks and the broken arms and the colds that wouldn't shift, to a cubicle all of my own. A nurse I could have married got me into a gown and put pads on my chest, and a cannula in my hand, and for the first time in, well, forever, I lay on a bed and gave myself over to the ministrations of others, and there was so much relief in that, in the gradually feeling better, that I could have wept.

Time passed. At first everything had happened quickly, but I became aware of the periods of lag, of measuring things out by hours. 'I'll come back in an hour,' the nurse said, several times. The curtain, a cheerful blue, was whisked back and forth. Blood was taken. Oxygen levels were tested. I saw other doctors. Notes were unhooked from the end of my bed, eyes flicked over them. Questions were asked: had I been ill recently? Any allergies? Cats? Dogs? Had I suffered from asthma before? Any unusual stress?

I was moved to a different bed, out of a cubicle and into the observation ward.

I was observed.

More time went by.

Can we call anyone, someone had asked early on: family? I'd shaken my head. I thought about my mother, the constant worries about her health; the way each passing pain, each tiny twinge, was subject to discussion and debate and investigation. I had a pang for my sister, then. A terrible, hopeless pang. One of the nurses wasn't happy. 'Is no one coming to visit you? Do you have support? Will there be someone to look after you when you get out?'

When the lights above the curtain rail were dimmed it

struck me how late it had got. I pushed the blanket off and stood up. A machine started beeping. A nurse came – a different one, less friendly – and when I told her I had to go, that I'd already been there too long, she told me I couldn't leave: the doctor wanted me under observation. I was here at least until tomorrow. I need to get home, I repeated. My dog's on her own. My dog depends on me. No food. No company. No visit to the garden. How long now? I looked at my watch. *Eight hours.* My throat began to constrict; my chest to feel tight. I tried to breathe again, to quell the rising sense of panic, the self-disgust that rises from awareness of neglect. Her voice softened then. Wasn't there a neighbour I could call?

I had no choice then. I found my phone in the bottom of my bag, and dialled her number. It took me four tries until she answered. There was music behind her voice, and chatter. 'Hello,' she said. 'Verity, I'm sorry I haven't been round. I'll pop in to see you tomorrow if that's OK?'

I told her briefly what had happened.

'You're in hospital?'

'I'm fine. I'll be out . . .'

The nurse was standing just across from me. I looked at her enquiringly. 'Tomorrow afternoon, I expect,' she said.

'Tomorrow afternoon.'

'Are you OK?'

I told her I was fine, but hoped she would be able to look after Maudie for me. I told her where the food was, and asked if she could let her out and take her home with her. She said she would and I directed her to the front door key that was hidden in the toolbox on the front porch.

'Which one?'

'The blue metal one.'

'The blue metal one,' she said. 'Is it obvious?'

'Yes. There are other keys. The front door key's the one

with the elephant tag. Not the Chubb, that's for ... Not the Chubb.'

'Got it.'

We disconnected and I lay down. I should have felt calmer, but the call had inspired other anxieties. She was out; I could tell that from the background noise. Did that mean there would be further delay before Maudie was rescued? Maybe she would ring Tom and ask him to go in? In that case *he would go into my house.* And, even putting that danger aside, other matters were unresolved. I hadn't specified water. She would give Maudie water, wouldn't she? Even a non-pet owner knew to give a pet water. And a walk? Should I ring her back and ask her to walk her? But maybe it would be better if she didn't. Ailsa was so lax. *Oh, let her off.* No sheep, or farmers with guns, but squirrels, and cars. If I rang her back, either way, it would annoy her.

All these thoughts churned. It strikes me now how odd it was that I didn't think more about the music behind her, the distracted snippiness of her tone. I think I had already begun to perceive I could be an irritation. She hadn't, for example, asked if she could visit me, or whether I needed anything. Does that sound self-pitying? I suppose it does. I had often had the sense that something was going on in her mind, that her reactions were fed by a deeper well. But I had become too wrapped up in myself. I just think if I had spent a bit more time wondering what was up with her, things might have turned out differently.

One more thing, too: would it have been so awful if Maudie had spent the night alone? It seemed unimaginable at the time. In the end the consequences of my efforts to avoid it were much worse.

Chapter Twenty-one

Blue mohair wool, loose

Disclosure, *noun*. The action or fact of revealing new or secret information; action of making something openly known; an instance of this.

I've been thinking a lot about what happened after I left the hospital – or rather, not about what happened, but about how to *report* what happened. I had thought all along that I might miss it out of the narrative. The books Ailsa reads, her TV shows, they're so often about 'secrets', as if secrets are something dangerous and invasive, like a deadly gas. Personally, I've always been of the belief that secrets are the natural state of affairs, simply an incident or action one chooses not to tell anyone else. Surely that is a basic human right? We all have our skeletons. So it is painful to tell this, though as I reach this point in the story, I realise anything that contributed to Ailsa's mental state, so close to the murder, is relevant.

It was a surprise to learn it was raining in the outside world. Proper August monsoon rain. A warm, blustery wind threw the drops sideways, like a dog romping with a much smaller dog – playful, but threatening; that kind of wind, that kind of rain.

I half expected to see Ailsa waiting for me. Stupid, really. She had no idea what time I was leaving. Grateful for my cardigan, I half ran, half lolloped to the bus stop, just as the bus was drawing in. The T-shirt of the boy in front of me in the queue was soaked, clinging to his shoulder blades. Inside the bus it was warm and humid, all summer dresses and furled-up umbrellas, the floor muddy and slippery. A woman at the next stop got on carrying a paper bag full of oranges, but the paper was so wet it disintegrated and oranges spilt onto the floor. I helped her pick them up and then sat on the back seat, watching the rain-streaked backstreets flicker by, clutching my bag and a package of medicine on my lap. I'd been shown what to do with the inhaler; I'd been given iron to take for anaemia; I'd make a follow-up appointment with my GP. All would be well and all manner of things ... And yet again I was filled with unnamed foreboding. Its focus was the dog, and probably at the back of my mind was delayed shock and a perfectly natural anxiety about my own health. But it was something else – call it instinct, or its plainer cousin, suspicion. I began to fiddle with the cardigan. It was loosely knitted in blue mohair. I'd found it on the station steps several months previously and it had become something of a favourite. But the mohair had become very bobbly and I pulled at the patches where the loose threads had bunched – which was easier to do because it was damp – until I had quite a sizeable ball in my hand.

When we drew close to my stop, I collected my things and stood up, and waited by the door until we reached it. As the door slid open, I glanced back at where I'd been sitting, and on the floor I saw a small patch of blue, the size of a robin's egg – and it took me a moment to realise it was the wool I'd gathered. I must have dropped it as I stood up. Not that it mattered, of course; it was nothing. I stepped out onto the pavement but as I walked along the last stretch of road, the sense of dread I'd experienced was compounded. It sounds ridiculous, but I felt a pang of regret for the wool, as if I'd separated it from a parent, as if I'd left something precious behind.

The gate to my front garden was wide open. A plastic cup from McDonald's had blown onto the path. A Tesco bag lay sodden, and I picked it up. In the porch the blue toolbox sat, innards exposed, lid cast aside. I saw immediately that both keys, the Yale and the Chubb, were missing. I put my own key in the lock, braced to exert the usual pressure, to force it open against whatever might impede its path. But it swung back easily.

In the hall, I expected to walk into post, junk mail, free magazines, bags of items, recent findings, including the stool and kettle, but a space had been cleared along the middle of the floor, and in it were two footprints, the outline pale brown against the dark wooden boards. No welcoming click of Maudie's claws. Her absence set up a dull tolling of disquiet. I closed the front door and laid down the wet plastic bag on top of the small pile that had collected there. It was warmer inside than out, the house full of trapped air, and it smelt different. The meaty sweetness that had begun to turn my stomach had something sharper in it, too: basil or citronella. I took a step and felt the walls rustle, brace in alarm, or warning. A flurry of rain rattled against the sitting-room window. The nozzle of one of the vacuum cleaners resting next to a mirror slid sideways.

I should charge my phone. Ring Ailsa. Or I could knock next door. I was thinking all this, but I didn't do any of those things. I took another step towards the staircase. I could tell, couldn't I? I could sense her presence. The anticipation, the anxiety, the *conviction* I'd held all morning had reached its apotheosis. I knew her so well. How could I have ever thought she wouldn't?

I looked up to the first floor. I craned my head, trying to see round the bend of the bannisters but I could only see the bathroom door and it was closed. And then I heard a sound; not an accidental sound – not an object slipping or sliding, or blown, not a rattle. This sound was purposeful, and human: the deliberate clunk of a cupboard being closed.

My chest tightened; I found it harder to fill my lungs, and I used the bannister rail to help myself up, the dirty wood rough beneath my palms. The row of books on the top stair had been disturbed, one of the A–Zs I'd found in Oxfam kicked side-ways, lying open at a map of Southall, and I could see as I approached that the blanket that ran along the bottom of Faith's door had been rolled aside. The door was ajar, reveal-ing a triangle of artificial light – surprising, I thought, even in my agitation, that the bulb still worked. Small, studied sounds came from in there: a shuffle, a rustle, a click.

I stood and waited. The ferns on the landing wallpaper were hands gesticulating, faces gurning in warning.

From my own bedroom on the next half-landing came the sound of water, the soft thud as each drop landed on the newspaper under the bucket.

I was about to write that my heart was in my mouth, but that is such a silly phrase. It would mean blood and liquid, pulsing life. My mouth was arid, empty, completely dry. I tried to swallow and I couldn't. My throat had seized up. The tightness was back in my chest; my hands gripped either side of my ribcage. I'd left the bag with the inhaler by the front door. I thought about going down to get it, but I knew if I did, I might leave the house, and I might never come back.

I put my hand against the panel and pushed.

It had been such a long time since I'd been in that room. It smelt of wet wood and apples and sweat and old perfume. The terrible smell, the one that got into your nostrils and set up home there, had long gone, though the Glade air fresheners were still strategically placed. Dust lay on every surface, as thick as underlay across the top of the chest of drawers, the desk, the surface of the pictures. Water had crept in through the broken window; seeped into the walls, peeling the wallpaper back, brown spreading to black below the cornice. One of the curtains had fallen away, the other hung in disintegrated loops from its hooks. Along the mantelpiece were nubs of an eerie yellow mould structure, which were the ends of the scented candles I'd lit. There were a lot of dead flies, too, but I didn't like to look at those.

A long thin mirror leant against the wall by the bed. It was an early skip find: it had plaster stuck to the back of it in swirly patterns. I used to sit on the floor next to it, watching Faith do her hair. I could see my reflection in it now; so pale it was as if death was coming into the room. Except death was already in the room.

She was sitting on the single bed, between me and the mirror, with her back to me. At first, I thought she didn't know I was there, but she spoke without turning round. 'Verity,' she said. She made my name sound like a groan.

I didn't want to look at what was on the bed next to her. I crossed my arms over my chest. I tried to make space in my airways, to clear my throat.

She twisted her head then. Her face was in the grip of what looked like a tremor. The lines above her eyebrows were pulled tight. She seemed to be fighting against something internal.

'What is this?' she said.

Thinking back, it shocks me that I didn't ask her the same question. Because she was the one who had let herself back into my house, who had watched and taken the key from its hiding place; she was the one who was trespassing. She was the one who had entered this, my most private place.

I took a step towards her. Her neck was twisted to face me, but her body was still rigidly turned away. I could see the sinews in her neck. Both hands were on the sides of the crate; knuckles white, clinging on. She was wearing a dark-coloured top, black leggings; I thought of her as a big black crow then, standing guard, a barrier, and I fought the urge to push her out of the way, to knock her sideways and gather up the contents of the crate, and hold it in my arms.

I still couldn't speak. My face felt as if it were swelling, my features like pinpricks, slashes, rough marks drawn on by a child. A flood, huge and unmanageable, unassailable, was waiting to gush through me. I tried to concentrate on her face, not on what was on the bed next to her. I managed to force my jaw to unhinge. My mouth was open, and a sound came out that I didn't recognise as belonging to me; a long drawn-out cry between a groan and a whimper. It didn't sound human, except I knew that it came from the most human part of me.

The shoebox. The scraps of pale-pink eiderdown, so soft, now rotted, darker. The white pillowcase I had used: grey. The bones.

'Verity?' she said again. It was still a question, more insistent than before.

I sank to the floor, falling forwards, my head in my hands. I dug my nails into my forehead. My hands were like claws. I wanted my forehead to bleed.

'Is it an animal?' she said.

Is it an animal? She didn't know.

'Is this a body?'

Tiny matchstick bones, tendons, muscles, the palest dark sheen of skin.

'Verity. What is this in the box?'

The head large, the limbs fragile. Veins. Blood: the mass and mess of it.

'Verity.'

I still didn't speak. I couldn't. I had begun to cry. I really didn't want to. My head bowed, my body convulsed. I was gasping for breath between sobs. She touched my shoulder as I did so, and I wished that she wouldn't, that she would take her hand away.

I began to intone the word.

'I can't hear what you're saying.'

When I raised my head, she said, 'You're going to have to stop crying. I can't understand what you're saying.'

The sobs had taken on a terrible rhythm, and even though I had forced them under control, they continued to rise.

I'd never said it out loud before, the word so round and full, so real. And my stomach clenched as if trying to draw him back. I wished I could bring the word back too, as soon as I had said it, because it wasn't right. I didn't deserve it.

'A baby.'

She stood up then; I sensed her tower over me. She knocked my thigh with the edge of her shoe as she passed. A noise at the back of her throat – disgust and horror, maybe trying to say something and failing – and then her steps across the floor, a clatter, almost a tumble down the stairs, through the hall and finally the slam of the front door.

I don't know how long I sat there with my forehead pressed into my knees; minutes, an hour? If I could have turned myself to stone I would have; anything but standing, picking up a life. All this time reality, and the exposure of it, had been waiting and I'd known it and yet I'd carried on. I had got up and gone out, and worked, and inhabited days and met people with whom I felt I could be friends, and at night I had slept. I didn't know how I could have done any of that. I was monstrous.

Eventually, I pushed my head off my knees and sat for a bit with my eyes closed. And then for a while I sat with my eyes open. And then, gradually, I began to wrap the bones back up in the pillowcase and laid it again in the shoebox, and I gathered the bits of the dried flowers that hadn't turned to dust and I scattered them on top. I put the lid back on the shoebox and I carried it through to my room and pushed it under my bed, way at the back against the wall. I wasn't hiding it this time; I just didn't want the police grabbing it straight away. I wanted them to take care. I wanted to know, when they did come, that I'd have a little more time, a few more minutes, to make sure of that.

The kitchen table was inaccessible again at that point so I sat at my desk in the front room. I didn't know how long it would be, whether she would ring 999 or 101, whether they'd come in a squad car or on foot.

When – how long later? An hour? Two? Time had extended, stretched, or suspended, perhaps I was beyond time – I heard the front door open, I was just sitting there, with my hands on my lap, crossed as if already in handcuffs, calm now, waiting.

She stood in the doorway to the sitting room. I could see the back of her head in the mirror behind. The space behind her expanded and hung, empty. The sounds in the street were normal, cars and vans, a single thundering lorry. I got to my feet.

She stared at me, calmly. 'I've been for a walk. Tom's at work or I'd have . . . I couldn't stay. You do understand. I had to get some air. I'm not sure what has happened here, or what

I should do about it, but as I was walking, Verity, I thought I should perhaps first give you a chance to explain. I'm not sure I want you to, but we are . . . we've been friends. I've become fond of you and you've done so much for Max and I owe it to you to listen at least.'

I nodded, hands still clasped. 'Yes. Yes. I will explain. I can.'

'So please could you tell me what that is up there? What's happened?'

I stood up then. 'Do you want to sit down?' I began to move the books and the piles of newspapers, the bags of clothes from the sofa.

'I'm fine here,' she said. 'I'm OK standing.'

'OK. Right. Yes.'

She was twisting her fingers, her eyes skittering about the room. The house was pressing in on her. 'So there's a baby there. A dead baby. Verity. Whose baby is it. *Was* it?' Her face scrunched; she was beginning to lose control. 'Was it Faith's?'

'No.'

'Whose, then?'

It came out, piercingly, like a cry. 'Mine.'

'Yours?'

'Yes.' I clamped my hands to my mouth.

'You killed your baby?'

'No. No.' I looked into her face, saw her expression: the terrible doubt, disbelief, but also a kind of savage, naked distress; and I realised what she thought, and it was so horrific I forced my eyes away. But I couldn't deny it. It was the truth, too; life and death, the line between them so fine.

I began to speak, hoping she would hear, that she would follow, that she would make sense of the hideous, dark, painful fragments in the wrong order, too linear, but it was the only way I could bring myself to say it. I told her about that night with Adrian Curtis, we'd slept with each other, the beast with two backs, when you know you know, and how I'd ignored him at work the following day and didn't answer the phone when he rang, and how I'd prayed that would be the end of it, and it seemed perhaps it was, and I'd put it out of my mind, thought nothing of consequences, and cause and effect, and then a few months later, I'd been changing Mother's dressings when I'd felt a terrible pain.

Her frown deepened. She thought it was a digression, a bid for sympathy. 'A pain?'

I kept going, despite the revulsion in her face: how the pain had stretched up and across my abdomen, and how it came out of nowhere and I'd believed it to be indigestion, not the curse, as my mother called it, because I was forty-four and I'd believed that to be over. I didn't tell her how frightening it was when it began to happen, when I realised what it was, sitting on the toilet on my own in the bathroom, because it didn't matter what I felt. Someone told me once you should grip the soft bit of flesh between your thumb and forefinger to keep an emotion under control and I did that when I was telling Ailsa.

There were pauses and long silences.

And at the end, when there seemed to be nothing else to say, I said: 'He didn't have a chance because he only had me and he was so small. I tried to keep him alive. I wrapped him in a towel and I pressed his chest and I held him, but he never even made a sound. I couldn't see a breath. His skin was translucent – you could see the light through it, but it got darker, like blood, like rust, as I held him and colder, and then he got even colder, even though I'd done everything I thought – I'd used nail scissors and tied the cord, and I wrapped him next to my skin, and tried to keep him warm. His eyes were tight. He was no bigger than . . .' I held up my hand, though I still gripped that soft bit of skin between my fingers. 'I tried to keep him warm,' I said again.

I looked across at her. She had sat down at the far end of the sofa. 'Oh, Verity,' she said. Her mouth had slackened, her shoulders slumped. 'Oh, Verity,' she said again. 'You had a baby. You lost a baby.'

Lost. *Lost*. It's a verb I held on to.

'I knew Mother would want her bath so I cleaned the floor. I used toilet roll and all the towels that were in there to scrub up the blood, and I held him to my chest the whole time. I didn't want to put him down. He was so light there was almost nothing to him. I was crying and bleeding and I was trying to keep quiet. And when I heard her moving downstairs, I took him into my room, and swaddled him in a pillowcase and laid him on the bed while I found a clean towel for her. I put a wash on then, while she was in the bath. And I cooked supper because she was expecting it, and later I put him in a shoebox and put that in the plastic crate. I'd filled it with soft things, and teddy bears.'

'Oh, Verity.' She had moved while I was talking and was sitting on the sofa in front of me now. 'How old was the baby? How many weeks pregnant were you?'

I knew what she was asking. 'Twenty-three weeks,' I said. 'We only did it the once. It was easy to calculate.'

I saw the relief in her face then. 'It wasn't your fault. He was too little. He couldn't have survived. Oh, Verity. You didn't tell anyone? You did it all on your own?' Her eyes were wide and full. 'You should have rung for an ambulance. You wouldn't have been in trouble. They'd have given you counselling. And you'd have had support. They'd have, you know . . .' She was squeezing her hands. '. . . taken the body.'

My voice broke. 'I didn't want them to take the body.'

'I can't believe what I thought.' She was shaking her head. 'When I saw the bones, that you . . . you'd be capable of that.

But Max is so fond of you. *I'm* fond of you. You're clever and sharp, and yet – *this*. I don't know anyone else who could have just . . . I don't know how you managed to carry on as if nothing had happened.'

As if nothing had happened. I didn't know how to tell her how the previous ten years had been an effort of engineering, how I had shored these fragments – this fucking house – against my ruin. 'I put his little bed in Faith's room,' I said, 'because he'd be safe there and no one ever went in. And I visited all the time at first, to make sure he was OK, but then I did have to stop.'

There were things I couldn't disclose. It had been a hot, dry summer. I'd done what I could to make it better, with the candles and the air fresheners, and I laid the rug along the bottom of the door. Mother kept saying she thought a rat had died under the floorboards. In the end it did go away, but I never went into the room again.

I sat on the arm of the sofa. I wasn't sure if she'd mind me being that close, but she didn't move away. Her hands fluttered in the space between us. I clasped mine on my lap. 'Is that when you began to collect things?'

'Maybe. Yes. I mean it's always been . . . but yes, it got much worse.'

'And not taking care of yourself?'

I looked up to the ceiling. 'I'm not worth taking care of.'

'Does Faith know?'

I shook my head. 'She was away.'

She said, 'I'm so sorry, Verity.' It seemed to encapsulate other things she couldn't say. 'I'm glad you've told me. You should have told me before. If I'd known the damage of this, it would have made it easier to help you.'

I got off the arm of the sofa and kneeled on the floor in front of her.

My voice cracked: 'Can't I just keep him?'

Ailsa's eyes had filled again with tears. 'I think we should tell someone,' she said. 'You should get help.'

'Do I need help?'

She looked at me then. I could see she was considering. 'Let me think what the best thing is,' she said.

'Please don't tell Tom,' I said.

She sighed. 'I won't. But maybe we should get in touch with your sister.'

I didn't speak. I couldn't. We sat there in silence for a bit longer. I was coughing a little.

She breathed in deeply. 'This house,' she said. 'It's even worse than before. You can't live here.'

I tried to make it look as if I were breathing properly. 'I'm going to have another clear-out. I promise.'

She stood up. 'Pack a bag and come home with me tonight. I want to keep an eye on you.'

Chapter Twenty-two

1 baby's plastic dummy, white

Contact, verb intrans. To come into, or be in, contact.

Today's appointment was at 2 p.m. but Ailsa was at the front door, waiting for me to unlock it, at noon. She was wearing her green silk – poignant that she chose that dress in particular, the dress Ricky Addison had so admired. It's a little creased these days, and it's a thin fabric; I made her wear tights with it, and the maroon puffer.

It was a smooth journey, though neither of us had checked the destination before setting off; the contact centre purporting to be in Vauxhall was, when we checked Google Maps, closer to Oval Tube: an easy diversion, though it did nothing for Ailsa's nerves.

I hadn't known what to expect. The centre has 3.4 stars on Google; though the staff seem to respond promptly to all complaints ('We're sorry to hear you found the experience "like going to prison". We do our best to ensure . . .'). It was a low, unimpressive building, 1980s-built, squeezed between tower blocks. Two boys of about eleven were pulling wheelies on small bikes outside. A black and white cat perched on a big green bin. The online gallery of pictures makes much of a garden, but that must be at their outpost in Solihull, because there was no sign of any outside space.

A social worker saw us coming through the doors and took us straight into a small room, made more mournful by the naked attempt to cheer it with a naïve mural: a tree, an owl, lots of pink and yellow birds. Nursery toys and books, a train set and a plastic miniature kitchen were placed along one side; on the other, a sofa covered in a red fabric like something you might stretch over a sports car. There was a low table, several mismatched chairs. The room smelt of boiled sweets and bad breath, and the carpet gave a scrunch as you walked across it. I hesitate to say it was sticky; it may have been underlay.

I sat on the red sofa and made weather-based conversation with the social worker, a friendly faced, grey-haired woman in a polka-dot dress and a man's black cardigan. Her person was rather cluttered: pins in her hair, and glasses on a string and an official lanyard around her neck which she kept flicking and rearranging. A book bag, overstuffed with papers and evidence of a half-eaten packed lunch, slumped at her feet. I experienced a welling of fellow feeling. Ailsa, hunched at the table, looking closely at her poor, raw hands, ignored us both.

We seemed to wait ages, though it was probably only ten minutes, until at last there were voices and movement in the corridor outside. Ailsa leapt to her feet and took a run at the door as Melissa and Bea came in, followed by another younger social worker. Seconds before, Ailsa had been dull, enervated; now she looked suddenly quite deranged. Her hair has become a bit of a bird's nest and her gestures were big, her expression contorted by eagerness. Both children instinctively recoiled, and Bea, rearing back, scraped her arm on the metal bit of latch. Ailsa threw herself at her, letting out a high keen, a sympathetic 'Oh oh oh', trying to kiss the scratch, to rub it better, until the new social worker, who was suited and pony-tailed, pulled her off and encouraged her to sit down.

'Where's Max?' Ailsa said, standing up again.

'He didn't want to come.' Melissa's voice was clear and defensive. 'He—'

'It's best not to push initial contact,' the young suited social worker interrupted quickly. She was looking intently at Ailsa, nodding. 'Next time.'

Ailsa stared and then slowly sat down, matching her nod. 'Next time.'

It's only a handful of weeks since I've seen the children, but they both looked different. Melissa's hair is white-blonde now, with dark roots, and she was wearing an A-line skirt and a blouse with a Peter Pan collar. Bea's hair was in bunches and her oyster pink frock was almost bridesmaid in its laciness and flounce. Clearly Cecily Tilson had had her terrible way with both of them. Their faces looked different, too. I was about to write older, but actually *younger*: bruised and vulnerable, with a strain around the eyes, but a looseness to the mouth as if emotion was close to the surface – which I suppose it was.

It was awkward, awful at first. I greeted the children warmly but then returned to the sofa and sat quietly, feeling it was best to stay out of the way. Both social workers perched on chairs near the door, writing notes, while Ailsa battled through a series of questions, trying to sound upbeat – bless her – like it was any ordinary day. How had they got here? So Granny was waiting outside in the car, was she? How was the school? Oh dear, why did Max hate it? Had they been riding? Or shopping? I averted my eyes, trying not to look as if I were listening, and my gaze settled on a white baby's dummy, abandoned in the corner, behind the plastic kitchen sink. I thought of all the other meetings that had happened here, fathers and mothers and babies – so many families broken by alcohol or drugs, or abuse or crime or acrimonious divorce.

Ailsa's voice, higher, more strained now: 'Any plans for Halloween?'

'Max and I are going trick or treating with Auntie Jane,' Bea said. 'It's going to be super fun.'

'That's nice.' The agony in Ailsa's response was palpable.

Melissa looked down at her phone. 'Auntie Jane thinks we should move in with her when it's all over. Lizzie's off to university and Charlotte will be on her gap year next year, so she's got space. Grandma's not so keen. She wants us to herself.'

When it's all over. Is that the way even *they* think it's going?

Ailsa didn't speak at first. She stared at Melissa. The older social worker looked up from her notebook. Someone's lanyard clattered. Outside, a large dog started barking. An aeroplane snarled. If you listened carefully, you could hear the traffic on the main road, the shudder of a bus. In the room, the silence yawned.

'What about Max?' Ailsa said.

'Oh, Max,' Melissa said. 'He says Auntie Jane doesn't like him.'

Ailsa's skin was so pale it was almost translucent. She looked at the social workers. 'Jane's not used to boys,' she said. Her tone was heartbreaking.

I decided to speak then, and I launched in, rather as one might plunge headlong into cold water. One of the contestants on *Love Island*, I'd read in the tabloids, was joining something called *TOWIE*. What did this mean, for the state of human civilisation?

Melissa and Bea looked across at me and Bea muttered something which Ailsa grabbed on to, managing to keep the subject going for a while. It was too awful to bear but at some point, Bea got up and slid over to sit on her mother's knee. It was self-conscious and fey; she was too big for it. I thought of that lunch in the pub when she'd sat with her arms around Tom's neck. But it was better, much better, than nothing.

When the younger social worker closed her notebook and got to her feet, Ailsa didn't groan or cry out as I'd feared. She tipped Bea off her lap and stood too, her head doing the same controlled, neat nodding as at the beginning. She hugged Bea to her tightly and then put her arms out for Melissa. I'd worried Melissa would shun her – she looked sullen again, her face closed – but she came round the table, jostling past the chairs, and the two of them stood, holding each other until the social worker gently peeled them apart.

'I'm never going to see them again,' Ailsa said as we left the building.

'Don't be over-dramatic. Of course you will.'

'Why didn't Max come?'

I wanted to say I didn't know, but I felt a tug at the back of my throat, as if my own disappointment was a solid weight, pulling the words down. Behind my eyes, I could see his face, his earnest expression, his habit of screwing up his lower lip when he was concentrating, his hair stuck up at the back. I could hear his voice in my head, the gruffness that undercut his laugh. Until that point, I don't think I'd realised how much I'd been looking forward to seeing him myself.

'Doesn't he want to see me?' Ailsa said. 'I wanted to see him. How do I know he's OK otherwise?'

I forced myself to sound easy. 'Maybe he had another commitment, a rugby match or something.' As I said it, I realised it was Tom who had piled on the pressure to play rugby and that Max no longer had that pressure. It's awful to admit it but, with an eruption in my chest, for the first time I was glad he was dead.

We were getting close to the main road, and it was noisy, or we'd have heard the car door. Thinking back, maybe I did hear it – a distant clunk above the rattle of a lorry. But it was the sound of rapidly advancing footsteps that made me spin my head.

Behind was the contact centre; people standing in a gaggle, and a car with its door open onto the pavement. The black and white cat was still there, down from the bin now, washing itself on the ground. The sun was out and had caught the windows on one side of the tower block. But none of that mattered, because running towards us, tripping over his feet slightly, gaining on us with every second, was Max. Darling Max.

'Mum!' he shouted. 'Verity! Wait.'

Chapter Twenty-three

3 pale-grey cushion covers

Abreaction, *noun*. Discharge of the emotional energy associated with a psychic trauma that has been forgotten or repressed; the process of bringing such a trauma back to consciousness.

Later, we learnt how he had struggled to get out of Cecily's car; that the child locks were on in the back, and he had banged on the window, scratched to get out. Not that she was trying to stop him. It was Max who hadn't wanted to see his mother; Max who, when he saw me, had changed his mind. Moments like that give me added purpose.

It's time now to go back to the morning Tom died. I need to think it through.

That scene in Lionel Bart's *Oliver!* (Faith's favourite) when he wakes up in Mr Brownlow's house and the light is pouring in, and flower girls are singing outside his window and you think everything is going to be OK: that was me, the morning of Tom's death. I woke in Ailsa's spare room, between something called a topper and the bounciest of duvets, finding the whiteness not actually sterile, but blissfully clean and sharp. It had rained again in the night; the crack of window between the curtains glistened with drops.

Maudie was sprawled on a sheepskin rug and I reached down to stroke her. Max had washed her; she was as white and fluffy as the dead lamb on which she lay. She licked my hand. The oatmeal carpet around the rug, if you looked closely, was made of little flecks of different-coloured wool: cream and ivory and taupe. It was actually quite attractive. I thought of the Herberts' beige carpet piled up in the skip like sheets of tripe, and I remembered how much I had hated the waste. Maybe I'd been wrong. Change could be good.

My body felt looser, from having rested, from breathing properly again, but also from something deeper and more fundamental. I thought about the birth, and the death; the tiny body; and I felt pain, but love too. Ailsa had called it a loss. *A loss.* I felt the enormity of what had happened, the relief of finally letting something go.

My clothes were folded neatly on the chair and I dressed and opened the bedroom door. Noises rose from the kitchen; the suck of the fridge door, the whoosh of the boiling-water tap, a murmur of voices. Tom was still in the house. I'd managed to avoid him the previous evening; like a child, I'd been put to bed at seven. Maybe I should wait until he left for Paris before I went down. But Maudie stretched and nosed my knee, and I stepped out onto the landing.

Ailsa's voice was at the back end of the kitchen, but Tom was closer to the kitchen door. I caught the odd tense word – 'disinfectant'; 'Eurostar'. He came out of the kitchen, and his voice got louder. He was a few feet below on the other side of the bannisters. I held Maudie by the collar, and shrank back against the wall. The scrape of wood, the brush of fabric, as he opened the cupboard under the stairs. He said: 'The dog stinks. Tell Max not to get any ideas.'

I got myself back up the two steps and into the bedroom. I sunk onto the floor, the door behind me. Maudie pushed her muzzle into my hand, and I stroked her head, which felt uneven and bony. Tom came up the stairs, inches from my face on the other side of the door, and climbed the next flight, and then up one more. 'Fuck's sake,' he said under his breath, two sibilants, two hard 'k's: a double-headed snake and the aggression of the voiceless velar stop. On Maudie's haunches I felt a couple of lumps. Fatty tissue – I'd Googled; idiopathic, age-related. Nothing to worry about. Nothing to worry about at all.

A door opened above my head, and his footsteps crossed the ceiling. A scuffle, the thump of feet, a heavy object falling with a clunk, Tom's voice, stifled but still distinct through the lathe and the plaster. 'Mud everywhere . . . Tidy up. Now.' A door slammed, and his footsteps clonked back down the stairs – that heavy tread I could hear through the walls in my own house – past my door and onwards, his hand banging on top of the bannister, down the staircase to the hall. Ailsa's voice, soothing. 'Have you got everything? Passport? Tickets? Phone? Calm down. I'll wash them.' The front door opened. 'See you tomorrow,' she called. And finally the front door closed.

Did she lean against it with her eyes shut, feeling the relief of his departure? The house had held its breath and let it go. The walls relaxed. The joists loosened. Upstairs, in the room above, I felt vibrations of steps, the sash thrown open, the closed air freed, and out of the window a high-pitched shout – a release of tension.

I splashed water on my face, took a puff from my inhaler and left the room.

Ailsa was in the kitchen, her laptop open in front of her. She was wearing pale-blue cotton pyjamas, with navy piping on the collar. The sun was throwing small box-like flickering shapes across the wall behind her. Maudie ran out through the open doors and crouched to relieve herself in the middle of the grass. On the terrace sat three black bin bags, bulbous with soil, spikes of green emerging from their gathered tops. You could hear the growl of next door's lawnmower. Andrew Dawson already preparing his betrayal.

She looked up when she saw me standing in the doorway. 'I've found a new website – Fat Flavours, Thin Thighs; this Indian guy was a serial dieter for years until he discovered an ancient Ayurvedic system which uses low-fat, high-protein superfoods – spices, which have natural anti-oxidising qualities, apparently also speed up your metabolism.' She tapped her stomach twice and inhaled deeply, squeezing it in. 'Chicken, with ginger, coriander and turmeric – my supper tonight. The kids won't touch it, but I'll make a big pot and batch it into portions and freeze them. I'm turning over a new leaf, starting today.'

She closed the laptop and stood up. She looked tired, dark smudges under her eyes like bruises. There was tension in her face, something poised to break. 'Did you sleep well?'

I nodded.

'Good. I'm so glad. You really needed it. Now what can I get you for breakfast?'

I sat down, feeling awkward, intensely vulnerable. I thought maybe we would talk as we had the day before, but she seemed to be pretending everything was normal. She started opening cupboards, finding cereal, a bowl, milk.

Outside, Maudie was sniffing at the base of one of the bags of plants. Ailsa watched her and said: 'I've brought back up a few cuttings from Somerset. I don't know if they'll live but I thought they'd be nice in the wild bit at the back. I'm not sure what Maudie can smell. Fox probably.'

I clicked my fingers and Maudie raised her head and tapped back into the kitchen, leaving footprints on the floor. 'You're a good dog,' I said into her neck. 'A very good dog.'

'So . . .' Ailsa sat down next to me, her feet on the crossbars of the chair, hands resting between her thighs. 'I need to talk to you about a couple of things.' She sighed. 'The timing isn't great. I wanted to talk to you yesterday, but obviously, well, it wasn't at all the right time. I could wait, but I don't want to risk you finding out from anyone else.'

I didn't like this. I shook some Bran Flakes into the bowl and poured on milk.

'Look at me,' she said.

There was a red speckle in the corner of her eye; a burst capillary. Her lips were dry, rough around the edges. She said, 'So, first of all, I want you to know I'm going to give you as much help as you need. We'll start with your GP, or social services. I can come, too. There are health issues – your chest, for starters. And you've carried this trauma, and probably grief for your mother; we'll get you help, some counselling. And . . . the box.' She couldn't bring herself to say 'body'. 'They'll take it away, you can properly put the baby to rest.'

I nodded. 'Yes,' I managed to say. 'OK.'

'And we'll really sort the house this time. We'll start again. Tom thinks you've got dry rot – so I think we should bring in professionals.' She smiled, raising her hand to halt my objections. 'The house, your hoard, your mental health – it's all connected. We'll confront both issues head-on.'

If this was what she was frightened of talking to me about, I could cope, I could manage. I'd make an appointment with the GP that day. I'd start clearing the house again then, that day, that minute.

I nodded. 'OK.'

'That thing you said yesterday about not being worth it. You *are* worth it.'

A breeze ruffled the drying-up cloth on the back of the chair. The shadow on the wall flickered, brightened. Did she really think I was worth it? It seemed such a huge and wonderful thought.

She looked at me, her eyes enquiring, waiting for me to answer, and I was about to speak, to bring into this world of revelation and forgiveness the thing, the final secret I had hoped never to have to put into words, when her phone emitted a little chirrup and she glanced at the screen. Wincing, she said, 'Sorry, shit. I do have to take this.'

She stood up and turned away from me, leaning into the island. Her left arm rested on the top of her head. 'Ah,' she said. 'I'm glad you rang. Could we rearrange this morning? Tomorrow – would that be OK? Great. Yup. So if you do the photos then, you can still get the brochure out by next week? And online?' A pause. 'No. We don't want anyone before the weekend. Yes, exactly. Working on it. OK, bye.'

She picked at something – a bit of dried milk, perhaps – on the marble top and then she slowly turned round, leaving the phone behind her.

She stroked the back of her hand across her mouth, rested it there and then took it away. She sat down again next to me and gripped the sides of the chair, her shoulders hunched, like someone walking on crutches.

'So what I have to say: I know you're not going to like it. And I'm not thrilled myself. It's just it's the best option.'

My mouth was dry.

'I don't know – maybe it isn't bad timing, maybe it's good. It'll galvanise us both. And nothing will change. I promise.' She picked up my empty bowl, clasped it in her hands, and then put it down in front of her, with a decisive clunk.

'What?'

She held her hands up in a comic demonstration of dismay. 'We've decided to flip the house.'

A shuffling in my head, a confusion. Flip the house? I was thinking mirror image. How would they do that? My house already *was* the mirror image.

She had returned her hands to her lap and she studied her fingers. 'It means moving sooner than we expected, but as you know Tom's company isn't bringing in quite the business we were expecting. We've got this horrendous bridging loan. It's time to do it.'

Inside me something broke, or was about to break; as when a bottle slips from your hand and hasn't yet reached the floor. 'Moving?'

Her hand went to the side of her cheek. She said something about investment and profit on return. I had a narrative in my head and her words didn't fit, but still when she paused, I said: 'Are you being forced to? Is the bank foreclosing?'

'It was always the plan. It's always been temporary. We wouldn't have moved here otherwise. Tom doesn't want to live on a main road. It's what we do, you know that: find fixer-uppers. I told you when we first met. It's not an easy life – it takes effort keeping a house *sellable*.'

I looked around me, seeing the room for the first time. 'So that's why . . . it's like this?'

She frowned.

'So spartan?'

A flicker of a frown. 'I wouldn't say *spartan*. Just not crammed like yours! There's no point having loads of knick-knacks, sentimental items cluttering up the place. It puts buyers off.'

'Where to?' It came out like a small sob.

She was smoothing the edge of the table, back and forth, with both hands, watching herself do it. 'We thought – madly – about Somerset at first, but it's too much disruption for the kids. Bea wouldn't mind, but Max – he hates change. He's angry enough as it is. He likes living here. He likes living next door to you.' A quick grin. 'And anyway – the country; I've already discovered that's not for me. No – we're thinking . . . Crystal Palace? Sydenham?'

I felt my insides crumbling. 'I don't even know how you get to Sydenham.'

'We'll pop back and visit.'

'But I'm used to seeing you every day.'

She put her hand on top of mine. I stared down at it. I could see the rough, raw skin creeping round the edges of her fingers. 'I don't see you *every day* now. More like once a week – if that.'

Was she right? Did I only see her once a week? I'd imagined we lived in each other's pockets; how cosy that cliché, reducing us to little dormice. Was the truth bleaker and more mundane?

She was watching me. Thoughts seemed to skid across her face. 'In the short term I wondered if the two of us could have another go out the front? Tom got a guy to clear some of the bigger stuff when you were with us in Somerset – but you seem to have collected more since. It's still unsightly out there.'

So that's where the rotary dryer went. The fridge.

'As a favour to me, could you make it a bit better? I'll help. Not this afternoon – I'm seeing Ricky to talk more about his garden – but tomorrow?' She took a deep breath. 'Unless of course, you want to sell us *your* house,' she said. Her voice was light, deceptively casual.

For one glorious moment it seemed like the answer. She was smiling expectantly, and I smiled back – trying to copy her exact expression. 'Where would I go?' I said.

'We could find you something much more manageable, somewhere down in Tooting, closer to the Dog and Fox. Or Colliers Wood. I bet we'd find a bargain there.'

'Or Sydenham,' I said.

She gave a soft laugh. 'Exactly.'

I felt myself redden, tiny pinpricks of mortification across my neck. It was grotesque that she should buy it off me. A fixer-upper. A project. The back ripped off, plaster hacked from the ceilings, peels of wallpaper, the foundations gashed, yawning open. My dear house, where I'd lived with my mother and my sister; the years I had spent putting it together, filling it, shoring it up. The bricks, the mortar; all my precious possessions, how could I think about 'clearing' them? They were part of me. I could feel their presence from here, feel myself cleaving to them.

'But of course, it's a big step.' She brought her hand to her forehead. 'I just thought I'd mention it, put it out there.'

She was gripping the skin on her forehead with her nails now. They were leaving red marks. The conversation had taken something out of her. There was a bruise on the inside of her wrist; how had that got there? Her nervous habit with the hair, her poor, raw hands, her disappearances, her diets: all evidence of suppression. And the huge unspoken thing between us loomed into my head; it had been lying dormant and now it raged to life. My heart began to pound. 'Tom,' I said. 'It's Tom who's making you do this.'

'It's not him.'

'I think it is. Instead of moving, why don't you *leave* him?'

'Oh, Verity.' She shook her head.

I had bitten my lip – I could taste blood. 'He doesn't deserve you.'

'We're stuck with each other.'

'No. You don't understand what I'm telling you.' The knowledge of what I could tell her, of what I'd seen, grew and expanded and when it exploded inside me, I felt the shock of it as if for the first time myself. 'I've watched him. I know what he's like.'

She was still shaking her head, little trembles of her neck. 'There's nothing you can tell me about Tom I haven't seen for myself.' She let out a hard, mirthless laugh.

I put my hand on top of hers. Now the moment had come, I wasn't sure where to begin – with the party, or the night in Somerset. She was staring at me. I would let her know first she was safe, that she had somewhere to go. 'You and the children,' I said. 'You could always move in with me.'

She took her hand away. 'I don't want to move in with you.'

'I've left Max and you the house in my will.'

'What? Why?' She let out a shocked laugh. 'What are you trying to do? Hoard me?'

'No. Of course not.' I didn't know what to do with my face. I'd lost all sense of what was happening. 'Please, Ailsa. Believe me. You should leave Tom.'

Her eyes seemed to disappear. She looked furious, desperate. 'I don't understand you, Verity. You're clever and interesting and kind. And yet your view of the world can be so simplistic. Life is complicated. Maybe if it wasn't for him we wouldn't be moving. But we've got kids together, and they love him and he loves them.'

She started screwing her pyjama top together at the neck, as if trying to strangle herself. 'I hated how he shouted at Max this morning. I wish he didn't act like he hates them . . .' Her eyes and cheeks suddenly changed to an expression of exaggerated delight. 'Darling!'

I turned my head.

Max was standing in the doorway. He was wearing track-pants and his smart shirt from the party, the buttons done up wrong. Maudie had padded over to greet him and he bent down to stroke her head. I couldn't see his face. 'I'm sorry I got mud on the sofa,' he muttered. 'Dad said I had to stay and tidy my room, but I've finished and I've come downstairs to help you wash it.'

'Oh, sweetie.' Ailsa was already halfway towards him. 'Don't worry. Dad's away until Thursday. We've got plenty of time to launder the cushions. They'll be good as new when he gets back.'

He was still crouched down and she stood next to him, opening and closing her hands. She murmured, *Did he hear?*

I wanted to shake my head, but I didn't know. I shook it anyway. I tried to settle my heart.

'Right, I've got to get on.' She looked around the room, her eyes desperate. 'I've got that chicken and ginger to cook, all those plants to dig in. Plus I'm working at Ricky's this afternoon.' She didn't look at me, and there was a grim set to her jaw. 'And you've promised to have another go at clearing your front garden.' She stood up, tucking her hair into the neck of her pyjamas. 'So God, what's the time? I'd better go and get dressed.'

'OK then.' I went to hug her but she kept her arms by her side; I remember that now.

Chapter Twenty-four

Pizza Express Romana Margherita Speciale, 3 for 2

Formication, *noun*. **An abnormal sensation as of ants creeping over the skin**.

This morning, when I got back from taking Max to school, she wasn't in the front room or the kitchen. I assumed she had gone back to bed and didn't think too much about it. I was preoccupied. I've started a project of my own: the back sitting room study. It's years since anyone has opened the door, but last week I managed to push it the foot or so necessary to squeeze in and I've been systematically sorting it out. *Ruthless*. That's me. Sue helped me organise a skip and I've nearly filled it. It's going to be a nice space when it's finished. Light. Spacious. All it needs is a sofa and a TV. Anything will do. I'm keeping my eyes peeled.

I was listening to Classic FM – Mozart's Horn Concerto No. 4. It wasn't until it had drawn to its end that I realised one of the horns – of the hunting variety – was coming from the front room.

She'd left her phone in her nest on the sofa. I found it under the cushions. 'John Standling' read the screen. I answered. 'She's not here,' I said. 'She's sleeping, I think. Would you like me to wake her?'

'Well. If you think she wouldn't mind.'

'Hang on.'

I took the phone upstairs and knocked on the door of her room. No answer. She wasn't in Mother's, now Max's, either – though there were signs she'd been there recently. The cupboards were hanging open, and the shoeboxes were on the floor, with their lids off. I could smell her deodorant.

An inch of soapy water sat in the basin, but the bathroom was empty.

My bedroom door was shut and when I tried to open it, it wouldn't budge.

'Ailsa?'

'What?' Her voice was close; she was just the other side, using the weight of her body to keep me out.

'What are you doing in my room?'

'I won't be long.'

I took a sharp in-breath. Perhaps I should have forced the door. I've got into the habit of appeasing her.

'It's John Standling,' I said, mouth into the wood. 'On your phone.'

'You speak to him.'

I sat down on the top stair, watching the door, and brought the phone back to my ear.

'I heard that,' he said. 'OK. Right. Fine. Perhaps you could just ask her to ring me back.'

And then, because I wanted to hear what he had to say, I said: 'She won't. She's being funny about speaking to people at the moment.'

He sighed then. 'OK. Well I'll talk to you then. First of all – Max shouldn't be with you. Not with Ailsa in the house. We need to take measures before we get into trouble. I was hoping Ailsa could maybe come and see me – perhaps even this after-noon. We've just received the bulk of primary disclosure from the CPS and there are several other things I'd like to go over with her before her consultation on Friday with Silk.'

He always calls Grainger 'Silk'. I've begun to find it irritating. It's awful how familiarity breeds contempt.

'I'm not sure she's leaving the house at the moment,' I said. 'It might be better if you came to me.'

'That could be arranged.'

'Is there anything new?' I said. 'Anything we need to worry about.'

There was a long silence. 'Couple of things – some new witness statements, for example.'

'About what? From whom?'

A long pause. A woodlouse was inching along the base of the wainscot, legs hidden beneath the tiny armoured shell of its body. 'State of the marriage stuff. Pippa Jones. Ricky Addison . . .' He trailed off. 'I'm not going to go into it all now.'

I put my finger to block the woodlouse's path and it disappeared sideways into the crack between the wainscot and the floorboards. 'Do they say Tom was a bully?'

He sighed heavily again. 'This battered wife stuff, it isn't going to play. You do realise that? That scarf you gave me; I had it analysed. The red marks? They were nail varnish. No further evidence has come to light. Nothing ever reported to the GP, to the police, to social services. Mrs Tilson's statements make no reference to it. My clerk spoke to Tom Tilson's parents, friends, ex-girlfriends – Delilah Perch included. No one has ever experienced or witnessed any behaviour from Tom worthy of note, just normal husband–wife bickering. Mrs Perch was particularly vehement. She says he was under a lot of pressure at work, and that Mrs Tilson, Ailsa, was difficult to live with, never happy.'

The noises from my bedroom – small knocks and slithers

– had resumed. *Battered wife?* How language, under pressure, reveals people's true colours. I said: 'She was the victim in that marriage.'

Standling, responding to my tone, sounded tart: 'It's looking at this stage as if she was anything but.'

'Please elaborate.'

'We can talk more later. If it's OK with you, I'll come this afternoon. Around 3 p.m.? I'd rather talk about all this with Mrs Tilson in person.'

'Let me ask her.' I stood up, gripping the bannister to keep my balance. I turned my head, as the door to my bedroom slowly opened. A crack of mottled wallpaper, the plaster behind it spotted like coal dust. Ailsa stepped onto the landing. She was wearing Faith's pale-pink fleece dressing gown. The cuffs were grey; I should wash it. Something was dangling from her fingers. It looked like a piece of silk handkerchief; no, something more forlorn, like a used prophylactic. Her hands separated, and I saw there were two, each one gripped in the pincer of her index and thumb.

She was shaking her head. 'I knew it,' she said.

I still hadn't fully understood. I bury things, literally and metaphorically. At the back of the wardrobe in this case, in my box of precious things.

I disconnected Standling.

'The gloves,' I said. 'You've found the gloves.'

The day Tom died, I was highly aware, as I sat at the desk, of the comings and goings next door. Ailsa went out mid-morning for half an hour and came back with a bag of shopping. Bea left with a friend soon after, swinging a tennis racquet.

I sat in the garden to eat my lunch. The rain had done nothing to clear the heaviness of the air. It lay thick on one's skin, pressed into one's temples. Screws seemed to be tightening my chest; I took several puffs from my inhaler. The undergrowth looked thick and knitted; a smell of mildew filled my nostrils. It was quiet on their side of the fence. We now know she didn't plant the Somerset cuttings as she had told me she was going to. She did put on a wash and cook the curry, but I didn't hear or smell any evidence of that on my side. No wafting scent of garlic, or chilli, or coriander, just rotting grass, festering apples, the usual stench of wet towel.

Mid-afternoon, I left the house and walked to the supermarket for some Nurofen. They were doing a three for two on Pizza Express pizzas so I bought some of those, as well as a packet of special offer Mr Kipling Almond Slices, which Ailsa loves. Outside the shop, a metal crate-like cage was stuffed with deconstructed boxes and packaging, including sheets of soft blue cardboard moulded to fit a line of oranges. Halfway along Wiseton, someone had left a couple of cans of paint; bashed, but not completely empty. I carried them home, my arms full, laden, dragged by the weight, heavy with self-loathing. But, as I crossed the threshold and piled them in the already cluttered hallway, it felt like rebellion.

A little later, I decided what to do. I found a packet of pale-blue notelets that Ailsa had placed in one of the desk drawers. I didn't practise, or pre-prepare. I wrote straight from the heart. 'Tom has betrayed you,' I wrote. 'He is not worthy of being your husband, or a father to your children. He is having an affair. Keep the house. Get rid of him.' The last two sentences were an attempt at levity, but I underlined them three times.

I put the letter in the matching envelope, closed but not sealed, as my mother always insisted was etiquette with hand-delivered mail, and I went next door.

Melissa answered. 'Oh nice,' she said, when she saw the

pizzas and cakes. 'I've got a party tonight, but I'll have mine tomorrow. Do you want Mum? She's out.'

'I know. She's doing Ricky's garden.'

'Really? She was wearing her posh green dress. Are you here to tutor Max?'

I had held out my packages, the envelope on top, but at this I withdrew them. It was Wednesday. I'd forgotten.

Melissa went upstairs to find him and I walked down into the kitchen. I put the pizzas in the fridge and left the cakes on the table, the envelope still on top.

It was stuffy in the room; the doors were closed. A tired bumblebee was humming against the glass close to the floor and I unlocked the doors with the key and folded them back. The bee, still low and heavy, floated off. The cushion covers, big white squares, were hanging from the line. On the terrace, earth seemed to have spilt from Ailsa's plastic bags, but on closer inspection the scattered piles of black soil were moving and seething, growing wings: ants doing their pre-swarm thing.

'Ugh.' Max had come out to look too. 'It's horrible when I see loads of tiny insects. It makes me feel all wriggly in my stomach.'

I looked at him. He'd grown over the summer; his limbs had lost their soft roundness. He had freckles on his nose, and his hair, tufted and mussed at the back, was touched with golden streaks. I noticed again how one of his eyes sloped down more than the other, and was overwhelmed by love. He'd crept into my heart, this boy. And now they were moving away. I wasn't sure I could bear it. I cleared my throat. 'Excellent sensory description,' I said.

'What are they doing? Why are they behaving like that?'

'They're fleeing the nest, I think – preparing to set up a new colony elsewhere.'

'Moving home?'

'Yup.'

I could hear his child's breath, quicker and more shallow than an adult's.

'She told you we're going, didn't she?' he said.

'She did.'

He kicked the plastic bag containing plants with his foot. 'I don't want to move. I hate moving house all the time. They don't care, though. Dad says it's nothing to do with me. He doesn't like this house, he says.'

'He doesn't like living on the main road.'

'He doesn't like anything. He doesn't like me.'

The word came to me unbidden. It's a word Ailsa had used. 'Well he's an arsehole.'

'He ruins everything. He always does.'

All my unhappiness and anger was focused on Tom. 'Some people just do,' I said. 'If only we could stop them, but we can't.'

We both stared into the crinkled black plastic – at the muddled green tendrils.

'They're dying,' I said. 'She should have planted them already.' I bent down to adjust the bag that he'd knocked, and peered in. One of the fronds, a small but robust thing with delicate fern-like leaves and a thick, circular stalk, looked familiar. I bent to smell it, and Max asked what I was doing. I told him I was seeing if it smelt like mouse. 'What does mouse smell like?' he asked, and I laughed and said actually I wasn't sure; I'd never smelt a mouse. I pulled away. If it was hemlock, I thought, how clever it was to have slipped in alongside these other almost identical plants. Aggressive mimicry. Just like people. Yes – just like the way people pretend to be something they're not.

The big black winged ants had begun launching themselves into the air and we backed into the kitchen. I shut a couple of the doors, leaving the others open.

'Do I have to do work?'

'Not if you don't want to.'

'Oh good.'

'Rude,' I said.

I could hear him laughing as I inspected the pot on the stove, lifting the lid and getting a waft of garlic and cumin, like underarm sweat.

'You going to be eating this?' I said, conveying the answer in my intonation.

'No way. Not now you've bought us pizza.'

I hugged him at the door. 'Got any plans for the evening?' I asked.

'Probably *World of Warcraft*,' he said. 'As Dad's not here.'

'Is life easier when he's away?'

His face darkened. 'Yes it is.'

It was maybe 4.20 p.m. by then. Ailsa had not yet come home.

The Dog and Fox was busy that night; Maeve and Sue were back from France and Bob had brought his brother along (divorcing and at a loose end). We didn't do as well as usual, stymied by a nasty sports round; not our collective strong point. Still: an honourable third.

I walked home, cool night air on my skin after the warmth of the pub. Bursts of music and conversation reached me from open windows; the clatter of plates, laughter from a group of people gathered on a balcony. A fire engine screamed up the hill, overtook a waiting car at the lights and branched right down St James's Drive. The peal of the siren was still ringing in my ears when I drew close enough to see the police car and ambulance ahead of me, the lights on the police car's roof set to a sliding flicker – a migraine blue-white strobe. I began to run, breathless when I arrived, pulse racing, fear spooling in my head. People on the other side of the road had huddled to stare. The Tilsons' door was wide open, and a policeman in a high-vis vest was standing at the top of the steps, legs apart, like he was standing guard. It's the thing I keep thinking about even now, actually: the chilling nature of that open door.

'What's happened?' I shouted. Sue and Andrew Dawson from two doors down were out on the pavement, both in shorts and flip-flops. Another officer was talking to them, I think, though it's odd: I don't remember the details, just a sense of the air turning blue-white, electricity in it, lighting the air, turning night to day. 'Who is it?' I shouted. Melissa had told me she was going out, Tom was away. So – Ailsa, or Bea, or Max. Sue and Andrew ignored me: they always do.

A female police officer must have stopped me going up to the house. I found evidence the following morning of physical force: a fresh blister on the base of my thumb torn open. Now I think of it, she simply took my hand to drag me away. I was crying, I know; maybe I was shouting. But was I a danger? No; an object of pity, an embarrassment.

Was I family? One of them asked.

I nodded, *because I was as good as*, but Sue was still there, and she told them I wasn't.

It seems odd, looking back, that they didn't tell me sooner. I mean you'd think, wouldn't you, that they'd want to put people's minds at rest? Or maybe they weren't fully informed, the policemen outside. Maybe they thought a death wasn't anything to put anyone's mind at rest about. Thing is, I didn't know Tom was home. I thought he was away. Something dreadful had happened – an accident. That's all I knew.

The police officer took me to my door and put the key in it, I remember that. She offered to come in and make me a cup of tea, but I told her I would be all right. I watched the rest from Mother's window, piecing together what I could, peering out through the ragged lace. Now, the police and the lawyers have gone over it so many times, I know the lingo: 'blue light' and 'unmarked' and 'quick response', who's qualified to certify death and who isn't. I know the Astra contained the inspector; the Ford Transit van the scenes of crime officer – that he brought cameras and tape, and gloves and protective packaging, to locate, record and recover samples. But I was innocent then. It was just arms brushing the fence, the squeak of boots, the rustle of combat trousers, the crackle of voices.

Lots of activity followed by nothing. All those vehicles still there, blocking the road, the lights flashing. My forehead was numb against the cold glass, when two men in green uniform came out of the house. And that's when I saw, that's when I knew for sure: they were carrying a stretcher and under a maroon blanket – a body.

I know I let out a shout. I know I banged my head several times against the glass because there were bruises later and I remember the sound of it, and the sensation; I wanted to bleed. I wanted my head to crack.

The ambulance doors closed, and the men got into the front and they drove away.

I went downstairs and opened the front door. For a moment or two I stood in the porch, unable to take a step further. There was just a single police car now. In the distance a motorbike accelerated. For a split second, I almost turned back. How much easier the last few weeks would have been if that had been my decision. But I left the porch and walked down my path and stepped out onto the pavement.

The Tilsons' front door was closed now, though all the lights were on in the house – I could see through to the far wall of Ailsa's bedroom, to the shadow along the top of the fitted cupboards. A policeman still stood guard, holding a folder, at the bottom of the steps up to the door. It was hard to see his expression under his hat. He'd half unzipped his yellow jacket and the plastic cover of the walkie-talkie pinned to his shoulder gleamed. I remember thinking how odd it was to see a person standing still like that, apparently idle, without looking at their phone. Everyone looks at their phone now, if they have a minute.

They had strung blue and white tape across the off-street area, attaching it at one end to the old gatepost, and at the other to a shower rail half embedded in the hedge on my side. They must have thought it was easier than trying to tie a knot in privet. Or maybe they were just in a hurry and it was the simplest thing to hand. The tape, which read 'Police Line Do Not Cross', had been hung upside down, and it was twisted in places, crinkled in others as if maybe it had been used before. Tom's car was half wrapped, tape clinging to its rear bumper, like a horrible pastiche of the fantasy birthday present.

The front door opened and an officer came out of the house, walked down the path, ducked under the tape and got into the driving seat of the car. I slunk back into the shadow of the hedge and waited. He was waiting. He flipped down the visor and inspected his chin for a few moments and then something got his attention – he bent his head to look once again in the direction of the house.

I stepped forward again so I could see what had caught his attention.

Ailsa. Ailsa then. Ailsa was unharmed.

She was standing in the doorway, clutching a plastic bag to her chest, the arm of a jumper trailing out of it. The oval of her face looked very white, as if the features had been drawn on porcelain; a Chinese doll painted on the back of a spoon.

Behind her was the police officer who had helped me earlier. She said something in Ailsa's ear and Ailsa nodded and the two of them walked down the steps and on to the path. When they reached the tape, the officer raised it and Ailsa bent her head to duck under it.

She saw me then – looked at me with an expression of complete blankness.

'Where's Max?' I said. 'Where's Bea?'

The police woman had taken her arm again and was pulling her towards the car. Ailsa was still looking at me. 'They're at . . .' She paused. 'Thingy came to get them.' She squeezed shut her eyes, trying to think. 'Rose's.'

'What's happened,' I said.

The police woman had opened the back door of the car and was steering her in, doing that thing with the head, pushing it down to make sure she didn't bang it.

'It's Tom,' Ailsa called. 'I've poisoned Tom.'

The police search advisor and his team arrived to do their damage the following morning, digging up the flower beds, combing the house. It was to be another few days before they had the result of the post mortem, longer for toxicology, but they quickly began to build a picture to fit the facts. They found the hemlock in the garden, the box of unused gloves, the receipt in the bag for life, the coriander in the fridge. Andrew Dawson had given his statement. They began to hear about the financial difficulties, the problems in the marriage, the life insurance. Nobody mentioned my note: I have wondered since about that.

They interviewed me, as part of routine door-to-door enquiries. Not that I had much to say. They were a lovely couple. And Ailsa? Everyone loved Ailsa. No. I didn't see them very often. Once a week? I'd seen her the previous day, yes; she'd been looking out for me. I'd been poorly, in hospital. Chest. Sorry, just a cough. I wasn't contagious. My eccentricity, and the state of my house worked in my favour. Did they want to come in? No?

I visited her at the station as soon as I could, fetching whatever she needed – a bag of clothes, hydrocortisone for her hands, the vial of black onion oil from beside the bed. It was harder when she was moved on; sometimes I caught only a glimpse – her feet climbing the steps of court; that terrible time she banged her head against the doors of the Serco van. I failed to see her completely at Bronzefield, as I've explained, though I did manage to speak to her once on the phone. She complained about the food, the noise, the heat.

You've got to hand it to Standling and Grainger. It was a stretch to get her bail, but they managed. No proven link, her previous good character. No fear of further offending. The court kept her passport, just in case. Stringent conditions would be met.

When I heard the application had been successful, I got the train to Ashford; walked out of the station and up to the mini-roundabout, right into Woodthorpe Road, and along past the Salvation Army to the Bronzefield entrance. I knew the way because I'd been once before, though, as I think I've said, they hadn't let me in. I waited until she came out, watched her stand, looking around, noticing how lost and small she looked in her oversized jumper, hair flat, grey at the roots, her face pinched. She bent down to fiddle with something at her ankle – the tag already bothering her skin.

It was only when she straightened up that she saw me, standing on the other side of the road, waiting to bring her home.

Chapter Twenty-five

1 pair of Vinoguard essentials vinyl, Medium

Discovery, *noun*. Law: disclosure of relevant facts or documents by a party to an action, typically as compelled by another party.

'I knew it,' she said. 'I knew they were here. You had them. I knew it.' She was shaking her head; her words were triumphant but her body radiated disbelief. 'All this time. They were here.' She took a step towards me. I pressed back against the wall, felt the damp fold of the wallpaper beneath my palms.

She was crushing them together now, moving them from hand to hand. 'Why have you got them?'

I didn't want to answer. I took a step down the stairs. But she followed. She was just above me. 'I just have,' I stammered.

'Did you kill Tom?'

'No? Did you?'

We stared at each other. I was the one who broke first. 'I found them,' I said.

'I don't believe you.'

'I did.'

'Where? In the bin? You took them from the bin?'

I dug my nails into my palm. 'No. Between the hedge and the planks in my front garden.'

I stared at her and as she stared back the muscles in her face seemed to slacken, a blankness came into her eyes. She was silent for a long time. She started shaking her head, back and forth. 'What time does Standling want to come?'

'He said 3 p.m.'

'OK. Tell him that's fine.'

She pushed past me and walked slowly down the stairs and into her room, and closed the door.

Standling arrived at 3 p.m. on the dot. It was raining out and he spent a few minutes flapping the water off his mac, folding it up and laying it over the bannister. I'd cleared the hall to make room for Max's bike and he waited there while I went up to fetch Ailsa. I was anxious she wouldn't come out, but the door opened. She'd changed into a long-sleeved black T-shirt and black jeans, her hair scraped back into a ponytail. 'You all right?' I said. She nodded.

I'd made the kitchen as nice as I could, even picked a bit of greenery and put it in a vase, and we went in there to talk. I stood next to the stove and the two of them faced each other across the small table. Standling kept his briefcase pressed to his trouser leg. He can be pedantic, and when he first sat down he insisted on going through the evidence we knew by heart – point by point. His language worked hard to distract from the weight of it. The circumstantial details – the plants and the not-eating, the coriander in the fridge – he described as 'a bit annoying'. Andrew Dawson's statement about 'a bloodthirsty cry' he dismissed as 'unlucky'; Ailsa's 'confessional' 999 call 'unfortunate but not catastrophic'.

When he mentioned the missing gloves, 'a distraction', I felt myself stiffen, a flush rise in my neck. I didn't know whether

Ailsa would say anything, but she didn't. She kept her body very still.

Standling picked up his briefcase then and laid it on his knee. 'CPS have produced a new piece of evidence,' he said. 'A note, retrieved from the kitchen bin.'

Clicking open the case, he flicked through a file and drew out a sheet. He laid it on the table in front of him. It was a photocopy. On it, words in my handwriting.

'Familiar to you?' he asked.

Ailsa nodded. 'Yup.'

'I understand from previous conversations you are not planning to contest imputations that your marriage was anything but satisfactory?'

Ailsa stared at him as if the sentence was confusing – which, to be fair, it was.

I edged forwards. 'No. She won't contest it.'

'So this note shouldn't cause any change in our perception of that. However,' he sighed heavily. 'Was it the first time you were made aware of the relationship between your husband and Delilah Perch?'

Ailsa shook her head. 'No.'

'But you received the note when?'

A flurry of rain hit the window, small stones against the glass. 'The afternoon of Tom's death,' I said.

'That correct?' He gave Ailsa a level look over the top of his glasses.

She nodded.

'It's better to get in front of information that might be used as evidence against you. When you were asked if there was anything you thought was relevant, this sort of detail is the sort of thing that was meant.' He was tapping the side of his briefcase now, keeping his emotions under control.

'I'd forgotten it existed,' she said. 'What with everything. I read it. I dismissed it. I just thought it was Verity being Verity. I don't even remember what happened to it.'

'SOCO found it screwed up in a corner of the kitchen.'

'I must have thrown it there.' She tipped her chair back, her eyes focused on the panel above the garden door. It looks like green marble because of the ivy pressing up against it on the other side. Rain dripped. It was like being under water.

'One other thing you could have mentioned . . .' He took his glasses off, and rubbed them on the edge of his shirt before returning them to his face, making a little pressing movement with his fingers to adjust the arms. 'Gavin Erridge. Is that name familiar to you?'

She was still looking up at the ivy-covered panel, her fingers tapping the dip in her throat.

Standling glanced at me, and back to her. 'Gavin Erridge coached the Kent Warriors, an under-10 tag rugby team in Tunbridge Wells. Following claims from Tom's mother that you and Mr Erridge became close, he has confirmed her allegation that it was Tom's discovery of ongoing sexual relations between you that led to your departure from Kent.'

Ailsa made a face, shrugging one shoulder up to touch her ear. Her face was blank, all the muscles loose.

My stomach clenched as if someone had kneed it. '*That's* the great mystery about Kent?' I said. 'That's why you moved away?'

She glanced over to me. 'It was ages ago,' she said. 'It's not relevant now.'

'Why didn't you tell me?' I said.

Standling seemed to notice the teacake I'd toasted and buttered for him. He took a small bite, then laid it back down on the saucer and pushed it lightly away. Cold. 'Another witness has provided rather more up-to-date evidence that you may have wanted your husband out of the way.' From a plastic folder he produced a single piece of A4 paper which he laid down on the table and spun round so it was the right way up for Ailsa to read.

She gripped it between her fingers as she read. It seemed to take a long time. I watched one particular raindrop slide down the window. 'Pippa,' she said eventually. 'Yes.'

'As you see, she claims that Mr Tilson had suspicions, before his death, of an intimate relationship between you and Ricky Addison, her husband. That Tom spoke to her on the phone about it, the night of 17 July and then again in person, by the swimming pool in Somerset on the day of 18 July. She claims that she believed Mr Addison's protestations of inno-cence – until last week when she discovered texts on his mobile. She confronted her husband and' – he produced another sheet from the folder – 'he has reluctantly come forward to corroborate the affair.'

It all slotted into place then, like something thin and sharp, a key in a lock, or a knife in a block. All this she had kept from me. Ricky's garden. Her mysterious disappearances. Tom asking for her at my door. Her guilt was like something solid and sharp-edged, like a pane of glass.

'Why?' It's all I managed to say.

'Oh God, Verity. Don't look like that. Is it really such a surprise?'

Standling let out a long, heavy sigh which he arrested with a humourless smile. 'Mr Addison's statement is very clear that as far as he was concerned it was a casual fling, but that you were more intense about it. None of this is proof. I've spoken to Silk and he still believes as I do that the strength of our defence lies in simple mistake. Unless you have anything else to add. Or,' he spoke very clearly, trying to get her to engage, 'you can suggest anything else, or *anyone.*'

She'd been biting her lip, her eyes downcast. At this she looked up and for the first time in minutes, she turned her head directly towards Standling and there was an appeal, a vulnerability, in her eyes that made me want to leap to her defence.

'Delilah was in the house that day,' I said. 'No one has thought of her.'

I thought he was ignoring me, but then he said: 'Other people were in the house that day, yes.'

'Including me,' I said.

Neither of them seemed to register I'd even spoken.

Standling returned his eyes to the file on the table. He had already closed it and now he lined it up with the edge. He kept his hands on it, making minor adjustments, while he said: 'The Crown has asked for a brief delay. They've requested an interview with a further witness.' His phrasing was short, and list-like; he was trying to sound matter-of-fact. 'Little bit different this time – not written, as the witness is underage. It would be an ABE – Achieving Best Evidence – interview, in the presence of an appropriate adult, of course. In this case, they're suggesting the grandmother, Mrs Cecily Tilson.'

Ailsa was still staring at him. 'Max.'

He looked up at her then, gave a small nod.

I'd been trying so hard not to think about Max. I felt a pain across my ribcage, a tight squeezing.

'Do you know why they want to talk to him?' She had begun very quietly to cry.

He gave her another very level look. 'Not yet, no.'

Chapter Twenty-six

Faith's pink jumper

Confession, *noun*. The disclosing of something, the knowledge of which by others is considered humiliating or prejudicial to the person confessing; a making known or acknowledging one's fault, wrong, crime, weakness, etc.

She went upstairs to her room while I was seeing Standling out. I heard the door shut. I stayed in the hall for a few minutes, thinking, and then I went into the back room study and took the last few boxes of papers and put them in the skip. The desk, now revealed beneath its piles, was dusty, and I found some Mr Muscle and gave it a good clean and then I shoved it against one wall to make space. I put two chairs in front of it; one each. It took less than half an hour; it's amazing how quickly you can make things nice if you put your mind to it. I didn't have long. Max would need picking up from school soon. And before that, I had other things to sort out.

I went upstairs to Faith's room, now Ailsa's, and knocked. Silence.

I knocked again. 'It's me,' I said. 'I think we should talk.'

I tried to push the door open. I met traction. A sleeve of

pink jumper was caught under the jamb. I kept pushing and it dragged out of the way. Boxes and bags covered the carpet. Over the last few weeks Ailsa has emptied every drawer, every cupboard.

She was sitting cross-legged on the bed, looking out of the window. I stood in the doorway, but she didn't acknowledge my presence so I picked up a chair, lifted it over the scattered clothes, and placed it next to the bed.

I was right up close to her, but still she didn't turn her head. 'Faith?' I said. 'Are you OK?'

There was a long silence. Wind threw a handful of rain against the window. 'Murder,' she said. 'The word sounds so awful. But when you know what happened . . . I mean, when you *know* someone, nothing they do seems bad.'

I was disoriented for a second. It was the way she was staring into the garden that threw me. She seemed to be looking past the rain, to the darkness way down beyond, beneath the brambles at the back, deep in the undergrowth, among the ants and worms and woodlice. I leant forwards, put my elbows on the bed, getting as close to her as I dared.

'I imagine a person can mean it in the moment,' I said, 'but it could be a terrible mistake, and they'd spend the rest of their life regretting it.'

She began pulling at the counterpane, plucking at the tufty bits that create the snakes in the pattern. A lot of threads were missing; the holes looked like tiny teeth marks.

'Oh, Faith, it'll be all right,' I said. 'We'll make sure it is.'

She looked up and for a second I took in the upward sweep of her almond eyes; the particular crinkle of her hair, the central points of her lips. 'Ailsa,' she said. 'You keep calling me Faith.'

'Do I?'

'Yes. You've done it before.'

'I don't, do I?' I tried to laugh. 'It's just you remind me of her. Here you are sitting on her bed, surrounded by all her things.'

She looked down at the items strewn across the floor. 'I was looking for the gloves and then – there's so much stuff.' She sighed, twisting slightly so she could rest against the glass, laying her hands on top of her head, elbows out, leaning back. 'Tom always thought you were hoarding her up here, or that she was dead; you'd killed her and buried her down there in the garden. No, no.' She put up her hands. 'Of course, now I know you, I don't believe that. I never really did. But Verity.' She made a billowing movement with her hand. 'It's all here: clothes, make-up, phone. Even her passport.'

I took a deep breath, feeling the air push against my ribcage. 'Old phone. Old passport. Everyone uses their parental home as a dumping ground.'

I looked up. She was still gazing at me and I saw it in her eyes: the doubt. I don't blame her. We both had secrets – she certainly did; all those lovers. I wondered about Tom; she wondered about Faith. We had sat across the table from each other, wondering. But we'd rubbed along regardless. The benefit of the doubt. Excuses. Extenuation.

Long ago, Faith carved her initials into the headboard and, though it has since been painted over, you can still see the shape of the letters. I pushed my finger into them. The room was so quiet you could hear the dust fall.

'Tom was right,' I said. 'I mean, it's true that she's dead.'

'What?' Ailsa hardly opened her mouth.

'She was killed,' I said. 'One of those ordinary things: a tragic accident – or so the police eventually concluded. It was the day we argued. She stormed out. I went after her, to plead with her, to apologise, but when I got to the station it was too late. It was dark, and raining. The platform was packed. No one saw what happened. They said she must have slipped or tripped. She was on her phone . . . The police, they were so nice. They said she would have died instantly.'

'Verity.' She pushed herself away from the window, and shuffled forwards to hang her legs over the edge of the bed. 'Why didn't you say?'

That pressure again behind my ribs. 'I try not to think about it. It makes me feel less alone.'

'But Verity,' she said, and her eyes were round and plaintive. 'You're not alone. You've got me. Us. We're your family now.' Her voice broke then; she breathed in deeply and when she sighed, it came out like a shudder, shaking her whole body. 'Bloody hell. What are we going to do?'

The parts of me I'd depended upon, that I'd shored up, were collapsing. I felt a hot flood of love for Faith, the lost baby, for Ailsa, but most of all for Max.

I must have said his name out loud, let it out in a cry, because she tipped her elbows forward so she was holding the weight of her head in her hands. 'I know,' she said. 'My darling boy.'

We sat there in silence for a bit. I wondered whether I should begin to say what I thought, to guide her, but she clasped her hands together, into a praying shape, and dug the tips of her fingers into her lips. 'Did you know all along? Did you guess?'

I nodded. 'I had a strong suspicion.'

'It's why you kept the gloves?'

'I picked them up when I found them – it was that afternoon. They were just *there*. Then later, I kept them because I assumed they were incriminating.'

'But it was their *absence* that was incriminating. It's one of the first things they held against me – that I'd hidden them. If you'd come clean earlier, explained that you'd stolen them . . .' Realisation hit her and she shook her head.

'Exactly. They'd have tested them. The simplest test distinguishes between male and female DNA.'

'I've been *hoping* it was me. I mean, that was what they kept telling me . . . I was sure I wore the gloves to chop the onions, and I can't remember wandering out into the garden for garnish, but I was hoping that I did. On autopilot. Not coriander. But parsley? Fennel? I don't know how but that's what I hoped.'

'I hoped that too.'

'He thought he hated his father. But he didn't.'

'He's a child,' I said.

'He didn't want to move. I mean he really didn't want to move. My fault. I should have listened. So many changes – he blamed Tom. But then your note.' She looked at me, a fierce frown. 'What did you write? I can't even remember now. "Get rid of him"?'

I dug my nails into the palm of my hands. 'I didn't mean like that. *He* takes things so literally . . . But it was meant for you, not him.' She was looking at me as though I held full responsibility. My eyes felt hot and small. I rubbed them, wiped my cheeks. Enough guilt. I said: 'If only you hadn't brought the hemlock back from Somerset. Then it wouldn't have been there for him to pick.'

She frowned again, but this time it was more surprised. 'What do you mean?'

'If you hadn't dug the hemlock up in Somerset and brought it back with you into your garden, then, well . . .' I shrugged. 'It wouldn't have happened.'

'But Verity, surely you know that's not how it got into the garden?'

'How *did* it get there then?'

I could feel the answer growing, coming, even before she turned her head and looked out of the window, past the rain, out to the wilderness. 'From there,' she said, pointing. 'It came

301

from there, from your side. It crept under the fence. Just one small plant. It's so damp – the high water table, all those underground streams. But Tom was right: your garden harboured secrets and death, just not the kind he thought.'

I was shocked; I'm not afraid to admit it. This information knocked me off course. But maybe it was a good thing, because I pulled myself together, remembered what I had to do.

I took a deep breath. 'Poor Max,' I said. 'I can't bear it for him.'

She started tugging again at the counterpane. 'I'll ring Standling, ask his advice,' she said. 'What do you think?'

'I think Standling has already guessed.'

'They won't send him away, will they? They'll understand. He didn't mean it. He's just a kid.'

The time had come. I needed to tread carefully.

I let out a sigh. 'I don't think he even knows what he's done. I'm sure he's blocked it out.' I went slowly, for I had rehearsed this. 'It's a shame they have to talk to him at all,' I said. 'I wish there was a way that they didn't.'

'Yes.' She sounded tentative. 'I can see. But I'm sure they will be kind. He's not a bad boy. He's a wonderful boy. He made a mistake, that's all it is. He isn't a murderer. They're not going to *put him away*.'

I was careful not to answer.

She started fiddling with her hands. 'And we'll start afresh. Move somewhere new, where people won't know.'

I nodded. *I knew it.* 'I can't bear it for him,' I said finally. 'He'll never get over it. His life will never be the same again.'

'They'll give him counselling – surely that will be their priority.'

'I wish I was as confident as you that the court will be so understanding.' I closed my eyes. 'I keep thinking about that contact centre, how grim it was.'

'You think they'll take him into care?'

I gave her a level look. 'I think they'll take him away,' I said.

'Do you mean lock him up? Prison?'

'I think they call them detention centres.'

'Oh, Verity.' It came out like a cry. 'What can we do?'

I stood up. 'You're right,' I said. 'There's nothing we can do. I'll ring Standling.'

I trod over Faith's stuff, stumbled on her pink jumper. I waited until I reached the door.

Raising my hand to hold the jamb, I paused. 'Unless . . .' I said.

'Unless what?'

I gazed at her. She was just like Faith. How could she have thought about moving away.

I spoke calmly. 'Unless you change your plea.'

Ailsa's jaw was set firm and her eyes were fixed somewhere in the middle distance, entirely lost to the room, and I wondered for a moment if she hadn't heard me. But as she continued to sit there, so still, her mind almost audibly turning, I realised she had heard me perfectly.

It had worked.

Epilogue

Max

**Resolution, *noun*. The action, or (in later use esp),
an act of resolving or determining; something
which has been resolved upon; a fixed or positive
intention.**

I've taken Maudie out onto the common and I'm sitting on
the bench at the top of the slope down to the pond. It's where
we sat that first day when Ailsa told me in detail about Tom's
last moments, when I first concocted a plan. It's cold, properly winter; the trees have lost their leaves – though a few
linger, gripping on for dear life – and I'm wrapped up warmly
in the maroon puffer and the black scarf. Perfume clings to it
now: lily and pomegranate. It smells of her. The bench is
damp; even though I wiped it with my gloves, I can feel it
begin to penetrate my trousers.

I won't stay long. I'm a few minutes early, that's all, for
meeting Max off the train. He's had Magic Club today – the
one I found for him in Streatham. He'll be practising some
little rope trick when he gets out, head down; but I'm already
looking forward to the moment he'll notice me and Maudie
waiting at the top of the steps, and he'll grin and run up to
meet us. How much happier he is these days.

With good behaviour, Standling thinks Ailsa should be out in ten years. It seems about right. It gives me long enough. We visit her often, Max and me – enough to keep the relationship going, not enough for anyone to feel *dependent*. I'm enjoying the sense of control. I'm allowed in these days. I've got my own photo ID. A provisional licence. When – if! – I pass, I might even drive us down. (I've got use of the little Fiat now.) She's in quite good spirits. She is learning Italian, she told us last time, and her work in the garden is earning her an RHS qualification, 'so Delilah can stuff it up her arse'. She is grateful to me, has no idea that in the end I betrayed her. Every time we leave, she tells me she's glad it's her and not him, and thanks me again for giving him such a wonderful home. 'I don't know what I'd do without you,' she says. 'You've literally saved my life.' And these days she actually means it. I'm family, she says, and at last it feels true.

Sometimes Max and I bump into Cecily Tilson and the girls. There's a cafe down the road from the prison that we like to retreat to. Cecily, 'Tom's bitch of a mother', is a poppet when you get to know her. I mean, grand and a terrible intellectual snob, but she and I get on pretty well now we've discovered shared interests – crosswords, Italian Renaissance art, the novels of Ann Patchett. She lets Melissa and Bea sleep at mine when they're up to see friends, though she insisted on inspecting 'the gaff', as Bea calls it, first. An excuse for one last massive clear-out. Sue and Maeve, even Bob, came to help. Cecily's standards are higher than mine, and she sent a man in to mend the staircase and the roof, but she appreciated I'd made an effort, that I was putting the children first. She approved of everything I had done in the back sitting room, now 'Max's den' – even the Xbox. The table tennis table was a particularly clever find. Someone had left it outside a house in Ritherdon Road. I persuaded the coaches at Max's football team to lug it back.

I worked out early on Max had killed Tom. I paid attention to him, you see, unlike anyone else. I knew how much he hated his father. Ailsa was too busy with her own dramas – her little dalliances. It took me a while to think what was best, to keep one chess move ahead. The priority was to keep the focus off Max. One word from me and they'd have released Ailsa. I only had to give them the gloves. I thought the case would be dismissed, that a jury, if not the police, would accept it was a simple mistake. But when the daubings began to appear on my front fence, when I realised how readily her friends would turn against her, I changed tack. There's been so much in the press about that woman who killed her husband and belatedly got out, I had hopes for a defence of domestic abuse. But it wasn't a goer. The silly stunt with the scarf – I regret that. He could be a bastard, Tom – I wouldn't have wanted to have been married to him myself – but she was difficult too. The more I thought about it, the more guilty she seemed. The restlessness, the greed – how jealous she was of Rose's seaside house – the self-aggrandising self-pity. I know I have my own secrets but, big secrets, when you lay them out on the bed, often turn out to be innocuous. More dangerous are the ordinary everyday lies, the million little shams and pretences between friends. Ailsa was good at that; she honed her own particular form of aggressive mimicry. All things to all people. The fact is she had mental health issues and was off her meds. She was repeatedly unfaithful. Desperate for male attention, for things to go her way. Guilty; it became the obvious solution.

I did consider one other option: telling the police that *I'd* killed Tom. I look the part, after all. The house, the dishevelled nature of my person. 'Odd': isn't that what people think of me? I had access to the food, to the hemlock (in my own garden, as I've discovered). Max, I think, though I haven't asked, added a frond to his father's plate, a little garnish. He wouldn't have risked hurting the rest of his family. I couldn't say the same about me but at least I could argue I bought pizzas to ensure the children were safe. The sticking point, of course, is that I believed Tom to be away. I'd have to have stated my intended victim was Ailsa. It's not so implausible. Love/hatred: they're sides of the same coin. I'd been weakened by my stay in hospital, still under the influence of those strong steroids. The previous day, finding my baby's bones, she'd forced me to confront the past. I was overwhelmed by grief and delayed trauma. When she told me they were moving, I had a sudden rush to the head, I made an impetuous decision on a hot afternoon? What did Ailsa say I had? Abandonment issues, that's it. I like to keep things close. I find it hard to let them go. It's happened before, though I might not have needed to mention that.

So, yes, I did think it through. But did she deserve that sacrifice? Would it really have been the best thing for Max? I realised the answer was no to both of those questions when she dismissed me from their lives – all that talk of a new start elsewhere. After everything I'd done for her. Turns out *she was just like Faith*. I had to work quickly. A guilty plea, clean, straightforward, the only safe solution.

She was easy to persuade. I showed her the results of a Google search. Nasty child murderers in Wisconsin or Lincolnshire ending up in hideous small specialist units being monitored, treated and assessed by psychiatrists. If I'd given her time, she might have realised Max, a nice middle-class boy, might not have been treated in the same way; a family court would probably have found a discrepancy between his actions and his awareness of their consequences. But one could never be sure. I told her we couldn't risk asking Standling for advice; the prosecution was already halfway there. Mother's love: the strongest thing there is.

I miss her. I thought she was the friend I'd been looking for all my life. And in many ways, thinking back over the last ten months, I do have a lot to be grateful to her for. She *saw* me, looked past the mess, treated me as a friend . . . But I mustn't be sentimental. She took advantage of me. I was a cover for her affair (she *should* have told me; she made a fool of me). A free tutor. (Well, she is paying *now*.) I never did get back my grandmother's Regency slope. The fact is she reached inside my house, and my heart, rummaged around in it, and threw me aside. The worst kind of betrayal isn't a major act of treachery, but a minor act of casual indifference.

Ten years stretch ahead of her now – long enough for her to have a jolly good think about her behaviour. Obviously, I've taken her out of my will; everything goes straight to Max whatever age he inherits. Her rehabilitation will probably coincide with his departure for university. Oxford or Cambridge, I have great hopes. His confidence has increased so much without Tom breathing down his neck, and with my help and encouragement. As I told the woman in the bookshop, he's twelve but has a reading age of seventeen; he's become a lovely little writer. I'll keep those hopes to myself – I'm not going to put him under pressure. If he wants Oxford Brookes, or to sit in his room smoking marijuana, so be it. He can be what, and who, he wants. At last I've learnt something my mother never wanted to face: that the dishonourable parts of us are as worthy of love as the good.

If he does choose further education – Fred says I'm mad to think otherwise – she could move back in. Fill the empty nest. It might suit us both. We'll see. I'll ask Max what he wants when the time comes. It's tricky, though. The guilty plea – he's come to believe it, buried his own responsibility way down deep. I'm careful how I talk about her. I'm not taking the place of your mother, I tell him. She is your mother, and she will always be your mother. It's funny, though: every time I say it, the words seem to mean a little less.

It's always best to be thinking ahead.

Above the pond, the clouds are dense and grey, but further over I can see a small patch of blue – well not really blue, more of a tinted white, but in the dark sky it's a little spot of clarity. It feels like that spot of light is what has been happening in my head, as if something massive has lifted. I've carried a weight of guilt for several years now, but I think finally it's gone. That aching hole has filled, too. My nerve endings have begun to tingle. Perhaps it's the cold. Or perhaps it's that I've realised for the first time in a long time, every day has a purpose; I have someone else to live for.

Right. It's time to call Maudie to me, and we'll go back round the pond, and across the road and down to the station. I'll wait for him as usual on the bridge. I try never to go down onto the platform, if I can help it. It's the one place memories can come up and swipe you. People trip so easily. All it takes is one shove.

Max was talking this morning about wanting a puppy. He says it would give Maudie a new lease of life. I was resistant but I've changed my mind. I'll tell him on the walk back. We'll start looking for a rescue.

Acknowledgements

It's always useful to have a few things to research to put off writing, and several people were kind and generous enough to indulge me. Thank you to Andrew Watson and Peter Gilliver (OED); Deborah Taylor, David Jeffreys, Hugh French and Michael Maxtone-Smith (the law); Susannah Buxton and Pete Westby (hoarding) and Jill Mellor and Julia Wylie (the habits of hemlock). For help in turning the research and prevarication into a novel, I am eternally grateful to my agent Judith Murray, my editor Joanne Dickinson, everyone else at Greene & Heaton and Hodder, and my husband and first reader Giles Smith.

Read on for an exclusive extract of
Sabine Durrant's brilliant new thriller . . .

Chapter one

The thing I keep telling myself is we shouldn't even have been
there. The business with the 'Picasso' napkin had gone to plan,
and St Cecilia sur Mer should have been a distant memory,
only I'd been ill for 48 hours and, when the antibiotics kicked
in, I'd persuaded Sean to stay one last day at the beach, sun
beds legit this time, maybe even a cocktail (on tab) at lunch.

Obviously, I wish now I hadn't.

The English voice caught our attention – the sub schoolgirl
French grappling with an order for a demi-carafe. We were, as
usual, close to the bar – you tend to pick up more there. She
was at a table in full sun. Rookie mistake (one of her shoulders
already going red). Fresh off the plane: always a bonus. A
British Airways tag hung from the leather straps of her powder
blue Longchamp bag (genuine logo: I'd checked), and the
paperback in front of her, spine unbroken, was part of a 3 for
2 airport deal. What other tells? New mani pedi – the neon
pink posh Brits were wearing en masse that year; ill-judged
white jeans, which she kept plucking at the thigh, and on the
sand next to her, a brand-new sarong, still furled in its store-
packaged ribbon. Also present: signs of the mild agitation
people often display on the first day of a holiday, a sort of
panicked eagerness already undercut with boredom. She
picked up the paperback, smoothing the front cover with her
thumbs, then turned it over and looked at the back. Again, it
was the texture of the paper that seemed to interest her.

When Sean went to the bathroom, I kept her in my line of

vision as she scrolled idly through her phone; then held it up, small lips pursed, for a selfie.

She was alone. I should have wondered more about that.

'Debit card: L Fletcher Davies,' Sean murmured, his chair sinking into the sand a little as he slipped back into his seat. 'Address on luggage: 11a Stanley Terrace, W11.'

'Lulu,' I countered. I couldn't help myself. The four letters were strung in gold on a chain around her neck.

He smiled, pleased with me, then jerked his chin at my phone, saying time to get working. I looked at him: *Really*? I wish I could say it was conscience that held me back, at the very least foreboding, that those instincts of mine he claimed to admire had switched on. I'd be lying. It was searingly hot. Music, some kind of jazz, swam against the murmur and shuffle of waves. I was lethargic; plus I felt the gnawing of a headache. 'Ali,' he said, coaxingly, warningly. It wasn't the money. There was enough in the hotel safe to get us where we wanted, even go our separate ways, which I'd been considering. No, he never could resist, that was Sean's problem. His fatal flaw – always wanting one more. And she was just the right sort of challenge. Tourists always are. The south of France may not be India, where 80 rupees pass through a person's fingers as easily as eight, and where you could say I'd become who I was. But a fish out of water is a fish out of water whatever water it's out of. We all make our worst decisions when we have a lot on our mind.

I adjusted the halter strings on my bikini top, pulling the knot so tight it bit at my neck. I'd been for a bathe and the towel between me and the wooden seat was damp. Sand slid silkily between my bare toes. I tasted salt on my lips, felt the loss of the heat-heavy afternoon. I'd been going to read my book, the Trojan siege told from the perspective of the women, which I'd found on a train, swim again. Maybe blag a Jet Ski.

Sometimes, though, he set little tests. Some bigger than others. I'd learnt not to fail.

Sean had flapped open his newspaper – a four days-old Sunday Times. I picked up my phone and started trawling. The usual forums. Facebook, Insta. Didn't take long to find what we needed. A double-barrelled surname's a gift.

Sean held my eye as I got to my feet.

Raoul's was the more relaxed of the bars that fringed this small crescent bay, no solid platform, but sand under foot, director's chairs, parasols, a bustling trade of goat's cheese salads and steaks haches carried aloft on oval trays. It was drawing close to lunchtime and the tables were filling up, mainly families wandering up from the beach, trailing damp towels and small kids in their cozzies. Boats were mooring up out on the water now, their occupants swimming or bobbing ashore, pushing their dry clothes ahead of them in blow up tenders. This was the rush, the razzle-dazzle hour. It'd be quiet again by four.

I screwed up my eyes as I walked from shade into brightness, worked my way through the tables towards her. Behind her chair, I crouched down. One of her striped espadrilles still had the price tag on the sole. Heat rose up from the sand. I could smell the coconut of her sun cream.

'Mademoiselle?' I straightened up. 'Je viens trouver . . .' I dangled a sliver of cotton decorated with glass beads and metal charms. 'Mademoiselle, est ce que c'est a vous?'

She turned to face me then and seeing her, for the first time close up, I felt a shock of recognition. 'Oh God.' She blushed. 'I don't understand. I don't speak French.' She was wearing more make up than me – thick eyeliner, sparkly bronzer - but the shape and position of her features, the *essence* of her face: we looked alike. The same nebulous green/grey/blue eyes, pale skin, the sort of almost colourless hair you could describe as 'honey' if you paid for highlights like she did.

She didn't seem to have noticed.

'Oh, you're English!' I let out a small exhausted exhalation of relief. 'Me too. I just found this – did you drop it?'

She looked at the bracelet and her wrist and then again thoughtfully at the bracelet. She extended her hand. 'Ah. Thank you.'

I hardened towards her then. It's not true you can't con an honest person, but I preferred not to. Sean didn't care whom he worked on; angels, devils, all grist to his mill. I was happier knowing that, in other circumstances, the person paying my wages might not be my friend.

'Let me,' I said, pulling back the tiny clasp with my fingers and holding it so as to attach it to her wrist.

'Thanks.' She smiled again, and I bent over her, feeling her eyes skate over my head, as I secured it. A pebble-shaped burn on the pulse point, quite recent, still red. Calluses on the back of the knuckles, a tiny ladder of white scars on the forefinger. Don't look; *observe*. Sean taught me that.

'There. Careful not to lose it again.'

She swung her wrist to admire the flash of tat. 'I won't.'

I straightened, tensing as I sensed his footsteps getting closer, small shivers of movement in the sand.

'Lulu?' His tone was both surprised and cautious, as one might gently admonish a small child. 'It is Lulu isn't it?'

Ray-Ban Aviators attached to the top of his white t shirt, he bent forwards, revealing a triangle of smooth brown skin. His dark hair was still damp, tousled, and the fan lines in the tan around his eyes brought out the blue in them; just the right amount of stubble (too much and he can begin to look louche). He was secretive about his age; I guessed him to be about 40, though he could pass for ten years younger.

'Or –' His elbow had rested on my shoulder, but he took a step back now. 'Am I wrong? Sorry. I thought I recognised you.' He looked at me, and then back to her. I wondered if he'd noticed the similarity between us. Maybe. His teeth dug into his lower lip.

She had twisted round completely in her seat to fix him, her fingers toying with the letters on her necklace. The strap of her meshy pink bra slipped out from under her vest top. 'No. No. Yes. I am Lulu . . . Who are you? Do we?'

'Val d'Izere?' he said, tentatively. 'I'm John Downe.'

'Val d'Izere?' Her eyes were searching his face. 'Were you a guest at the chalet. No. I'd remember. The Bar d'Alpine? Um. Oh God. Le Petit Danois! Carrie Bowman's last night party?'

He tapped his forehead, a small dramatic movement, a magician producing a bunch of flowers from his sleeve. 'Carrie Bowman's last night party!'

'Oh my God. That's so weird. *Yes*. How do you know Carrie? Were you part of the Marlborough crowd?'

He had moved around so she no longer had to strain to see him. 'Yeah. I *love* Carrie.'

'John Downe. God. Sorry, it was the end of a long season. I was wrecked that night.'

'Weren't we all!' he said.

I rolled my eyes. 'John. Honestly!'

A tiny pause as she looked from him to me, and back again, calculating. 'So, you two here on holiday?'

'Yes, I suppose you could call it a holiday.' He hooked his arm around my neck, squeezed it. 'Ellie's on her way home from a course in Florence and I've come out to join her for some R and R.' He poked me in the ribs. 'She's totally gassed to have the chance to spend time with her big embarrassing brother.'

I watched the zygomaticus major, the muscle on the side of the mouth that's impossible to control. It twitched, causing a tiny quiver in her lower lip. She was relieved, but also satisfied at being proved right. He was older than me, yes, but in her judgement way out of my league.

'So, what kind of course?' she asked.

'Cookery,' I said. 'Italian pasta.'

I knew, fresh from the Picasso sting, Sean was thinking history of art. But I'd seen her Instagram feed – the bread stretching from bowls of fondue, the ceremonial racks of sacrificial lamb, the totteringly flamboyant meringues. And I'd run my thumb over the scars.

'Not Mansaro's?' she asked.

I shook my head. 'I *wish*. Nothing so grand. Nona's kitchen?' I plucked the name from the ether. 'Basically, home-made pasta.'

'How wonderful.' She looked amused. 'I'd love to eat Nona's home-made pasta.'

Sean's breath warmed my neck. 'Come on, then we should probably –' He hooked one thumb back at our table. 'Order food before the rush.' He reached his hand out to shake hers, with a heartfelt, 'Lovely to see you again Lulu.'

We began to move away. Our bare feet sunk into the sand. The waiter with the lazy eye, the one who had snuck me a free croissant with my morning coffee, was standing aside for us to pass. A small boy had run up, his splayed feet sending little cascades. Disembodied sounds reached up from the beach like the chatter of birds. A woman somewhere screamed.

'Unless . . .' Lulu's voice was soft, a caress. Sean's nails were digging sharply into my skin. I turned before he did and caught the eagerness in her eyes, the vulnerability. I tried to slacken my face as an appeal or warning. It was too late. For her, and for me. She gestured, fingers fluttering, at the empty seats to either side of her. 'You'd like to join me?'

*

It's not rocket science, grifting. Mostly, it's bread and butter stuff – literally, a roof over your head, food in your mouth. You can big the language up, talk about your smacks and your tats and your wires, go to town with your hooks and your convincers, but really, there's no 'art' to it. Sean liked to call himself the aristocrat of crime, but it's living a life at the expense of someone else, just thieving, when it comes down to it, with extra psychology.

Sometimes an opportunity falls into your lap; other times you work hard for not very much. Usually it's somewhere in between. A free lunch – it feels stupid now, looking back; naïve – but that's all I had in mind that day. It had been pretty textbook so far. The conman's genius, Sean once told me, lay in figuring out precisely what it is a person desires and then presenting themselves as the perfect vehicle for delivering on it. Lulu Fletcher Davies was on her own, hot and bored, hoping for an experience St Cecilia sur Mer had so far failed to deliver Handsome, single John Downe, with his safe, friendly, faded sister as chaperone, were here to provide it.

She started talking as soon as we sat down – a little bit nervous, keen to entertain. She was here for two days, before starting a job on Saturday: a private cook in Provence. She'd done it the year before, for a really cool young couple, Olly Wilson, the guy who started the food delivery service, and his wife Magda, the fashion designer? She mentioned names, I noticed, in the form of questions – expecting us, now she thought us part of her social circle, to know the lot of them. 'They're friends of friends, but they told the owner about me, and somehow I've got roped in to doing it for the people who are renting the Domaine this year. I said yes because I wanted to get away – I'm coming out of a bad relationship. And I've scored a couple of nights with the house to myself at the end. But I've so gone off the idea. I mean, the money's *nothing*. It's loose change. I'm missing a 30th I really want to be at – Boo Watson? Do you know her, too? She was at St Mary's with me, but her brother Will was at Marlborough.'

Sean wasn't sure, but the name was familiar.

I picked up her book, a bestseller about two sisters growing up in war-torn Sudan - and asked her how she was finding it. I'd cried when I'd read it, but I caught the fleeting upturned quiver of her nose and, before she could answer, said, 'I gave up, too hard to get into.'

'I *know*, right?' She slipped off her espadrilles, getting comfortable.

'I mean give me a good magazine any day.'

She pulled out the copy of Vogue I'd already spotted in her bag. *Tra-la.*

'Ooh,' I said, as if it was an enormous bar of chocolate she'd produced, or a small puppy.

I could feel Sean's eyes on me. When I glanced up, he gave me a tiny nod of approval. He'd taught me how to do it, reflect a person back at them. The more closely your interests or opinions align to theirs, the more likely they are to trust you. It's human nature, really. Every time you agree with someone just to stay on their right side – 'oh yes I loved that film'; 'yeah, I know, you're right, she's such a bitch' - you're conducting your own little mini con. Us grifters, we just take it one step further. The Chameleon Effect, he told me it was called, or Egocentric Anchoring. As I say, he liked his poncy labels.

When our order came, she ate like a woman who loved her food, cracking open claws, pulling at the flesh, sucking greedily at shells. She turned down the bread – some sort of intolerance – but she snaffled down the chips, chomped at the chargrilled chicken. 'These prawns', she said, bringing her mouth to a quiver of a pale pink, 'are as good as the ones in Ibiza last summer.' Her lips glistened. 'Have you been?'

'No, but I really want to,' I said.

'Oh my God, you must. Todd and I had a ball. You'd *love* it. It's just one long party.'

The breeze dropped; the heat sank and turned to something solid like jelly. She changed into her bikini, using the cubicle out the back, and we took our coffees down to the beach. Sean persuaded her to take his sunbed, and he sat between us, facing the sea, cross-legged, under the parasol. She lay down before undoing her sarong, unfolding both sides like a fancy menu. Closing her eyes, she let out a small sigh. Her eyelashes were blue black against her freckled skin. Her stomach was pale and curved. Sean lent back and caught my eye. He was enjoying himself. I didn't like it. It wasn't normal attraction. I'd begun to notice how he liked to get one over a certain kind of woman. Something in his past – maybe back in New York where he claimed to have been brought up.

I'd been looping back and forth. I'd felt bad because she had a low paid job, and then OK again because her parents lived in Dubai 'for tax reasons', so, she didn't need the money. She'd had a tricky break up, some guy called Todd who was still hassling her, but she didn't seem too traumatised. I liked her appetite, the way she ate, her zest, but then she'd say something snooty about Essex girls or 'the French' and I'd think you deserve what you get. I ached to read my book, but I thumbed through her magazine, all those expensive clothes, and ridiculously strapped sandals. It contained a free sample of face cream which I peeled out of its metal foil. It stank. Anyway. Different world.

The sun had lowered into a pinky haze on the horizon, the water melted to liquid silver, when the waiter came down with our bill. Brown seagulls were teasing the waves. Up at the bar, they were raking under the tables now, clearing and clattering, getting ready for the evening shift. Lulu was leaning on her side, her elbow doing the heavy lifting, her eyes watching Sean's mouth as he prepared our escape, seeding thoughts of the following day: a plan to take a boat out to the islands, where we could find a quiet bay, swim, get away from the crowds. There was a lovely hotel with a restaurant, though stuck in the mud little sis Ellie here wasn't keen. His arms rose lazily to encompass the emptying beach, the pockmarked sand, and then paused in mid-air, as if welcoming the man into our midst.

'My shout,' he said, scrambling to his feet. 'Definitely on me.'

She demurred – 'no, no, I ate so much. I drank all that wine . . .'

But Sean had ducked out from under the parasol and, reaching into the back pocket of his navy shorts, produced the CDG black leather holder he'd filched from the American student in Madrid. He handed his credit card to the waiter, then keyed in the number, and stood back, already bored.

I watched him. He'd timed the boat trip mention just right; not overtly inviting her, but leaving the possibility hanging that we'd meet again, that the relationship had a future. The bill he'd treated casually – hadn't even checked the amount - and how deft his finger-work with the wallet: the way he flipped it open with the thumb of one hand, cursory, practised, as blasé with the contents as any arrogant hedge fund manager or whatever he'd told her he was.

The waiter – the older one with a crucifix nestling in his salt and pepper chest hair – was having trouble. He apologised in French; Sean unconcerned, told him it didn't matter. The waiter tried a second time, and a third, and then, shaking his head, handed the card back.

Sean tutted in frustration. 'Damn. It's got damp I think.' He rubbed it on the side of his shorts and then looked at it closely.

'I dunno.' Flicking open the wallet. 'The other's Amex and I'm not sure that you . . .?'

I took up a handful of sand and let it run out through my fingers.

The waiter shook his head.

I breathed in slowly and pushed myself up. 'I'll go back to the room,' I said. 'Get my wallet.'

Lulu stirred into life then. 'No,' she said. 'Stay there,' she said. 'It's fine. Let me.' Finding her card in a dinky hessian purse ('LOVE' spelt out in silver beads), she slotted it into the machine. She didn't even glance at the bill, still scrunched in Sean's hand, with its itemised list of our day's expenditure: the early morning grand cremes and sunbeds, and ice creams, the aperitifs, the cocktails, the rose, the food, *les petits cafes*. 'Pay me back another time . . . tomorrow.'

'You're a doll.'

'Or,' she began. 'I don't know if you're doing anything later. I mean we could go back and shower and then....'

'Sorry to be a wet blanket,' I said, putting on a pouty disappointed little girl's voice. 'John – you know we've promised . . .?'

He nodded slowly. 'Damn.'

I explained, underlining the weight of the *previous commitment*, about the aunt who lived up in the hills, a bit of a recluse, with whom we'd promised to have dinner. I was sorting my rucksack, while I talked, handing back the magazine, and her fancy lotion, not looking at her, not quite ready to see her disappointment. Sean was dusting the sand off his legs and shaking his hands through his hair. Lulu flapped her sarong out, rolled it and re-wrapped it, and then the three of us walked back up to the beach, round the side of the bar, and to the road.

St Cecilia sur Mer was at the less fashionable end of the French Riviera. Monopoly villas scattered the dark green hillside above. The main port was lined with nice restaurants and shops, rows of clattering white yachts in the harbour, the occasional Russian oligarch moored up on some gleaming monstrosity. We were round the headland from there, at the blue-collar, low rent end of town, in a dusty, utilitarian stretch: the hotels that straggled along the main drag modern, box-like buildings with ragged out-buildings. A few of them had palm trees and patches of grass, maybe even a fenced off pool. I thought Lulu would head for one of those, but she stayed with us – moaning again about that impending job of hers – until we reached the flat, unprepossessing entrance of La Belle Vue.

'Oh, you're here too?' she said as we went through the sliding doors. The small Reception was usually un-attended but that evening a neat blond young woman was sitting behind a desk. It was hot in the room and she was fanning herself with a Hertz car hire leaflet. 'Were you also late to book?' Lulu said. 'I don't know whether there is a convention in town, or whether it's just the French's absurd obsession with August, but when I tried there was just *nothing*.'

'Beggars can't be choosers.' I tried to speak softly. The receptionist, pausing her fanning, looked up.

'I'm this way,' Lulu said, pointing to a fire door on the right leading to a staircase.

I gave her a careful, damp hug and turned to the back door. My skin felt sweaty and tight; in my head I was already crossing the courtyard towards the cheaper annexe and our quarters overlooking the car park. I would run a shower. It was over. Our day on the beach was gratis. All expenses paid. The best kind of scam when the victim doesn't even realise they've been scammed. Tomorrow, Lulu would find a note; a family crisis that meant we'd had suddenly to leave. By the time, she read it, we'd be long gone. On to the next place. Sean had talked about Monte Carlo.

But Sean hadn't moved. One palm was propped against the wall, the other roaming beneath his t-shirt, massaging his chest, the pressure of his palms both efficient and sensual.

'I mean, I don't know what time we'll be back from visiting the elderly relative,' he said. 'But maybe if it's not too late and you're still up for it, we could have a night cap?'

'Oh. Well…' She brought her hand to the back of her hair, and twisted the clip, turning her hair into a fresh knot. 'I'll probably have supper at Raoul's so . . .'

A couple of mosquitoes were floating up and down against the glass of the back door. 'We'll be lucky to escape from Aunt Marie,' I said. 'You know how she talks.'

Sean still didn't move. 'Perhaps now she's getting older she'll fancy an early night.'

'It's not that close,' I said. 'A longer drive up into the hills than we always remember.'

I was expecting him to step towards me then. He didn't and I felt foolish and then angry, like when you trip on a paving slab and you want to blame the pavement not yourself. Things between us had been off since Barcelona, when maybe I'd taken a trick too far.

I put my hand against the glass and pushed. The door swung open more easily than I expected, and I knocked over a pot of geraniums. The earth spilling looked like seething ants.

I could hear them laughing as I bent to scoop it up.

Read on for an extract of the Richard and Judy
Book Club pick and *Sunday Times* top ten bestseller

LIE WITH ME

August 2015

It struck me in the night that it might have started *earlier*. I sat up in horror and, in the darkness, used my fingernail to scratch the word 'BOOKSHOP' on the inside of my forearm. It has gone now: the skin is inflamed due to an infected insect bite, which I must have further scratched at in my sleep. Still, the act of writing did the trick, as it tends to. This morning I can remember well enough.

Hudson & Co: the secondhand bookshop in Charing Cross Road. I have been assuming it began there – that none of it would have happened if my eye hadn't been caught by that silly little shop assistant's red hair. But am I wrong? Were the forces already in motion, in the weeks and months before that? Does the trail of poison lead back, long before the bloody girl's disappearance, to university? Or before then, even – to school, to childhood, to that moment in 1973 when I struggled, puce-faced, into this unforgiving world?

I suppose what I am saying is, how much do we collude in our own destruction? How much of this nightmare is *on me*? You can hate and rail. You can kick out in protest. You can do foolish and desperate things but maybe sometimes you just have to hold up a hand and take the blame.

BEFORE

Chapter One

It was a wet day, one of those grey, drizzly London afternoons when the sky and the pavement and the rain-streaked buildings converge. It's a long time since I've seen weather like that.

I'd just had lunch with my oldest friend Michael Steele at Porter's in the Charing Cross underpass, a wine bar we had frequented since, at the age of sixteen, we had first discovered the discretion of both its location and its landlord. These days, of course, we would both have much rather met somewhere less dank and dark (that chic little bistro on St Martin's Lane specialising in wines from the Loire, *par example*), but nostalgia can be a tyranny. Neither of us would have dreamt of suggesting it.

Usually, on parting from Michael, I would strut off with a sense of groin-thrusting superiority. His own life restricted by the demands of a wife, twin boys and a solicitor's practice in Bromley, he listened to my tales of misadventure – the drunken nights in Soho, the young girlfriends – with envy in his eyes. 'How old's this one?' he'd say, cutting into a Scotch egg. 'Twenty-four? Saints alive.' He was not a reader and a combination of loyalty and ignorance meant he also still thought of me as The Great Literary Success. It wouldn't have occurred to him that a minor bestseller written twenty years ago might not be sufficient to maintain a reputation indefinitely. To him I was the star of 'Literary London' (his phrase) and when he picked up the bill, which he could be depended upon to do,

5

there was a sense less of charity than of him paying court. If an element of mutual bluff was required to sustain the status quo, it was a small price to pay. Plenty of friendships, I am sure, are based on lies.

That day, however, as I returned to street level, I felt deflated. Truth was, though I had kept it to myself, life had recently taken a downward swerve. My latest novel had just been rejected, and Polly, the twenty-four-year-old in question, had left me for some bum-fluffed political blogger or other. Worst of all, I had discovered, only that morning, that I was to be evicted from the rent-free flat in Bloomsbury I had, for the last six years, called home. In short, I was forty-two, broke and facing the indignity of having to move in with my mother in East Sheen.

As I have mentioned, it was also raining.

I trudged along William IV Street towards Trafalgar Square, dodging umbrellas. At the post office, a group of foreign students, wearing backpacks and neon trainers, blocked the pavement and I was pushed out into the gutter. One shoe sank into a puddle; a passing taxi soaked the leg of my corduroys. Swearing, I hopped across the road, wending my way between waiting cars, and turned up St Martin's Lane, cut through Cecil Court, and into Charing Cross Road. The world juddered – traffic and building works and the clanging of scaffolding, the infernal disruption of Crossrail. Rain continued to slump from the sky but I had made it doggedly beyond the Tube station before an approaching line of tourists pulling luggage thrust me again out of my path and against a shop window.

I braced myself against the glass until they had trundled past, and then I lit a cigarette. I was outside Hudson & Co, a secondhand bookshop specialising in photography and film. There was a small fiction section in the back where, if I remembered rightly, I had once pilfered an early copy of *Lucky Jim*. (Not a first edition, but a 1961 orange Penguin with a Nicolas Bentley drawing on the cover: nice.)

I peered in. It was a dusty shop, with an air of having seen better days – most of the upper shelves were bleakly empty.

And then I saw the girl.

She was staring through the window, sucking a piece of long, red hair, her features weighted with a boredom so sensual I could feel it tingle along my fingertips.

I pinched the lit tip off my cigarette, put the remainder in my jacket pocket and pushed open the door.

I am not bad looking (better then, before everything happened), with the kind of face – crinkled blue eyes, strong cheekbones, full lips – I've been told women love. I took trouble over my appearance, though the desired result was to make it look as if I didn't. Sometimes, when I shaved, I noticed the length of my fingers against the chiselled symmetry of my jaw, the regularity of the bristles, the slight hook in the patrician nose. An interest in the life of the mind, I believed, was no reason to ignore the body. My chest is broad; I fight hard even now to keep it firm – those exercises I picked up at Power Pulse, the Bloomsbury gym, over the course of the free 'taster' month continue to prove useful. I knew how to *work* my look, too: the sheepish, self-deprecating smile, the careful use of eye contact, the casual deep-in-thought mussing of my messy blond hair.

The girl barely looked up when I entered. She was wearing a long geometric top over leggings and chunky biker boots; three small studs in the inside cartilage of one ear, heavy make-up. A small bird-shaped tattoo on the side of her neck.

I dipped my head, giving my hair a quick shake. 'Cor blimey,' I said in mock-Cockney. 'Rainin' cats and dogs out there.'

She rocked gently backwards on the heels of her boots, resting her bottom on a metal stool, and cast a glance in my direction. She dropped the spindle of ruby hair she'd been chewing.

I said, more loudly: 'Of course Ruskin said there was no such thing as bad weather. Only different kinds of good weather.'

The sulky mouth moved very slightly, as if vaguely in the direction of a smile.

I lifted the damp collar of my coat. 'But tell that to my tailor!'

The smile faded, came to nothing. *Tailor?* How was she to know the coat, bought for a snip at Oxfam in Camden Town, was ironic?

I took a step closer. On the table in front of her sat a Starbucks cup, the name 'Josie' scrawled in black felt tip.

'Josie, is it?' I said.

She said, flatly: 'No. That was what I told the barista. I tell them a different name every time. Can I help you? Are you looking for anything in particular?' She looked me up and down, taking in the absorbent tweed, the cords, the leaking brogues, the pathetic middle-aged man that wore them. A mobile phone on the counter trembled and, though she didn't pick it up, she flicked her eyes towards it, nudging it with her spare hand to read the screen above the cup – a gesture of dismissal.

Stung, I slunk away, and headed to the back of the shop where I crouched, pretending to browse a low shelf (two for £5). Perhaps she was a little too fresh out of school, not quite my audience. Even so. How dare she? Fuck.

At this angle, I smelt damp paper and sweat; other people's stains, other people's fingers. A sharp coldness in here too. Scanning the line of yellowing paperbacks, phrases from my publisher's last email insinuated themselves into my head: 'Too experimental . . . Not in tune with the current market . . . How about writing a novel in which something actually *happens*?' I stood. Bugger it. I'd leave with as much dignity as I could muster and head off to the London Library, or – quick look at my watch – the Groucho. It was almost 3 p.m. Someone might be there to stand me a drink.

I have tried hard to remember if the door jangled; whether it was the kind of door that did. The shop had seemed empty when I entered, but the layout allowed anyone to hide, or lurk – as indeed I was now. Was he already in the shop? Or not? Do I remember the scent of West Indian Limes? It seems import- ant. But perhaps it isn't. Perhaps it is just my mind trying to find an explanation for something that may, of course, have been random.

'Paul! Paul Morris!'

He was standing on the other side of the bookcase, only his head visible. I took a brief physical inventory: close-set eyes, receding hairline that gave his face an incongruously twee heart shape, puny chin. It was the large gap between the two front teeth that sparked the memory. Anthony Hopkins, a contemporary from Cambridge – historian, if I remembered correctly. I'd bumped into him several years ago on holiday in Greece. I had a rather unpleasant feeling that I had not come out of the encounter well.

'Anthony?' I said. 'Anthony Hopkins!'

Irritation crossed his brows. 'Andrew.'

'Andrew, of course. Andrew Hopkins. Sorry.' I tapped my head. 'How nice to see you.' I was racking my memory for details. I'd been out on a trip round the island with Saffron, a party girl I'd been seeing, and a few of her friends. I'd lost them when we docked. Alcohol had been consumed. *Had Andrew lent me money?* He was now standing before me, in a pin-stripe suit, hand out. We shook. 'It's been a . . . while,' I said.

He laughed. 'Not since Pyros.' A raincoat, pearled with drops, was slung over his arm. The shop assistant was looking over, listening to our conversation. 'How are you? Still scribbling away? Seen your byline in the *Evening Standard* – book reviews, is it? We did love that novel you wrote – my sister was so excited when you sold it.'

'Ah, thank you.' I bowed. His sister – of course. I'd hung out with her a bit at Cambridge. '*Annotations on a Life*, you mean.' I spoke as loudly as I could so the little scrubber would realise the opportunity she had passed up. 'Yes, a lot of people were kind enough to say they liked it. It touched a nerve, I think. In fact, the review in the *New York Times* said—'

He interrupted me. 'Any exciting follow up?'

The girl was switching on a blow-heater. As she bent forward, her silk top gaped. I stepped to one side to get a better view, caught the soft curve of her breasts, a pink bra.

'This and that,' I said. I wasn't going to mention the damp squib of a sequel, the disappointing sales of the two books have had that followed.

'Ah well, you creative types. Always up to something interesting. Not like us dull old dogs in the law.'

The girl had returned to her stool. The current from the blow-heater was causing her silky top to wrinkle and ruche. He was still prattling away. He was at Linklaters, he said, in litigation, but had made partner. 'Even longer hours. On call twenty-four seven.' He made a flopping gesture with his shoulders – glee masquerading as resignation. But what can you do? Kids at private school, blah blah, two cars, a mortgage that was 'killing' him. A couple of times, I said, 'Gosh, right, OK.' He just kept on. He was showing me how successful he was, bragging about his wife, while pretending to do the opposite. Tina had left the City, 'burnt out, poor girl', and opened a little business in Dulwich Village. A specialist yarn shop of all things. Surprisingly successful. 'Who knew there was so much money to be made in wool?' He gave a self-conscious hiccupy laugh.

I felt bored, but also irritated. 'Not me,' I said gamely.

Absent-mindedly, he picked up a book from the shelf – *Hitchcock* by François Truffaut. 'You married these days?' he said, tapping it against his palm.

I shook my head. *These days?* His sister came into my mind again – a gap between her teeth, too. Short pixie hair, younger than him. I'd have asked after her if I'd remembered her name. Lottie, was it? Lettie? *Clingy*, definitely. Had we actually gone to bed?

I felt hot suddenly, and claustrophobic, filled with an intense desire to get out.

Hopkins said something I didn't completely hear, though I caught the phrase 'kitchen supper'. He slapped the Hitchcock playfully against my upper arm, as if something in the last twenty years, or perhaps only in the last two minutes, had earned him the right to this blokeish intimacy. He had taken his phone out. I realised, with a sinking horror, he was waiting for my number.

I looked to the door where the rain was still falling. The red-haired temptress was reading a book now. I twisted my head to read the author. Nabokov. Pretentious twaddle. I had a strong desire to pull it from her grasp, grab a handful of hair, press my thumb into the tattoo on her neck. Teach her a lesson.

Turning back to Hopkins, I smiled and gave him what he wanted. He assured me he would call and I made a mental note not to answer when he did.

THRILLINGLY GOOD BOOKS
FROM CRIMINALLY
GOOD WRITERS

CRIME FILES BRINGS YOU THE LATEST RELEASES FROM TOP CRIME AND THRILLER AUTHORS.

SIGN UP ONLINE FOR OUR MONTHLY NEWSLETTER AND BE THE FIRST TO KNOW ABOUT OUR COMPETITIONS, NEW BOOKS AND MORE.